Through the d... a woman standing in the sun. Tall and slim, dressed in a well-fitted gown of lapis blue, she had her back to him, but she stood apart from her guard. She'd brought no maid with her, and by the strength in her shoulders and by the way she held her veiless head, she was confident and strong-minded. And she was young. Her hair, dark and as shiny as polished jet, fell in a loose braid below her hips. She turned her head to see his horses, though she didn't seem to realize *he* was watching.

Robert took a deep breath. God's bones. She was not at all what he'd expected. She was a beauty with fair skin, lips the color of new wine, and dark, intelligent eyes. Eyes that drew him in and made him wonder what magic she possessed.

<u>BOOK YOUR PLACE ON OUR WEBSITE</u>
<u>AND MAKE THE</u>
<u>READING CONNECTION!</u>

We've created a customized website just for our very special readers, where you can get the inside scoop on everything that's going on with Zebra, Pinnacle and Kensington books.

When you come online, you'll have the exciting opportunity to:

- View covers of upcoming books
- Read sample chapters
- Learn about our future publishing schedule (listed by publication month *and author*)
- Find out when your favorite authors will be visiting a city near you
- Search for and order backlist books from our online catalog
- Check out author bios and background information
- Send e-mail to your favorite authors
- Meet the Kensington staff online
- Join us in weekly chats with authors, readers and other guests
- Get writing guidelines
- AND MUCH MORE!

Visit our website at
http://www.kensingtonbooks.com

DARK RIDER

Kathrynn Dennis

ZEBRA BOOKS
Kensington Publishing Corp.
www.kensingtonbooks.com

ZEBRA BOOKS are published by

Kensington Publishing Corp.
850 Third Avenue
New York, NY 10022

All Kensington titles, imprints, and distributed lines are available at special quantity discounts for bulk purchases for sales promotion, premiums, fund-raising, educational, or institutional use.

Special book excerpts or customized printings can also be created to fit specific needs. For details, write or phone the office of the Kensington Special Sales Manager: Attn. Special Sales Department. Kensington Publishing Corp., 850 Third Avenue, New York, NY 10022. Phone: 1-800-221-2647.

Zebra and the Z logo Reg. U.S. Pat. & TM Off.

ISBN-13: 978-1-4201-0047-1
ISBN-10: 1-4201-0047-5

First Printing: September 2007
10 9 8 7 6 5 4 3 2 1

Printed in the United States of America

To Steve, for your unfailing support.
Love and thanks.

Chapter 1

*Born in the saddle, he loved the chase, the course,
and ere he mounted, kissed his horse.*

—William Cowper

Dover Beach, England, 1269
Eve of the Eighth Crusade

The warm ocean breeze, damp and heavy with the scent of brine, pasted Sir Robert Breton's muslin shirt against his broad chest and lifted the dark hair that curled at the nape of his neck. But neither his skin nor his temper cooled.

"Have they been whipped?" he asked, his voice tight. He wrapped his fist around his sword's hilt and drew small circles with his thumb on the end of the handle, a place so worn from rubbing it shone like a silver mirror.

The royal clerk, a narrow man with shrewd eyes, licked his lips before he answered. "The sergeant-farrier beat them to make them walk. I intervened before he'd done his worst, knowing how you abhor the lash."

Sir Robert's gut slammed into his backbone. As a knight-for-hire in Prince Edward's wartime service, he'd witnessed cruelty aplenty. The visions crept into his dreams and kept him up at night.

But this was too much.

He clenched his jaw shut, the muscles in his neck and shoulders as tight as a loaded crossbow. God's bones, these horses were his most prized possessions. The only living beings on earth he could trust. He'd whip the sergeant-farrier if the coward dared to show his face. Any fool could see the poor beasts had foundered—so footsore they couldn't move. The bay, the chestnut, and the dappled gray stood stiff-legged in the back of the wagon with their necks extended, their tails lifted and their anxious eyes filled with pain. The sergeant's whip had only added to their agony.

The ocean beat against the shoreline, unrelenting, and a slow burn smoldered in Sir Robert's belly. His throat tightened in response, and he got that heavy feeling that plagued his soul whenever someone whipped a horse—the savaging of skin and muscle by a weapon one could not escape. He'd known that kind of pain, better than most men of four-and-twenty.

A string of oaths erupted from his throat as he jerked his shirt over his head and split the garment down the middle, the fabric shredding in his hands like parchment. Garbed only in his black leather breeches and his thigh-high riding boots, he strode past the clerk to the wagon, dunked the tattered shirt into the water bucket, then took the soaking cloth and spread it over the gray's trembling haunches.

An idle crowd gathered round and watched while he soothed his horses—pilgrims, washer women, men-at-arms, knights, and clergy all distracted from the tedium of waiting for the tide. They'd come to gawk at the knight once called the Dark Rider, come to get a glimpse of the horseman who rode for five seasons undefeated on the lists, until the day, a year ago, when he'd been unseated and almost killed, his horse knocked off his feet by the force of their opponent's blow.

Sir Robert rubbed the jagged scar that tracked across his neck, the old wound a grim reminder of how close he'd come to death, of the unfinished business he would leave behind in

England. But service to the crown and God precluded personal vendettas. His enemy would have to wait, but he would not be forgotten.

Pivoting on his heel, Sir Robert spun around to face the royal clerk. "We sail at dawn, and my mounts aren't fit enough to make the journey. My horses are critical—to me and to the Holy Cause." He wiped the sweat from his brow with the back of his large hand, then thrust his chin forward. He gestured to his horses. "Their affliction is suspiciously severe. I suspect they have been poisoned, though God knows with what. I've heard rumors a horsewitch is on the beach. I need her counsel."

At the mention of the word "horsewitch," the crowd gasped.

The clerk's face turned grim. "Sir Robert, she's the daughter of the Earl of Crenalden. He would not let her come, and she might refuse to give assistance, especially to a Breton. Do you really think—"

Sir Robert's fist gripped his sword's hilt. He shot an urgent glare at the clerk. "My destriers might die. She will be safe with me. You may give the earl my promise."

A hard line of disapproval formed around the clerk's mouth. He said not a word, though he studied the horses as if considering all alternatives.

Sir Robert drew an impatient breath. Truth be told, he loathed the Earl of Crenalden as did every member of the house of Breton. To seek assistance from the man's daughter, a woman called a horsewitch, was an act of desperation that stabbed his conscience.

But if anything happened to his horses, his soul would be torn apart, and all hope for the future would be lost.

The clerk looked up, his face full of reservation, but his tone acquiescent. "She might do as much harm as good, but if you are determined . . . the prince can persuade the earl and his daughter to be compliant. You need only give the order."

Sir Robert's head ached with a peculiar knowing, a sense that the rising wind would soon be more than just a salty breeze.

A gale was coming.

His heart pummeled against his sternum. He planted his feet squarely in the sand, clenched his fists, then said the words loud enough for all to hear. "Fetch the horsewitch."

Her father's words, spoken not an hour past, pounded in her ears. "Do nothing to attract attention. Do not set foot outside our camp, and most of all, do not lay a hand on a horse."

Her hands shaking, Eldswythe pulled the cork from the leather wineskin, then forced a hollow length of cane into the spout. "Mother Mary, please forgive me. But there is one who needs my help. I must go."

With the ocean winds whipping at her veil and her fine blue tunic, she hurried toward the haggard horse tethered to a wagon not twenty feet away. Placing the heel of her hand beneath his chin, she raised his muzzle. "Just a draught to help you breathe." She slipped the cane into his mouth and squeezed the wineskin like a bellows.

The horse closed his eyes, as if he savored the taste of the mare's milk, ale, and honey. Then a cough erupted from his head. The outburst was followed by a fit of retching. Medicine spewed from his mouth and nostrils—splattering Eldswythe's face.

She dropped the wineskin and wiped her cheeks. "*Jesu!* Swallow what is left and be at peace. Else you'll get me discovered!"

From the corner of her eye she caught a glimpse of a scarlet tunic headed toward her. A soldier. A royal guard. Fear paralyzed her legs as a rough hand caught her elbow. "Are you the Lady Eldswythe? The one they call the horsewitch?" The soldier smelled of sweat, roasted pig, and wine. His fingers dug into her arm. "I've orders to find her. They say she bears the mark of the devil's horse on her backside. Will you make me look?" He leaned closer. "Horsewitch?"

Her throat tightened, impeding her ability to swallow or

move her tongue. *Horsewitch*. That word could still undo her, even after all these years.

She cast a furtive glance at the tent behind her where her father slept, resting after a long day's journey. Mother Mary, she hated being called a horsewitch, but if he awakened to *that* word, he would be furious. And the very mention of her mark would inflame him. He would fight the man to defend her reputation. She could not have her father risk his life again—for her.

She glared at the soldier's small eyes, then lowered her gaze to the dirty glove that held her arm. "Unhand me, sir. You overstep your bounds. I *am* the Lady Eldswythe, the daughter of Aldrick, the Earl of Crenalden. Don't force me to wake him."

Instantly, the soldier's grip relaxed. Without another word, he wheeled around and headed in the direction from whence he'd come, his booted feet kicking up the chalk-white sand.

Emboldened by his fast retreat, she cupped her hands around her mouth and yelled, "I am *not* a horsewitch, or else I'd cast a spell and make you grow a horse's tail. And that, good sir, would much improve your backside."

She hurried to the refuge of her father's tent. "At times I wish I had some magic," she mumbled to herself. "Then I'd conjure a home, a handsome husband, and children of my own. A normal life like any other woman's."

Leaning against a stack of oaken chests, she drew a deep breath and brushed a straying curl off her forehead, tucking the recalcitrant lock of hair beneath her veil. The old horse had finally stopped coughing, and above the ocean's rumble, her father snored like a man who could sleep a thousand years. Endless waves rolled to the shoreline and for a moment, all was calm. Like the days she spent as a girl, playing and working in the stables, caring for her father's horses. She knew no greater joy than the hours she spent with them—or with Safia, a servant woman with a talent like her own. Her teacher and a woman who had loved her like a mother . . .

Eldswythe shook her head, fighting back the black mood and dark fear that surfaced when she dwelled on the past. *Horsewitch*. The very name they'd called her beloved Safia the day they drove her out.

Overheated, she pulled her veil from her head and scanned the crowd. A vast assembly, an army of a thousand men, congregated on the beach. Heraldic silks in vibrant jewel-tone colors beat against the bright blue sky. The sounds of horses, men's shouts, and war drums pounded in the air. Swords clanked and armor glinted in the sun, while pilgrims prayed and peddlers hawked herbs against seasickness and holy relics meant for luck.

Eldswythe reached for the sugared plums she always carried in her satchel. The treat soothed her like no other sweet, and she chewed while she watched a royal clerk, a thin-faced man with bags beneath his eyes, weave his way between the jumbled rows of tents. He tromped in her direction. His brown velvet robe, too warm for summer, billowed in the wind and wrapped around his wiry legs. Pink-cheeked and breathless, he stopped to shake the seaweed off his pointed shoes and smooth his lank blond hair.

He stepped beneath the awnings of her father's tent and bowed. "Lady Eldswythe, Prince Edward sends his greetings. I am here to ask you to come with me to Sir Robert Breton's camp. He has need of your assistance."

Eldswythe straightened. She dusted sticky sugar from her hands, knowing that her fingers and her lips bore a plum-colored stain. She swallowed, then tugged at the neckline of her tunic. The rose-and-laurel stitching there prickled as if it had suddenly sprouted thorns. "Sir Robert Breton asks for my help?"

Despite the feud between their families, her heart thumped with secret pride. He was her enemy by birth, but he was a gifted knight, renowned for his horsemanship and his exquisite horses.

Armor clattered and a stream of curses erupted from within the tent behind her. The clerk stepped backward as her father strode forth. His young squire, Malgen, stumbled out behind him.

Her father grabbed her hand and pulled her to his side. "What does Robert Breton want?" He glared at the perspiring clerk. "Lady Eldswythe is not some strumpet to be summoned to his tent for his amusement."

Malgen, sweet-faced and easily embarrassed, stepped beside his lord in a show of support, but a faint wash of color rose to his pale cheeks.

The clerk's jaw muscles began to twitch. "Someone has poisoned Sir Robert's horses, my lord. He knows of the lady's equine expertise and has need of her assistance." He lifted his chin. "And, my lord, Prince Edward has named Sir Robert as commander of the mounted guard. An honor for a knight not yet twenty-five years old. A man so favored by the future king can surely be trusted with your daughter."

Eldswythe bit her lower lip, struggling to contain her excitement. It would be an honor to examine horses as fine as those belonging to Sir Robert, even if he was a Breton and the scandalous younger son of her father's greatest enemy, the Earl of Hillsborough.

Eager for the chance to prove herself, she pried her father's hand from hers. "I wish to go, Father. Perhaps I can be of some assistance." She gestured to the surf, where men readied rowboats that would ferry them to waiting ships. "I'll be back before you finish loading."

She forced a smile, knowing her father disapproved. He'd been tolerant of her gift so far and sensed he watched her with the scrutiny of a father who was proud, but wary of her skill and uncertain of what to do with her. She'd no doubt he would have liked her better if she'd been a boy.

Yet she could not deny her calling. She had a gift for rooting out the cause of equine maladies. Only a month ago, she had cured Sir Hallard's stallion of chronic pizzle rot after many men had tried and failed. The grateful knight had gifted her with a fine lady's saddle cut from the finest leather.

Pride emboldened her. "Please, Father, I want to—"

The earl held his hand up. "Hear me out on this, Eldswythe. I know you well enough. You are headstrong, though well-meaning. You'd go marching to Sir Robert's camp, to do what you felt you must, heedless of my warnings or of the consequences of your actions. But no daughter of mine will give audience to a Breton—thieves, blackguards, scoundrels, every one of them. Robert Breton is the worst. He's filed a petition with the king, claiming Crenalden land east of the River Greve. *Your* dowered land. And he's the swine who ruined Margaret of Suttony—"

The clerk's voice rose above the wind. "My lord, Sir Robert did not—"

"You dare refute me?" the earl bellowed. "Robert Breton does not abide by the code of chivalry expected of a knight. Lady Eldswythe is just a year from the convent, and soon to marry. I've not kept her so protected to have her ruined on the whim of the Breton horseman. She is here today to see me off, to say goodbye. I've brought her here for no other purpose."

The clerk squared his shoulders. "Good sir, it is *Prince Edward's* strong desire that your daughter assist Sir Robert with his horses. He asks that you remain behind, since your presence in Sir Robert's camp might incite a riot. I've brought the royal guard to escort us. Your daughter may bring her maid. They will be safe." His voice was stern and strident, his manner unflinching as he tipped his head toward the soldiers who stood discreetly in the distance.

Eldswythe held her tongue, certain the king would not give away her land. That would alienate her father, his rich and staunch supporter. And her father, as much as he hated the House of Breton, would not go against a royal command. Best she did not tell him her maid, Bertrada, lay prostrate in the sick tent, suffering with the others who could not take the heat.

His face creased with frustration, her father let out a long breath as he rubbed his forehead. He glowered at the clerk. "Because our prince desires it, and for the sake of the Holy Cause, I will let her go—with her maid." He jabbed a thick finger at the sweating clerk's chest. "Tell Robert Breton if she comes to any harm, he will pay the price."

The clerk grimaced, then nodded once, but his head barely moved.

Eldswythe tossed her leather satchel over her shoulder. "I'll be careful, Father. I've long learned to be wary of a stallion in a box."

She pecked a kiss on her father's cheek, feeling wise and independent. Then she looked away, lest something in her face reveal it was not just Sir Robert Breton's horses that flamed her interest. The man intrigued her, too. All of England knew of his extraordinary gift for training horses.

The truth be known, she craved a glimpse of this so-called master horseman. She'd heard he was a man who could tame a vicious destrier with his gentle touch and soothe its troubled spirit with his voice. And he could ride a horse as if he had some special insight into the equine mind. Perhaps he, too, was blessed with a powerful connection to the greatest beasts that ever roamed the earth.

This man she had to meet. But she would be cautious. 'Twas rumored Sir Robert Breton was a knight who held his horses dearer than he did a lady's heart. His charm, 'twas said, was especially appealing to women who thought themselves immune.

But I am not just any woman, and after a few short hours it is doubtful that I will ever lay eyes upon him again.

She gathered up her trailing skirts and hurried toward the clerk. "I am ready. We can fetch my maid along the way."

Sir Robert Breton paced, the air inside his tent cool and still, though it did little for the ache that burned inside his belly. His horses were his livelihood and his steadiest companions. He'd seen to it that they had water and shade, but still they sweated and trembled when they tried to move.

Damnation. He'd had no choice but to send for the horsewitch, the daughter of the murderous Earl of Crenalden—the man who had found his father barely breathing with a dagger in his back, then left him in the woods to die.

He clenched his jaw so hard his teeth ached. As a boy, he detested his father, even as he tried to please him. The Earl of Hillsborough used his whip as often on his sons as he did his horses. But he never sought to see him murdered. Now he was forced to serve a lesser man, his older brother Harold, a carousing, careless leader and the heir to Hillsborough.

Every muscle in his neck taut, Robert took a swig of ale, the drink warm and thick enough to chew. Hell to the devil, the old scar where the monks had stitched his head back onto his shoulders ached tonight, a grim reminder of the injury that nearly killed him. Hate and anger had kept him alive. A year of his life had been lost while he laid on what should have been his deathbed. From there he learned his father had been murdered, the woman he had sworn to marry broke her oath, and his jealous brother let his parcel along the River Greve, land rightfully deeded to the second son, fall into the hands of the treacherous Earl of Crenalden.

Robert gulped down the foul-tasting ale, punishing his throat and his stomach. He could not resurrect his father, nor the love of the woman he'd asked to be his wife, and without royal intervention, he could not stand against the powerful Earl of Crenalden. Without that land he had nothing. He'd do anything to win his birthright back.

Robert lowered his head, the bitter aftertaste of the rotten drink sobering his thoughts.

This holy war was not to his liking either, but at least it provided an opportunity to win a cache of coin, and an even bigger prize—a title and land of his own, and a place to raise his horses.

His horses.

Who had poisoned them and why? And why should he trust the horsewitch, the daughter of the Earl of Crenalden, to set them right? The prince, by his own decree, had ordered

Crenalden's camp to be pitched as far away from the Breton tents as possible, intending to minimize chance encounters between their households and the violent outbreaks that inevitably followed.

The tent's flap billowed. Thrown partially aside. Light flooded in and the hazy form of the prince's royal clerk appeared.

"She's here, Sir Robert."

Through the darkness in the tent, Robert saw the figure of a woman standing in the sun. Tall and slim, dressed in a well-fitted gown of lapis blue, she had her back to him, but she stood apart from her guard. She'd brought no maid with her, and by the strength in her shoulders and by the way she held her veiless head, she was confident and strong-minded. And she was young. Her hair, dark and as shiny as polished jet, fell in a loose braid below her hips. She turned her head to see his horses, though she didn't seem to realize *he* was watching.

Robert took a deep breath. God's bones. She was not at all what he'd expected. She was a beauty with fair skin, lips the color of new wine, and dark, intelligent eyes. Eyes that drew him in and made him wonder what magic she possessed.

Eldswythe stood in front of the entrance to Sir Robert's tent. A few feet away, Breton soldiers dressed in blue and white gathered around three horses standing in a flatbed wagon. A dappled gray courser, a smaller bay, and a massive chestnut destrier with soulful eyes stood as still as statues. Solidly built and yet refined in conformation, all three horses were a good two hands taller than the average mount and were well suited to a tall rider. To the untrained eye they were fit and journey-ready, unless one were to notice the signs of equine pain—their flaring nostrils, their shallow rapid breathing, and the sweat behind their ears.

She raised her hand, palm upturned, and softly clucked. The great chestnut swung his head around, looked at Eldswythe, and nickered. The men who stood beside the wagon turned to face her, one or two at a time. They pointed and whispered, their voices muffled by the wind. A knight with a belly like a gourd laughed out loud and jeered. The sergeant-farrier, a burly man with a leather apron tied around his waist, stepped directly in her path. He folded his arms across his beefy chest and stared at her, eyes filled with resentment.

Eldswythe gritted her teeth, ready for a confrontation, but the smell of vinegar and goose grease liniment that lingered on the sergeant-farrier turned her stomach. She had a notion to inform him the concoction was worthless. She was about to tell him his treatment did nothing more than make the horses stink when a flash of white caught her eye.

Tent flaps parted. A man emerged. No, not a man. An archangel. A horseman, the darkest of the four described in the Book of Revelations. Tan and swarthy, he bore a cleft chin and stubble on his cheeks, but with a face so perfectly proportioned, surely he'd been made in heaven.

He was uncommonly tall, tall enough to ride these mounts. And, blessed saints, his horseman's tunic, black as a moonless night, was split up the middle, from the hem to his waist. He had the legs of a rider, long and lean, with thighs that looked like they could crush a silver cup between them.

Eldswythe's breath caught in her chest.

She slowly turned to face the towering horseman and the commotion in the camp ceased. She forgot about the crowd, the guards, and, for a moment, the horses in the wagon.

Sir Robert strode from his tent, his stride powerful and long, his legs encased in deerskin boots, dyed black, that rose above his knees. He stopped in front of her, folded his arms across his broad chest and spread his feet, standing as if he owned the beach.

"Lady Eldswythe?" he asked, as if she did not look at all like the woman he expected.

"Sir Robert." Her eyes locked with his.

His mouth crooked into a lazy smile. He moved his gaze from her face to her shoulders, then lower. Her braid had unraveled, beaten by the wind, and he stared at her hair, fanned across her chest. Saints forgive her, the nuns who had tried so hard to instruct her on modesty would be ashamed.

Cheeks burning, Eldswythe ducked her head. God's peace! How could she have forgotten her veil? And how was she to know Sir Robert Breton would be a man like this? A man who elicited a stirring deep inside her, something that made her want to touch him, to put her hand on his arm and make certain he was real. The way he looked at her—as if he enjoyed seeing a woman so disheveled by the wind—made her toes curl inside her slippers and her stomach flutter.

"I had no idea that the daughter of the grizzled old Earl of Crenalden was such a beauty," he said. "Lady Eldswythe, you are comely for a horsewitch. I am surprised."

That word again.

Her hands balled into fists and she straightened her back. "I am a healer. Not a horsewitch. A healer."

Sir Robert drummed his index finger on his lips. His smoldering dark eyes sparked with challenge. "Pray tell, my lady, what's the difference?"

She glared at the man, then lifted her chin. "A horsewitch uses magic, and may inflict an equine sickness, if it suits her purpose. I have no magic. And no horse will ever suffer at my hand."

His eyes narrowed. "Rest assured, Lady Eldswythe, I am watching your every move."

Indignation swelled inside her and erupted like an angry gale. How dare the man threaten her! She was the daughter of an earl, here at the request of the prince. To insinuate she would harm his horses was reprehensible.

She forced a brittle smile. "Sir Robert, I am a healer. I would never harm a horse, even those belonging to a Breton. But I, too, am surprised. I had no idea a man as famous for his horsemanship as for debauchery could feel compelled by God to take the cross and lead the prince's troops."

The crowd gasped. The clerk took renewed interest in the seaweed on his shoes.

Sir Robert grinned. His sensuous lips parted, revealing strong white teeth. "Perhaps I seek our Lord's forgiveness." He held up one finger, pointing to the sky. "Yes! This crusade will be my penance. Surely, Lady Eldswythe, you can understand how burdensome the sin of desire can be?"

The crowd cackled. Eldswythe's cheeks burned.

Sir Robert sobered, then pointed to his horses. "They are so footsore they cannot walk and must be carted. I believe they have been poisoned, since no other horses are affected. What is your opinion, Lady Eldswythe?"

"First, I must examine—"

She stepped in the direction of the horses. A gust of wind whipped her gown. The toe of her slipper caught in the hem, and the fabric trapped her foot, pulling her down. Eldswythe landed on her knees, bowing in the sand before Sir Robert. Absolute humiliation doused her pride and drowned her dignity. Unthinking, she grasped at the first outstretched hand that offered her assistance.

Sir Robert's strong fingers wrapped around her hand and squeezed lightly. She shuddered as she stood to her full height, his touch strong with reassurance and warmth. His eyes captured hers, then he glanced down at their clasped hands. A hint of bewilderment flashed over his face, as if he, too, felt the strange sensation that passed between them. Eldswythe snatched her hand away, praying no one noticed their exchange. "Thank you," she muttered.

God's bones, she should have insisted Bertrada leave the sick tent and come with her. The plump and pious maid had a way of deflecting scandal.

Without another word, Sir Robert spun around and strode to his horses. He leaned across the wagon sideboard, brushed the forelock from the dapple's face and rubbed the horse's neck. The horse lowered his head and closed his eyes. The touch of his horseman's hands, long-fingered and strong-boned, seemed to soothe the animal.

Good God. She knew how that horse must feel. The very thought of Sir Robert's fingers sent goose bumps up her arms.

The great chestnut destrier that stood beside the dappled gray nickered as if he, too, begged for Sir Robert's attention. Were he any other man, Eldswythe would have asked him how he'd won such keen affection. At the moment, she was disinclined to gratify his horse-sized ego.

She squared her shoulders. The leering crowd parted slowly as she passed, each man reluctant to give her space to walk. She'd endured such treatment many times before, though men dared not display such disrespect when her father was at hand. She rarely told him when it happened, fearing he would challenge the offenders and either be killed, or kill.

Sir Robert's voice boomed. "Silence yourselves. Let the Lady Eldswythe pass."

The cackling ceased. Men stepped aside.

Eldswythe stopped before the wagon and peered across the sideboard. Their flanks drawn and muscles trembling, the horses struggled to bear no weight on their front feet.

Clucking and cooing in a low voice, she pushed up her dangling sleeves, then climbed into the cart. She knelt beside each horse and pressed her hands against their hooves, one by one.

Their feet were warm. Too warm.

She squatted close beside the dappled gray. With her thumbs, she probed the soft spot, where hair met the hoof wall, and felt his pulses throbbing at the fetlocks. She bent down for a closer look, undeterred by the pungent smell of fresh manure and soured straw. The horse lowered his head and sniffed her hair.

"What's she doing?" asked the sergeant-farrier. "Listening for voices?"

Men chucked. Sir Robert grunted.

Eldswythe pinched between the horse's tendons. At her fingers' insistent command, the animal lifted up his front foot. She pulled a hoof pick from her satchel, raked the bottom of the hoof, then tapped the toe. The horse switched his tail, pinned back his ears, and jerked his foot from Eldswythe's hands.

She tucked the hoof pick back into her satchel. "I agree, Sir Robert. Your horses have been poisoned. They are foundered."

A small voice cried out. "I didn't do it! 'Twas but eggs and barley gruel I fed them to settle their guts before they board the ships. I know naught of poison."

Soldiers tossed a barefoot boy at Sir Breton Breton's feet. Shaking with fear, the boy clasped his bound hands, bowed his head, and squeezed his eyes shut. "Have mercy, Sir Robert. I didn't poison your horses. I only meant to help."

Sir Robert's gaze turned icy.

Eldswythe jumped from the cart to stand between the boy and Sir Robert. The boy crouched behind her skirts, trembling. She spread her arms to shield him. "What he fed the horses is not the cause of their condition. I am certain."

"Then what, Lady Eldswythe, has caused their affliction?"

Eyes downcast, she studied the toes of her leather slippers. Causes, remedies, and outcomes galloped through her mind, each idea fleeting, too quick to catch. Shaking her skirts to rid them of the clinging chaff, she stalled to rein in her thoughts while she plucked at the dark bits of bedding stuck to the bottom of her dress.

"She doesn't know, Sir Robert," said the sergeant-farrier. "But I'll wager that the lad knows more than he is telling."

The boy began to sob, tears trickling down his grimy cheeks. "I do not, my lord. I am just a mucker. I was about to clean your horses' bedding afore they dragged me here."

Eldswythe dropped her hem. "I've found the cause!" Triumphant, she scooped up a handful of bedding. "This." She shook the darkened shavings mixed with bits of straw into her hand.

"It's just straw and wood chop, Lady Eldswythe," said the sergeant-farrier. "It cannot make a horse lame or every horse in England would be sore." He let out a hollow laugh, but fell silent when no others joined in.

"The problem is the kind of wood, good sir. The chop is brown, but it has a mauve tint and the grain is straight and short. There is only one tree that looks like this. The black walnut tree." She pinched a curled shaving between her fingers and dropped it into Sir Breton's open hand.

A hush descended over the crowd.

"Sir Robert, the oil in the wood of black walnut trees is bad for horses. It rubs off on their feet and quickly makes them lame."

The sergeant-farrier narrowed his rheumy eyes. "What is this black walnut tree? I have never seen nor heard of it. How do you, Lady Eldswythe, know what it looks like?"

"I have seen this wood, sir. My father commissioned our chapel's altar to be built with it and my copy of the *Hylica* describes the syndrome. The trees are not native to English soil, but were brought here from the Holy Lands and planted by the Knights Templar."

Sir Robert raised his eyebrows. "I've seen this text, an ancient treatise written by a Greek surgeon in the Roman army. You can read Latin, Lady Eldswythe?"

"Yes." She patted her satchel where she kept her book. "The nuns at Covington insisted on it."

That Sir Robert could read Latin, too, was a quality she did not expect in a man who earned his living by the sword.

Sir Robert turned to his sergeant-farrier. "Who brought this bedding?"

The man paled and lowered his head. "Horsham Manor. 'Twas sent as a gift, my lord. Three wagonloads."

Sir Robert's face reddened. "Horsham? God's teeth, you fool. The baron there fought with Simon de Montfort, the Earl of Leicester, against the king!" He gripped his sword's hilt. His thumb rubbed furiously over the hub of the handle as if the motion served to keep him from striking the farrier.

He spun around to face Eldswythe. "What is your prediction? Will they recover?"

"Stand the horses in the surf tonight. Let the sand support

their soles while the cold water takes away the heat. By tomorrow morn, Christ willing, they should be sound."

The boy stopped sniffling. "I will stand with them all night, my lord, and do exactly as the Lady Eldswythe says."

Sir Robert massaged the furrows etched into his forehead. "Lady Eldswythe, I pray to God that you are right. We sail for Acre in the morn, and I intend to take them with me. I can scarce ride against the infidels without my horses." He pointed to the sergeant-farrier. "Consider yourself lucky that I've no time to replace you. I should have your ears removed for your inattentiveness, but you might bleed to death. You will spend the journey in the bottom of the ship with my horses, eat what they eat, drink what they—"

The farrier slinked into the crowd as the royal clerk cleared his throat and stepped beside the entrance to a second tent, not fifty feet from Sir Robert's. He pulled aside the canvas flap. "My lord, Prince Edward wishes to confer with you. He is waiting."

He pointed inside, where ruddy-faced men sat around a table strewn with maps and drinking cups. Edward, the red-haired Prince of Wales, stood sipping from a gem-encrusted chalice, one booted foot resting on an oaken chest.

But it was his lady wife, the faithful Princess Eleanor of Castile, who caught Eldswythe's eye. Dressed in white damask and pearls, she sat beside her husband, her hands resting on her pregnant belly. She looked directly at Eldswythe. Even the fatigue on her drawn face could not hide the strength and understanding in her eyes.

Eldswythe knelt into a reverent curtsy.

Sir Robert shot a withering look at the sergeant-farrier, then started toward the prince's tent. "See to my horses, Lady Eldswythe," he said over his shoulder.

She jumped to her feet. Arms akimbo, she called after him. "Sir Breton, I am not beholden to you or to any member of your rude house. If you have further need of my assistance, you must ask for it politely."

The crowd fell silent. Princess Eleanor's gentle laugh tittered from within the tent.

Sir Robert whirled around. "I will overlook that you insult my family name, that your family has for generations wrongfully claimed the rights to waterways on Breton land. For my animals' sake, I will put aside our differences. Therefore, fair lady, I beg your pardon, but would you be so kind as to help my horses?" He bowed, his face intent, almost scowling. He strode into the tent, not waiting for an answer.

Eldswythe offered no retort. The man was delusional, his accusations unfounded. But she would have helped the horses no matter what. She could not let them suffer.

The mucker boy, still kneeling, clutched Eldswythe's hand and kissed her on the wrist. "I'm in your debt, my lady."

She pulled the boy up. "What's your name?"

"Simon One-Ear." He lifted up his hair to reveal a withered ear. "I was born with it this way. Works fine, though, and they named me on account of the other one." He proudly displayed his normal ear.

Eldswythe took his hand and squeezed, glad to have someone on her side. "Simon, we have a long night ahead of us." She scanned the scene before them. Sweaty, grunting men dragged and pushed the three reluctant horses from the cart and herded the miserable looking beasts into the water.

Until she watched them try to walk, she had been certain she could help. Now, she was not so sure.

Chapter 2

Robert Breton stood outside his tent and warmed his hands beside the evening campfire. A yellow gibbous moon hung at half-mast and waves rolled into the shoreline a few feet away. The quiet rhythm of the water's ebb and flow should have calmed him. Instead, it hammered in his ears.

He watched his horses, the sea lapping at their legs. They weren't moving very much, content, it seemed, to stand and let the water bathe their feet and let the Lady Eldswythe scratch behind their ears.

He stood transfixed by the sight. Never once in all his days had a woman handled his horses with such familiarity. His animals were not accustomed to a woman's touch, or to a woman's voice. It surprised him very much indeed, when his gray courser lowered his head and rubbed his face affectionately against the Lady Eldswythe's shoulder. He found himself envying his horse. He could almost feel the warmth of her shoulder beneath his mouth, imagine the softness of her white wrist, taste her fingers on his lips . . .

The shadow of an approaching figure caught his eye, interrupting his thoughts. He turned to see Sir Hugh of Watham lumbering across the sand.

His friend handed him a wooden cup. "A final celebration,"

he said, pouring golden liquid from a flagon into Robert's vessel. "'Tis the last of this we'll share on English soil for months, perhaps years. Drink up, my friend, and dream of the day when we return to Dover Beach, rich and triumphant, basking in the glory of our Lord."

Distracted, Robert made no comment. He kept his eyes on the Lady Eldswythe as he drank. It was the same swill he'd tasted earlier today and just as hard to swallow. He tossed the cup aside, then ran his fingers through his hair.

"Hell to the devil, Hugh! I did not expect disaster before we even left the beach." He pointed to his horses. "The men are declaring their poisoning an omen. They say it is a sign that this campaign will fail."

Hugh, a monster of a man with legs like tree trunks and a chest as sprung as a barrel, stroked his wooly brown beard. "I've heard the rumors, and I don't believe 'em." He grunted and pointed to the surf. "But, *Jesu*. Your chestnut stallion looks bad."

The big chestnut destrier switched his tail and lifted one foot at a time from the water, as if he were standing on hot coals. Robert shifted, too, commiserating with his horse.

Sir Hugh shook his head. "I've never seen beasts as sore as yours that didn't lose their hooves. My friend, I think you should have a plan. If they're crippled in the morning, you'll have to find another set of horses."

The dying fire sputtered, its glow dampened by the heavy fog that drifted down the beach. Kicking the sand, Robert swore. "God's blood, when I get my hands on Horsham, I'll make him pay. The coward. Who else would inflict such torture on a horse? The king should have hanged him when he had the chance, not granted pardon." He stared intently at his horses and rubbed his aching neck. "As for a plan, I don't have one. I can't replace my mounts. They are priceless, and I spent my last chink of silver to buy my passage."

"If the horsewitch fails, you can choose a horse of mine. I

know you like the sorrel. You can have him. Take the piebald, too. He's not the smartest, but he never balks in battle."

"She will not fail." The words slipped past Robert's lips and hung in the air. He had no reason to believe that she could cure them, and he entrusted few with the care of his horses, relying on his own experience and general knowledge. Certainly, he'd never relinquished their control to a woman before, yet she seemed to understand them and their pain.

He leaned his head back and inhaled the damp, briny fog, waiting for salt to clear his head. He did indeed hope the Lady Eldswythe would cure his horses. He simply refused to accept the possibility of any other outcome.

Bolstered, he clouted Hugh across his solid back. "I'll not be needing your mounts but, Sir Hugh of Watham, you are the best of friends. There is no finer man in the service of the crown."

Hugh smirked, but his eyes glinted. He pointed to Eldswythe. "She is tall for a woman, eh? And she moves around your horses as one who knows them should, slowly and with deliberate purpose."

Robert watched the shadowy figures in the surf. The fog swirled around them as the moonlight shimmered down, casting an ethereal glow over Eldswythe's captivating form. Her hair, loose and wild, crimped from the plaits, added to her aura. Water and sea spray soaked her skirts, the wet fabric adhering to her legs, fully outlining her graceful figure.

She withdrew a treat from her leather satchel and held the morsel in her hand. She hummed a lilting tune as the great chestnut horse devoured his sweet, then pestered her for more. He licked her fingers, then nibbled at her skirts while she stroked his neck and whispered in his ear.

Robert stifled a groan. "Good God. I am almost jealous of my horse."

Hugh gulped the rest of his drink, then wiped the foam from his beard with the back of his hand. "'Tis a good thing the wise old earl kept his jewel of a daughter hidden from the likes of you, an errant knight and a Breton."

Robert studied Eldswythe, pondering what kind of woman showed no fear of a beast with a head as big as a church bell, and teeth to match. "She is naive, overconfident, and I sense that she is much too trusting. Of horses and of men."

Hugh's bushy eyebrows lifted. "Hah! At last you're thinking about another woman. Good. 'Tis time you put that business with Margaret to rest and make another match."

Robert folded his arms, the blood in his chest and limbs chilled by the mention of her name. "I'm not looking for another match."

He paused, staring straight ahead. Yet, he saw nothing. Not Eldswythe. Not even his horses. Only fog. A minute, maybe two, passed, then he turned to his friend. "I would have given anything to have stopped Margaret from—" He let his voice trail off, and he looked away, having no intention of revealing the depth of his regret to Hugh.

"You did what you could, given the circumstances and what you knew at the time. What honorable man can understand the kind of wickedness that lurks in a beautiful woman's heart?"

Robert took comfort in knowing he could rely on his friend and his horses. He straightened. "What's done is done, and I cannot afford to be distracted by a woman, especially a horse-witch. The spoils of war are waiting for me. Riches beckon."

A chortle rumbled from Hugh's throat. "There are only three ways for a younger son to make a fortune—or in your case, win it back. War, tournaments, and marriage." He looked at Eldswythe and smiled. "Marriage is the easiest, I think, though some might argue. Too bad she is the Earl of Crenalden's daughter and you are a Breton. She is fair, her father is rich, and her dowered lands border yours. Not a large tract, but rich and stragegically placed along the river. You could appeal to her father for her—"

"Her dowered lands *are* mine, stolen from my family. And

there's enough bad blood between our houses to fill the ocean. There are things I will not do for the money or for the land."

Hugh squatted beside the fire. "So you've decided to leave England and seek your fortune in the deserts of the East? Bide your time, Robert. You'll have the wealth you covet. I'm old. Acre will be my last adventure, my last attempt to win my riches. I've got nothing much to lose. But you should stay. Retire the Dark Rider from the tourney circuit and marry well. There are women out there. Prepare for the day when you must take your brother's place and rescue what is left of your family's estate. Don't risk your life again on the lists, and especially not in a war you do not believe in."

"I took the oath to fight for Christendom. I'll keep my word and sail to Acre."

"I say this as your friend. Stay here. The king needs you. Hillsborough needs you."

"No. I've had a year to think on this. I've no ties to keep me in England. Henry is sick and ailing, and pays no heed to my petition. The time is right for me to rise in Edward's court."

Robert's chestnut horse whinnied in the awkward silence. The mist formed a hazy white wall between the shoreline and the surf, making it hard to discern distinctly the figures of the horses, or the boy, or Eldswythe's shadowy form.

Instinctively, Robert stepped closer to the surf. What was the horsewitch doing behind the veil of fog?

Hugh showed no sign of concern, stretching out in the sand with his hands behind his head. He stared up at the black night sky. "Tomorrow, then, we sail to Acre."

Without another word, he lapsed into a snore, his cup resting on his chest.

A festive tune, the merry timbre of a lute, and the faint sounds of women's voices rose from the camps where other knights were feasting, saying last goodbyes to beloved ladies, wives, and daughters. Fires blazed. Men laughed and sang and the smell of roasting meat drifted down the beach.

Robert stood in silence, cloaked in fog and darkness. Remembering Margaret. The lance splintering just above his heart. Searing pain ripping across his shoulder and his neck. The agonizing whinny from his horse and the ladies' screams from the dais beside the list. The last thing he recalled before his broken body slammed to the ground that day was the sound of the crowd yelling, "The Dark Rider has been felled!"

His body had healed, but the tightness from the wound that nearly severed his head from his neck made a full range of movement difficult. And he still bore the raw scar of treachery. Since that day a year ago, he trusted or needed few people, preferring the company of his horses. Tonight there was no one who had come to feast and say goodbye to him— but it didn't matter. There was peace in the solitude and ocean's darkness.

Staring into the mist, he watched Eldswythe and listened. Her voice soft and soothing, she sang to the chestnut, then loosened the horse's halter and scratched beneath his chin.

Robert rolled his shoulders and leaned his head back. He imagined Eldswythe in his warm bed, her long fingers sliding lightly down his back, her silky legs wrapped around his own. The muscles beneath the jagged scar on his neck relaxed and softened as the tension drained away.

Then the bulge between his legs began to throb.

Damnation.

He grabbed a wineskin and pulled the cork off with his teeth. He needed a strong drink to put the horsewitch from his head.

Standing at the shoreline, Eldswythe watched the dawn crest the horizon, the morning air clear and quiet, the sky void of clouds or gulls. The tide retreated. The white sand, smooth and shiny, looked like melted snow. She inclined her head, sensing the horses were getting restless. They shifted and flagged their tails.

The mucker boy stood beside her, holding the three ropes.

He looked at Eldswythe, his face tight with worry. Eldswythe smiled reassuringly, but she hid her shaky hands behind her back. What if she had missed the diagnosis? Failure would be humiliating, and the horses would still be hurting.

Bleary-eyed and hungry, she turned and looked behind her. Men had gathered by the hundreds, lining up along the beach, their faces filled with skepticism. A group of knights huddled round the sergeant-farrier and talked amongst themselves, voices low and hushed. Her father, stern and solemn, surrounded by royal guards, paced in front of the prince's tent. The clerk stood beside the empty wagon. His eyes darted back and forth among the scores of men, Eldswythe's father, and Sir Robert's horses.

Eldswythe swallowed. The palms of her hands went slick with gritty dampness. Sweat mixed with sea salt.

Prince Edward, Longshanks himself, dressed in a scarlet tunic emblazoned with brilliant yellow lions, stood in silence at the front of the crowd, his private council, somber-looking earls and barons, at his side. He stared expectantly at Eldswythe.

Sir Robert stood beside the young prince, his bearing every bit as regal and commanding as the man who would some day be king of England. He too stared at Eldswythe, his eyes daring her to fail and, at the same time, pleading for her to succeed.

Sea-soaked skirts clinging to her legs, Eldswythe took a lead rope from the mucker's hands and led the chestnut from the water. The boy followed with the dapple and the bay in tow. She jogged down the beach, her bare feet padding in the soft sand as the chestnut trotted along beside her. The boy and the other horses followed close behind. All three horses clipped along, with nary a misstep, nor any sign of pain or lameness.

The crowd broke into resounding cheers.

Eldswythe took a deep breath, sucking in relief, wanting to hold it inside her chest for a moment. She waved to her solemn father. But the joy drained away as Sir Robert strode across the sand and stepped in front of her.

His face filled with skepticism, he took the chestnut's rope from her hands. "He looks sound enough without a rider on his back. Now I will put him to the test." He led the horse away.

Eldswythe huffed. She knew a doubting Thomas when she saw one, for she had seen many. Sir Robert Breton would not be her first, nor would he be the last.

He tossed the rope across the great horse's neck and leapt atop its back. As if on cue to some silent signal, his destrier started into a canter, then broke into a gallop. The horse thundered down the beach, his long dark tail streaming in the breeze like satin ribbons, his heels leaving trails of inverted V's imprinted in the sand before the waves erased them.

With every surging stride, Sir Robert's supple spine rolled in rhythm with his horse, in perfect synchrony. His hands were still, his shoulders square and facing straight ahead as his strong legs hugged the horse's sides. Not a hint of light shone between his buttocks and his mount. His spurless boots swayed to the beat of his courser's pounding gait as horse and rider raced along, churning up the beach with grace, agility, and power.

Some two hundred yards away, they came sliding to a halt, the horse skidding on his muscled haunches, nearly squatting in the sand. Sir Robert leaned slightly to the left, and the great horse lifted up his forelegs, wheeled around, and landed facing Eldswythe.

As if to show he loved to do it, the horse sat back on his haunches and spun around again, this time executing a complete circle, pivoting on his hind feet, carving craters into the sand. All the while, Sir Robert sat securely, steadily, melded to his horse's back. So in control and in perfect balance with the steed, never once did he need to move the rope or lower his hands to touch the horse's withers.

Good God! It was remarkable to watch.

Entranced and awestruck, Eldswythe didn't think to step aside as Sir Robert and his mount thundered toward her. The great horse came crashing to a stop just beside her, splattering sand and water across the bodice of her blue gown and speckling her face. The horse pawed and snorted, its hot breath blowing.

Sir Robert jumped down, tossed the rope across the chestnut's neck. "You are trusting to the point of foolishness, Lady Eldswythe. I could have run you over."

"And you could have stopped much sooner. I have studied many riders, sir. After that display, I knew full well you could." She cocked an eyebrow and put her fists on her hips.

A hint of mischief danced in Sir Robert's laughing, gray eyes. "Barstow and my other horses thank you, Lady Eldswythe. You have cured them, and I am in your debt. Unfortunately, having just invested everything I own in this crusade, I have nothing much to offer you for payment." He pulled off his gloves and tucked them into his belt.

"I expect no payment, sir."

"Then please, accept a token of my appreciation." He took her hands into his, then lowered his face to hers.

The morning sun formed a glaring halo of white-gold light behind his head and shadows blurred his features. Blinded and surprised, Eldswythe stood rigid in her place. Before she could protest, he kissed her—once on each cheek, in the manner of the French court, with all the formality and deference a noble knight should show a lady.

Yet his delivery was sensual and rich. Subtle and exciting.

Her arms, as limp as ropes, fell to her sides. The scent of him, of horses, and of leather, filled her nostrils as she drew a startled breath. His lips barely touched her face, yet it was enough. Enough for her to wonder what he would taste like and to savor for an instant the warmth of his mouth on her skin. He didn't close his eyes, and she was shocked to realize she had not closed hers. His breath quickened and she could see the rapid rise and fall of his chest.

A languid heat rolled up from her belly, melting what was left of her indifference. She had no idea this was what it felt like—to have a man kindle such want, such desire. A sensation she'd never known before and didn't understand.

Just from a kiss on the cheek.

Alarmed, she stepped away and looked at her father, his face stern and impassive. If he detected any impropriety, there was no sign of it, thanks be to God. But the prince's guards still watched him with their hands on their swords.

The clerk, carrying a stack of ledgers, stumbled to her father's side, speaking in a low voice. Then he motioned toward the prince's tent. Her father took a single step, then stopped and shot a warning look in her direction before he proceeded with the clerk.

Sir Robert's soft voice echoed over the waves. "Lady Eldswythe, I would not taint your reputation, nor risk a challenge from your father by kissing you more—more intimately— in public. But I must admit, I wonder what those ruby lips of yours would do if I answered their unspoken invitation." He smiled and gestured to the audience, still boisterous with their approval. "You have saved the day. Their morale has much improved, as has mine." He grinned, his white teeth more perfect than any she had ever seen.

But ruby lips? Unspoken invitation?

Her face grew hot. "I offered my assistance, and you mock me? You are thankless and arrogant, Sir Robert, and not at all repentant."

She stepped in front of him, planted both hands on his chest and pushed, throwing her full weight against him, knocking him backwards.

His face froze, eyes wide and lips slightly parted. His feet flew out from underneath him. He landed on his arse with a splash as a low wave swamped his legs and lower body.

Barstow snorted and lowered his head to look at his master, then lifted his eyelids, as if he were both surprised and bemused.

The crowd roared with laughter. Men slapped their thighs and hollered, clapped, and whistled.

Eldswythe took a short step backward, shocked at her own behavior. Then she covered her mouth with her hands to hide her grin. "I'm, I'm . . . sorry," she mumbled from behind her fingers, stifling a laugh. She hadn't meant to knock him down.

Sir Robert stared up at Eldswythe. "God's breath, Lady Eldswythe, you are wrong about the water taking away the heat. It is cold enough, but after kissing you, I am on fire below." He threw his head back and laughed, a deep belly laugh that made his wide shoulders shake. Then he crossed his legs, his long thighs heaped one on the other, and wagged his booted, criss-crossed feet. "I think, Lady Eldswythe, that I should sit here for a minute, lest I reveal more than I intended."

Eldswythe gasped, heat rushing to her face. The laughter from the men behind her rose to a fevered pitch.

Sir Robert suddenly jumped to his feet, water dripping off his tunic and streaming down his booted legs. "You may be sorry, but I am not repentant, Lady Eldswythe. For my actions, past or present, I have no regrets."

Without warning, he took her hands into his again and said in a low voice. "No regrets but one, my lady. That I must leave you here." He squeezed her fingers. "I will not forget the horsewitch dressed in blue who cured my mounts and kissed me with her heart, if not her lips."

Eldswythe jerked her hands away. She shouted, "I am not a horsewitch, Sir Robert, and I did not kiss you! Not with this," she put her hand against her breast, "nor with any other body part!"

The words escaped her mouth before she realized what she said. She covered her eyes with her hand, wishing Jonah's whale would rise from the surf and swallow her right up.

The crowd erupted, whooping.

Sir Robert laughed. "Lady Eldswythe. So intelligent and yet . . . unschooled. A charming combination."

Determined to salvage her dignity she took a deep breath, then crossed her arms. "Sir Robert, your horses are restored. You can take them with you. Godspeed."

He leaned in close and brushed a lock of hair from her forehead. "Lady Eldswythe, mark my words. We will meet again," he whispered. "Be safe while I am in Acre. Pray for my return."

He bowed and walked into the parting crowd, Barstow following behind him.

Eldswythe bit her lower lip. Bewildered and confused, she looked at the prince, who stood watching from the dunes, his pale wife standing quietly beside him. He stroked his oranged-red beard, then tipped his regal head and grinned, as if he had heard everything.

By mid-morning, with the tide in full retreat, tents, armor and provisions had all been packed onto the baggage-laden rowboats that would transfer men and goods to the waiting ships.

Eldswythe held her father's hand. Together they watched young Simon One-Ear lead Sir Robert's dappled destrier into deeper water. He climbed atop the horse and, clinging to its neck, set the animal swimming. Once they reached the ships, she knew, the task of getting the horse aboard would test the patience of man and beast alike. If the dark shadows beneath young Simon's eyes were any indication, he was already exhausted. He had two more of Sir Robert's horses yet to transport, though she had seen none of them taken out as of yet. She had kept watch, telling herself she only wished to know they were still well. Eldswythe lowered her head. "St. Eustace, take care of Simon and the horses."

Tired and hungry, she rested against her father's shoulder, grateful that he had not mentioned the scene with Sir Robert. There was no time left to waste on argument and conflict, as these last minutes with her father would be her last for months or years to come. Perhaps forever. She swallowed the lump in her throat and squeezed her eyes shut, refusing to watch the sail on the distant ships unfurl and fill with the wind that would take away her father.

The earl wrapped his arms around his daughter's shoulders. "Eldswythe, know how much your mother loved you. You were just a child when she died, then sent as our God-gift to the convent. I should not have let you languish there. I've always hoped for a son. But that was not God's will. This last year you have made me proud, a daughter ready to take her place in the world. Do not wait for my return. Marry the Earl of Gloucester. William is a good man. King Henry retains him at his side to help him keep his grip on England. But as soon as he receives the king's permission, you two must wed. You need a husband."

Eldswythe lowered her eyes to hide her reluctance. The Earl of Gloucester, her father's closest friend and the only man ever to offer for her hand, was more than twice her age. She regarded him with fondness, but she knew that he'd suggested marriage at the urging of her father. Though the earl was kind and gentle with his horses, his touch did not make her feel the way Sir Robert Breton's did, warm and wanting.

The edge of a wave rippled across her feet, chilling all hope for a love-matched marriage. It was wrong to wish for that from the Earl of Gloucester, or any man. Who would want a horsewitch for a wife, tainted by suspicion and unlovable. She should be grateful anyone wished to wed her at all.

She looked into her father's pleading eyes. She would not disappoint him and refuse her mother's last request. "I will marry the Earl of Gloucester, Father," she whispered. "And you *will* return. I know it." Hot tears welled up on her lashes and she wiped her eyes. She hated crying. She hated knowing her father brought her home from the convent because he feared his death in Acre, and he feared the death of his wife, Isolde. He needed someone he could trust to stay with the sickly Isolde, someone with a rightful claim on Crenalden who could act as chatalain.

Her father patted her hands. "With God's grace, we all will. Take care of Isolde and tell her I know she'd be here if she could. I take comfort knowing she is resting safely at home."

He stared into the churning sea. "The babe was not meant to live and his birth nearly cost her life. I blame myself for that. I fear she still might die."

She rested her hand on her father's arm. "Father, 'twas no one's fault. You love each other, and she wanted you to have a son. She will not die." She hoped her reassurance was convincing. Isolde, her father's second wife, was a fragile soul and weak in body and in spirit. But Eldswythe considered the kindly older woman her friend.

He sighed. "Eldswythe, it all falls to you now. Consult with my seneschal on matters of business. Sell the horses if you have need of coin. Keep the Spanish stallion if you can." He pulled her close against his chest.

She nodded with grim understanding. The stallion's stud fee could buy a winter's worth of wood or, God forbid, help pay a sultan's ransom.

She pressed her face into her father's chest, inhaling his musky scent, wanting to remember it forever. She longed to beg him not to go, not to leave her here alone.

Malgen, her father's fair-haired squire, eager to begin this grand adventure, tugged her sleeve. She loved him like a brother and prayed he would be safe.

He grabbed her by the hand and pulled her from her father's arms. "When I return," he said, twirling her around, "I'll be a knight with golden spurs, and I will finally have a horse. I'll race you to the honey hives and may even let you win!"

She managed a weak smile. "I'll beat you squarely, Malgen. And you will be mortified, because by then you will be a knight." She kissed him on each finely whiskered cheek. "God bless, and take care of my father," she whispered, then waved goodbye as the two men traipsed into the water and waded to the boats.

The rowboats, laden with men and cargo, heaved and rolled atop the swells, lurching farther and farther out to sea. Soon they were nothing more than specks that bobbed on the brilliant blue surface, and then they disappeared. Far off, two of the ten ships that carried Longshank's army had already set sail.

The strength ebbed from her core. Her legs trembled, and it took every ounce of courage she could muster to keep herself upright. Good God. Her father never understood how much she needed him, or else he wouldn't have left. What circumstance had compelled him to answer the call? He'd done this service to the king, once before. Surely the great Earl of Crenalden had already secured his place in heaven.

Numbed with uncertainty and loss, she barely noticed the clerk who shuffled to her side. He tapped her on the shoulder, then handed her a small scroll. "My lady, Prince Edward sends you this. A reward for your services today. A gift sanctioned by the king."

Jolted from her worries, Eldswythe unrolled the parchment. "An endowment writ? My father told me to watch over Crenalden; he said nothing of giving it to me . . ."

"If your father dies, he leaves no son as his heir. You are his only offspring. The writ formally declares your entitlement, stamped with the royal seal. You are loyal to the king. Crenalden Castle and its properties are yours, and thus will remain within the crown's entailment."

Eldswythe felt the blood drain from her face. The writ smacked of planning for the death of the person she loved most in the world, a possibility she was not willing to face.

She thrust the scroll at the clerk. "I know the law, good sir. This is premature. My father is not dead. There is time enough for him to have another son. This will not sit well with him."

The clerk let out an exasperated sigh. He pushed the scroll away. "Take the writ. The crown has deemed you capable and worthy. In your father's absence, there *must* be no dispute concerning ownership of Crenalden Castle or its lands."

The worry on his face sent a shiver down her spine.

Her voice cracked. "What has happened? What do you mean there must be no dispute?"

The clerk's lips parted as spurs chinked and chain mail rattled behind her. Eldswythe spun around to see Sir Robert striding across the beach, directly toward her.

What in the devil's name is he doing here? He should be sailing to Acre!

His black tunic snapping in the wind, he gripped his sword hilt, his thumb working in circles at the end of the handle. The veins on either side of his neck throbbed and his face flamed red. He stopped next to Eldswythe and glowered at the clerk.

"Why has the mucker boy not returned to swim my other horses to the ships? The groom left them, the bay and my chestnut, standing hobbled on the beach. And my own row men did not wait for me despite my orders. I am deliberately being delayed. I demand an explanation!"

The clerk cleared his throat and wiped the sweat from his brow. All traces of hesitation and weakness vanished from his demeanor, as if the news he'd been entrusted to deliver empowered him. "King Henry's runner arrived this hour past. John Gilroy is on the march. He has taken Billingsworth, a minor but royal holding. He has garnered allies. His appetite for stealing from the crown must be curbed."

Sir Robert's eyes lit with rage. Instinctively, Eldswythe stepped backward to put space between her and this man who looked like he could snap the clerk in two.

A bitter, vile taste came to the back of her throat. John Gilroy proclaimed himself a bastard—her father's—and his name was forbidden at Crenalden. Those who dared to utter credence to the man's claim were banished, or worse. That Sir Robert had so visceral a reaction to John Gilroy, too, surprised her.

The clerk pulled a folded letter from his velvet sleeve. "The king has appointed *you*, Sir Robert, to stop John Gilroy. You have the skill as well as a reason to want him vanquished. With you leading Hillsborough's mighty army, he can be defeated."

He handed Sir Robert the letter.

As Sir Robert read the missive, the anger faded from his face. His lips set with hard determination, he glanced at Eldswythe, then folded the note and tucked it into his boot top. "John Gilroy," he said, the hatred in his voice unmistakable and deadly.

The clerk pointed to Eldswythe. "You must ready Crenalden's defenses, Lady Eldswythe. Gilroy is marching toward your land even as we speak. Sir Robert will escort you home and join the Earl of Gloucester, who waits with the king's army for the preemptive attack and Sir Robert's command."

The air rushed from Eldswythe's lungs as if she had been hit with a board. "Crenalden under attack? And you knew an hour ago, before my father got in the boat? Why didn't you tell *him*? He would not have left. This is why you gifted me with a writ!"

His voice level and steady, the clerk answered. "Exactly, Lady Eldswythe. The king wants the earl to stay with his son. Prince Edward needs your father, a warrior who has traveled to the Holy Lands before, and lived to tell about it. Your father knows the devil-infidels and their godforsaken country. Had he been told of Gilroy's actions, he would never have set foot outside of England. The king needs him to guide and keep Prince Edward safe. Surely you can understand? And England needs to know that you are the earl's sanctioned heiress. Crenalden is not to be had for the taking."

Seagulls screeched and circled overhead as Eldswythe tried to catch her breath. She searched the sea for any sign of her father's vessel. All but one waiting ship, a small sloop with a single mast, was gone. The finality of the day weighed on her heart like a boulder. Yet, she could not accept this situation.

She stepped toward the clerk, the pitch of her voice matching the furor of the rising wind. "But I saw the mucker boy swim Sir Robert's dappled courser out to the ships!"

The clerk inclined his head. "Sir Robert made a gift of the horse to your father's squire."

Eldswythe looked back at Sir Robert. He had actually given one of his prized and costly horses to her father's squire? He was a Breton. Not the kind of man who would give his enemy a present. What was he up to? What did the missive say?

She glowered at the clerk. "I acknowledge I cannot assume this responsibility alone, but how in good conscience, sir, can the king order *him* . . ." she poked her slender finger at Sir Robert's chest, "a Breton, to defend Crenalden? Did he forget the enmity between our houses? Sir Robert's foundless claim to Crenalden land? My land. And I've heard his accusations about my fath—"

Sir Robert erupted. "He let my father die, mayhap even killed him himself. Then watched while marauders from Crenalden killed our shepherds and fifty of our cattle and claimed my land and—"

"How dare you accuse my father of such a crime? Those men were not from Crenalden. We are not murderers, or thieves. Your villeins set Breton cattle free to graze along the east bank of the river, our richest parcel, my dowered—"

The clerk raised his hand. "Hold! Both of you!" he bellowed. "The sovereignty of the King of England is at stake. He cares not for your squabbles. Put aside your differences. King and country must come first."

He pointed to the sandy dunes a few feet away, where two mounted knights wearing equally dour expressions sat side by side. Eldswythe's maid, Bertrada, pale and sweating, stood quietly beside them, wringing her hands.

The clerk continued. "Sir Hugh and Sir Thomas have been recalled as well. Now go, Sir Robert. Make haste to Crenalden with the Lady Eldswythe and her maid, and take the task to hand. Your horse and the Lady Eldswythe's mare are saddled. All is ready."

Sir Robert scowled, then stormed toward the waiting party. "I will honor my king's request. I relish the opportunity to vanquish Gilroy, but as for escorting Crenalden ladies 'cross the countryside, we could make better time without the women."

The clerk's voice boomed. "You cannot leave them here alone. I know you hate that you must forfeit your investment in this campaign. But you will find another way to fill your empty coffers."

Barstow whinnied and pawed, champing at the bit, his tail held high. Bertrada cringed. Sir Robert slowed and spoke in a low voice to his destrier. The horse stomped, then settled.

The fine hairs on Eldswythe's arms lifted. She'd never seen a horse like Barstow, so in tune with his master. She recognized Sir Robert's power—the power over his horse and, if she wasn't careful, over her. She swallowed, biting back her fear. She wasn't ready for this and never really believed she might one day have to run Crenalden Castle. God's bones! Why did her father have to go? Staring at the wrinkled parchment in her hand, she raised her arm, then turned toward the ocean, the blue-green water less than twenty feet away.

The clerk's voice rang out. "Lady Eldswythe, do not blame the prince for giving you Crenalden and sending Robert Breton to your side. 'Twas Her Highness, the Princess Eleanor's idea."

She lowered her arm, stunned by the clerk's pronouncement.

The clerk glanced at Sir Robert and sighed. "I believe the princess thinks the two of you deserve each other." He rubbed his sunken eyes. "After dealing with you both, I agree."

Sir Robert swore beneath his breath. Eldswythe heard his fury and frustration, though he kept the words discreetly muffled. How could the Princess Eleanor believe that a Breton and the daughter of the Earl of Crenalden should fight a mutual enemy together? She didn't want a forced alliance, and Sir Robert had made it clear he'd rather carry out the king's command without her by his side. On this she and Sir Robert were in agreement.

But Crenalden Castle was her home, the only place she'd ever truly loved. Now the whole of it was her inheritance, and she had promised her father to protect Isolde and his prized horse, the Spanish stallion, Khalif. No false-claimant murderer like John Gilroy would wrest it from its rightful owner. By hell or heaven, she would preserve the place just like she promised, and stand on the gatehouse battlement, waving to her father on the day of his return.

She shoved the writ into her satchel. She would rather fight beside a Breton than let John Gilroy win. The crops and villages Gilroy would destroy would decimate her people.

The clerk stepped into the last rowboat, the one that brimmed with stragglers and the knights who'd had second thoughts. "One last thing, Lady Eldswythe," he called as they cast off. "The princess asked me to inquire. How did you learn your equine skills? Who was your teacher?"

Eldswythe wiped the briny sea spray from her face. "A Saracen," she said, "who came from Acre."

The clerk raised his eyebrows with surprised respect. "A learned man?"

"She," answered Eldswythe. Her eyes locked with Sir Robert's. *"She* taught me everything I know."

Sir Robert held her horse's reins in his outstretched hand, his voice impatient. "Make haste, Lady Eldswythe. Gilroy's army is advancing." He knelt, offering his bent knee as a step to help her mount.

Her chin lifted, she stepped around him. Gripping a handful of Ceres's mane, she swung into the saddle by herself, then reached down and took the reins from Sir Robert's hands. "Then we, sir, shall set the pace."

Digging her heels into her horse's sides, she raced ahead.

Chapter 3

God's bones, her rump was sore! They had ridden hard for hours and barely stopped to let the horses rest. Eldswythe shifted in her saddle. Dusk was falling, the last rays of daylight filtering through the canopy of elder vine and gnarled oaks. The air in the forest had grown cool, dampened with the scent of moss and rotting timber. A sharp contrast to the dry winds and the radiant warmth of the sun beside the sea.

She pulled her mantle over her shoulders, and scanned the woods beyond the hedgerow, where gray mist floated just above the emerald ferns that carpeted the ground. Ordinarily, she considered this part of Belway Forest a sanctuary. But this evening the woods felt eerie and foreboding.

Crows cawed and took flight from the treetops. Big wings beat against the sky and the horses pricked their ears and lifted their heads. Black clouds gathered, obscuring the setting sun, and further darkening the forest. Eldswythe looked at Bertrada. Riding pillion with Sir Hugh, the poor maid had her eyes closed, her face pale and fearful.

Sir Hugh grunted. "Is there a faster way to reach Crenalden, Lady Eldswythe? I would rather camp in hell than spend the night in Belway."

Bertrada opened her eyes and sat up. "There's witches in these woods, Sir Hugh. Horsewitches. My sister told me she seen one jump from a tree onto a destrier while the knight who owned him was busy pissin'. The good knight never saw his mount again and was too afeared to look for it. And I—"

Sir Hugh laughed, his eyes twinkling. "I'm not afraid, Mistress Bertrada. I fought a dragon once and whacked his wagon. Grabbed a gryphon by the tail and ate his wings for supper."

Bertrada's mouth gaped.

Sir Robert chuckled as Eldswythe cast a reprimanding look at Sir Hugh. "There's no shorter way, Sir Hugh. I used to play here as a girl and I never saw a horsewitch. Lord knows, if anyone would see one it would be me, since everyone seems to believe I am one."

Bertrada interjected. "But they live here, my lady. You know they do. A whole coven of them. All women. The Weeping Women, they be called, on account they suffered some abuse and took refuge here. Some are horsewitches and they're the leaders. All hiding from the church and godly men who would rout them out if they could find them. Commanding the mind of a horse is the devil's work, a special kind of witchcraft. It's forbidden. It's not right that a woman should have power over destriers. What if the king was riding and a horsewitch made his mount toss him in the river? He would drown and who would lead his army? Where would England be if we didn't have a king?"

Sir Robert sidled next to Eldswythe. "We would be fighting off more John Gilroy's and the woods would swell with Weeping Women. It behooves a horsewitch to keep her spitefulness in check." He shot a warning glance at Eldswythe.

She shook her head, dismissing the nonsense of it all, and pointed to the hilltop that rose above the tree line. "We are but half a league away from Crenalden Castle. You, Sir Hugh, and Sir Thomas and Sir Robert are welcome to spend the night beside the hearth if you can stand to set foot inside my father's home."

Sir Robert slowed his mount and glanced at Eldswythe. "If there's a warm fire and food, we gladly accept your invitation.

Let's hope the people of Crenalden can tolerate Bretons in
their midst."

Eldswythe did not responed, annoyed that the man implied
her father's house was anything less than hospitable. She
pulled her mantle closer. Sir Robert sat straight in his saddle,
leaning forward, with one hand on the reins and the other on
the hilt of his sword. He turned his head, scanning the woods.
His eyes, keen and wary, flashed with a hint of agitation.

Being ordered to leave the Holy Cause and to defend a
rival house would have to rankle. And riding with a so-called
horsewitch through a damp and inhospitable Belway Forest
must be a needling annoyance. At least he wasn't afraid of
her. Of that much she was certain.

She touched her cheek. He had kissed her there. A bold and
sensual kiss, for all that it must have looked so tame. So
unlike the tepid attentions of Gloucester, who had held her
hand once, his fingers trembling beneath his glove. Eldswythe groaned inwardly. God's breath, how could she be a
wife to a man who did not wish to touch her?

Exhausted, she eased her head from side to side, stretching
the muscles in her neck and shoulders. Crenalden Castle was
just beyond the hill, but the lack of sleep and thoughts of Sir
Robert Breton, and her new responsibility threatened to over-
whelm her. Eight hundred people, maybe more, lived in her
father's keep and the village, and all would look to her to lead
while her father was away. How would she manage if John
Gilroy attacked? In the convent she'd studied Latin and Greek
and learned to cipher. She could read prayer books and
poetry. She had mastered the use of herbals and the medicines
and could keep the household accounts. But she'd never studied war plans. She'd only just begun to learn the ways a
woman might be expected to help when defending a castle.
Such was left to her father's deputies and captains, and his
trusted seneschal. Now the responsibility fell on her, and with
most of the king's army off to Acre, Sir Robert Breton, a man
she was born to despise, was her only ally.

Bertrada's voice shook as she pointed to the clearing

ahead. "Thank the Lord, Lady Eldswythe, we are about to leave these woods."

Relief flooded over Eldswythe as she searched the darkening sky for Crenalden's green and white banners on the castle's crenellated walls. She had just nudged Ceres to a canter when the effort was cut short.

Sir Hugh and Sir Thomas reined in their mounts and drew their swords. Grabbing her horse by the reins, Sir Robert drew the mare to a skidding halt.

She jerked her horse's reins from his grip. "Let go. What's the matt—?"

He pointed to the hill beyond the trees.

Eldswythe sat rigid in her saddle. The sound of a battering ram hammered in the air and the rumbling of masonry echoed like distant thunder. From the high point in the road, she saw the catapult. And an army, thick and churning, stretched across the fields, as far as she could see.

Crenalden Castle was under siege.

Smoke curled up from the gatehouse and the smell of burning oil and charred wood filled the air as a surge of soldiers threw ladders against the curtain wall and ascended by the hundreds. Steel clashed on steel and stone cracked while cries of agony and assault echoed across the sky.

She gasped, her jaw agape.

Bertrada raised the cross she wore around her neck and pressed it to her lips. "God help them," she sobbed.

Sir Robert motioned to the woods. "Hugh, take the women off the road and back into the forest. Wait there while Thomas and I look for Gloucester. Bloody hell, where's the king's army?" Wheeling Barstow around, he thundered down the road, Sir Thomas close behind.

Eldswythe's stomach lurched. How had Gilroy's army gotten here so soon?

Sir Hugh drew his sword, his face filled with concern. "Ride to cover, Lady Eldswythe." He grabbed Ceres by the bridle and pulled the horse beside his own, racing into the woods. Not until they were deep beneath the trees did they stop and face the hill. Bertrada cried soundlessly, shoulders shaking. She slumped against Sir Hugh, her face buried in his hood.

Her chest heaving, Eldswythe fought to remain composed, fear surging from her gut. "Sir Hugh, what will Gilroy do to the people in the castle?" Deep in her heart she knew the answer. But she needed to hear the words.

"Kill the folk he has no use for. The young, the old, and the sick. The rest will be forced to swear fealty to him, or they will face the sword." His tone was laced with the resignation of a seasoned warrior and frustration etched the lines of his hardened face.

A wave of nausea rolled up from her stomach. There were children in the castle. And Isolde, sick with childbed fever. Khalif, still ailing from the illness that kept him from accompanying her father, was in the stables.

Her chest tightened. She fought back a scream. "Why, Sir Hugh? Why did the king not stop Gilroy sooner?"

Sir Hugh averted his eyes. "Gilroy is a robber baron. 'Til now, his actions have been overlooked or forgiven because he gives money to the crown." He took a deep breath and looked at Eldswythe, his face solemn. "Gilroy paid for the ships Prince Edward needed for the Holy War."

Mother Mary. How could the King of England be so foolish, so desperate? Was he not a wise and honest man like her father?

Bold resolve raced through her. Consequences be damned. She could not sit here and do nothing. Hands trembling, she lifted the reins, and spurred Ceres into a gallop.

Sir Hugh's voice boomed. "Lady Eldswythe, stay with me!"

She glanced across her shoulder at Sir Hugh. With Bertrada clinging to his back, and a packhorse tethered to his side, he was already far behind, his curses faint and growing distant.

Feet pounding against her horse's sides, Eldswythe yelled. "Keep Bertrada safe. I'll find Sir Robert. I know a way to get Khalif, Isolde, and the others out."

* * *

Darkness shrouded the woods as Eldswythe and Ceres picked their way down the narrow trail to the edge of the clearing. She had searched for Sir Robert and Sir Thomas for hours without success and now the air around her crackled with the threat of rain. A storm.

There was no going back to Bertrada and Sir Hugh. The woods behind her were swarming with soldiers who were searching for survivors. She could hear their voices, their horses, and the sound of their swords slashing at the bushes. Campfires, hundreds of them, flickered in the open fields and the smoky battle-haze that rose above the castle blurred the moonlight. Her throat tightened. With every rustle in the bushes, she jumped and Ceres skittered. The foolishness of her attempt to find Sir Robert and Sir Thomas was as clear as a new day.

Swords clattered. Horses snorted directly behind her. Soldier's voices. Good God! She had been spotted!

With soldiers streaming from the woods and an army camped across the fields, there was only one place left to run. In the shadows of the tree line—toward the river. Hunching low over Ceres's neck, Eldswythe spurred the mare into a gallop and headed toward the graveled riverbank.

She glanced behind her. A lone rider was gaining, a knight in a scarlet cloak and a helmet that obscured his face. With every stride, the distance between them was growing shorter. She could hear the ragged breath and the hoofbeats of the horse beneath her—and the one behind.

Then a cracking blow across her back sent her toppling from her mount.

She prayed she might at least land in the river.

She hit the rocks. Hard.

Rolling to land face down, her satchel ripped from her shoulders, her hose around her ankles; and her legs sprawled. She lay there, barely breathing, the ground spinning. Moaning, she tried to lift her head.

A male voice warned from overhead, "Do not move."

A horse's massive hooves stomped and scattered stones.

Booted feet thudded to the ground, spurs clinking at the heels, and stopped just inches from her face. "Are you the Lady Eldswythe?"

The voice, hard and unfamiliar, echoed in her muddled brain. Dazed and aching, she flinched as cold steel grazed her calf and slipped beneath her gown, lifting the hem.

"'Tis said the Lady Eldswythe bears the mark of the devil's horse on her backside. If you will not answer, I have another way of extracting from you what I wish to know."

He dragged the fabric upward. With her legs apart and hose around her ankles, she was naked from the waist down.

She shivered as the cool night air rushed against her bare legs. She slurred her words. "I am not her, sir, I swear it. Have a heart, sir. Do not do this."

"I have no heart, my lady. Without one I am a better judge of women and of liars. If you think you can deceive me, you are wrong."

He rested the tip of his blade on her bare bottom.

Fear streaked through her. Eldswythe closed her eyes and waited. *Oh God, I am found out. Please make my end swift and let me keep my dignity.*

Much to her amazement, the knight did the one thing she did not expect. He laughed.

"God's teeth, I began to doubt that you were she, since the famous Lady Eldswythe, renowned for her equine expertise, would not have been so easily knocked from a horse. But you are she, most definitely she. This lovely little double row of scars, four above another, proves I am correct."

He laughed again and rolled her over, her skirts wrapping high around her thighs. He straddled her and pressed the point of his sword to her breast.

Eldswythe gasped, struggling to bring air to her battered lungs. "Who are you?" she demanded, glaring at the eyes that leered from beneath his helmet.

"I am a man who knows a horse bite when I see one. And you have a pretty one right on your arse that must have hurt like the devil, though I doubt he gave it to you. Mind you, it

does nothing to diminish the perfection of your backside."
The corners of his mouth turned into a wicked grin.

"Name yourself. I would know the hand that has yielded
this injustice."

"I am John Gilroy, commander of the army that swarms
Crenalden like bees on honey." He pushed the tip of his sword
into her chest, the threads of her blue dress giving way. "I
have been looking for you."

Eldswythe fixed her eyes on his. "The Earl of Gloucester
is on his way with reinforcements. He leads an army from the
king. You will not succeed."

He laughed. "Gloucester? He is captured. And the king's
bedraggled troops have retreated. Between the Holy War and
the battle with the Scots, King Henry's attentions have been
diverted—to my advantage."

Eldswythe turned her head, attempting to hide her fear. Her
satchel lay close by and she sensed that Gilroy's gaze followed hers.

Sword tip still resting on her breast, he lurched and
grabbed her bag. Deftly, he unclasped the iron buckle,
grasped the scroll and shook it open.

His eyes narrowed as he read. "An endowment writ? Pro-
claiming you the earl's heir? Did he know Isolde of Albany
died two days ago, cold in her bed before I even got here?"

A cry broke from Eldswythe's throat. "Isolde!"

Gilroy shoved the writ into the satchel, then hurled the bag
into the river, where it swirled, then sank, swallowed by the
current.

"The writ! My *Hylica*!" The blood drained from her limbs
and left her weak.

Gilroy moved his sword point above her heart. The cold
steel pricked her skin and threatened to make a deeper cut if
she so much as flinched.

She stared into his face. "Even if you kill me, Crenalden
will not belong to you. My father is alive!"

"He'll not survive the journey. My assassins will see to
that." He rucked her skirt above her waist and forced her

thighs apart. "By right of conquest I claim Crenalden Castle, and my sister."

Unable to escape the sword point at her breast, Eldswythe screamed and kicked as Gilroy groped at the slit in his breeches. Then from the corner of her eye, she caught a hint of movement in the moonlight. A horse, fast approaching. The earth shook beneath his hoofbeats. In an instant, Gilroy whipped his head around, his eyes widening.

His face vanished from her sight.

Eldswythe scrambled to her feet. Gilroy rolled across the ground, gripping his dented helmet. His sword, sent spinning from his hands, sparked across the rocks and teetered on the river's bank before it fell into the murky water.

Wiping mud from her eyes, she squinted to see Barstow shaking his giant head, the bit between his teeth, straining.

Sir Robert sat astride, his long legs braced for action. He drew his sword and pointed it at Gilroy. "Had I not reined in my horse, his blow would have killed you. But the king has promised gold to anyone who brings you in alive. You are worth more with your head attached to your body. Otherwise I would remove it."

Gilroy wrestled his crushed helmet from his head. He grimaced, his face pinched with pain, though he kept his eyes riveted on Sir Robert. "Ah, Sir Robert Breton, the Dark Rider. The last time we met was on the lists at Smithfield. I spared your life that day. Now return the favor and let me go."

Sir Robert, his face menacing and deadly, inched Barstow closer. "I will not bargain with a man who has no honor, a man who cheats and uses women." He lifted a coil of rope from his saddle and kicked his feet from the stirrups. "Get on your knees and put your hands behind your back."

Gilroy dragged himself onto his knees and bowed his head. But only for a moment.

Seizing Eldswythe by the hair, he whipped a dagger from his boot, then raised his weapon to her throat. "My freedom for her life."

Barstow suddenly reared and snorted, his front feet slicing

through the air, then pounding the ground. An ear-piercing whinny peeled from his throat.

Eldswythe felt the hard, cold steel against her neck. She gripped his forearm and rasped, "Please. Please . . ."

Gilroy pulled her closer. He lifted her chin with the edge of his blade. "Call off your beast, Sir Robert."

Sir Robert didn't move, but his great horse stepped backwards, hooves grating across the rocks.

Pressing his lips to Eldswythe's cheek, Gilroy nuzzled a trail of kisses to her earlobe. "Pity we never got to know each other . . . your father knew my mother very well."

He flung her aside.

She gasped, then wiped her face with the heel of her hand. "What vile lie—?"

Gilroy laughed. "No lie, Lady Eldswythe. I've had my eyes on Crenalden Castle since I was old enough to piss straight. In our father's absence, I've come to collect my due."

He spun around, grabbed his balking horse by a mulish ear and tried to pull him forward. The horse refused to move.

She staggered backward, unable to comprehend Gilroy's words. It wasn't possible that this traitorous murderer was her father's son. Her half brother.

Sir Robert edged Barstow closer to Eldswythe. He pointed to the approaching torch lights, their glow lighting up the fields. "Get on," he commanded, reaching down to her, holding out his hand.

Gilroy tightened his grip on his horse's ear, forcing the destrier to yield. He spoke to Eldswythe. "You are riding with the devil in disguise, sister. Do you wonder what Robert Breton hopes to gain by coming to your aid? I win my wealth by war, but he prefers to take it from unsuspecting women. Think on Margaret of Suttony. Has he seduced *you* yet?"

Her fingers touched her cheek. Heat rose to her face.

Gilroy smirked. "Good God, Breton! I thought there simply hadn't been time. How do you do it?"

Anger flared in Sir Robert's eyes and he raised his sword, his arm tense and poised to strike.

Gilroy stepped backward, then tossed the reins over his be-leaguered horse's head and slipped his foot into the stirrup.

A glint of steel caught the moonlight. The flash of a weapon, a knife jutting from his boot top.

Eldswythe lunged before the agitated dun and waved her arms above her head, shrieking, "No!"

The horse reared and ran backwards, dragging Gilroy with him. When at last his foot slipped from the iron, he came crashing to the ground some fifty feet away, his dagger lost. His panicked horse trotted down the riverbank, snorting and bucking.

Eldswythe trembled. Pain stabbed her temples, then moved behind her eyes and made her squint. She raised her hand to her forehead and pressed her fingers to her brow. God's breath, what had just happened? She had not expected the horse to react with such extreme fright. It wasn't natural.

Gilroy staggered to his feet, wiping mud and blood from his mouth. "Horsewitch! I have Crenalden and I swear to you I will have your head hanging from a pike." He pointed to the fields. "You have nowhere to run."

Arrows rained down as men shouted, running from the fields onto the riverbank.

Sir Robert grabbed Eldswythe by the arm and hauled her up beside him, as arrows flew by. He turned his mount toward the river.

She flung her arms around his waist and clamped her legs against his horse's barrel. "The current here may take us under. Give Barstow his head."

Sir Robert leaned back in the saddle as Barstow skidded down the muddy bank toward the river's edge. "I can ride, Lady Eldswythe. I pray we all can *swim*. Now hold on tight!"

Barstow bounded to the river's edge and leapt, leaving Gilroy and his soldiers splashing in his wake.

Chapter 4

Thunder rumbled from the night sky. Barstow staggered from the river, his ribs heaving. Water ran in rivulets down his chest and haunches while he coughed. A sodden Eldswythe slid from his back, then dropped to her knees and slumped in the mud and reeds.

Robert jumped down and doubled over, his hands resting on his thighs. He fought for every breath, his lungs burning. The rush of river a few feet away, powerful and as black as midnight, reminded him of how close they had come to a watery death. Thanks be to God, and to Barstow, they had survived the crossing.

He watched Eldswythe's breath slow as she covered her face. There amongst the weeds, she let out a soft and mournful sound, muted by her trembling, pale hands. Her shoulders rounded and her head lowered, she looked nothing like the proud, tall woman who earlier that day stood before the clerk and challenged the wisdom of the king.

He knelt in front of her. For some inexplicable reason, seeing her defeated and so vulnerable made him uneasy. He hesitated, then wrapped his steady fingers around her arms and helped her to her feet. Taking her chin in his hand, he turned her face from side to side. "Are you hurt?" he asked softly, pushing her hair from her forehead. "Did Gilroy . . .

did he . . . ? So help me God, if he laid a hand on you I will flay the man alive before I drive a sword through his heart."

"I'm not hurt. I just, just . . ." Her red-rimmed eyes looked hollow and exhausted.

Relief flooded through him and despite himself, Robert wrapped his arms around Lady Eldswythe, pulling her close. His heartbeat slowed as she rested her forehead on his chest and drew a long breath.

Then a gasp escaped her lips and she touched his face.

Robert worked his jaw, his fingers next to hers. Deep pain throbbed from the gash on his chin and blood, mixed with the pelting rain, flowed down his wrist.

Eldswythe pressed the edge of her long sleeve against the wound. She straightened, her face transformed into that of a woman back in control, who decided what needed to be done. "You need a stitch." She dabbed at the wound. "I'll find some wormwood for a dressing."

Thunder cracked and a white flash of lighting scarred the dark sky.

Robert tensed with the reflex of a warrior, like a knight who knew what it sounded like when castle gates gave way beneath a battering ram, when stone walls breached and crumbled.

God's feet! What was he doing? They were in the middle of a war. Now was not the time to be coddled by a willful and impertinent woman, nor was it right for her to coax from him one iota of tenderness or caring. That scared him more than any enemy he'd ever faced in battle.

He drew his eyebrows together, then hastily set Eldswythe out of his arms and took refuge in his growing anger. The king had been a fool to let Gilroy advance this far. He stepped back a pace and glared at her. "God's peace! What in the devil's name did you think you were doing? I gave you orders to stay with Sir Hugh!"

Eldswythe narrowed her eyes. "I went to find you, to show you the way inside the castle. To save Isolde, Khalif, and the others. Surely you didn't expect me to stand and watch while the people of Crenalden were being slaughtered?"

He shook his head, resisting any sort of sympathy and understanding. "And what did your defiance accomplish, other than almost getting yourself raped or killed, or both? Now we're separated from the others."

"What do you mean?"

Robert raked the hair from his face. "Sir Hugh and your maid are gone. I didn't have time to look for them. I saw you dashing toward the river, with Gilroy close behind."

Eldswythe took a sharp breath. "Blessed saints, I pray they're safe. Where will they go?" She bit her lower lip, as if she feared to inquire any further. "What has happened to Sir Thomas?"

"I sent Thomas on to Hillsborough to ready my army. Hugh will take your maid and travel north along the coast to Hillsborough, too. They will all be safe, but your imprudent attempt at a rescue complicates things for us."

He stared across the river, where campfires glowed around Crenalden Castle's walls like beacons. "We need to get to Hillsborough. Get you out of Gilroy's reach."

He took Eldswythe by the hand.

"No! I cannot leave."

Robert clenched his fists. Irritation threatened to make him hoist her over his shoulder and throw her across his horse's back. "I told the king I would assist and protect you. There is nothing I . . . we can do from here. We are both in danger. Now get on my horse."

"You've no right to be angry with me."

"I'm not angry just—"

She shot a glance at his fist. "You are. I can tell by the way you're worrying your sword hilt."

Robert's thumb froze in place. He released his weapon, his fingers splayed. He hated his habit of rubbing his sword's hilt. It signaled his anger to the enemy and gave them the advantage. Though Lady Eldswythe bore no arms, she certainly was combatant.

He let out an exasperated breath. "Just get on my horse, Lady Eldswythe. I'll not ask you again."

She lifted her chin, making her refusal clear. If he didn't know better, he would think behind that proud façade she was fighting back more tears. Damnation. Noblewomen of the court at Hillsborough were soft and gentle. Pliable. Eldswythe of Crenalden was not like any of them. What was he supposed to do with her?

He shuddered to think what she would do if she knew the contents of the king's letter, the document tucked securely in his boot. She'd be furious when she learned the king had promised the choice Crenalden acreage that was her dowry land, the tract that was once his until confiscated by her father, as a reward. Better to reveal that secret after the deed was back in his hands. At the moment, he needed to convince her that what he wanted was truly in her best interest and in the best interest of Crenalden.

Winding Barstow's reins around his hand, Robert lowered his voice. "Lady Eldswythe, I admire your courage, but you must accept my counsel. You should not have left Sir Hugh's side. Because you did, we are alone, without provisions, and Gilroy is breathing down our necks. Now, if you please," he paused and took a slow breath, "get on. We must keep moving."

Trembling, she hobbled toward him, rubbing her thigh. "My leg is aching where you grabbed me when the current took us under. I really would rather ride than walk but, Sir Robert, your horse is exhausted." She hoisted her soaking skirt over her arm. "We should both walk and let him rest. There's a hermit's hut not far from here where we can find shelter."

Stricken, Robert winced with her every step, then looked at Barstow. The great horse's head hung low and his heart was beating hard beneath his ribs. Lady Eldswythe was right.

He took a deep breath and strode beside her, Barstow moving slowly but close behind.

"I did not mean to hurt you. Had I been swept from

Barstow's back, it would have been the death of me. Many men have drowned in armor, even those who can swim."

Eldswythe kept walking, her shoulders tense. The fine blue veins beneath the skin at her temples stood out. She said not a word but shot him a despising look.

Robert picked up the pace, his patience tested to the point of snapping. "Believe me, Lady Eldswythe. I would rather be on a ship to Acre then traipsing round in the rain with a head-strong horsewitch who is hunted by her murderous half brother, and who is addled enough to believe she could slip inside and rescue the occupants of a castle under siege. To complicate matters, I've sworn to protect her and now I've no shield, no helmet, both swallowed by the river. Not to mention that *I* . . . *we* are on our own, both soaking to the bone, with no real prospect of a decent meal or a place to dry our clothes until we find a village."

She slung a rope of wet hair behind her shoulders. "Gilroy is not my brother and I am not a horsewitch!"

Long, jagged arcs of lightening streaked across the sky and rain started to spit again. Barstow stopped, snorted, and blinked the water from his eyes. The horse was still heaving, his head low, his tail clamped between his legs. His muscles quivered beneath his skin.

She tilted her head, studying the horse, her face soften-ing, indifferent to the downpour. Then she pointed at Sir Robert. "You. 'Twas you. You were the Dark Rider, the knight dressed in black at Smithfield tourney, summer last. I had just come home from Covington Abby, and so excited to sit on the dais above the lists with my father. You were knocked that day roundly from your saddle, a lance buried in your shoulder. Barstow here—he stepped on your head and crushed your helmet to your skull. I recognize him now. I heard his whinny, a frightening sound, then I saw him standing at your side, and he looked just like this."

Robert rubbed his neck. Blood streamed down his jaw onto his hand. "I have been unseated only once, Lady Eldswythe.

That day at Smithfield. My opponent had to cheat to do it." He yanked his gloves up by the cuff and jammed his thumbs into his belt. "You should be thankful, horsewitch, that I lived, that I was there atop my destrier *today* to save your arse before Lord Gilroy and his men got to it."

Eldswythe dropped her skirts. The sopping garments puddled at her feet. "I'm not a—"

Sir Robert arched an eyebrow. "Not a horsewitch, Lady Eldswythe? Today I witnessed a seasoned battle horse spook at your command. He was either very poorly trained, or he did exactly as you ordered. A destrier would never run from a shrieking woman, unless she was a horsewitch."

"It has never happened before. I swear it!"

Corpus bones. Why was she so unable, or unwilling, to acknowledge that she possessed the gift?

In spite of her assertion, there was a hint of hesitation in her voice. Robert rocked back on his heels. "You mean to tell me you've never done before what you did today to Gilroy's horse?"

"Of course not! I've never needed to."

"Then I am correct in asserting that the blustery and self-assured Lady Eldswythe has never known real fear until today? Or real hatred? Stirrings in the soul that are reputed to ignite the power in a horsewitch?"

The look of fierce denial swept from her face, replaced with a look of sudden recognition. "I . . . I got mad at my pony once. I raised my hand and he veered away. He stepped on my puppy . . ." She turned away, shaking. "My little dog died. I think that was the first time . . . It doesn't matter. My father sent me to the convent soon after that and the good nuns didn't keep horses."

"It does, Lady Eldswythe. You're scared and it's your fear and the hatred of your brother which forced you to call upon the magic you didn't know you had. You *are* a horsewitch, a woman who can command a horse with just her thoughts, a power evoked by deep emotion. I read about it in the Persian text of Equus Magus. Why do you deny it? Your father didn't send you away because you spooked your pony. You were just a child, and he could not have suspected then that you were any more than ordinary."

Eldswythe swayed, forcing herself, it seemed, to keep upright. Eyes sunken, her weary face drawn and shallow, she answered slowly, as if this time she carefully considered her response. "I'm not a horsewitch. I've read the Equus Magus, too. There is no evil in me, like the legends claim. And the only person I ever knew who was accused of being a horsewitch was abandoned by my father. They said she was a horsewitch and accused her of a heinous crime she did not commit. She did not struggle with an inborn wickedness that tempted her to evil. Nor do I." She lowered her head, her words almost inaudible. "When I returned to Crenalden last year, she was the first to befriend me. I loved her like a mother. She taught me everything I know, and said I had a gift for healing horses. Then they cast her out and my father didn't help her. He could have stopped them but he did not. I think because he was ashamed he harbored a so-called horsewitch in his house." She lifted her eyes to his. "He knows I am not a horsewitch, and though he does not entirely approve of my skill, he begrudgingly allows me to tend to his horses because he loves me. I'll never give him cause to stop."

Robert stood for a moment, speechless, processing her confession. She didn't seem at all the type to harbor wickedness. He'd known gentler nuns with greater world experience than this woman and suspected even novitiates had a stronger sense of self. So fearful of losing her father's love, she denied her talent. Lady Eldswythe had much to learn—about herself. And about her ignoble father. Perhaps with time and experience, she would recognize that *everyone* is capable of evil. But it was not his place to teach her. At the moment, his job was to keep her alive.

He let out a deep breath, then clucked to Barstow, urging him forward. "We cannot delay here to discuss this. We all have our cross to bear. You must accept who you are and master your gift—"

"Tell me, Sir Robert, what cross do you bear?"

Robert stopped and faced her. "I want what I was not born to. Power and position. Yet, I work to earn my wealth and a title from a capricious king who oft forgets his loyal servants until he needs them, who underestimates his enemies, who binds my success to a recalcitrant horsewitch, the daughter of the man who killed my father and stole the land that is my birthright. That is my cross, Lady Eldswythe. Now keep walking, or I'll be forced to carry you."

Eldswythe increased her stride. "What did the king promise you if you should, by chance, remove Gilroy from Crenalden? Gold? A title? Land?" Her eyes widened. "My land? What's in the letter from the king?"

Robert kept his stride. Barstow in tow, he watched her out of the corner of his eye to make certain she stayed close. "The content of the letter is private. At any rate, Gilroy is winning, so whatever the king has promised me is moot."

She slowed. "It's not to me. Crenalden is a fine holding with water rights along this river. I promised my father I would take care of his estate, his horses, and Isolde . . ." Her voice cracked, the rainfall now steady and unrelenting.

He hated to see her weaken, though he didn't understand why.

Robert took her by the hand, pulling her ahead. "I realize you've suffered much this day. But all is not lost. You have an ally. Me. We can defeat Gilroy, but the people of Crenalden will need a champion. Who better than the Earl of Crenalden's daughter, the one they call the horsewitch?"

Eldswythe shook her head. "I am not so revered or beloved as my father."

"You have magic. Use it to help me squash Gilroy's rebellion."

"I told you I do not. And even if I did, how exactly do you propose I use it?"

"I'm a horseman, not a horsewitch. You must find the way. Now where is that damnable hut? Are we walking in circles?"

Eldswythe stared at their clasped hands. "I hope you're not like other men, who fear . . . who fear the darkness of these woods."

Damnation. The woman was like horsehair stuck in the seat of his breeches. He glared at her. "I am not afraid and I am not like other men, Lady Eldswythe. Of that you can be sure."

"Then you have but to ask for directions."

She pointed toward a mound of thatch and mud barely visible through the rain-soaked foliage. Then she muttered beneath her breath, but with a voice loud enough for him to hear. "Not like other men? Humph."

She hoisted up her skirts and strode forward, clucking for his horse to follow.

Eldswythe waited while Sir Robert tied Barstow to a tree, then she ducked beneath the ragged blanket that hung across the doorway of the hut. The rain had stopped and streams of moonlight filtered through gaps in the patchy roof, casting feeble rays inside the damp interior. A pile of ashes in the center of the floor marked the fireplace and the chimney hole above. Other than a battered earthen pot and the remnants of a tattered pallet, there were no amenities.

Sir Robert followed her inside. "'Twill serve," he said, scooping up the pot and dumping out the ashes. "This will be useful for our dinner. I'll try to find some wood that's dry enough to use for a fire." He stomped from the hut.

Eldswythe collapsed onto the pallet, her feet and fingers numb with cold and her soaking clothes stuck to her like a chilly second skin. Tiredness consumed her strength. She wilted, closed her eyes and drew a deep breath, as if she could somehow force the dismal day to end. It was hard to imagine life as it was just a day ago, privileged and comfortable.

When her greatest troubles were the couched gibes of men who called her horsewitch.

Nothing would ever be the same.

Sir Robert's footsteps pounded across the threshold. He strode into the hut with a bundle of sticks beneath his arm and the water-filled earthen pot in his hand. He dropped the pile of kindling to the ground, pulled his gauntlet from his belt and dumped the contents of the glove, mushrooms and sprigs of wild thyme, into the vessel.

Eldswythe leaned forward and studied the floating herbs.

His head a few inches from hers, Sir Robert gave her a wry look. "Checking for poison, my lady? Do you fear eating food cooked by a Breton, or mayhap, you think I am a wizard, a horse lord here to steal your power?"

Eldswythe leaned back and wrapped her arms over her chest. "Don't be ridiculous. The herbs are safe. And common knowledge has it that a horse wizard is born only once every hundred years. By my recollection of the rumors, he was born about five years ago. He won't come into his powers until he reaches manhood. You are too old already."

Robert chuckled. "Too old indeed. In ways you cannot begin to understand."

Within minutes, small flames jumped from twig to twig. A vein of white smoke curled upward. Sir Robert tilted his head back and studied the chimney hole. "I'll keep the fire small, just enough to heat a little soup and dry our clothes, lest we send a signal of our whereabouts."

He sat back on his heels and wrestled with his sleeves, attempting to withdraw his arms from his hauberk, but it was clear that he had no intention of asking for assistance.

Eldswythe barely had the strength to rise, but she moved beside him. She pulled on his sleeves until his arms were free, then helped him lift the bottom of the mail shirt and draw it over his head. From the weight of his hauberk alone, he would have drowned indeed.

But it was not the heaviness of his armor that made her

heart go still, or the way his wet shirt clung to his well-formed chest that made her breath refuse to leave her lungs. No, it was something else entirely. It was that hint of vulnerability that made her want to trace the long column of his neck and run her fingers through his thick, dark hair. A nameless pull that made her want to fill the space between them, though he stood barely a hand's breadth away. She wanted to breathe the same air he breathed. She wanted his warmth and his masculine scent wrapped around her and to feel the strength of his powerful-looking arms.

He lifted his chin and shifted, leaning back slightly, and his eyes locked with hers, searching, challenging, puzzled. Without averting his gaze, he peeled off his padded shirt and faced her squarely.

The rise and fall of his chest quickened at her inspection and a sheen of moisture glistened on his skin, even on the battle scar that marred his shoulder. His torso, lean and tight, so well-honed that she could see every rib, tapered to a narrow waist with rippling muscle on each side that met in a V and dove downward beneath the front of his breeches.

Without another word, he rolled the breeches past his hips, down his muscular thighs.

Astonished and speechless, she studied him, all of him, unabashedly, though she knew she should look away. But she could not avert her eyes. Behind him, the low fire danced and cast a golden glow on his nakedness. His buttocks were as strong and as round as a stallion's haunches, and his long hard legs, as taut as bowstrings. There between his thighs rested . . .

Eldswythe's breath quickened. Goose bumps rippled up her spine. She felt a strange sensation in the pit of her stomach and bit down on the inside of her lip to keep from looking lower. It wasn't seemly that she should inspect him so, but in truth, she could not tear her eyes away.

A guttural sound rumbled from Robert's throat. He yanked his damp breeches back up. He stepped forward, consuming the last measure of space between them, and lifted the armor from her arms, his gaze never wavering from hers. He tossed the hauberk on the floor beside him and in an instant his arm wrapped around her waist.

He pulled her close. "Damnation," he swore beneath his breath. "What spell have you cast on me?"

A small gasp slipped past her lips. Her breasts molded against his chest, she could feel his heart beating and the rush of his breath on her cheek.

"Eldswythe," he said, his voice ragged and husky. "God's bones, you've tempted me since I first laid eyes on you. I exercised restraint when I kissed your cheeks this morning, but at this moment, I choose not to."

He tipped her head back by lifting her chin, then slid his hand up from her waist to cradle the nape of her neck. "I want your lips on mine, to feel their pliant softness, and all they promise."

His mouth touched hers and her body trembled. Modesty and decorum melted away. She could offer no resistance. He was kissing her senseless, and she was powerless to stop him.

His tongue, wet and silken, tasted her at will. She leaned against him with languid relish, and let her hips meld into his. She wrapped her arms around his neck and threaded her fingers through his damp, slick hair. All of her senses centered on the pleasure of his mouth, and the thunderous sound of his heart beating close to hers.

Her brain hazy with desire, Eldswythe sensed his movement down below. His hard shaft, growing larger, pressed against her thigh. It startled her, and yet she could not find the strength to protest. Indeed, she was *not* protesting. She was kissing him back. Saints preserve her! She had not the will to stop.

Robert abruptly ended the embrace. He pulled his mouth from hers and set her from his arms, his eyes intense and flaming.

A sharp cry of disappointment escaped her lips. The space between them felt cavernous and vast.

He stood there staring at her with his chest heaving, hands

clenching into fists, and the fire crackling behind him. His arousal was evident and he made no attempt to hide it. He let out a frustrated groan and raked his fingers through his hair. "Damnation, Lady Eldswythe. Have you no fear of men? Did they not warn you in the convent? At first I meant to show you, to dissuade you from such reckless behavior. God's feet! I did not expect your response, though I thoroughly enjoyed it. Have a care!"

The hut suddenly felt warm. Too warm. And the wisp of white smoke that drifted upward from the glowing tinder made Eldswythe's eyes start to burn. She put her hand to her neck and lowered her gaze, uncertain of what to say, regretting what she had just done. He was right, of course. She'd had no real experience with men, but the nuns had spent hours teaching her the deprivations of carnal sin. She should not have her first real kiss with a man who'd been born to despise her, as she did him. Especially a man who would not, could not be her husband.

Robert let out a long, ragged breath. "What just happened—was an aberration, Lady Eldswythe," he said evenly, though the tightness of his voice belied his struggle. "The trials of this day have resulted in our unguarded passion. It isn't wise or conducive to our mission. Promise you will forget this, as will I."

Eldswythe swallowed. As if she could forget the flaming torch he'd just ignited. As if denying what had passed between them would make her feelings go away. Well, if he could be so damnably detached and controlling, then so could she. After all, their kiss was just an aberration. One that would not be repeated.

"Of course, Sir Robert," she answered coolly. "And I pray that you'd keep *my* honor and never mention this to my father, or to the Earl of Gloucester."

She'd said the words hoping her indirect reference to the disgraced Lady Margaret would prick his conscience. But she was surprised to see the hurt flash across his face, before his eyes narrowed with sullen anger.

He glared at her. "Lady Eldswythe, when a woman studies a man with such intent as you did when I undressed, she invites such attention as that kiss between us. And more. Much more. Is that what you want?" he asked, in a throaty whisper.

Heat rose to her cheeks. "No, I, I . . ." She lowered her eyes.

She what? She didn't mean to look? More than anything, she had *wanted* to look, wanted to see everything. Good God, she was weak and she could not promise to forget what had passed between them, even if his lips never touched her own again. She could not forget his kiss. And the sight of him unclothed would forever be burned into her memory. She would lie abed and think about this night, long after she was wed to the Earl of Gloucester.

Robert eased himself down on the pallet beside her. "I'm not blameless for what just transpired between us, but you are too trusting. It took all of my will to keep from granting what you seemed to wish for."

Eldswythe let out a little huff. At least things between them were getting back to normal. "I don't wish for anything, except my castle back."

He reclined on his elbows and looked distractedly at the roof hole. The corners of his mouth turned slightly upward. "Ah, but you do . . . I saw it in your eyes, Lady Eldswythe. Beautiful eyes, like the forest, dark and shimmering green. They promise a place where a man could lose himself and take refuge from the world."

Was he teasing?

Flustered, Eldswythe absently spread her wet skirts across her legs. "You flatter yourself, Sir Robert. Not every woman swoons with the flowery words that cross your soft lips."

She felt the heat twinge her cheeks. Why did she turn into a peg-brained dolt when he egged her on?

He threw back his head and laughed.

Eldswythe looked away, but not before she caught a

glimpse of the wicked scar that rode across his collarbone and traveled up his neck, ending just beneath his ear. Blessed saints. Someone had tried to lop his head off. It was a miracle he lived.

She cleared her throat, forcing her thoughts to cooking. She scooted closer to the fire, turned her back to him and stirred the brewing soup, letting the warmth caress her hands and face as the pungent aroma of wild thyme filled her head.

Without warning, a tingle prickled inside her nose and her eyes began to water. She turned her head and sneezed. And sneezed again.

Robert sat upright. "I suggest you dry your gown and shift lest the chill settle in your lungs." He snatched the ragged blanket from the doorway and tossed it to her. "Here, I'll leave you to your privacy." He strode out of the hut, wearing only his breeches. "Call me when you're finished."

Relieved not to have to remove her clothing in front him, Eldswythe kicked off her soggy leather slippers and unlaced the ties of her ruined tunic and let it fall to the floor. Her once white chemise, finely woven and trimmed with blue ribbons and silver thread, was now gray and stained with mud. The fragile garment, translucent with water, clung to her hips and breasts and twisted around her legs. She let out a long breath. The blue tunic and this chemise had once been her best. Her favorites. All she had left of her former life, they were ruined now beyond repair.

Shivering, she stepped out of the chemise and reached for the blanket. The tattered woolen coverlet, brittle with age, was barely big enough to cover much below her thighs. Barefooted and naked beneath the blanket, she settled on the pallet and let the smoky warmth in the hut swirl around her.

Thoughts of Crenalden Castle filled her weary head. Towers rising, overlooking rolling pastures where fat, glossy horses ran and grazed. Her father whistling as he rode Khalif across the drawbridge. Hounds barking in the yard where knights trained and armor clanked and flashed in the sun. Isolde laughing and waving from a narrow window slit in the keep. . . .

Eldswythe pressed her arm across her forehead and closed her eyes, clinging to hope that the Earl of Gloucester was still alive. That Khalif was unharmed. That Crenalden could be retaken.

That somehow, Blessed saints, Sir Robert had been wrong about her magic.

Robert strode from the hut into the cluster of silver-barked beech trees where Barstow was tied. He kept an eye on the doorway to the hut. God knows he couldn't trust the woman to do as she was told and stay put.

He slipped his hand into his boot and withdrew the king's letter. The damp parchment, warm and soft, made no sound as he unfolded it and reread the contents, relying on the dim light of the moon to help him decipher the smeared ink. Not that he had to actually read it, for he'd memorized the message.

> *Upon the dispatch of John Gilroy, traitor to the crown and to England, Sir Robert Breton, second son of Raulf, the Earl of Hillsborough, is to be awarded two hundred hectares of land along the River Greve, bordered to the north by Shropshire, and to the south by Taddingly. To the west borders Crenalden Castle, twenty-five miles, and to the east, the county Willow, fifty miles. This tract, entailed to Henry II, King of England, along with the fifty hectacres once bequeathed to the second son of the Earl of Hillsborough, now in the possession of the Earl of Crenalden, is to be Sir Robert's knight's fee, bestowed upon John Gilroy's defeat.*

Robert slipped the letter back in his boot, as satisfied by the terms as he had been when he first read the words on Dover Beach. The tract was far from the whole of Crenalden, but it was vast and included the parcel traditionally passed to the second son of the Earl of Hillsborough—before Henry had allowed the Earl of Crenalden to claim after he'd perfomed some favor to the crown. Harold hadn't bothered to contest the exchange, but the king had made it clear: the only way to win the parcel back and an even larger promised tract was to earn the right by beating John Gilroy.

Robert rubbed his neck. The king's so-called reward was more than he could have hoped for, the boon richer than any manor house or farm belonging to Hillsborough. He would, at last, be on equal footing with his brother. With the proper patronage and pledging, he might even buy himself an earldom. Henry had a penchant for granting rank for gold.

Damnation. He hadn't counted on being saddled with the heiress to the land he hoped to claim. It would have been easier to swallow his revulsion for her despicable father and marry her right now, but that was impossible. She was betrothed to Gloucester and their impending match had been sanctioned by the king. Who could know what plan Henry and the Earl of Crenalden had launched by arranging such a match.

He ran his hands through his hair. *Marry the Lady Eldswythe?* Good lord, what was he thinking?

He could almost hear her ranting in response to the letter. By God, if he wasn't careful, he might find a hoof pick in his back. She would not easily give up what she desperately wanted to reclaim. And to complicate things, he found her enticingly attractive. Alluring. He'd had to leave the hut because he could barely stand being alone and almost naked with her. 'Twas a good thing his breeches were wet and chilly. They kept his loins from burning.

Hell to the devil! His fate was tied to a comely horsewitch who didn't want to be one and who had no idea of the effect she had on him. Never once in all his life had he resisted the urge to take a woman in his arms and kiss her senseless. He had never needed to. Women had always been so willing. Certainly Margaret of Suttony had never objected. And that was the trouble. The Lady Eldswythe had not objected either, until it was almost too late. She did not know, could not have known, what might have happened.

Guilt boiled up from his stomach, at the thought of bedding another woman who had clearly never been with a man. A dalliance with Eldswythe of Crenalden had far too many other complications. She was his enemy and if she discovered that he worked to win her land—it was hard to predict what she might do. Anger in Eldswythe might provoke injury to him, or worse, to Barstow.

That thought was the most disturbing.

Robert rubbed his forehead. He must tread lightly, neither denying nor confirming her suspicions. He'd been careful so far. But he had a weakness to confess when he felt it was the honorable thing to do, and the consequences of this admission might prove costly.

Spinning on his heel, Robert headed back into the hut. She had had ample time to change. Damnation, he was cold and he was hungry. He stormed inside.

He found her snoring, curled up beneath the meager blanket, feet poking out at one end and at the other, a mass of dark hair spilling onto creamy shoulders, draping over the swell of her breasts.

Robert reached to brush a tendril from her forehead, then pulled his hand away. He had no wish to wake her, but felt the need to touch her hair. 'Twas a shame she ever wore a veil.

Eldswythe stirred, reaching to scratch her neck. The blanket slipped, fully exposing one exquisite breast.

Robert pinched the bridge of his nose and squeezed his eyes shut. God's feet. Why was he here? Had the horsewitch cast a spell on him? Her voice resonated in his head, usurped his thoughts. He could recall almost every word she'd said.

Sir Robert, I had no idea a man as famous for his horsemanship as for debauchery could feel compelled by God to lead the prince's troops on a crusade.

He'd nearly laughed aloud when she said that on the beach. He nearly laughed now.

Robert drew a breath. Struggling to command his mind, he gulped the dregs of the soup, then stretched out and reclined just close enough to Eldswythe to feel her body's heat, but not close enough to touch her.

She moved, her bare leg slipping out from beneath the blanket, her foot brushing against his own. A slow burn spread up his calf, behind his knee to his inner thigh, then higher. The ache between his legs suddenly grew hard and insistent, longing for release.

Then he saw it, the black-and-blue hand print that wrapped around her upper thigh.

Damnation. He had not meant to hurt her. Forcing his eyes shut, he rolled away, wishing he could sleep.

A damp chill had settled in the hut. Sometime in the dark hours of the night Eldswythe nestled against the man who lay beside her, his breathing slow and rhythmic. Her eyes snapping open, she suddenly realized his bare arm rested across her naked breasts. She didn't dare move.

God's peace. Why was he lying so close?

Carefully, she lifted Robert's arm and placed it at his side. Wrapping the blanket tight around her chest, she rose from the pallet. Robert groaned as she slipped into her shoes, but he didn't move as she padded out of the hut. The cold night air burned her lungs and forced her wide awake. She scanned the woods, praying Gilroy's men weren't lurking, then she ventured forward, tiptoeing over the soft forest floor. The night hummed, crickets chirping. An owl hooting. Barstow's ears pricked as she came to stand beside him, then pressed her face into the hollow of his neck. Inhaling the familiar equine scent, she rubbed her cheek across his soft hair. "I've lost Ceres and Khalif. Two of the finest horses I've ever known."

She smiled, but tears flooded down her face. Choking back

a sob, she sucked in a deep breath, then wiped her palms across her eyes. "No more tears. What's done is done." She scratched the great horse on the jowl. "You deserve a rest. Thank you for saving us today," she said, tossing the iron stirrup across the saddle's seat. "'Tis hours until dawn."

Her fingers moved with assuredness as she pushed and pulled the saddle girth. She unbuckled the breastplate and left it swinging in between the horse's legs. She strained to lift the saddle, pads and all, from Barstow's back.

Sir Robert stepped behind her. "Let me help you."

Eldswythe started. Trapped between the saddle and his arms, she turned and faced his chest. "How long have you been standing there?"

Sir Robert whispered. "Long enough to miss my bed and my bed partner. Come back with me. It isn't safe. Gilroy's men will be scouting." He lifted the saddle from her. "Barstow is a warhorse, Lady Eldswythe. He is accustomed to standing under tack. It would be better if we left him ready, should we need a quick departure."

Eldswythe ducked beneath his arms and clutched the blanket to her chest. "You were spying on me?"

His eyes roamed the length of her. He pointed to the blanket and glared his reproach. "Go back to the hut. You risk much coming out here alone."

Acutely aware of the shortness of the blanket, she spun around and headed to the hut. Once inside, she leaned her head back and closed her eyes, taking a deep breath to fight off the pain of humiliation and restore her pride. Perhaps he had not seen her cry. She dearly hoped not. It was a useless thing to do. Once beside the river was quite enough. She clutched the blanket to her chest and squared her shoulders.

Blessed Mary. Why did she care what Sir Robert thought, that he spoke to her as if she were a child who needed scolding? The Earl of Gloucester had always treated her with respect, even if he was fearful of her. But the foggy image of Gloucester faded, suddenly replaced with one more intense, more enduring. Waves crashing on the salt-white beach. Sir Robert thundering toward her.

Eldswythe touched her cheek. God's peace. Why couldn't Gloucester have kissed her once like that? With feeling. Even if it was only on the cheek.

Heavy footsteps approached. Eldswythe dropped the blanket and grabbed her chemise and tunic. She pulled the damp garments over her head and tried to smooth her tangled hair. Sir Robert marched into the hut, dropped his saddle by the fire, and arranged the saddle pads.

He sat down on his makeshift pallet. "My bed," he said, stretching his legs. "You're right, Barstow deserves a rest. It is a long way to Hillsborough." He rested one hand on his sword. "Go back to sleep, Lady Eldswythe, and don't even think about leaving the hut. If you have to take care of necessities, I will go with you."

Exasperated, Eldswythe let out a hissing sigh and lowered herself to her pallet. A pair of linnets warbled in the distance and river rushes whispered in the breeze, but no matter how she tried, she could not force herself to sleep.

Barstow's great hooves suddenly scraped against the ground, raking iron on stones.

She sat up straight, as did Sir Robert.

The horse was worried. She could feel it in her bones.

Chapter 5

Robert grabbed his sword. "Let's go," he whispered, "There must be soldiers in the woods." He motioned to the door.

"Your saddle?"

"Leave it."

Barstow danced around the tree, his anxious eyes flashing white at Robert. Robert freed the reins and swung onto the horse's back, pulling Eldswythe up behind him. "Which way?" he rasped in a low voice.

She pointed to a rocky path that twisted up the tree-covered hill behind the hut. "To the bluff. There's a pass between the rocks."

Picking his way around the boulders, Barstow slipped and scrambled as he climbed. Robert looked back, holding Eldswythe's arm at his waist. Gilroy's men swarmed into the hut. Two fought for his saddle and his mail. Two others, still on horseback, had spotted Barstow on the trail.

Eldswythe grabbed the reins from Robert, jerking the horse's head to the left. "Behind the trees. The opening is there."

"What the devil?"

"This way." Eldswythe reined Barstow around the jutting rocks stopping at the opening, a cave tall enough to let a man pass, but too narrow for a horse and rider both. She jumped off and grabbed the bridle. "Get down. 'Tis not wide enough."

She led them through a rock-walled passageway so tight that Barstow's hips scraped against the sides. Eldswythe coaxed him on and Robert followed, urging Barstow forward when he balked.

"Lady Eldswythe, any man with sense would not bring a horse in here," he said as he pressed his shoulder into Barstow's rump and slapped him on the hip.

"I'm counting on exactly that." She craned her neck to see ahead. "There is light!"

Emerging from the passage, he squinted at the harsh morning sun lighting up the sky and the valley just below the bluff.

Eldswythe dusted cobwebs off her limp gown. "I think the village of Whickerham is but a day away, depending on how fast we travel. I cannot tell you more. I've never been this far from home save to see my father off to the Holy Land."

A soldier's voice echoed from within the passage. "You bloody horse! I'll tie a hedgehog to your tail. Move on!"

Robert leaped onto Barstow's back, then offered Eldswythe his hand. "To Whickerham, my lady, or wherever the path below may take us."

The sound of clanking armor and angry men faded in the distance as Robert spurred Barstow down the hill with Eldswythe clinging to his horse's back.

Mahaut held Ceres's reins in her gloved hands. The horse whinnied at the wild ponies with long hair on their legs and chins. The rugged little beasts romped in the moonlight beside the lake, not fifty feet away.

Ceres stomped and edged away from Mahaut. She tightened her grip on the horse's reins. She'd found the Lady Eldswythe's mare wandering with the ponies and contemplated sending the worrisome horse out of the woods. But Safia, her mentor and her leader, had asked her to bring the mare to her.

"There, there." Safia clucked. The mare settled.

Jealousy tugged at Mahaut's heart. She was not her mistress's first pupil, or her best. Would Safia ever love *her* the way she had loved Eldswythe of Crenalden?

She shifted the bow she wore across her back. "Mistress, Lady Eldswythe fled the hermit's hut. She's with the knight Sir Robert Breton, the horseman from Hillsborough Castle."

Safia didn't answer, her gaze fixed on the women bathing in the lake. Bubbles percolated from its surface, steam wafted upward. Eight women, battered and beaten, had fled Crenalden Castle to the forest, seeking refuge with the Weeper Women, the ones who called Safia their leader. Young and old, wives and maids, few women from Crenalden had escaped the soldiers without being raped. Most had not. Their wails carried in the breeze.

But the ritual would heal them. It was the same for all who joined—restored by a purifying bath, the relinquishing of possessions and the gifting of weapons. The bathing women emerged from the water, renewed and cleansed. Each received a bundle of clothes, a bow and arrows, or a short sword.

Celeste, Mahaut's sister, took the scissors to their hair and tossed the shorn tresses onto the pile of discarded clothing— shredded gowns and shifts, veils and hose—and set a torch to the heap.

In the glow of the bonfire, the women dressed in the clothes that symbolized their new life amongst the Weeper Women—a short tunic, breeches, leggings, and a hooded mantle. From a distance, it was difficult to discern their female form. That was the intention.

Mahaut cleared her throat, hesitant to intrude on her mistress's thoughts. "My lady," she whispered. "I've brought her horse, as you requested. Should we bring the Lady Eldswythe to you as well?"

Safia pushed back her hood, her face serene, her dark eyes sad and wise. Mahaut marveled at her smooth skin, skin that never seemed to age. Her shorn silver hair framed her delicate face, her body slight but willowy and graceful. She was dressed in a tunic of forest green. The gold torque around her neck and the bangles on her wrists glinted in the moonlight. She is as beautiful as the day we met, thought Mahaut, the day she came to the camp sobbing. Safia had fled Crenalden Castle with snarling dogs at her heels. Like so many members of the camp, she'd been accused of witchery and casting spells. Here, all sins—real or not—were forgiven. Even those of a horsewitch.

Safia took Mahaut's hands. "Was the Lady Eldswythe safe?"

"She was, mistress."

"Has the horseman caused her distress?"

"No. He helped her escape John Gilroy and the soldiers who swarmed the hermit's hut."

Safia took a deep breath, then turned to watch the women. Their wailing had ceased, as it always did. Occasionally, one or two would cry throughout the night. But with time, their spirit would return. 'Twas wrong that the local villagers and hunters called their little gathering the Weeping Women. For they were neither. They did not pass their days weeping, nor were they small in number. Several hundred women lived in the protection of these woods, and all looked to Safia, the horsewitch, as their leader. It was a task that had taken its toll on Safia. She had grown tired of the fight and Mahaut knew she would not stay much longer. She spoke too often of returning to her homeland.

The new women followed Celeste down the winding trail leading to their camp.

"Mistress?" Mahaut asked in a quiet voice. "Should we bring the Lady Eldswythe to you?"

"No," said Safia softly. "She does not need me. Yet."

Mahaut shifted, relieved that she would not be asked to bring Eldswythe of Crenalden to the camp. There could be only one horsewitch to replace her mistress as the leader of the Weeping Women. And she intended to be that woman. Mahaut folded her arms. "And what of him, mistress?" she asked. "Do we let the horseman be?"

Safia motioned to the herd of ponies that had wandered

into the lake to drink, a rough-looking mare and two foals, a rare set of twins. The foals, kindred spirits stood side by side. One nibbled the withers of the other.

"Yes, Mahaut. Tell the others to let the Lady Eldswythe *and* her horseman leave. But exact from John Gilroy's men the usual penalty for venturing into our woods. Lure them to the lakeside. Draw them into the water. Let them try to fight in armor."

She pulled her hood over her head and started along the trail in silence.

Mahaut mounted Ceres, then galloped the mare down the path that led toward the hermit's hut, where a hundred able-bodied Weeper Women were hiding in the woods and watching unsuspecting soldiers.

The noonday sun baked down as Eldswythe and Sir Robert traveled through the common fields that bordered Belway Forest. Barstow's back, slick with sweat, made it hard for Eldswythe to keep from sliding forward. Horsehair prickled through her gown and scratched against the insides of her thighs. The sweltering humidity only added to her misery. She hiked her gown up to her knees and fanned herself. It was as hot here on the open road as the air in a smithy's shop.

Sir Robert turned to watch the soldiers who still followed. "By the saints, 'tis a good thing their horses are as tired as Barstow. But rest and water will still have to wait," he said, as if he had read her mind.

Eldswythe twisted around in the saddle to get a better look at the men behind her. Their persistent presence had been unnerving, and yet now they seemed to have fallen farther behind.

The soldiers behind them suddenly stopped in the middle of the road and argued for a moment, then turned their mounts around and rode back. Excitement rippled up her spine. "They're giving up, Sir Robert!"

"Odd. Gilroy is stingy with his pay and the men he buys in service are not inclined to overly extend themselves, but why would they bother to pursue us this far, then decide to turn around?"

He was right to be suspicious. Her intuition agreed with him, even if outwardly she remained the skeptic. She scanned the fields beside the road. No cows or sheep wandered on the land—there was nothing much for them to eat, the ground brown and dry. There were no people about, either, no travelers, no commerce from the village.

Smoke drifted from the pastures ahead, blanketing the road in a haze of ash and cinders.

Sir Robert moved one hand to his sword. "The common pastures have been burned."

Eldswythe feared the devastation was more of Gilroy's work. "God help them."

In the village, the shops and houses that were not burned had been abandoned, doors left open, shutters ajar. Carts and wagons lay upturned, their contents strewn about.

Sir Robert dismounted, then led Barstow to the center square.

Eldswythe jumped from the horse's back and raced to the well. She filled a dipper and splashed her face and neck while Sir Robert filled a bucket for Barstow.

"The people here were not attacked by Gilroy's army, or these would not have been left behind." Sir Robert nudged at coins, silver spoons and plate with the toe of his boot. "I have need of coin and silver, but I am not so greedy as to try and pocket these."

Eldswythe, woozy from heat and hunger, lowered herself to her knees. Sir Robert knelt in front of her, water droplets sparkling in his hair. He stared past her, his eyes searching the square. "Lady Eldswythe, we must not linger."

Eldswythe squinted, shielding her eyes from the sun. "Why is the place deserted?"

Sir Robert shook his head. "I can only guess what made the villagers depart in such a hurry. Any reason I come up with does not bode well for us."

He pulled her to her feet and helped her onto Barstow's

back. "We need to leave this place," he said, as he mounted behind her.

Barstow trotted past the empty houses of Whickerham toward the village church. Stark and white, the tiny structure was unmarred by fire. The tower bell was still and silent, pigeons roosted on the gables and the sanctuary doors hung ajar. A wagon piled with wooden benches and gold-embroidered vestments was parked at the bottom of the church steps. Still strapped to the wagon's hitches, a horse, lying on its side, paddled in the dirt and struggled to get up.

Eldswythe tensed. Even from the distance she could see the scarlet trickle running from its nose and mouth, and oozing from beneath its tail. Eyes red and bleeding at the corners, it gasped a final breath and was still. Eldswythe shivered at the sight, and shrunk back from the staring eyes of the dead horse.

Sir Robert drew his sword. "There's someone in the chapel."

Eldswythe grabbed Sir Robert by the sleeve. "Sir Robert, we must ride from here as fast as . . ."

She watched in horror as the priest, his white robes speckled with red, staggered from the chapel and fell beside the wagon. Blood running from the corner of his mouth, he clutched a crucifix and pressed it to his lips. His eyes rolled upward. He fell limp against the wagon wheel and crumpled in a heap beside the horse.

Sir Robert drew Barstow to a halt. "If I were a religious man I would plead with the heavens, too, though little good it did the priest."

Her fingers tightened around Sir Robert's arm. "It is the Black Bane. I've seen it many times in horses. It killed a stable boy at one of my father's manor houses. Once the bleeding starts, there's nothing to be done."

"This is why Gilroy's men retreated." He slapped his thigh and swore. "Damnation! I was distracted. We should have gone another way."

"Which way would you suggest? To the east? The west? The disease may have already spread there. We have no way of knowing."

She glanced at blackened pastures just beyond the chapel, where carcasses of sheep and cows and horses littered the landscape. She covered her nose as a rotting stench wafted across the road. "They moved the animals into the fields they thought were safe. They were mistaken. I suspect that's what made the people panic. I saw this once on one of my father's farms. The unburied dead are the most contagious. We must be away from here, Sir Robert!"

"Go back and face Gilroy's men or stay here to sicken, bleeding from the inside out? We have no choice but to go forward." He steadied his chin atop her head, then handed her the reins. "You set the course, Lady Eldswythe. We have nothing much to lose."

How very wrong you are. It will be a miracle if we, or Barstow, do not sicken, too.

Eldswythe leaned down to pat Barstow on the neck, glad to see woodlands just ahead that offered respite from the heat. "When we get to Glensbury, I want a bath," she said, as she lifted her hair off her neck and fanned herself. "And I want to sleep."

Sir Robert swatted at the flies that pestered Barstow's flanks. "I want a stew, a hearty stew so thick I have to spread it on my bread."

Eldswythe twisted round to face him. "You should bathe first, sir." She wrinkled her nose.

He laughed and pulled Barstow to a halt. "Have a care," he said, suddenly serious as he drew his sword and pointed to the riders who approached.

The two men halted their horses in the middle of the road. Mounted on fine palfreys, they wobbled in their saddles and yanked the reins to keep their balance. Their rich attire, ill-fitting and mismatched, was clearly not their own. Saddlebags bulged from the horses' sides.

The older man smiled and spit through broken teeth. "Give

us yer horse and yer blade and we'll be on our way." He slurred his words.

Sir Robert lifted his sword. "Let us pass," he said, with a deadly tone.

The man chuckled and swayed in the saddle. "There are two of us and only one of you, milord. It's really just yer horse we want." He pointed his sword at Eldswythe, then licked his lips and winked. "But yer pretty lady sweetens up the pie."

Sir Robert whispered. "They are drunk and they intend to fight. Get down and run. I'll distract them." He gestured to the left, where the field beside them still smoked and a bloated horse lay upside down in the ditch beside the road.

Her throat tightened. Leaving the protection of Sir Robert seemed unwise. But she understood it would be hard for him to fight with her clinging to his back. Sliding off Barstow, she picked up her skirts and ran across the road, jumped into the ditch and scrambled up the other side, struggling for a foothold. She slipped, sliding backwards in the dirt, and almost landed on the bloated horse. Panicked, she scrabbled to her feet, then bounded from the ditch and ran into the smoking field, praying that the robbers horses would not ride through smoke.

The thieves descended, swinging wildly at Sir Robert. The drink had left them fearless and they fought without regard for life or limb.

Sir Robert raised his sword. Steel clashed with steel and one long swipe, passed just inches from the man's unprotected head. The robber swayed, the look on his face that of someone who'd almost lost his life. Then called to his accomplice. "I'll get the girl!" He spun his horse around and headed for the field.

The younger of the two, not nearly as stout, or as drunk, kicked Barstow in the face and thrust his sword at Sir Robert's chest. Barstow reared as Sir Robert, leaning backward to dodge the jab, threw him off balance. The great horse nearly toppled.

Eldswythe gasped.

Then she saw the other horse and rider by the ditch. The man used his reins to whip his horse about the neck and head. His horse refused to jump and the man whacked its rump. The squealing horse bucked and danced around in circles but would not venture near the ditch.

Eldswythe, running farther into the field, searched for cover. She gasped for air, sucking in the acrid smoke that burned her nose and her throat, coughing to the point of retching. When at last she caught her breath, she wiped her burning eyes. She stepped behind a burning line of grass, then let the smoke envelop her. She could not outrun a horse.

Through the haze she could barely see the horse still balking at the ditch, its rider striking blow after blow about its head.

Anger surged through her veins and a blackness, powerful and intense, filled her heart. She would not allow the horse to jump, and neither would the rider be allowed to beat the poor beast senseless.

She focused on the blurry image of the horse and with all the strength her voice could summon, she bellowed. "No!"

With one great buck the horse slung its rider from his back, tossing him into the air. The man landed in the ditch, blood running from his wounded arm, his neck twisted at an awkward angle as his horse galloped down the road.

Eldswythe gasped. She'd not meant to kill the man!

A second horse and rider thundered in the haze across the field and headed toward her. Reeling from what she'd done, she braced herself, certain that now she would meet the wrath of her maker. And she deserved it.

A voice boomed. "They're gone, Lady Eldswythe. Gone." Sir Robert leapt from Barstow's back and wrapped his arms around her.

Eldswythe flung her arms around his neck and buried her face in his the folds of his tunic. "Did you see what I did? I killed a man! Oh, by the saints, it's true—I am a horsewitch."

"Shhh," he soothed her, stroking the back of her head. "The man meant to kill you. And he would have killed his horse."

Her voice cracked. "I am tired of running, Sir Robert."

Robert picked her up. He lifted her onto Barstow's back. "You'll be safe behind the walls off Hillsborough soon, and I'll keep what I witnessed here today to myself." He leapt onto Barstow and took a seat behind her. "I find your talent fascinating, and mayhap I am a little jealous I do not possess it."

Wiping her soot-smeared face, she leaned into Sir Robert's chest. "Perhaps I . . ." She searched for the right words. "Perhaps I misjudged you."

"On what level? My artful wielding of a sword? My expert horsemanship?" he teased.

"You could have left me to them. Even if I don't survive, the king will reward you if you put down Gilroy's challenge. What does he care if I live or die? Why do you care, that you would risk your life defending me?"

"Your life, my lady, is important to the king. He has a plan for you. You are also important to the people of Crenalden, who wait for you to free them. You are important to me— because it will take a horsewitch to get us safely home to Hillsborough." The humor faded from his voice. "The Earl of Gloucester, no doubt, is living for the moment when he can take you as his wife. Were I in his situation, it would be what was keeping me alive." Sir Robert leaned close, pressing his broad chest against her back.

Eyes downcast, Eldswythe sank against him, taking comfort against his solid presence. "Thank you, Sir Robert Breton, for saving my life." Uncertain what else to say, she busied herself, inspecting the sticky substance smeared across her fingertips and streaked across her sleeve.

She sat up straight and held up her hands.

Blood.

Fresh blood.

Eldswythe pulled Barstow to a stop. "Are you injured?"

Sir Robert looked perplexed. "No, why do you ask?"

She grabbed his hand and turned it over. A slice across his last two fingers, caked with dirt, gaped across the knuckles.

She felt the blood drain from her face. "This must be tended to."

He laughed. "'Tis just a scratch. It will heal." He rubbed the red wound on his jaw, then massaged his neck. "I've suffered worse."

Eldswythe lifted up her skirt and ripped the bottom of her blue-stained shift. "I fear it could be more than that." She spat onto the cloth and scrubbed at the wound. She wound the cloth around his fingers. "Keep it covered. The Black Bane spreads from cows and horses and then to sheep . . . and men. The disease arises from putrid blood exuding from the sick that mixes with the air."

Sir Robert pulled away his hand. "Then do not tend to me, Lady Eldswythe. You risk your own life."

He leapt down and strode around Barstow, inspecting. Lifting the horse's tail, he stooped and ran his hands up and down the inside of the horse's legs. "Thank God, Barstow has no marks."

"Mayhap he won't get sick. Let us pray he does not." *Though many horses die of infection of the lungs even if they have no wounds.*

She took a deep breath. "Sir Robert, there is a house ahead. Perhaps we can find some food and rest. I can better tend your hand."

"Lady Eldswythe, may we dispense with formality? We might not live long enough to know each other better. Call me by my Christian name."

Indeed, the danger of their journey had just increased tenfold. Polite address seemed frivolous. "Please, call me Eldswythe. I prefer my given name to . . . the other."

He pushed her hair from her face. "'Tis hard to resist calling you *horsewitch* when I see what I have just seen," he protested.

"Try, please. Else I shall have to call you something equally repugnant and it will not be Robert."

Chapter 6

They rode in silence into the empty yard of the mud-and-wattle manor house. The midday sun filtered through the apple trees on the perimeter and Barstow's long black shadow stretched across the ground.

The house boasted two stories and a thatch-and-timber roof and a tall, stone chimney. Laundry dangled from the window on the second floor but, other than the pigeons that cooed beneath the eaves, there was not a soul about.

Robert lowered Eldswythe to the ground. "It seems the news from Whickerham has scared them off. At least they did not burn the place."

Eldswythe followed him into the barn. There were no animals inside, but the stalls were clean and there was fresh water in the trough.

Barstow found the manger and filled his face with hay. Robert laughed. "Barstow, rest awhile and eat your fill, as I intend to do."

Taking Eldswythe by the hand, he drew his sword and approached the house.

It came as no surprise to Eldswythe that Robert found the kitchen first, where a great slab of salted venison still hung from drying hooks. An oaken cask sat beside a cider press and the smell of apples lingered in the air. Wooden cups lay strewn across the kitchen table beside half-eaten loaves of bread and chunks of cheese, all left in haste.

Robert pulled up a bench and offered Eldswythe a seat. "A feast." He filled two cups with cider and raised them up. "And a two-day ride from here to Hillsborough." He handed Eldswythe a cup.

She sipped the aromatic cider, cool and tangy-sweet. Robert carved a slice of venison and slapped the meat between two slices of bread. "Not a stew," he said, "but 'twill serve." He winked and took an enormous bite.

Her stomach was as hollow as an empty drum. Cheese and bread had never tasted so good. Satisfied and full, she filled a bowl with cider. "Give me your hand, Robert."

He put his swollen hand down on the table and watched her as she unwound the bandage. Flexing his fingers, he seemed to be indifferent to the pain such a wound would cause. Relaxed, his hand in hers, he allowed her complete inspection.

"You have a horseman's hands," she said, running her fingers across his swollen knuckles. "A strong but gentle touch, with a knack for knowing how much pressure to apply and not abuse a horse's mouth."

Her heartbeat quickened. She looked up to find Robert staring at her, his gaze smoldering. Unnerving.

The heat rising to her cheeks, she submerged his fingers into the bowl. Rattled, she averted her eyes and looked around the kitchen. "If we had prunes, I would make a poultice with them. They are most effective against the Black Bane. But cider will have to do." She massaged the wound, cleaning off the dirt and dried blood.

Robert leaned his head back, the creases at the corners of his eyes softening. His breathing slowed as he slumped into the chair. In the quiet of the house, Eldswythe feared he could hear her heart beating. She had dressed the Earl of Gloucester's wounds once, when he was thrown into a bramble bush by his horse. But her skin had never tingled where she touched him, as it did when she touched Robert Breton.

Her chest tightened.

Robert opened his eyes and caught her staring.

God's teeth, she'd been holding his hand in the liquid longer than she'd meant to. Longer than necessary. She quickly pulled her hand away, and sloshed cider from the bowl. Fumbling, she dried his fingers with the corner of the tablecloth.

"Thank you. I am not accustomed to a woman's care," he said, his voice husky.

He pulled her to her feet. "One good turn deserves another." He pointed to the small tub beside the cooking hearth. "Within the hour you shall have your bath. Go find a scrub brush and some drying cloths. Meet me in the hall."

Eager to be clean, she wasted no time. Her arms piled with clothes and linens from the rooms upstairs, she hurried to the hall.

Two benches and a dining table sat before a narrow stone hearth, where the fire within had warmed the room and cast a golden glow against the whitewashed walls. Robert filled the tub with steaming water and settled in the chair beside the hearth.

Eldswythe set the linens on the table. "I found these in the sleeping quarters upstairs. Fresh clothes that hopefully should fit, and a soft scrubbing brush and drying towels."

Robert smiled. "If there are actually beds up there, 'tis more than I could hope for." He stretched his legs and leaned forward in the chair. "You go first." He gestured to the bath. "The water won't stay hot for long."

Eldswythe crossed her arms and glared, shooting him her best reproachful look.

"I'd leave you to it, save that we don't know who may be about. Thieves. Gilroy's men. The owners of this place would be not be pleased to find us here, I'm sure. I've pledged to keep you safe. I must stay, but I'll turn my back. Call out when you are done." He got up, turned the chair, and sat down in it again, this time facing the door.

Eldswythe hesitated, then kicked off her shoes and pulled off her filthy blue dress. She stepped into the steaming water and then dropped her shift on the floor as she hastily sat so that he could not see her. She almost melted as the warmth penetrated to her bones, then she set to scrubbing, washing her hair, pulling river weeds from the tangles. Satisfied that she had washed away the muck, she climbed from the tub and dried herself until her skin turned pink, careful to keep the drying cloth covering her as much as she could.

She slipped the borrowed shift and a baggy olive gown over her head, and sat barefoot beside the fire. The clothes were soft from wearing, and smelled of lavender and mint. Absently, she rubbed the towel through her hair and contemplated curling up in bed, but turned to dragging a comb through her hopelessly tangled hair.

Robert strolled over to her, pulling off his tunic and his padded shirt. "I thought you'd never finish." He kicked off his boots. They landed by the fire that glowed in the hearth.

Heat prickled over her skin and warmed her cheeks.

Balling up her wet towel, she sent it sailing at his chest. "Were you watching me? How else would you have known that I was done?"

Robert dodged the towel. "I wasn't watching you, really, I just grew tired of waiting. And if I don't do this soon, I'll fall asleep in all my filth. A fine straw and horsehair bed is waiting." He untied his breeches. "Unless *you* want to watch *me*, I suggest you turn your back."

Eldswythe backed away, pretending to ignore him—but the last thing she could do was ignore him. When he'd taken off his clothes in the hut and she watched, she could not control the urges that filled her head with thoughts about a man a lady shouldn't have. Yet, once again, she couldn't turn her eyes away.

Robert scooped up the towel. He tossed it and his breeches into her lap. "Look away if I offend you. Though 'twould be hard to get a look at me, through all the dirt," he said, stepping into the bath.

Legs pulled up to his chin, he reached out. "Would you be so kind as to hand me the scrub brush?"

Eldswythe picked the brush up off the floor and chucked it at him. "You didn't give me time to leave or even avert my eyes!"

Robert laughed and splashed water in his face. "The water in the tub is black enough from you. You cannot see a thing." He dunked his head and scrubbed his hair. "Besides, you could have closed your eyes in the time it took for me to drop my breeches. I'm not so quick. If you saw anything at all, my lady, it's because you wanted to look!"

Eldswythe stood, her mounting fury as black as the bathwater. "Sir Robert, I am—"

He placed his hand over his heart. "I know . . . you are betrothed. But it has not kept you from looking, nor me from having thoughts I should not have about a promised lady."

She threw the comb and hit him on the head. It bounced off and clattered to the floor.

Robert chuckled and rubbed his head. "Eldswythe, I was once betrothed. But that did not stop me from looking either."

"I'll wager that your roving eyes and other indiscretions are the reason for your unmarried state. If that is your inclination, 'tis better for all women that you stay that way."

Robert stepped out of the tub, slopping water everywhere. "I intend to," he said. He grabbed a shirt from the pile of clothes and pulled it over his head. "When a woman claims to love her future husband and then looks at another man the way you look at me, perhaps she should reconsider. There will be consequences to her actions."

Speechless, Eldswythe shoved past him. "I am going to bed." Her footsteps pounded up the stairs. She slammed the door and pulled the iron lock-bar down.

* * *

Robert slumped into the chair before the fire and swallowed cider. He did not have the energy to pull on his hose and could not be bothered to lace his shirt. Propping his feet up on the footstool, he closed his eyes, remembering the vision of Eldswythe bathing. True, she was tall and thin for his taste, but her hips hinted of a woman's softness. Her breasts were big enough to make him yearn. He should not have looked but the temptation had been impossible to resist.

He examined his throbbing hand. It was such a minor wound that he never would have bothered tending to it. He found it puzzling that it hurt at all.

Shivering, he rubbed the scar across his neck. After a year, the jagged pink skin was still stiff and unforgiving, a wound that would have killed most men.

Mercifully, his brain had blotted out the pain of that initial injury. How he wished that Eldswythe had been the one to stitch him back together then, rather than the monks at Mont Agrew. They were diligent and competent. Never gentle.

He turned his neck to flex the aching muscles. He'd passed the days in the cold stone monastery cell, not giving thanks that he survived, but devising ways to kill the man who had stolen his horses, his armor and the thing that mattered most—the woman he loved.

Margaret of Suttony.

Damnation.

All of Hillsborough had been witness to his defeat.

He chucked the cup across the room. The wound across his neck had healed, but the anger after his betrayal still festered in his soul. He closed his eyes. The vision of Margaret with her legs wrapped around John Gilroy's waist, his naked buttocks pumping hungrily against her as she moaned beneath him, was more than he could bear.

He downed another cup of cider.

The fire blazed and his skin began to roast. It felt good at first, then turned warmer than he wanted. But he was too exhausted now to move. He let his head roll down, his chin rest against his chest.

He thought of Eldswythe. The water droplets trickling down her legs, her damp dark hair curling round her face. Her body pressed against his chest as they rode on Barstow's back . . .

God's peace, her gentle curves and the look of exquisite pleasure on her face while she soaped her firm, young breasts was enough to drive him insane with desire.

"Eldswythe," he called, aware that his voice was but a mere whisper, though it rang in his ears like church bells. "Eldswythe."

He listened. But she did not answer.

Chapter 7

Light streamed through the narrow window as a cock's crow pierced the morning silence. Eldswythe rubbed her eyes and rolled over. When the fog cleared from her brain, she realized she was alone. She jumped from the bed and raced to lift the iron bar that locked the door to the tiny room. Barefoot, she stumbled down the steps into the hall.

The fire was cold, and Robert lay draped across the chair, snoring.

She laid her hand on his shoulder. "I'm sorry, Robert. I should have gone into the children's room and slept in the small bed, or at least thrown some covers down the stairs."

He didn't stir.

Eldswythe tapped him on the shoulder. "Robert?"

He moaned.

She took his chin between her hands and pressed her palm against his hot skin, his face flushed and burning. Her pulse raced. "Oh, God. No!"

Robert lifted his heavy lidded eyes. "Good, you're still . . . still here," he said, holding up his hand, his fingers purple from the knuckles to the tips. "I fear 'tis more than just a scratch."

Eldswythe dunked a towel in the dregs of the chilly bathwater, then wrapped it round his head. "I'll help you to bed. The big one."

Robert leaned against her, his knees buckling beneath his own weight. When he reached the master bed, he collapsed.

Lifting his hand, she inspected the pustules along the margins of the wound. Her calmness eroded, she worked not to show her alarm. "I'll get more towels and water."

He touched her hand, his fingers weak and trembling. "Eldswythe, last night . . . I'm sorry. You did not deserve my harsh words."

"Nor you mine. Save your strength." She laid her palm against his pink cheek, hot with fever. "I am going to the kitchen. I'll be back."

He closed his eyes and she raced from the room knowing full well he might not survive the day. Blessed saints! His life meant more to her than she'd ever dreamed! If he died, she would be stranded here alone. But if she stayed here with him, she might get sick herself in the hours still to come.

She stopped at the doorway that opened into the yard. Barstow was in the barn. It would be easy enough to ride away. Leave Robert Breton. It would be safer than staying here exposed to the contagion.

Eldswythe's gut rolled, her insides churning. If she left him, he might survive. Most likely he would not. His chances were only a little better if she nursed him.

Hesitation drummed at her conscience. She glanced up the stairs toward the bedroom, then back to the door. Yet she could not find the will to command her feet to move. What hold did Sir Robert Breton have on her? Was it strong enough to keep her here and risk her life?

She closed her eyes to steady her thoughts. God's teeth. She was a healer. She could not walk away from one who suffered, nor could she bear the thought of never seeing him again.

She hurried past the door and toward the kitchen.

Rummaging through pantry boxes, she searched for herbs and tools. There was nothing she could use except a carving knife. God willing, it wouldn't come to that.

She pounded up the stairs.

Robert lay sprawled across the bed, his borrowed shirt barely covering his hips. Eldswythe lifted his head and held a cup to his lips, dribbling weak cider into his mouth.

He raised a limp hand and wiped the cider from his chin. "Tell me, will I die from this, fair horsewitch, or can you cure me?"

"You cannot die. I will not let you." Hot tears welled up in her eyes.

He rasped. "My lady, someday you will admit you *are* a horsewitch. You'll have no peace until you do. From me, or God. I've seen you cure my horses, and spook a destrier, then make it run. You should embrace your gift, not deny it." He smiled, his grin weak and pale. "Now tell me the truth about the devil's mark you have on your lovely rump. 'Twill help to keep the demons at bay while my brain is cooking."

Eldswythe bit the inside of her cheek to fight back her alarm. She would not let him know how scared she was. "'Tis not the devil's mark! My father's horse bit me there when I was little. I've never turned my back on a horse again. It was a painful lesson that left a scar." She pulled up a stool beside the bed.

Robert rolled his head in her direction, as if to signal understanding.

She dabbed his forehead with a wet towel. "What else I know I learned from Safia, a Saracen and converted Christian, who came to Crenalden with my father when he returned from his first visit to the East. He said he'd brought her back because she was good with his horses and she wanted to come. She kept the stables for him, and rode a stallion as black as jet, a horse with a fine head, a dish-shaped nose, and small curling ears. Khalif, she called him. A small horse, faster than any in father's stables. Khalif could travel miles before he needed rest."

Eldswythe lowered her head to listen to Robert's chest. She wiped his neck and shoulders with a cloth and then continued. "Safia struck a bargain with my father and took up residence in exchange for lodging in the stables. As a horse healer and a trainer, she proved invaluable. Safia took me underneath her wing, taught me almost everything I know."

Robert grunted. "What happened to her?"

"A year ago, she was accosted by a crowd of castle folk who chased her down with sticks and pitchforks. They yelled 'horsewitch' and threatened to drag her behind a horse until she died if she did not leave. She screamed for my father. He turned his back, and the crowd drove her from the castle. I don't know why he would not help her. No one would tell me, but she was not a horsewitch. I missed her so. I cried for days. She was so desperate to save her life, she left her books, her *Hylica*, and Khalif behind. I don't know where she went, or even if she is alive."

Eldswythe pressed her hand to Robert's forehead. He was hotter than just an hour ago. She covered his forehead with more wet towels, and layered as many soaking cloths as she could over the rest of him.

Her voice wobbled as she bathed his neck and cheeks. "Khalif grieved for her as much as I did and stopped eating. He got so sick he almost died. He sweated and foamed at the mouth and many said he was possessed by the devil. I knew he was not. But I could not diagnose his illness. Finally, when breeding season started in the spring, his attitude and appetite improved. He is all I have left of Safia." She lowered her eyes. "The *Hylica* Gilroy threw in the river was hers."

Robert's eyes glazed beneath half-closed lids. Eldswythe doubted he heard a word. She fought back tears while she dunked more towels into the water and packed them beneath his arms. "Please," she whispered, "please, don't leave me, too."

"Thirsty," he rasped.

She held a cup of cider to his lips. His opened his eyes, hazed and vacant, and stared at her. "Is it enough?" he asked, the look on his face beseeching.

"Is what enough?" She stroked his brow.

He raised his hand and laid it on her arm. "Am I enough?

'Tis all I have to offer. No gold, no title. My brother is the earl, not I."

Eldswythe arched an eyebrow and held her breath.

His fingers tugged at her gown. "Margaret, what else do you want? A castle? A kingdom? I would give them to you if I could."

Mother Mary! He thought he was talking to the Lady Margaret.

She searched for the words to comfort him, fighting to ignore a pang of jealousy. "Robert Breton, you are a master horseman, the finest I have ever seen. That is enough for me."

Robert dropped his hand. A look of calm slipped across his face as his breathing slowed. His head lolled to the side, his face pale.

Exhausted and overcome with weariness, Eldswythe sat on the bed. She slumped, and without thinking, rested her aching head on the pillow next to him. She draped her arm across her forehead and closed her eyes. *Jesu, please don't take him.*

If only Safia were here. She had seen the Bane many times before, both in England and in Acre. Eldswythe knew there were other things to try for treatment, if only she could remember. If she only had her *Hylica*. Curse John Gilroy for destroying her book. Without it, she felt lost, adrift without the woman who'd been her teacher, her friend, almost her mother.

The pain of loss gripped her soul. Her mind reeled and suddenly, she was pleading with her father to find Safia and bring her back. The sun was warm that summer day and the horses were in the yard, readied for transport to market. Their coats gleaming, hooves blackened and their manes and tails plaited for the trip. But her father was preoccupied. He dispersed the crowd that threatened Safia and ordered her to leave. Even his daughter's pleading didn't move him. Not only did he not seem to hear her, he smiled at a handsome washerwoman as she flounced by, resting a basket on her generous hips. Skirts pulled up between her legs and tucked into her apron, she pranced, revealing shapely legs and nicely turned ankles.

Eldswythe sat upright and clapped her hand over her mouth. She'd seen her father smile that smile before. At the washerwoman. Lady Beatrice. Chloe, the brewer's daughter. At a string of women who hovered round whenever he was near.

Mother Mary! Her father had had many women, right before her eyes. She'd been too innocent to comprehend, kept too long in a convent to understand what she'd seen—or else she'd blocked it from her mind. Tears welled beneath her lashes.

Her father was not the saint she'd pictured him to be. Had she ever known what was in his heart? Did he love her mother? Or Isolde?

Did he love her?

She lifted her head and studied Sir Robert's face. Strong chin and jawline. Sculpted cheekbones and deep set eyes. Full, pale lips. Even near death he was a handsome man. How many women, she wondered, had smiled at Robert Breton?

He had loved at least one woman. Margaret of Suttony, the woman her father said Sir Robert ruined.

Though the thought was oddly painful and made her wince, she was glad Robert had loved Margaret, so passionately, it seemed, that he'd let her claim his heart.

Everyone should experience that kind of love once before they died.

A tear slipped down her cheek.

Her soul ached for Robert Breton, to the horseman from a rival house, to the man she suspected of plotting to take her land. So many reasons to leave this place and take her chances. Yet she could not.

She would not.

She was falling in love with Robert Breton, a man she should, by all rights, hate.

A man who might not live out the night.

* * *

Robert's whole body ached, his legs and arms as heavy as lead weights. It took every ounce of strength he had to keep breathing. He squinted against the dim but painful light from a single candle, burning low in the darkness.

His skin was hot and his bandaged hand throbbed. But at the fingertips of his other hand, he could feel silken hair and gentle breath.

A woman! Margaret?

No. The scent that lingered by his bed was too earthy and too clean, not at all like the heavy sweetness of Margaret's perfume.

Corpus bones, it was the horsewitch.

He wanted to reach out to her, touch her, hold her in his arms. Her nearness gave him comfort in a way that Margaret's never had.

Images raced through his mind—Eldswythe standing at the beach, hair whipped by the wind, sun shining on her smooth skin. Her laughter. Her smile when she pushed him and he landed in the water. Asleep by the fire in the hermit's hut and standing in a smoky field, gripped by terror, but determined.

God's bones, he admired her spirit, her knowledge. She knew things about a horse he'd never heard of. And by the saints when she leaned against him in the saddle, it had taken all of his willpower to ignore the fire she ignited in his heart—and below.

If he could have smiled, he would have, but his lips were parched and cracking.

A spoon of cool cider pressed against his mouth. He was grateful for the oval face and dark green eyes that seemed to loom out of the fog around him. Someone cared enough to make him drink.

Lady Eldswythe. She had risked her life to stay with him.

He half wished the Earl of Gloucester had been scared off by the prospect of marriage to a horsewitch. Then she would be free. Free to ride with him. He would make her *his* wife, then fill their stables full of horses and their nursery full of children. Children.

His head ached, but not from fever. From the sickening thought of Margaret's betrayal. Treachery that no man or woman should have to suffer.

God's breath! How could he tell Eldswythe that the king had promised him Crenalden land, the very plots along the River Greve their families had fought over for years? She would hate him if she knew, and would *never* agree to marry him. He'd never be able to convince her it wasn't her land he wanted.

Guilt racked his burning body. It would serve him right if she let the Bane take him. He knew if he lived to defeat Gilroy, he would take her land and in doing so, kill his soul— and hers.

Regret fogged his fever-racked brain, but of one thing he was certain. Eldswythe of Crenalden would despise his duplicity.

Jesu. Don't let her find the letter.

He hoped God listened, and not the devil.

The sound of the wind in the trees awakened Eldswythe. Robert lay exactly as he had before she fell asleep with her head on the pillow beside him—arms at his side, legs straight and feet nearly hanging off the mattress. His skin hot and dry, his face turned ashen.

Eldswythe ripped the bandage from his hand. The pustules were larger and his fingertips black. She tumbled from the bed and groped on the table for the kitchen knife, then lanced the boils around his knuckles. Gathering up the linens, clothes and anything she'd used for dressings, she tossed it all into the smoldering fire. She shed her borrowed gown and burned it, too, then fled naked from the chamber to the hall.

She stepped into the tub. The cold water sent goose bumps

up her arms, but she scrubbed herself with the last scrap of soap, scrubbing until her skin turned red and burned.

It kept her mind off the terror that galloped over her bones.

Skin slick and squeaky, she stepped out of the tub and donned the only other gown that she could find, a baggy, rough-hewn garment the color of a wheat sack.

She hurried back up the stairs. It didn't matter now that she had come in such close contact with the blood and putrid discharge that accompanied the Bane. It didn't matter that she danced with the devil every time she entered Robert's room. She knew what she had to do.

Even if he did not live, and her courage almost shattered at the thought, Sir Robert Breton, the man who held her heart, did not deserve to die alone.

Eldswythe moved across the floor, toward the bed. Her knees shook as she threw the covers off his almost lifeless form. She worked his arms from the sleeves of his shirt and pulled the garment over his head, revealing his broad, hairless chest, his smooth skin hot to the touch. His ragged breath was shallow and slow and his ribs flared as he breathed.

Rolling his breeches past his hips, she wrestled to work his legs free. When she finished, he lay naked, a statue of manly perfection. Despite the raging fever and the deep sleep induced by the Bane, he looked vital and very much alive, as if at any moment he might leap from the bed.

She lifted his arms to feel the underside, probing for telltale lumps beneath the skin, moved to check beneath his ears, and along his throat beside his scar. No bumps or nodules there.

Her breath whistled from her lungs. She pushed her hair behind her shoulders and took another deep breath. There was one place left to check. She ran her hands down his ribcage, to his waist and down below his hips. His manhood settled in between his legs, long and thick, resting in a nest of wiry hair.

Hands trembling, she explored the creases of his groin, the

places where she knew the Bane would spread. His skin was warm and smooth, his hair prickly and thick.

"Sweet Mother of Mary," she said beneath her breath, "he's as big as Barstow!" What was she thinking? The man was at death's door, yet she couldn't resist the need to explore.

She pulled her hands away, embarrassed by her actions and thoughts, but satisfied with the inspection. Letting out a long, deep sigh, she pulled the covers up and sat on the bed, resting her palm against his chest.

She leaned close. "The Bane has not spread. Please, stay with me, Robert," she whispered.

Free of fear or hesitation, she lowered her head and lightly kissed his lips, his musky scent strong and familiar, his mouth soft and warm.

Fatigue consumed her, overwhelmed the strength that kept her bones and muscles working. She stretched out beside him on the bed, then laid her hand on his chest again.

She prayed his heart would not stop beating.

Barstow whinnied. His shrill call echoed from the barn, across the yard through the window of the tiny bedroom. He then greeted the morning by kicking the stall door, jolting Eldswythe awake.

She rubbed her eyes, not daring to look at the man she'd spent the night with, fearing she would not see life. But his arms were warm, and the length of his legs next to hers emanated a gentle heat.

She felt for Robert's heartbeat. It was faint, but steady. For the first time, she allowed herself to hope.

A low voice rumbled beside her. "Barstow sounds alive and well." He held up his bandaged hand, turning it over to examine the thickness. "It hurts like the devil." He yawned. "How long have I slept?"

Eldswythe scrambled up, straightening her tunic and

smoothing her tangled hair. "I'm not sure. A day. Two, maybe. I've fed and watered Barstow at least six times"

She felt the blush spread across her cheeks. At the same time, she wanted to throw herself back into the bed and cover his face with kisses.

Robert groaned and tried to lift his legs, the effort draining him of breath.

He fell back, then reached out and took her by the hand. "Did you sleep beside me every night?"

She lowered her eyes. "No, but last night I was exhausted, and you looked so pale. I must have fallen asleep without realizing where I was."

His fingers gently squeezed her hand. "Your presence gives me comfort. I thank you, Lady Eldswythe, for my life."

He interlaced his fingers with hers, the strength in his touch unmistakable. His life force entwined with hers. A shiver raced up her arm. Eldswythe swallowed, fighting back the powerful connection that drew her to Robert Breton, its source one she couldn't quite define. His probing eyes captured hers and in that instant, she knew her fate was bound to the life of this man. The only man who understood her struggle. The one person on the face of the earth to whom she'd as much as admitted what she long denied. She was a horse-witch.

He released her fingers, then he groped beneath the covers and his thick eyebrows arched with a look of mock surprise.

She stammered, "I burned our clothes. They carried the contagion."

"Ahh-hah." He smiled weakly. "Did you . . . tend to my every need?"

Eldswythe felt the heat rising to her cheeks again. She ignored his question. "Are you hungry?"

"No." He winced and rubbed the scar across his neck.

She dipped her fingers in the butter pot on the table and sat beside him. "This will soften it." She rubbed the butter on the scar and felt his tension ease beneath her fingers.

Robert moaned and closed his eyes.

"The fever nearly killed you. But I see it's not the first time you've been so close to death. How did you come by such a wicked wound?"

"At Smithfield," he mumbled.

"The day you were unseated from the saddle?" Her hands slowed until she stopped massaging altogether. "But the lance tips that day were splayed for sport."

"Not every tip. Some chose to ignore the rules."

She frowned, knowing that a pointed lance could pierce the weak spot between the coif and shoulder mail, killing a man as quickly as any sword. "Did the judges know your opponent charged you with a gimlet tip?"

"No, and the only one who could make the accusation lay bleeding in the grass, his helmet stomped and crushed into his head."

"Who was the knight who almost killed you? He should be held accountable."

He barely moved his lips. "You know him."

Puzzled, Eldswythe tried to recollect the field of challengers that day. "Who?" Then her eyes widened. "John Gilroy?"

Robert nodded and closed his eyes. "I need to sleep again," he said, his voice barely above a whisper. "I would like it very much if you would sit beside me. No need to worry. I've never forced a woman into my bed."

Eldswythe smiled. He hardly had the strength of a newborn kitten, but he was game enough to jest. It pleased her that he wanted her to stay beside him.

She dragged the stool from beneath the window and set it by the bed. "I will stay, Robert, as long as you need me."

Chapter 8

John Gilroy sat back in his cushioned chair, dangled one booted leg across the other and sucked his little finger. Crenalden Castle was not much to his liking, but the beehives were full of honey and the hearth was big enough to roast a deer. Otherwise, the place was too Spartan for his taste.

A soldier knelt before him. "What of the horse, my lord, the Spanish stallion?"

"What of it?"

"What should we do about it? Someone set it loose in the woods. It will not let us come close enough to get a rope around its neck; we've tried for days."

He shrugged. "I have no interest in it. When you catch it, sell it and bring the coin to me."

The soldier bowed and trotted off as Gilroy pulled a dagger from his belt and speared a chunk of stewed fish. Chewing carefully, he made a sweeping gesture. "From the looks of things here, the old earl spent his resources on his bloody horses." He picked up a battered wooden cup and held it out for refilling. "For God's sake, why not hang a tapestry or two or paint the flagstones at the hearth? And where's his gold and silver plate? I was told he entertained the king!"

He did not expect an answer. His men were focused on their food.

A waif-like serving boy, begrimed and barefoot, filled his cup and then produced a ram-shaped ewer. He dipped his fingers in the vessel, then wiped them on the linen tablecloth, his mustached lips curling in disgust. As the victor he'd expected finer things as booty. Silks perhaps, or at least velvet runners on the table.

At thirty years of age, he had become accustomed to certain luxuries. War, he determined, was the most efficient way to obtain almost anything a man desired. It didn't hurt that he had inherited his father's cunning knack for sniffing out the weak, including a king distracted by his conflicts with the Scots, and a crown prince who felt the need to stay away, fighting in the Holy Lands for God knew what.

Circumstance and wars, thankfully, provided unexpected opportunities. It was no coincidence his holdings were vast and growing, his wealth an example of his prowess. Hell to the devil, if the father who'd denied him could see him now. He laughed at the irony of finding Crenalden Castle devoid of silver plate. All hidden, he suspected, and sooner or later, he would find it. And if he did not, it didn't really matter, since the land and the water rights along River Greve were now in his control. There was the real wealth. Even the king paid tariffs.

Gilroy rolled the watered wine around in his mouth. He expected no punishment or retribution for his activities because he fully planned to swear allegiance to Prince Edward following his coronation when he returned from Acre or Damascus or wherever he might be. What new king would not want access to the coffers of a rich and powerful subject?

He sniffed. Yes, he would be forgiven. It was the way of politics and war. Too bad it was not the way of women.

A freckle-faced servant girl knelt beside him. "My lord, do you wish for company tonight?"

John Gilroy fingered the golden hair that tumbled freely down the girl's shoulders. He slipped his hand behind her neck and squeezed. "You remind me of someone I used to know," he said. "Braid your lovely blond hair and wear a veil tonight, a veil as white as you can find, then come to me before you say your evening prayers."

The girl kissed his ring. Her eyes were full of hope and anticipation. She bowed and hurried back to the kitchen.

Gilroy lowered his head to inspect the flecks of dried blood on his tunic sleeve. Just a few small spots which could have been his own, but blood had always bothered him. He scratched until they flaked away. *Good God, combat is such a messy business.* And after all the killing, his half sister, the Lady Eldswythe, was still alive.

He pounded his fist down on the table and roared. "Crenalden Castle is my birthright! I am the Earl of Crenalden now. Is there anyone who challenges my claim?"

His soldiers paused from eating and stared at one another, then went back to feasting. Gilroy rubbed his face in frustration. Food would always win the war between a stomach and decorum. But at least he had captured the Earl of Gloucester, though he doubted the old man's kin would choose to pay the ransom.

Sitting back in his chair, he surveyed the room and laughed at the middle-aged serving woman who dashed around the table, screaming. Her portly rump bounced beneath her flouncing skirts as two drunken knights chased her. This one, who had somehow managed to survive, might wish that she hadn't in the hours to come.

He scratched beneath his tunic, his own shaft starving for attention. He had had enough of washerwomen and camp whores. He longed to share a lady's bed again. At least the kitchen maid was fresher, and just as willing. And she resembled a woman he had once adored.

The fire raging in the hearth, he called for his serving boy. "Reynaud?"

The boy stepped forward from the shadows. "Yes, my lord." He cringed and bowed at the same time.

Gilroy laughed. "Make the new Earl of Crenalden's chambers ready."

* * *

At dawn, Gilroy paced the floor in the great hall, surrounded by the men he was certain he could trust. He unrolled a map onto the table and stabbed his knife into the symbol of his next acquisition.

His senior retainer, Richard of Lisbon, cracked his knuckles. "'Tis not three days' ride from here, my lord. Faster if we move some men on boats along the river." He traced a line up the River Greve with the tip of his dagger.

Success was imminent. Gilroy clouted Lisbon on the back. With Crenalden Castle in his possession, he had his base camp. He would need one in the winter months when he moved his army through the countryside, heading for the real prize. Hillsborough Castle.

Hillsborough Castle, three times the size of this one, could not easily be taken by siege, though he suspected the new Earl of Hillsborough, Lord Harold, was not the warrior his father was. But nonetheless, the best way to conquer Hillsborough was to draw its army to the battlefield.

The very thought of drawing that blackguard, Sir Robert Breton, to the battlefield made his palms itch. Robert Breton did not deserve to walk the earth, and this time he would finish what he meant to do a year ago at Smithfield.

He smiled and tossed pieces of his breakfast to the dogs that panted at his feet, stroking the elegant ears of his favorite hunting hound. "I know exactly how you feel, snatching morsels here and there. You would rather feast on the entire table, knowing that you are the one who rightfully deserves to do so."

He tossed a glazed egg into the pack, which set them all to baying. Stroking his mustache, he chuckled. Soon enough, Robert Breton would be begging at his table, just like these dogs. And the horsewitch would be hanging from chains in the dungeon. The thought was so sweet that he could taste it. He poured his private stock of claret from a flagon into a wooden cup, then raised it to his lips. Somewhere in this hellhole, his black-hearted father must have hidden all his silver plate.

He swallowed. His face pulled into a violent pucker. He swore a string of curses, then sent the cup flying, splintering against the wall. The blood-red liquid trickled down the stones and puddled onto the floor. The hounds were on the spot, lapping with slobbering pink tongues.

Gilroy wiped the dribble from his chin. What a disservice, he thought, to drink his finest wine from so crude a vessel. It tasted like a musty wooden shoe.

The sergeant-at-arms grimaced with the insult of having his sword and dagger removed at the doorway. He pushed past the men and strode into the hall, summoned to recount his men's failed attempts to catch the Lady Eldswythe.

He knelt before his lord and commander, John Gilroy. "She rides with Robert Breton, my lord. They traveled into Belway Forest and then to Whickerham, where the Black Bane runs rampant. We dared not venture there."

Looking down, Gilroy flicked a bread crumb from his leather jerkin. "How unfortunate. I'm sad to say that this failure marks the end of your career."

Guards dragged the sergeant from the hall. Feet kicking and arms flailing, he bellowed. "Gilroy, rot in hell! Your mother was a whore! You are a bastard, and all of England knows it!"

"Hang him," answered Gilroy as he rose from his seat. "And his men."

Indifferent to the condemned soldier's protests, he sauntered to the hearth and pulled down the lance that hung against the wall.

Fingering the tip, he turned to face his burly captain, who snapped to attention. "Alberts, did you hear she rides with Robert Breton? Strange that he should be the one coming to her rescue." He set the lance up on its end. "Then again, perhaps not. I am sure the king has offered him a chest of gold to try and stop me. Take your best men and set out for Hillsborough. Capture Lady Eldswythe before she makes it to that fortress, then bring her here. Alive."

Captain Alberts nodded, his face impassive. "What of Robert Breton, sir?"

Gilroy picked up the lance and snapped off the wicked-looking gimlet point. "Give this to Robert Breton. Tell him I said that all is fair in love and war, then kill him. Let those be the last words he hears." He laughed and stroked his hound beneath the chin. "He'll know exactly what I mean."

Chapter 9

A dusky evening light filtered through the open windows of the kitchen and carried with it the sweet fragrance of apple blossoms and the chattering of sparrows. Eldswythe leaned across the table, layering slices of cheese and salted meats onto a wooden tray. Bootless and sleep disheveled, Robert ambled into the kitchen and leaned against the hearth.

She smiled and handed him the tray. "No more lolling in the bed. Follow me."

She'd swept the hall and set the table with cups and wooden bowls filled with nuts and apples. Over the past week, she'd grown accustomed to talking with him while they ate, about horses and the teachings of masters such as Xenophon and Alexander. Roberts's easy banter about horses he had trained and ridden gave her comfort.

Robert stretched his arms above his head, then pulled out the bench and took his seat. He, too, seemed to look forward to being with her. They'd spent hours while he lay abed resting, discussing horses, horsemen and tales of valor before he drifted back to sleep.

No longer a man on the brink of death, he cut a handsome figure in the soft evening light. His broad chest strained against the seams of the borrowed rust-colored tunic. His gray hose stretched across his long thighs and calves, and molded to their form. His swarthy color had returned, and his steely eyes were bright.

Eldswythe found it hard to forget the image of Robert Breton lying naked on the bed. It was a sight she thought of often. Too often. His newfound vigor and ill-fitting clothes only seemed to exacerbate her obsession with the man.

She concentrated on her cheese and hoped he hadn't noticed she'd been staring at him.

Robert wolfed down his meat and reached for an apple. "A fine meal, Eldswythe. I don't remember one much better." He bit into the apple and smiled. "Perhaps it's the company."

Eldswythe ignored the compliment, struggling to broach a subject that they each had avoided. It was time to leave, though she wasn't ready. In truth, she wished they could stay. But she worried about Crenalden. And Khalif and the Earl of Gloucester. Bertrada would be waiting for her at Hillsborough, and Robert had an army waiting for him. She could sense his impatience, his body forcing him to rest and wait while urgent business was at hand.

She lowered her eyes and crumbled her cheese between her anxious fingers.

He cleared his throat. "Eldswythe, I am well enough to ride. It's time for us to leave."

Disappointment washed over her. She knew he was right, but *she* wasn't ready. There were so many things she wanted to talk to him about, not the least of which was the letter. He never mentioned the king's missive, and she avoided asking him about it. Neither did she broach the subject of her land or her father. She'd no proof that Robert was out to steal her property and she knew in her heart that her father had no part in the old Earl of Hillsborough's death. Yet Robert believed it true. No, it was best to leave some things unspoken. She wanted to enjoy the newfound peace between them. She was happy and he seemed glad to be with her.

"Your health is not yet up to spending hours in the saddle. Hillsborough is still a two-day ride from here."

He pushed his food away and stood up. "Eldswythe, an

army waits for me. And Gilroy will track us down. It isn't safe to stay. The people who own this place will return. I've seen merchants on the road, headed for their shops in the village."

A thin wind rattled the shutters and Eldswythe looked to the window. She steeled herself to face the truth. She and Robert Breton had obligations and responsibilities that reached far beyond the confines of this cloistered manor house. Here they were removed from politics and war and from the conflict in her heart. She had to distance herself from him, from this place and from the contented quiet hours they had shared. She would focus on her duty while she still could.

She scooted from the bench and gathered up their utensils, but she kept her eyes on the table, intending to hide the misery that swelled inside her. "Then we should leave as soon as possible. Let me have a few minutes to put things right . . ."

She hurried toward the kitchen, relying on her instincts to tell where her legs were going.

She tripped beside the hearth.

Food, platters, and one of Robert's boots went spinning across the floor. Her gaze followed the yellow parchment that fluttered from his boot top and came to rest at her feet. A letter, half unfolded. The king's missive. Open just enough for her to read.

A jolt of pain shot through her soul. So that was Robert's secret—her dowered land and two hundred more hectacres of Crenalden properties, as well. The king had promised him what he knew Robert wanted more than anything on earth. Good God. How had she come to care so deeply for Robert Breton? A covetous knight who helped her at the king's bidding in exchange for a royal boon. A mercenary to the core.

Robert snatched the letter up. A light sheen of sweat glistened on his forehead, and he clenched his fists.

She closed her eyes, her mind racked with confusion and with anger.

How had this happened? Had she forgotten she was honor

bound to marry the Earl of Gloucester, the man her *father* chose for her?

Robert spoke, his voice barely above a whisper. "Eldswythe, I cannot deny I want what the king has promised. I grew up expecting to inherit the tract along the River Greve. My brother all but gave it to your father while I was laid low after the Smithfield tourney. I would do anything to get my parcel back. I cannot tell you I do not want it, but I promise once it's mine we will live in peace, your house and mine."

Eldswythe looked away. Mother Mary. Was it possible to hate the man you loved? Slowly, she rose from her seat. "I've nothing more to say to you, Sir Robert."

Blackness filled her heart, an ocean of distrust, hatred, and hurt as wide and inhospitable as the sea that stretched from England all the way to Acre.

Miserable and numb, she spent the rest of the evening putting the house in order, intent on leaving things as she'd found them while Robert worked in the barn. The darkness would soon drive him back inside, but she'd kept busy, planning to be occupied when he returned.

When there was nothing left to do in the hall, she beat the lumps out of the mattress and lowered herself to the bed, thinking about the hours she'd spent at Robert's side, feeling his closeness, drawing on his strength to keep them both alive. Never once during his sickness had he mentioned the letter—and the silence that passed between them since she'd discovered it just hours past was cold and as hard as stone.

She pulled a wooden comb from her belt and dragged it through the tangles in her hair. She closed her eyes, in part from the pain in her scalp and in part to keep the tears behind her lashes from spilling down her cheeks. God's peace! She'd been a fool. To think he cared for her, a horsewitch.

The door to the hall below banged against the wall, rattling the plates and cups.

Eldswythe wiped her face and pinched the color back into

her cheeks, then descended the narrow stairway. She prayed that Robert could not tell she'd been crying. Perhaps without a candle, her red-rimmed eyes would not be so obvious. She stood at the entrance to the hall, and stared at him with an icy look she knew to be her coldest.

Robert knelt beside the hearth, intent it seemed on stoking up the fire, though it was late now. He held up a hare, dressed and gutted. "I snared our supper for the road. I'll cook it tonight and we can take it with us tomorrow."

He ran the carcass on the spit and motioned to the flagon of wine sitting on the table. "Have a drink, my lady. It will do much to improve your mood."

Embarrassed that he'd noticed she'd been crying, Eldswythe kept her head down as she poured the wine. "Where did you find this?" She held the flagon up. The vessel was already half empty.

"There's a cellar in the shed behind the barn." He grinned and settled himself in the chair beside the hearth. "It's potent stuff, so be careful how much you drink. We leave for Hillsborough at dawn. I need you to be awake early in the morning."

Two subjects she was in no mood to discuss: leaving and the king's missive. In just the hour last, she decided she needed Robert and his army to retake Crenalden. Without him, her castle and her land, including the tracts the king had promised to Robert would be lost. Cutting off a part of her father's estate would be better than losing all. She would hold fast to the belief her land would not be awarded to a Breton once Gilroy was ousted, and her father could persuade the king to offer Robert gold instead.

She eased down on the bench and aligned the spoons, stalling for time to find a topic for conversation which would not lead to an argument. "Tell me, how did you come by Barstow?" she asked without looking up. "Did you win him in a tourney?"

Robert laughed. "Hah! God, no. He hails from the South of France. I was there for a tournament when I heard the story of a horse that rescued drowning men."

Eldswythe raised her eyebrows. "You are drunk and telling tales."

"'Tis true. A shipwreck happened off the coast of Saint Raphael. His owner saw the sailors drowning. He jumped on Barstow's back and braved the waves, swimming from the shore to the wreck and back, with two and sometimes three men hanging from his boots and two from Barstow's tail. Fifteen times Barstow braved the ocean waves. On the last trip out, his owner was swept away and drowned."

Robert took another swig, then sat quiet quietly, rolling the stem of the pewter chalice between his fingers. "Barstow made it to shore. I found him running wild in the barren hills, hungry, but unapproachable. Not even the locals could catch him. Eventually, I was able to befriend him. I bought a few of the villagers a cup or two of ale and persuaded them to let me keep him."

"He suits you."

"He's worth his weight in gold. It would kill my soul to lose him."

She swirled her cup and watched the wine spin in circles, wondering what had happened to her own horse, Ceres. With any luck, she had joined with the herd of wild ponies that grazed beside the banks of Belway's lake, deep inside the forest. She took another drink and let the oaken taste of the wine fill her head before she swallowed. If she learned as much as she could about Robert Breton, what he really cared about, she might be able to persuade him to accept coin for a reward in lieu of her land.

"I know how much a warhorse means to a knight," she stated carefully. "Why did you give your dappled destrier to my father's squire? It was generous. An act of kindness I did not expect. Tell me why you really did it. I want no more secrets between us."

Robert studied Eldswythe's assessing face, worried that whatever he answered might reveal too much. He desperately wanted her to believe in him, to trust him, though his every action since they met could be questioned. Even the gifting

of his destrier to her father's squire had not been entirely al-
truistic. But that was weeks ago. He felt different now.

He left his chair and knelt at the hearth, pretending to be
occupied with the fire. Maybe it was the wine, but his stomach flipped with self-reproach.

Damnation. She was too trusting. She thought him generous. Well, he wasn't. He'd given the destrier to her father's
squire because he knew Edward needed every mounted
knight he could muster. It was as much a favor to the young
prince as it was a token of his gratitude to Eldswythe. Since
the moment the clerk had handed him that damnable letter,
he'd kept his real intent—to win Crenalden lands—from Eldswythe. But he hadn't told her so. Nor did he wish to speak
of it now. In truth, he didn't want to disrupt the quiet bond
that had started to form between them before she'd read the
missive. He hated himself for his ambition, for misleading
her and coveting a boon that he could only win at her ex-
pense. But neither could he let it go. Anger and frustration
flared in his soul.

Tell her the truth about the horse gift and be done with it.

He pulled the spit from the fireplace and set it on the table.
The meat sizzled in the platter, and the rich smell of cooked
game fat filled the air. "I gave the horse to your father's squire
as a favor to Edward. Edward needs every man and horse he
can get. He will someday be the next king of England. I want
him to remember me." He paused and waited for her response.
When none came, he turned and faced her, expecting the disappointment he read on her face. "The rabbit is done now," he
said without emotion. "When it cools, I'll wrap it up in cheese-
cloth and take it with us."

An awkward silence fell across the hall. The fire crackled, burning orange and blue. In the soft light, Eldswythe
looked enchanting. Robert studied her as one would study a
newly painted fresco, a complex painting rich with color and
layers he'd not yet explored and couldn't understand. He
wanted to know more. "You won't accept I intend to take your
land, I can tell by your silence. But will you finally admit,

since we are being frank with one another, that you are a horsewitch?"

She didn't answer but he could see her eyes flicker with uncertainty. Softening, he stooped beside her and rested his hand on her knee, regretting he'd caused her more distress. "Eldswythe, what is it that you fear? If you are one, declare yourself. I won't think less of you. I don't think you capable of the wickedness Equus Magus describes in those who have the gift."

Her voice shook. She spoke so softly he could barely hear her reply. "I don't know what I am. I've never met a horsewitch. I've no one to ask. I don't know what I . . . what *they* can do. The book says they are usually women, for women share a bond with the beasts. Unlike men who can use brute force to make a horse yield, a woman has not the strength. She must rely on the power in her heart and mind, and use a kind of magic unavailable to most men. I read that a horse wizard, as rare as he may be, will someday challenge that myth. But I don't know anything for certain. Safia never broached the subject, I swear it."

Robert arched an eyebrow. "You spooked Gilroy's warhorse. Didn't it seem strange to you that a seasoned destrier, accustomed to the sounds and cruelties of a battlefield, would run from a shrieking woman? And then you did it again to the robber's horse. The beast bucked the robber off because you willed it. Can you think of other times a horse has behaved as you would like?"

Eldswythe lowered her eyes. "Once Khalif was so sick, fighting for his life. I don't know what happened to him, but I mixed a draught and made him drink it, when no one else could get anything past his lips. And there was the time when Ceres . . ." Looking up, she locked her eyes with Robert's. "If my father ever knew, he would cast me out. He would not have a woman as unholy as a horsewitch in his presence."

Her hands balled into fists and her shoulders started to shake. Robert felt her anguish. Damnation. She was scared. Scared to admit she had power she didn't know what to do with and afraid she would lose the love of her father if he knew. He would cast her off forever if she lost any of his castle or estate—to a Breton or to John Gilroy. At this moment, she probably considered one man as bad as the other.

He doused the embers and plugged the flagon with the cork. Rising, he offered his hand to Eldswythe. "Forgive me. I should have told you about the king's reward. Better that you knew at the start of this, than to find out when you did. I will never take more from Crenalden than what I have been promised by the king, but our houses will live peaceably, thereafter. You have my word on this."

Eldswythe did not take his hand. She stared into his face, her eyes unreadable.

Robert lowered his arm. "We will not be allowed to share quarters once we've reached Hillsborough," he said softly. "I want to keep you near me for a little while longer, horse-witch or no. Not every man fears your power, Eldswythe. I wish to prove it to you. Let's go to bed. Enough talk of politics and land."

She shook her head, her eyes raised to his and the inflection in her voice that of disbelief. "I cannot. I am the Earl of Crenalden's daughter, and you believe he killed your father. You are bound by the king to protect me and you will take what is mine for the privilege. You do not have to prove anything to me. Do not pretend to care for me. It will do you no good. I am pledged to wed another. I cannot sleep beside you."

Robert laced his fingers with her own. "Eldswythe . . ."

"No, Robert, please don't." She pulled away.

Robert leaned against the table, his heart heavy. He locked his eyes with hers. "I would never have fathomed being laid low by the Bane and recovering at the hands of Lady Eldswythe, the Earl of Crenalden's daughter, that I would survive and find myself so attracted to . . ." He hesitated, then gritted his teeth. "You cannot expect a man, any man, to turn down what the king offers. You cannot expect a man to spend day and night with you and not. . . . Eldswythe, there is more between us now than either you or I can admit. Despite the reasons not to, you and I share a connection between a man and woman that's . . . that's . . ." He let out an exasperated sigh and ran his hands through his hair. "Good God, the words escape me. Don't you know how beautiful you are?"

She shook her head. "It's the wine talking. Sweet words that make me call on every ounce of strength I have to refuse you. But you pursue me hoping I'll concede my heart and thereby not object when you've won my land and come to claim it." She turned and started up the stairs. "I'll sleep in the children's room. Alone."

Robert bounded across the room and to her side. "No, you won't." He scooped her up into his arms.

Eldswythe bucked and fought. "No! You said you'd never force a woman."

She beat her fists against his chest as he stomped up the stairs. He held on tighter, his arms locked around her like a vise.

He kicked open the master bedroom door and sent it swinging as he thundered into the room, then tossed her onto the bed. "For days you have tended to me like a babe," he growled. "Fed me, washed me, and lain beside me." He folded his arms. "Do you really think I would repay your kindness by forcing myself upon you? Have I been so horrible or mistreated you in any way that would make you think I'd hurt you? Drunk or no, I've never forced a woman. It wounds me to see the doubt in your eyes, Eldswythe. Sleep in here tonight, alone, and sleep well." He stalked from the room and slammed the door behind him.

His voice roared from the other side of the door. "I'll sleep in the stables."

His feet pounded down the stairs.

Eldswythe, breathing hard, leaned against the bedpost. The thought of spending the night without him left her cold. She slid down onto the lumpy mattress, then rolled onto her side and drew her knees to her chest. The hardest thing for her to do was to keep from Robert what she wanted. She wanted him, a Breton and a man she could not trust. Damn the king's letter. She wished she'd never read it!

From below her window, the barn door hinges creaked. Barstow whinnied and a deep rich voice rose up from below, carried by the gentle wind.

She could not be sure, but she thought she heard Robert call up to her. "I'll not forget the horsewitch dressed in blue, who kissed me with her heart if not her lips."

Robert stomped into the stables. A bed of straw was softer than a stone floor. He kicked an empty bucket and sent it sailing. At least his horse would keep him company.

If she found him so unappealing, why did every signal he could sense tell him that she wanted him as much as he wanted her, despite her protests? Tonight she acted as if she had not just spent her days tending to his every need and sleeping close beside him. Why could she not accept he agreed to a deal proposed by the king, an arangement between two men who sought opportunity in war? What was wrong with that, especially since a portion of the land he fought for was rightfully his?

Damnation, would he ever understand a woman's mind?

Barstow hung his head across the stall door and nickered. Robert stroked his horse's nose. "Thank God. You are a sane and steady companion."

He stretched out on the hay that would be his makeshift bed. It prickled and made him cough, but it was better than sleeping with the she-witch inside. He closed his eyes. At least the wine had made him groggy, though it set his mind to spinning.

The vision of Eldswythe standing in the firelight filled his mind. Her gentle curves, her dark hair spilling down her shoulders . . . even a wheat sack of a dress could not disguise her breasts. He wanted to bury his face in that place between her neck and earlobes, to kiss the softness of her silken skin and breathe in her scent.

A mouse skittered across his boot. Rain pattered on the

roof, then splattered on his forehead. He shifted his position and threw his arm across his eyes.

God's teeth, why did she have to look the way she did? The ache in his loins was more than just the cold. It was lust, pure and simple.

Lust, desire, and wanting—those he understood!

Thunder cracked as more water droplets dotted Robert's forehead. He ran his hand across his face, and looked up. The roof leaked directly on the spot where he had made his bed. He moved away, but was wetted down again as the rain found its way through the patches of aging thatch. He contemplated taking shelter under Barstow, but then the great horse flagged his tail and peed a gush that splattered in the straw and steamed. Damnation. He would not tolerate a barn when there was a warm, dry bed inside. At this point all he really wanted was sleep.

He barreled into the house, climbed the stairs three at a time and bounded past the children's room into the master bedroom.

Eldswythe sat up. Her lips parted and a gasp slipped past.

Robert met her glare directly. "The barn roof was leaking and the children's beds are too small." He shook the water from his head, pulled off his wet shirt, then flopped down beside her. "If you will stay on your half, I will stay on mine."

Eldswythe lowered herself back down, then hugged her arms across her chest. She stiffened, trying not to roll toward him as the ropes beneath the mattress sank with his weight.

He could hear her breathing and he watched the rise and fall of her chest from the corner of his eye. Her scent of apples and herbs clung to the sheets.

"Robert," she whispered tentatively, "had we met years ago, before your father . . . before my father . . . Things might have been different between us. But now it is too late and I—"

His face moved above hers. A warm current rippled over him, emanating from the point where their shoulders touched. Guarded desire shimmered in her green eyes, eyes that asked a question and probed his soul.

Robert lowered his mouth to hers. Eldswythe did not pull

her head away, but let her lips open just enough for him to taste her. Red wine and spice.

He stopped and pulled his head away, staring into her eyes, giving her the opportunity to push him off or roll away.

She lay perfectly still, then he felt her hands sliding up his back, until her fingers buried in his thick dark hair. She pulled his face to hers. "Damn you," she muttered against his lips.

He moved on top of her, her softness warm and inviting. He explored her mouth with his tongue and let his hands roam, moving down to the neckline of her gown. "I want to feel you, Eldswythe, and see you. Will you let me?" He slowly slipped the tunic and chemise off her shoulders and exposed her white, rounded breasts, nipples erect and jutting.

Eldswythe shuddered. He feathered kisses down her neck and brushed the tips of her breasts with his lips. Arching her back, she pressed herself against him, warmth spreading from between his legs, to his belly. It made him ache for more. He didn't want this to stop, wanted it to last forever.

Damnation, he should have claimed her for his wife and had the clerk marry them right there on Dover Beach. The king would have been furious, but Gloucester could find another heiress. He wanted this one, this amazingly tantalizing woman called a horsewitch. "Eldswythe," he whispered, his voice husky. "If our houses were united, if we married the feud would be over and I would . . ."

In an instant, she pulled away, struggling to cover her breasts. "No. I am pledged to marry. I will keep my vow." She clasped the bodice of her gown to her chest. Confusion and alarm stole across her face. "I have forgot myself and who I am. I have forgot who you are and what I think you really want. It isn't me."

Robert groaned, and lay as still as a statue.

Minutes passed, and then he raised himself and kissed her softly on the lips. "I want you, Eldswythe of Crenalden. You use the Earl of Gloucester as a barrier between us. With the patience of a horseman, I will wait for you to come to my bed willingly and with an open heart."

He got up and settled in the chair beside the fire, propped his feet up on the stool, and folded his arms. His head lolled backward and he stared at the rafters, knowing sleep would evade him tonight.

Trembling, Eldswythe turned to face away from him. "Don't kiss me again. I hate that you covet my land and you work to take it from me. I hate that you do not speak to me of . . . love. I know from your ramblings on your sick bed another holds your heart. I hate that I am not her, that I am not the Lady Margaret."

The air in the room suddenly turned cold, brittle.

Utter devastation flooded the last of Robert's checked reserve. His feet slammed onto the floor. "No, you are not Lady Margaret, *Lady* Eldswythe. If you were, you would not be here. Nor would I."

Eldswythe flung herself on her side to face him. Tears rolled down her cheeks. "Gilroy said you have a penchant for wooing women you think might make you rich. I know you fell in love with Lady Margaret and her dower was a duchy. Tell the truth. Do you want me, or my land?"

Robert seethed, the veins at his temples throbbing. "You do not know the whole of it. Have you ever given heart and soul to someone, and then later learned that they did not want it? That they did not care if you lived or died?"

Her face went pale at his admission. She didn't answer.

"I thought not," he said. "Until you do, you have no right to judge me." He clenched his fists. "You and I, Lady Eldswythe, are bound by the king's command to work together. So I will do my best from now on to keep myself in check where your person is concerned. I ask you to do the same. It will make things easier for both of us."

He stormed from the room and slammed the door behind him with such force the sound cracked through the whole house.

Chapter 10

Mother Mary. She'd never seen him so angry. He was furious and she knew she'd no right to bring up his painful past. What kind of woman was the Lady Margaret, who incited love and hatred from Robert Breton? It sparked her curiosity. Most of all, it made her jealous. Thoughts of another woman in Robert's arms had kept her up all night, and the chamber alive with shadows that were anything but restful. At dawn, Eldswythe dragged herself from the bed, her attention distracted from her anxious thoughts to the clamor in the yard. She pushed the oilcloth from the window, then threw back the shutters and watched a squattish man lead Barstow from the barn. A strapping boy followed close behind, carrying a whip.

A withered-looking woman in a drab brown dress trod into the yard and labored beneath a large pack that toppled from her back. She sat down on the baggage, surveyed the grounds, then rubbed her rump. Villagers straggled down the road, then filed into the yard, sticks and pitchforks in their hands.

Eldswythe dragged her dress over her head and bounded down the stairs to the hall. Robert snored in the chair beside the dying fire, his hair tousled and his face creased with fatigue.

"Wake up! The owners of the house are back," she whispered as she shook him by the arm. "There are villagers, too, armed and ready. They have Barstow. Make haste!"

Robert leapt from the chair and strapped his sword to his side. "Stay here," he commanded, then bolted from the room.

Ignoring his direct order, Eldswythe followed.

Robert kept his hand on his sword as he strode into the yard. He stopped and bowed nonchalantly to the villagers. "Good morrow. I see you have my horse."

A stout man with copper-colored hair and a wiry beard handed Barstow's reins to the round-faced boy. Some ten other men, each with a weapon, stood shoulder to shoulder, blocking Robert from his horse.

The man tightened up his rope belt and rolled up his sleeves. "And you've helped yourself to our belongings." He pointed to the gray woolen tunic and bacon-brown shirt that Robert wore. "I figure for the food you ate and the wood you burned, your horse will make us even."

The woman looked at Robert's bandaged hand. A look of alarm shot across her face, then vanished. She adjusted her wimple, then cleared her throat. "Magnus, I am tired. I have carried all our valuables on my back for miles. We left nothing much worth taking. Let them go along their way. They were just leaving." She looked at Eldswythe, then tipped her head and averted her eyes toward the road.

Barstow snorted and pawed, startling the boy who jumped and dropped the reins. The boy squealed, and stepped closer to his mother. "The devil of a horse! It tried to bite me!"

Peeking from behind his mother, he pointed at Eldswythe. "Uncle Magnus, she be the horsewitch from Crenalden. We saw her at the summer fair. She gave a poultice to Jules Whitby and claimed 'twould cure his horse's thrush."

A feeble voice called from the crowd. "And it did! And I sold the horse, sound and able, for a half a shilling more than the knacker woulda gimme for it, lame and stinking."

The crowd murmured and backed away, their faces filled with the kind of caution that bordered upon outright fear.

Barstow moved over to the grass beside the barn. The horse lowered his head and started munching, his white teeth ripping a thin patch of green. A villager with a coil of rope beneath his arm attempted to approach him. With every step the man took, the great destrier turned his rump and kicked, sending clots of dirt whizzing by the man's head.

The boy, apprehension on his face, spoke again. "Look, mama, she wears your birthing dress."

Eldswythe patted down the stomacher of the drab dress. Crudely cut, it sagged and hung off her shoulders. She stepped forward and lowered her head. "I am sorry to have borrowed this one. My own is ruined." She hesitated and then continued. "I . . . I am with child. We travel on to Hillsborough, but I asked my new husband to find a place to rest. We spent the night and ate a little of your food and drank some cider." She turned to the boy. "I am not the horsewitch. You are mistaken."

Surprised at how easily she lied, Eldswythe kept her eyes downcast and prayed that no one else would recognize her and that no one would search and discover missing clothes and linens, and empty flasks of wine.

Magnus growled. "Get my hoe, Timothy." The boy ran into the shed, fetched the hoe and tossed it to his father. Magnus took a battle-ready stance. He looked at Robert. "You say you travel on to Hillsborough? From which direction did you come? From Whickerham? 'Tis the only road here."

The villagers gasped. Several stepped away, breaking rank.

Robert drew his sword. "Let us be, good sir, and we'll be on our way."

Magnus gestured to Eldswythe. "The magistrate has offered a reward for anyone proved to carry the contagion, man or beast, or woman. 'Tis known by all, that she is a horsewitch. I saw her at the fair, and everyone was pointing. Maybe 'twas her that loosed the Bane upon our village. 'Twas the devil's work and the church and magistrate are looking for the culprit."

The crowd started chanting "horsewitch," and circled Eldswythe.

Magnus raised his hoe. "I say we put the horse and the horsewitch in the lime pit with the others and bury them." He tipped his head toward Robert. "You can go. I've no inclination to fight a man who wields a sword." He turned and spoke to the villagers. "But I'll split the magistrate's reward with any of you that wants to help me with the horsewitch and her horse."

The old woman shook her head. "Magnus, you fool. You and the men here have killed every horse and cow in town, even the healthy ones. And a couple of the folks you thought were sick. But the Bane's still with us. 'Tis an act of God, not of a horsewitch." She pointed a gnarled finger at a tall man with a scythe in his hand. "The Lord's curse on you, Thomas Locksmith, for drinking and beating your wife half senseless, and on you, Richard Fromeby, for sleeping all day and whoring at night, and on the rest of you, too, for who knows what else. You should have built the church this year, like you promised the bishop you would."

Smirks spread across their faces. These men did not fear God enough to give up the prospect of the magistrate's reward.

Barstow snorted, cornered between the fence and a line of men with ropes and sticks.

The shepherd and the blacksmith stepped forward, taking Eldswythe by the arms. She screamed as Robert lunged and charged the group.

The cold steel of a hoof knife suddenly pressed against her neck. "Drop your sword, Sir Knight." The blacksmith held the blade at her throat, pressing the tool into her windpipe.

Robert halted. He studied the group, then dropped his sword, and raised his hands. "I am unarmed. Release her."

The men gave no answer, though the shepherd kicked Robert's weapon to the side. In an instant, the wheelwright and his three strapping sons descended on the fighting Robert and finally wrested him to the ground. He lay in the dirt on his belly, with four strong men sitting on his back and legs.

Magnus tossed a rope on Barstow's head and slid it down the

horse's neck. Barstow reared. The noose tightened as the horse wheezed and stood straddle-legged with his head extended.

Eldswythe pleaded, the hoof pick at her throat gouging into her skin. "Please, the horse is not sick, nor does he bear the contagion. He has not grazed the fields outside the village, and they were already burnt to the ground in Whickerham. We did not stop there." She looked up at the shepherd, a tall man who gripped her by the arm with a claw-like hand. "Good sir, how many of your sheep have died from the Bane?"

He shook his head. "None, so far."

"And why do you think that is, when so many have lost all their horses and their cattle?" asked Eldswythe. "Could it be, good sir, as any knowledgeable shepherd would know to do, that you wisely moved them from the fields and into your cottage when it began to rain?"

The others focused on the shepherd. Their faces clouded with suspicion.

The shepherd answered, his voice couched with caution. "I brung 'em in from the common pastures, and kept 'em in my hut with me to keep their wool clean and dry for shearing, and ready for market."

"Exactly," said Eldswythe. "The unlucky horses and cattle that stayed outside grazed on grass, already thin and brown from last month's sun. They grazed it to the nubbin. Didn't they? So starved for roughage that they ate the weeds. The land is so drenched and muddy, even the worms came up from the earth to breathe."

The shepherd's eyes grew wide. "'Tis true. The morning after the hardest rain, the worms were everywhere; so many that I could not walk a foot without stepping on 'em."

Magnus spit and pulled the noose on Barstow tighter. "What of it, horsewitch? We've had droughts and rains, and all seen worms before."

Robert shifted. "But not so dry a spell as this one, nor one that was followed by such heavy rains. It has not happened since ten years ago, when the Bane last swept across the land."

The shepherd raised his eyebrows, as if struck by the realization. The villagers eased in their formation and shifted.

She folded her hands together. "The contagion is an act of nature, not an act of God, or of witches. It follows droughts and rain, and has happened here before. I was just a girl when the summer fair here had to be canceled." She pointed to Jules Whitby, a man close to sixty, if a day. "Master Whitby, you remember when the Black Bane last came. The fair was canceled that year for fear it would spread the sickness. You were a younger man then, and I remember my father planned to bring our finest horses. The best place, he always said, to see our stock, was at Whickerham's summer fair."

Magnus cleared his throat. "I think it's more than just coincidence that the Bane is all around us and we've a horsewitch in our midst." He turned and addressed the crowd. "And what's more, she's brung her familiar, a devil-dark horse that isn't even sick!"

Magnus handed the rope, still tied around Barstow's neck, to the man beside him. He sauntered up to Eldswythe. "I'll keep your horse for the goods you and your husband owe me. As for you, we will be taking you before the magistrate. Only a horsewitch could bring the worms up from the earth. You're still worth a gold piece."

Eldswythe felt the blood drain from her face. "I'm not a horsewitch!" She glanced at Robert, hoping he would keep her newly discovered powers a secret. "Even if I were, what reason would I have for killing horses by the Bane?"

Magnus grabbed her hands and tied a rope around her wrists. "I dunno. Mayhap you made a bargain with the devil and the babe you carry is the devil's seed. I'll leave it to the magistrate to make you tell us why you did it. He has ways of getting a confession."

Robert laughed. "You know her to be a horsewitch and yet think to test her? You would lead her to her death, when you believe she can summon worms from the earth and bring the

Black Bane to your town? Aren't you afraid of what she will do to you if you are foolish enough to go forward with this?"

The men stood still and looked at Magnus.

Hesitation passed across the shepherd's face. "Her potion cured Whitby's horse of thrush." He lowered his eyes. "I reckon she could make us and our horses sick, if she chose."

Robert eased himself up. "She is a horsewitch. Let her prove it to you. She bears the mark of the devil's horse on her backside. Show it to them, Eldswythe."

Sweat dampened the back of her neck. She lowered her eyes, her cheeks hot with shame and anguish. "No, Robert, I cannot."

Robert folded his arms. "Go on, horsewitch. Show the men your mark."

"Robert, I . . ." Eldswythe stammered.

Robert yelled. "Do it, Eldswythe. Some of them do not believe you are a horsewitch. If they did, they would be disinclined to kill you, considering the havoc and the haunting that you would inflict on the men who caused your death."

Eldswythe cringed inwardly. She had never willingly showed her scar to anyone. And Gilroy was the only person who'd ever subjected her to the humiliation of inspection.

She turned away from Robert and the villagers, then lifted her skirts. Her face burned, but her backside turned cold.

The old woman gasped. The boy squeaked again, but no man spoke, stunned to silence. Magnus grunted. "So, she has a horse bite on her arse. What's she gonna do? Call the devil's horse to dance before us? Let's get her to the pit and collect our money."

Robert cleared his throat. "Do you want to see what she can do?"

Eldswythe dropped her skirts and wheeled around to face him. Puzzled, she raised her hands.

The frightened villagers gasped. The four men who sat on Robert jumped to their feet. Robert scrambled up, then picked up his sword. "Release the horse. Else the horsewitch will cast a spell and hex your livestock. The Bane will strike every sheep and cow you have left."

"Let the horse go," the wheelwright called to Magnus. "I've got three sons to feed and a wife who's soon to birth another."

"Aye!" The blacksmith jerked the rope from Magnus's hand. "'Tis bad for business. I've no way to pay my taxes if I've no livestock to tend to."

Magnus swore an oath, but stepped aside as Barstow trotted past him, and stopped in front of Robert. Robert leapt onto the horse's back. He raised his arms above his head and held his sword in the air. "I will show you she's a horsewitch!" He spun Barstow round to face Eldswythe. "Make him dance, horse-witch. He will do as you command."

She arched an eyebrow, not certain what to do, and lifted her hands a little higher, her palms upturned.

At that, Barstow began to dance. Haunches drawn beneath him, his great head collected, chin tucked so that it nearly touched his arching neck, the horse began to move up and down, trotting in place, neither advancing nor retreating.

The villagers gasped.

Robert sat still and balanced with his arms above his head. Barstow transitioned from the cadence of the slow but ele-vated trot to a gait that Eldswythe had never seen before. His forelegs traveled at a canter while his hind legs trotted. The movement was staccato-like and at the same time, bizarre. Barstow began to ride in rings around her.

Eldswythe folded her arms across her chest and inclined her head. This was quite a show. She pressed her lips together to keep from smiling.

At the change in her position, Barstow came to a halt. His head came up, but he kept it vertical to the ground, from his poll to his nose. Crouching, he shifted all his weight onto his fore-hand, and then exploded and erupted upward. He thrust double kicks with both hind feet into the air. Again and again he jumped and kicked, clearing villagers, Magnus, and the old woman and her son from the yard. Robert kept his legs clamped around the horse. He held on, holding fistfuls of the horse's mane. Barstow broke into a canter, riding in circles around Eldswythe, while Robert sat on the horse's back and waved his sword above his head. "You see," he called to Magnus, "only a horsewitch could make a horse dance and kick and jump a jig."

With one acrobatic leap, Robert leapt down, while Barstow never missed a stride and continued to canter round in circles. Robert knelt before Eldswythe, kissed her on the hand, then looked at Magnus. "In case you think that I had anything to do with that performance, you can see that it continues without me on his back." He pointed to Barstow. "He is the devil's horse but here on earth he answers to the horsewitch. He is the horse that marked her. I would not want to be the man to part these two from each other."

Eldswythe tensed, not in fear, but from an unexpected surge of power.

Mother Mary! She'd felt this way when she spooked Gilroy's horse beside the river, when she'd forced Khalif to drink the draught that saved his life. God's feet. What was happening? Could she channel fear, anger or courage to summon up her power?

Barstow slid to a stop. He turned and ambled to the center of the yard, where Robert still knelt before Eldswythe. The great horse lowered its head and knelt beside his master, facing Eldswythe. Haunches jutting up and nose to the ground, he nickered as he offered Eldswythe his salute.

Surprise flashed in Robert's eyes. He looked at Eldswythe, eyebrows arched. Then he jumped to his feet and, with the ceremony of a knight carrying a princess, he lifted her onto Barstow's back.

Hauling himself up behind her, he scabbarded his sword. "Now, good men, my wife and I will take our leave. She tells me the Bane will pass. Give thanks to God that you have seen a horsewitch and the devil's horse, and lived to tell the tale."

Magnus lunged at Barstow but staggered as the old woman

grabbed the back of his shirt and yanked him back. "Magnus, old fool, the man's a knight and a horseman like I've never seen. You've no business fighting 'em. Now let 'em go." She poked a finger at Eldswythe. "Good riddance to you. We want no quarrel with a horsewitch."

Eldswythe, still shaking from a power she did not understand, twisted to face the men. "Good men of Glensbury, build the village a church, like you promised. Hang a horseshoe over the door and, I swear, no horsewitch will ever pass this way again."

Robert cleared his throat and kicked Barstow into a trot.

Eldswythe gripped Barstow with her knees and held on to the tuft of mane above his withers. She leaned against Robert, her courage fading, replaced by relief and hesitation. She wasn't certain if what she'd just felt was real or if what she'd seen Barstow do was compounded by her imagination, or her fear.

Barstow was Robert's horse, trained to his command. It was foolish, to ask, but she had to know. "Robert, is it possible that *I* had anything to do with Barstow's performance? Anything at all?"

There was a momentary silence. Not a sound except the soft thudding of Barstow's hoofbeats on the earthen road.

Robert drew a deep breath. "Though I am loath to admit it, I've never seen Barstow perform with such aplomb and I've never seen my horse kneel—before anyone but me."

Eldswythe glanced behind them, where the old woman still stood in the road, watching.

"Make haste, Lady Eldswythe. Get away from here, but take heed. There's trouble on the road ahead. I can feel it in my bones."

She could have sworn she saw the woman wink before she hauled her bundle back onto her shoulders and strode into her house.

Chapter 11

Weaving his way around the wagons, mules, and people traveling afoot, Barstow trotted down the road. Eldswythe kept her head bowed, hoping not to draw attention. The rains had washed away the Bane. Peasants, tradesmen, merchants, and their families headed back to their towns and homes.

She pressed her hand to her lower back. Riding pillion behind Robert with her legs aside, as was necessary for a pregnant lady and wife, was not for the weak of spirit. It was even harder riding sideways without the benefit of a planchet to rest her feet on. She clung to Robert's middle to keep her balance, but her left buttock was numb and tingling and her right leg cramped. To add to her discomfort, Robert had barely spoken to her since they left the farmhouse. Mayhap she'd been too harsh and misjudged him. Her comment about the Lady Margaret had apparently hit a nerve he'd not been willing to discuss.

She fidgeted. "Robert, I need to stop and stretch."

Robert pointed to the crowd gathering by the roadside shrine. "Too many people. I prefer that you remain sitting where you are, at least until we pass these pilgrims. Gilroy's men, no doubt, will be searching for us amongst the travelers."

"But they are looking for a girl in a blue dress, not a pregnant woman dressed in drab sackcloth who travels with her husband, a farmer in a brown tunic and ragged hose."

Robert grunted. "They will recognize the horse. And what farmer carries a sword and wears riding boots like these?" He stuck out his feet.

He steered Barstow around a decrepit, heavily loaded cart that sat in the middle of the road. Grunting men, their backs against the wheels, tried to rock it free of the muddy ruts. Their feet sank in the quagmire as they struggled. He kept an eye on the gypsy boys who watched from the trees and tightened his arms around Eldswythe. "Have a care," he whispered, "we are being watched."

He smiled but shook his head at a rumpled-looking lad who held out his hands, begging.

Eldswythe, sorry they had nothing to offer the abandoned youth, patted her stomach. "Safia would have loved to see me round and waddling. It was her greatest wish to see me happy with a husband and children."

"There is still time, Lady Eldswythe. Time for us both to have everything we want. Your Earl of Gloucester is waiting, and once I've put Gilroy from your castle, I may ask the king for land in the North. Perhaps he'll even grant me a title."

She held her breath. Did that mean he wouldn't claim her father's land? It was the first time he had indicated a possible change of heart where his reward was concerned.

Robert pulled Barstow to the side of the road. A gypsy girl sashayed by, balancing a baby on her hip. The baby giggled as the girl scurried off the road into the woods and waved, signaling them to follow.

Reining Barstow to a halt, he helped Eldswythe dismount, then pressed his hand into the small of her back, guiding her to walk beside him. "We'll join the gypsies. I smell food."

Eldswythe stopped. "You are overly concerned with your stomach, sir. And what makes you think that they will welcome us?"

"They are old friends. Besides, staying off the road is safer. There's likely to be trouble."

A slurring, drunken voice called from beside the fire. "Sir Robert, 'tis good to see you. I figured you'd be with Long-shanks, gone to fight for God. What brings you here?"

"The king's business."

The brown-skinned man with bushy eyebrows shrugged indifferently. He belched and danced a jig, hopping from one foot to the other, nearly stepping into the fire. He stopped and staggered dizzily, then pulled the scarf from his head and bowed to Robert. "Welcome to our camp."

Robert laughed, took a mug of ale from a barefoot woman with striking black eyes, and pecked a kiss on her cheek. An orange scarf stretched across her ample waist and her red skirt fell just below her knees. Her feet and calves were bare. She drew X's in the dirt with a beringed big toe and grinned at Robert. "I still wear your present, my lord. I would not sell it for anything, though I've had plenty of offers for it." She pressed her hand against an opal amulet that dangled from a silver chain and rested in the crease between her bulging breasts.

Eldswythe arched her eyebrows. "Good sir, do you know these gentlefolk?"

Robert took a long drink from his cup and motioned to the gypsy man. "This is Filo," he said, then pointed to the young girl who dipped a curtsy, the boy balanced on her hip. "This is his little sister Joan and his nephew."

Eldswythe stroked the giggling baby's cheek.

Robert winked, then bowed to the buxom woman with the wanton eyes. "This is Filo's other sister, Gunnora."

She laughed a rich deep laugh and shook her skirts. "The most famous member of our gypsy troop. We travel now and then to Hillsborough and do business in the town."

"What kind of business do you do?" asked Eldswythe, as the woman handed another cup of ale out to Robert.

"Oh, we do this and that, odd jobs and whatever's needed.

Joan here can sing. She takes care of my baby boy while I tend to business."

The young girl kissed the baby's dark head and trilled a clear, melodic tune. She smiled at Eldswythe and then wandered toward the lopsided tent beside the fire. "'Tis time to put the little one to bed," she said, singing softly as she went.

Robert rubbed his neck. "Would you mind if we shared your camp tonight? We travel on to Hillsborough in the morning."

Gunnora answered before Eldswythe could object. "Of course, my lord. You are always welcome by my . . . er, our fire. Isn't that right, Filo?"

Filo's head bobbled back and forth. His hair flopped across his eyes. "I see you've lost your saddle and your armor, sir. Must have had a time of it so far." He smiled at Eldswythe. "Is this your wife, my lord?"

Eldswythe froze in place. She looked at Robert.

"Yes, this is the Lady Margaret." He picked up Eldswythe's hand and held it between his. "She is with child and weary from our travels. Ruffians set upon us and stole everything we carried. Could she have some meat and ale?"

Eldswythe forced a smile. "If I might sit down now, I would appreciate the rest."

"Certainly, my lady," said Gunnora, and gestured to the stool beside the fire. She put some chicken on a slab of black bread and handed it Eldswythe, along with a tall cup of ale. "The wagon has a bed. You eat, then get off your feet. I'll tend to your husband."

Robert grinned, then tied up Barstow before sitting down next to Filo.

Filo spoke from behind the wide brim of his cup "Guess you won't be needin' Gunnora's services this evening, will you, sir?" He handed Robert a piece of bread and a chicken leg.

Eldswythe choked, spilling ale down her chin.

Robert swallowed, ducking his head. "No, I won't. Best not to mention our previous transactions." He smiled, took a bite of chicken and chewed.

Eldswythe watched Gunnora shoo another man from the wagon's berth.

Filo poured himself another drink. "There's Jacques. He joined up with us when his kinfolk died of the Bane. The women love him and he knows how to pinch a penny if you know what I mean. He comes from fine gypsy blood, he does, though." He tossed the dregs of his cup into the fire, then called across the camp, "Jacques, you can sleep in the tent tonight but keep your hands off both my sisters."

Bleary-eyed Jacques raked his fingers through his dark curls and stumbled into the tent. "Move over, Joan, you get to have me for the night." The girl giggled.

Gunnora sauntered over to the campfire. "Your bed is ready, my lady. Is there anything I can do for you, or for your husband? I haven't had much of what a man can offer since my dear husband died. Maybe you would like me to pleasure him tonight, given your condition?" She ran her fingers lightly across Robert's forearm, and batted her cow-like eyes.

Eldswythe felt the heat rising to her face, stunned by the woman's proposition. The very thought of him with another woman made her chest tighten until it almost hurt to breathe.

Robert stood and brushed the crumbs from his tunic. "I am married now, Gunnora. But I still struggle with temptations like any man, and my wife is not so far along with child that we cannot enjoy each other." He held Gunnora's fingertips and kissed her lightly on her knuckles. "I must be strong and resist your charms. Good night, fair lady." He winked at Filo, then took Eldswythe by the hand and led her to the wagon before she could protest.

The inside of the wagon was sumptuously appointed, although the bed in the middle was narrow and small, barely wide enough for one person.

Eldswythe felt the gentle push of Robert's hand against her waist as he urged her inside.

"'Tis a smaller place to sleep than I remember," he said beneath his breath. He climbed in behind her.

Eldswythe stumbled into the heap of blankets and coverlets piled atop the narrow pallet. Some were velvet and so fine that she was uncertain if they were meant for sleeping or for hanging on a wall. She slipped off her shoes and wiggled her toes in the fox fur coverlet at her feet. These people lived in greater comfort than most of her father's villeins, even if the sleeping quarters were a bit cramped.

She sat and hugged her knees to her chest. The pallet squeaked beneath her with the weight of Robert, who sat beside her and took off his tunic.

An alarm sounded in her head. Surely, he did not intend to sleep here, too?

"This place is too small for both of us . . ." Her voice almost stuck in her throat. She searched the confines of the wagon for an inch more space. There was none, and the air inside suddenly grew thick and heavy with his male scent.

The image of him naked came crashing into her brain. The thrill of his touch every time he reached for her hand, the softness of his lips on hers, thoughts she'd tried to put from her head. He would take almost everything she owned, if he proved the victor over her enemy. But was it wrong for her to wish that, just this night, she and Robert Breton really were peaceably married? Who would ever know? Yet the thought of yielding to temptation with Robert scared her. If she once gave in to her desire, she could not go back. A Breton coupled with the Earl of Crenalden's daughter? Impossible.

She could not love him. He could not love her.

Robert fumbled in the darkness. "I am sorry to impose my presence in such close quarters." He unbuckled his sword belt and stretched out his legs. "But I seek refuge from Gunnora. Even she would not venture into my bed with my wife at my side."

He laughed and slid down next to Eldswythe as if it were his natural place. "I trust you find these accommodations to your liking?"

Conscious of his nearness, Eldswythe didn't answer. Every-where he brushed against her, she felt like she was on fire.

Robert rolled to hover just above her. "Don't be jealous of Gunnora. The bauble that she wears was a gift given years ago by a lonely lad who was grateful she would take him to her bed."

He brushed a lock of hair from Eldswythe's cheek.

She pushed his hand away. Her skin tingled where he'd touched her. "I'm not jealous. But I don't think it's wise that we should sleep here together." Her breath quickened. There, she had said it. As much as she hated to admit it, the attrac-tion was too difficult to deny, too hard to keep in check. "We need to get to Hillsborough. I want my home back and to free the Earl of Gloucester. And you want . . . Well, we both know what you want."

She closed her eyes and leaned her head back, confused. Longing, desire, and guilt all played havoc with her heart.

A whisper of a kiss caressed her temple. "Yes, I want what will be my due when the time comes. Forgive my ambition, Lady Eldswythe, and forgive me for wanting you. I know you asked me not to kiss you again, but I cannot have you so close beside me and not do this." His lips trailed down her neck, then he pulled away. "I agree, I have to leave. But it will look suspicious if we do not share a bed. We are supposed to be man and wife. You must kick me out."

Confusion muddled Eldswythe's brain. "What are you asking?"

He looked into her eyes, his own burning with desire.

A slow, sly smile spread across his face. "Pick a fight with me. A loud, screaming fight. A reason to send me from the wagon and let you sleep in peace. Tell me every thing you hate about me. All that you dislike. Throw a pillow and a fur out of the wagon, so I can at least have something to keep me warm when I go." His breath was so close it sent shivers down her spine.

"I'm not a puppet on string!" she yelled suddenly. "You cannot make me dance anytime you want!"

Robert laughed. Loudly. "You are my wife. You will do as I command."

"No, I will not, you vile man. Like all the men of the House of Breton! You are a thief and a murderer and a player of women! You've bedded every wench who ever crossed your path. Is there no gypsy in all of England who has not had your sword between her thighs?"

Robert's face twisted with surprise, but his eyes shone with approval. "Good God, woman, if it weren't for your dower lands, no man would have you. You have a pretty face but with it comes the temperament of a witch and the constitution of an angry boar. Thank God for your father's money and his property. Without it, I never would have agreed to this mockery of a marriage. You can hate me all you want but, bloody hell, you have wifely obligations!"

Eldswythe's palms suddenly turned damp. "No," she cried. "You will not force me, you lout, to lie with you! Once was quite enough!"

He roared. "What's that?" The sound of his voice was deafening, and loud enough to wake the entire camp.

Eldswythe lifted her chin. "I said no!"

Robert slapped the side of the wagon. The canvas billowed with the impact and the wagon creaked. "By God, if you weren't such a *she-witch* and carrying my heir in your belly I would throw you to your hands and knees and lift your skirts—"

Her cheeks began to burn. The very thought of what Robert threatened to do to her sent her pulses racing. "Robert Breton, I will make you rue the day I ever let you touch me. You care more about my dowered land and your bloody horse than you do your wife!"

"You hate me? Well, my lady, I would rather sleep with my horse than with you again. He keeps me warmer and he isn't nearly so pious. He breeds when he feels the need and his mares are always willing. They feel no shame in the act. Even the ones who need a twitch and chain around their nose when he mounts eventually learn to like it!"

Eldswythe shrieked, "They are animals! How dare you compare me to the beasts! You do not have breeding rights! The devil take you, Robert Breton!"

She sent two pillows sailing from the wagon, flying past Robert's head, and chucked a fur cover in his face. "Rot in hell!"

"You, Lady Margaret, are enough to send a man directly there!"

Robert leaned in toward her, took her hand and gently kissed her fingers. "Well done," he whispered. "Now sleep peacefully tonight." His chest heaved, his eyes still aflame with the heat of the moments past. "Eldswythe, I am sorry. I should not have turned on you last night. But you needn't worry over Margaret. I do not love her. And it's pointless to argue over the king's reward, your land. I haven't won it yet and Gilroy is a formidable enemy. Pray I can defeat him."

He tossed the blanket across his shoulder and climbed out of the wagon.

Spent and confused, she threw herself into the pallet and buried her face in a velvet cover. There would be no sleeping peacefully tonight. Not without Robert. The emptiness of the wagon already felt vast and hollow, the narrow pallet felt as wide and lonely as an ocean.

Mother Mary, where would Robert sleep tonight?

She pounded the pillows in frustration. Unable to put the agonizing thought from her head.

Robert might very well go to Gunnora.

The rude morning came early and shone with a vengeance on the wagon. Eldswythe, glad to be awakened, hurried down the ladder to find a place to wash. Where Robert spent the night she had no idea, but she managed to convince herself it didn't matter.

She knelt and stared at her reflection in the slow-moving stream. The purple circles underneath her tired eyes made her look as fragile and uncertain as she felt. She splashed cool water on her face, but as refreshing as it was, it didn't lift her spirits.

A smooth stone skipped across the water, then another plopped into the stream, sending ripples to the banks.

"Good morrow, Lady Margaret," said a cheery voice. "How do you fare today?"

A dark-haired man squatted close beside her, scooping pebbles from the water. He sifted through the stones and rolled them around his open palm, picking out the colored ones, smooth stones of earthen blue, and orange, and green.

He dropped the pebbles into his pouch, then smiled. A golden hoop glittered in his ear. "Gunnora's made some pottage, if you care to break your fast. If you have morning sickness it'll cure it, and if you don't, it'll give it to you!"

He laughed and bowed with all the elegance of a knight who'd been to court. "Jacques de Littean," he said, lifting her hand to his lips. "I was glad to give my bed up for so fine a Christian lady. I have heard of your miracle at Smithfield. If any woman could save the life of Robert Breton by praying for divine intervention, you were the one to do it. But I heard the spat last night between the two of you. And I know that folks don't fight like that unless they love each other. I bet he comes back a-begging for forgiveness. If nothing else, he won't be wanting to sleep beneath the wagon again."

Miracle at Smithfield? Lady Margaret had been there?

She'd seen Robert carted from the lists and carried to the tents that day, but she'd not heard of any miracle associated with his recovery. 'Twas true, it was an act of God he'd survived. The Lady Margaret must be well on her way to sainthood.

Eldswythe looked away, hoping to hide her face. "Thank you, sir, but God hears the prayers of everyone and no doubt many prayed for my good husband." She dried her hands on her skirts. "I must return to the wagon. He will be up by now."

Jacques scurried beside her. "I thought it odd that he should sleep beneath the wagon, Lady Margaret. But I know it can be difficult to sleep beside a woman who is new with child. I hope you both got rest." He smiled. "We also planned on leaving this morning, but my mare that pulls the wagon is having trouble with the farcy. We will have to stay a day or two until the swelling in her leg goes down. I'll tie a colored talisman around it." He patted his pouch, stones rattling inside. "With rest, she should be good as new."

Eldswythe stopped. "Is that what those stones are for?"

"Yes, my lady." He looked sheepishly at his shoes. "That and for the travelers on the road." He pulled a handful of pebbles from the pouch. "See, the orange ones here will protect a man from the Black Bane and the blue ones keep their women safe. Had my kinfolk been wearing them when the Bane hit our camp," he said with a saddened tone, "they'd be alive today. I can attest to that." He showed her the umber stone suspended by a braided thread around his neck.

"What do the black stones do?" she asked. "Keep the horses healthy?"

"Yes, my lady. This one here would bring a half a penny."

She took the stone, rubbing the smoothness between her fingers. She believed none it, of course, but would not raise suspicion and tell him so. "And the green ones?"

Jacques lowered his voice and looked around as if he was about to share a secret. "Lady Margaret, these are very potent." He pulled a leather string from his pocket and tied it round the stone. "When a lady's lover wears it round his neck, their devotion to each other will never falter." He pressed it into her hand.

She held it in her open palm and smiled. "I suppose it would fetch a pretty penny?"

"At least a fiver," he said, and laughed aloud. "But you can have it." He turned toward the camp. "I need to check on Winnow. The poor mare's not had her breakfast yet."

Eldswythe tucked the green stone into the pocket of her

baggy dress and walked behind him, to the wagon, where a swaybacked mare stood with her head down and her eyes closed, right rear foot cocked beneath her.

Jacques tied the oat bag to her nose. "Ahh, poor Winnow." He stooped and rubbed his hand up and down her cannon bone. "Too bad you suffer so." He took a small black stone from his collection and tied it around her hock.

Kneeling, Eldswythe touched the flaking skin on the front of the horse's swollen leg. In places it oozed with golden serum, and the hair had fallen out. "Some days it looks better?" she asked.

"When the swelling goes away, she walks fine."

Dusting her hands, she replied. "It isn't farcy. A good scrubbing with a salve of tar and tallow should cure it in a month. But you should buy the proper mixture from an apothecary." She grinned and slipped her hand into her pocket to feel the stone that he had given her. "Spend some of the coin you earn from selling pebbles to help your poor horse." She laughed, then tied the stone around her neck.

"Lady Margaret, I had no idea that ladies reared in convents learned so much about horses and the like."

Eldswythe felt the blood drain from her face. "I was in charge of the Mother Superior's horse. Both the horse and Mother Bromely had the same condition. I can still smell the tar and tallow every time I set foot in chapel."

"I see," said Jacques, smiling.

Robert emerged from the trees, buckling his sword belt, his face red, his brows knitted. "Where have you been? Hillsborough is but a day away. I am eager to depart."

Jacques stepped up to the wagon and lifted up the lid to the driver's seat. He pulled out a loaf of bread, broke some off and handed it to Eldswythe. "The Lady Margaret could not stomach Gunnora's pottage, sir. Neither can I. So I offered to share my private stash." He winked at Eldswythe.

She snatched the bread and chewed. "If I do not eat something in the morning, sir, I will be sick." She swallowed. "I am ready to leave. As fine hosts as your friends are, I miss the comforts of our solar."

Robert pulled Barstow to his side. "We bid you goodbye, Jacques," he said, lifting Eldswythe onto the horse.

Robert waved goodbye to Gunnora, who held her smiling baby to her breast. "Here, my lord," she offered him a small cloth pouch with her free hand. "Take these figs and almonds. Your wife will need to keep her stomach settled."

Eldswythe arched a brow. Figs and almonds were expensive and had to be imported.

Gunnora actually blushed. "A Spaniard gave 'em to me for some chores I did for him." She smiled. "'Twas a fair trade."

Robert tipped his head in thanks and handed the small pouch to Eldswythe. "I am sure it was, Gunnora. *Adieu.*"

Feeling guilty for the woman's kindness, Eldswythe smiled and waved to Gunnora.

Filo waved from the beneath the awnings of his tent. "Be careful on the road, Sir Robert. Watch your lady wife. There are bad men about in times like these."

Robert patted his sword and wrapped his arm around Eldswythe's waist.

Filo put his hands on his hips and his eyes searched the woods. He yelled, "I need some help taking down this tent. Where'd everybody go?"

Eldswythe scanned the camp.

Gunnora sat in the wagon nursing the baby. Joan waved goodbye and turned to washing pots beside the stream.

Jacques was nowhere to be seen.

Chapter 12

The soldier wore a scarlet tunic, and a painted iron badge, a gryphon with a dragon in its talons. He picked his teeth with his dagger as he leaned against the tree. "Are you sure 'twas her?"

Jacques de Littean wiped his forehead with his kerchief. Soldiers always made him nervous, especially the ones who promised they'd pay for information but kept their knives ready. "As sure as a man can be," he said. "The lady traveled with Sir Robert and they pretended they were married. I could tell they were not."

Another soldier cackled and moved to stand behind him. "How was that?"

"The way they was looking at each other. 'Twasn't natural for a husband to be lusting after his wife like that. They even pretended to be fighting." He grinned. "But this lady, she weren't Lady Margaret of Suttony. I've seen her and she be fair and slight. This one is tall with dark hair, looking like she is with child."

The leader of the troop yawned. "Your information is not helpful. Lord Gilroy did not say Lady Eldswythe of Crenalden was pregnant. The woman that you saw with Breton is not her. Be off with you." The soldier pushed Jacques de Littean aside and stomped in the direction of his horse. "Mount up!" he commanded to the others who watched with boredom.

Desperate to be heard, Jacques clutched the man by the arm. "There is more, good sir. For a coin I will tell you."

He knew immediately his demand had been a grave mistake.

The soldier swung around and grabbed Jacques by the throat, pinning him against a tree. "Did she tell you who she was? If she did not, unless you lifted up her skirts and saw the mark that scars her arse, you do not know who she was."

With his arms pinned behind his back, Jacques cared little for the coin, but now feared for his life. He knew the men could extract the information and leave him empty-handed. Or worse, without his head. "She said as much, sir. She took an interest in my horse's swollen leg and told me how to treat it. The Lady Margaret wouldn't do that," he rasped. "The woman with Sir Robert is the horsewitch."

The soldier moved in closer. "You say they are on the road between the hamlets of Cavendish and Lackford?"

"I followed them there myself, sir. They did not see me."

The soldier let him go and turned to mount his horse.

Jacques rubbed his throat and backed away. "The coin you promised, sir?"

It was the last thing he said before he felt the thud that cracked his skull and knocked him to the ground.

Thankful to be riding in the noonday shade, Eldswythe rested her head against Robert's back and closed her eyes. The argument they'd played out the evening past kept creeping into her brain like a disturbing dream.

Robert sat stiffly on Barstow's back. She could feel both the horseman and his horse were tense, and tired.

He cleared his throat. "Seeing you so cheery this morning with de Littean did not sit well with me. I don't trust the man. I am eager to get you to the safety of Hillsborough."

She fingered the green stone tied around her neck. "You were jealous?"

He stared at the road ahead. "If I could deny wanting you,

Eldswythe, I would. It would make things easier between us. That said, the sooner we get to Hillsborough the better."

Eldswythe lowered her eyes. "Agreed."

But the very thought of not seeing Robert Breton on a daily basis, riding next to him, or even sleeping with him again left Eldswythe shaken. She was not ready to part company. They would be in Hillsborough tomorrow morning. These past few hours alone with him she knew would be her last.

Barstow's gait rocked her gently. She let the swaying, rhythmic motion of his gait soothe her and she barely noticed the slight bobbing of his head. The lifting of the favored foot. Then a stumble.

Robert swore. "Damnation."

She straightened, every muscle in her back taut. "He's lame!"

God almighty. How she wished she'd noticed sooner.

Robert reined the horse beneath a towering oak and dismounted. Eldswythe slid down beside him, where he knelt by Barstow's giant hoof. He tapped the horse's tendons. "Up," he commanded.

Barstow lifted his huge foot and Robert braced it on his bended knee. Drawing his dagger from his belt, he poked and scraped the dirt from the bottom of the horse's hoof. The steel tip grated against the shoe iron as bits of trodden earth and grass fell away. The cause of the problem was revealed— a river stone big as an acorn, blue as the summer sky, wedged between the iron shoe clip and the heel.

The breath hissed from Robert's lips as he carved the horny sole away, working to free the stone. "*Jesu*. It looks like someone put this here on purpose. I've never seen a pebble so firmly stuck."

Eldswythe bit her lower lip to keep from blurting out her suspicion. Mother Mary! Why would Jacques do it?

She knelt beside Robert and peered at the bottom of Barstow's foot. Already the soft white sole was turning purple where the stone had lodged.

"He's bruised but he can walk now." She lowered her head to get a better look as Robert brushed away the last of the debris.

"We'll have to—"

The thud in Eldswythe's ears sounded like a club that whacked against a block of stone. Robert lurched forward and fell face down.

She shrieked. Hands suddenly wrenched hers behind her back. A mail-covered knee knocked her to the ground.

Barstow reared as steel rattled, a sword sliding from a rusted scabbard.

"Horsewitch! There's no escaping this time."

Eldswythe scratched, clawing at the man who held her down.

"Grab her feet! I'll bind her hands!"

She glimpsed a soldier standing over Robert's still form, sword poised to strike.

"No!"

In an instant, Barstow's head came crashing across the man's back. The great horse whinnied as one giant hoof cut through the air and landed squarely on the soldier's head, pounding at him, driving his face and helmet into the dirt.

A second soldier sprang from the bushes and grabbed the other one by the arm, dragging him to his feet. "Mullins, you fool! Get up. Get the horsewitch. Sure as hell, if we don't, we're as good as dead. Gilroy or this beast will kill us! "

He pushed his friend aside but kept a wary eye on Barstow, who now bared his teeth. "A present to Sir Robert Breton from Lord Gilroy," said the soldier as he tossed a gimlet tip to the ground. "He says to tell you all is fair in love and war."

He hauled Eldswythe toward his waiting horse.

The other soldier stumbled to his mount, his helmet dented, his face covered with mud and blood. His left arm hung limply at his side as he crawled into the saddle. "Bloody horse! My collarbone is broken!"

Barstow snorted and pawed, threatening to charge while

Robert lay unmoving, blood trickling from the corner of his mouth, his sword in his fist.

"Robert!"

Rough hands jerked her by the hair and then hoisted her up. She landed with a rib-jarring thud across the back of a horse, tossed like a sack of beets and trussed like piglet sent to slaughter. Ropes wrapped around her hands and ankles, cutting like blades.

Barstow whinnied, his shrill cry sending sparrows from the trees.

"Let's go!" yelled the soldier. "Afore the devil's horse there decides to come after us!"

Eldswythe rolled her head aside, a wad of filthy cloth stuffed into her mouth. She gasped, struggling for breath while the horse beneath her spun around and raced into the woods.

Through blurry eyes she caught a glimpse of Robert. He wasn't moving, and she wasn't certain he was breathing. Powerless to help him, Eldswythe sliently pleaded with Barstow to stay by his master's side. The great horse pawed and snorted, as if he understood.

Chapter 13

Eldswythe moaned and rested her aching head against the horse's sweaty flank. She rode face down across the destrier. Their captain seemed to have little regard for how fast they traveled or for the brambles that scratched her face and legs. The woods grew darker and with every hour that passed, she gave up hope.

She squeezed her eyes shut but, no matter how she tried, she could not put aside the vision of Robert lying still on the ground. A surge of panic rose from her stomach and she fought the urge to retch. She prayed to God he wasn't dead.

A soldier on a rat-brown horse rode up beside them. "Are you sure you didn't kill her, Captain? She hasn't tried to scream or move in near an hour."

The captain shifted in the saddle. He poked his thumb across her shoulder. "She's still breathing. And I am tired of chasing her around the countryside. Now that we finally got her, I want her still and silent. I want a good night's sleep tonight."

The other man rested his hands on the saddle pommel. "I hope we got the lady Lord Gilroy wants, the one they call the horsewitch. Shouldn't we be checking that?"

Eldswythe tensed and lifted her head. *Please no.*

The captain drew his horse to a stop beneath a cluster of trees and climbed down. "You're right, Wellesley, we ought to look. Lord Gilroy'd not be pleased with us if we bring him the wrong woman." He turned to Eldswythe and jerked up her skirts, throwing them across her back to expose her naked rump. She felt the sting of his leather glove slap across her bare buttocks. "Looks like we got the right one." He laughed as the other two men jumped down from their horses to get a better look.

"Would you look at that?" said Wellesley, stroking Eldswythe's scars. "She does have the mark of the devil's horse." He licked his lips. "And what an arse, smooth and pink and . . ."

The captain yanked her skirts down. "Don't be getting any ideas about riding this." He slapped her rump again. "If Lord Gilroy plans to take her, he ain't one for sharing."

The captain dragged Eldswythe from the horse. "Here's as good a place to camp as any." He set her down and checked the gag.

She locked her knees to stay upright as he wrapped a rope around her waist and tied her to a tree. "Now don't be thinking you can run, my lady. Sit here while we cook our dinner. We may let you have some. If you're good to us." He winked.

Eldswythe leaned against the tree and closed her eyes. Her body ached and her head throbbed.

The soldiers went about the business of setting up camp. One built the fire, while the others set off to hunt for dinner. By sunset, they returned with squirrels and woodcock, cleaned and gutted. They sat beside the fire and drank as their bounty roasted in the flames.

The captain squatted and pulled the gag beneath her chin. "I'll take the rag from your mouth so you can eat and have something to drink, but if you think to get away, well there are lots of ways to keep you still and quiet that won't leave a mark on you. If nothing else, I'll tie you like a hog and leave you that way until I turn you over to Gilroy." He poked a piece of meat in her mouth and held the wineskin to her lips.

Eldswythe coughed and spat. "Gilroy is a bastard. I'll die by my own hand first before I submit to him."

The men laughed and the captain smiled broadly. "Don't say as I blame you, my lady. Lord Gilroy *is* a bastard—your father's!"

The men whistled.

The captain laughed, his tone almost sympathetic. "If I were a woman, I would rather spend eternity condemned in Hell with all the other suicides than spend the night with Gilroy. He's your half brother and likes it rough. I've bet you heard, too, that his privates are as twisted as his mind. Even the camp whores hide when he comes looking for it."

The soldiers howled.

Eldswythe swallowed. Every thought of Gilroy was repulsive. "He will never touch me. It is a mortal sin, an abomination. The Pope and God will both condemn him!"

The captain popped a piece of meat into his mouth and chewed. "Lord Gilroy doesn't care much for the church, my lady. And plenty of great lords have bedded their relations. I dunno what it is Lord Gilroy intends to do with you—make you his wife or put you in his prison. He doesn't share his plans with the likes of me."

"I'm pledged to marry the Earl of Gloucester." She spat the words.

The captain grunted. "The last time I saw the Earl of Gloucester, Lady Eldswythe, he was looking pretty poorly. Lord Gilroy won't do much to help him, unless his family chooses to pay a very hefty ransom."

He belched and tossed the bones from his dinner into the fire. "Check on the horses, Wellesley. Gerrod, you take first watch." He leaned to retie Eldswythe's hands, then check the rope around her feet and waist. "You're a pretty thing," he said. "If Lord Gilroy had no interest in you, 'twould be hard to keep my men away from you tonight. But I suspect Sir Robert's already had you. You been too long by his side, not to take a tumble in his bed."

Eldswythe felt the heat rising to her battered face.

"Too bad, Lady Eldswythe, because if Sir Robert's gotten

to you, he did it out of spite." He chuckled. "It serves ol' Gilroy right. He had it coming. After all, he plucked the bloom from Sir Robert's lady love. Them two been trying to settle the score between 'em over Lady Margaret now for near a year. If Breton wants you, Gilroy won't care if your petals are already missing."

Nauseated by the revelation, she slumped against the tree and let the ropes that bound her hold her up. Was it true? Was she a pawn, caught between two vengeful men and their private war over another woman?

It wasn't possible. Robert would not use her thus. He coveted her lands, that much she knew and she fought to keep from hating him for that. But she could not believe he used her to settle a score with John Gilroy over a woman.

The full moon lit the forest in hues of dusky blue and green and by the time Robert opened his heavy-lidded eyes, the egg-sized lump behind his ear felt as if it might split his skull wide open.

He moaned and lifted his hand to feel Barstow's velvet muzzle nuzzling his palm. The great horse sniffed his hair and nudged him on his cheek. Crawling to his hands and knees, Robert tried to focus, his vision blurred. But he could barely make out Barstow's massive form. He grasped his horse's bridle and pulled himself upright. He scanned the woods, bleary-eyed, searching frantically for any sign of Eldswythe.

Then he saw it. A glint of steel shimmered in the grass beside him.

Anguish gripped his chest. He closed his hand around the broken lance tip, a gimlet like the one that had pierced his shoulder a year ago today. He felt no pain, not the sharp points that dug into his palm or the pounding that hammered in his head.

An angry roar exploded from his throat. "Gilroy!" He

leaned against his horse, unsteady, but determined to remain conscious. "I will not rest until I see this buried in your heart."

They had been easy enough to track. Three men on three horses, wandering through the woods at a pace slow enough to catch. The man who followed them with rage boiling in his chest and hatred eating at his stomach never slowed or wavered from the pursuit. Even when the deadly pain that throbbed in his head made the world go dark, he held on to his horse and entrusted the animal to find the way until his vision returned.

Crouching in the bushes with his sword drawn, he could see the captain drinking by the fire, Eldswythe tied to a tree.

The lone guard pulled aside his scarlet tunic with one hand and leaned against another tree to take a piss, not suspecting he had an audience.

Leaves rustled and Robert, battle ready, raised his eyes to see the hooded figure perched on a tree limb directly over the guard. Jacques de Littean pressed a dagger to his lips, signaling to Robert to hold his place. With a fell swoop, he dropped from the tree onto the soldier's back, yanking back his coif, then held the dagger to the soldier's throat. "Those who do not deal fairly with gypsies," he whispered, "face the consequences." With an expert swipe, he slit the soldier's throat. Blood gushed from the wound and sprayed across the bushes.

The soldier slumped to his knees, then fell flat on the ground. Sliding from the man's back, de Littean pushed back his own hood and faced Robert.

Robert bounded from the bushes. Sword drawn, he pressed the tip against the gypsy's neck. "Tell me why I should not cut you down. 'Twas you who set Gilroy's men upon us."

Jacques de Littean backed away and looked toward the camp. "Shhh, my lord." He held his fingers to his lips. "I am here to help you set the Lady Eldswythe free."

Robert's eyes narrowed with suspicion. "You turned her

over to them and now you want to help? I should kill you," he hissed.

"Aye, I tried to earn a coin in exchange for giving Gilroy's men some information. But this fellow here did not live up to his part of the bargain. They cannot have what they did not pay for. 'Tis my honor as a gypsy I am seeking to restore." He put his hand across his heart.

Robert scoffed. "A gypsy code of honor?"

"A man should know never to cheat a gypsy. The captain and the others need to learn that lesson." He grinned. "The odds are in our favor if we work together. You will get what you want and I will get what I want."

"I won't go dropping out of trees and slitting throats. I fight face to face."

Jacques scrambled back up the tree. "You'll be getting yourself killed then. Here comes the other one."

Gilroy's soldier drew his sword. "Wellesley, what's taking you so long?" He stalked through the bushes and held his shield beside him. "Speak up, man."

Robert jumped in front of him, and brought his sword down atop the man's head.

Helmet knocked askew, the soldier staggered backward.

Steel clashed with steel as Robert skirted around the wildly slashing soldier. Splinters flying and branches snapping, Robert dove behind a tree trunk as the blade slashed before his face.

His sword embedded in the tree, the soldier growled and put his booted foot against the trunk. He pushed backward. When the sword suddenly pulled free, he stumbled, then gasped and clutched his chest. The man sank to his knees. His mouth agape, he fell, Robert's dagger buried in his back.

With a soft thud, de Littean landed next to Robert. "He almost knocked me from my perch, sir. Thank you." He turned and trotted into the woods. "You can get the last one, too. He should be ready for you now."

Robert thundered after him. Much to his surprise, the captain slumbered inches away from Eldswythe.

Her eyes grew wide and she cast an anxious glance at the captain.

De Littean pushed the limp body of the captain over, then cut the purse from his belt. "Bit of gypsy magic in your brew, Captain. Hope you liked it."

Robert scrambled to Eldswythe's side and cut her ties away. He kissed her bruised and bleeding wrists, then drew her into his arms. "No matter what they've done, I will make it right," he whispered. "Gilroy will pay for this."

She buried her head on his shoulder, a whimper on her lips.

Jacques tapped Robert's shoulder. "You're not leaving yet, are you, sir? I still need your help."

"What more do you want from me?" asked Robert as he looked closely at the sleeping captain. "You've drugged him, haven't you, de Littean?" He kicked the wineskin from the man's hands.

"I would have drugged the others, too, but I didn't get the chance. The captain set his drink beside the bushes to tie up Lady Eldswythe. The others took theirs with them."

"You killed his men and got his purse. What's left to do?"

Jacques grinned. "Don't you recognize your mail and saddle?"

Robert studied the saddle on the captain's horse's back.

Jacques motioned to the captain. "Help me strip him down. You can get your mail, and then take your saddle back."

"De Littean, what exactly is your plan?" Robert pulled his mail shirt and padding from the captain's body, then un-hitched his saddle from the horse's back.

"I'll take their horses with me. There is a horsemonger in Billington that don't ask no questions. They'll fetch a pound or two." He grinned. "I'll take the captain's clothes here and give 'em to a village they sacked. The people there will be needing a decent pair of boots and hose for winter."

He stepped back and put both hands on his hips. "Leave a

naked man afoot to wander in the woods for a day and he'll have lots of things to worry about besides chasing after us."

He pulled his golden earring from his ear. "Just in case there's any doubt, I want him to remember the gypsy he cheated and left for dead." He hung his earring on the captain's ear and stepped back to admire his handiwork. He laughed. "Don't he look pretty?"

Jacques lifted Eldswythe's hand to his lips. "Lady Eldswythe, forgive me. I've tried to set things right. No harm was done to you?" He pointed to the smooth green stone that hung around her neck. "It's another bit of gypsy magic that keeps him by your side. Not as strong as horsewitch magic, but it works." He winked at Robert.

The captain stirred from his stupor, grunted and rubbed his naked belly.

Jacques jumped onto the captain's horse and kicked, pulling the other two horses by his side. "I'll see you springtime next, my lord, at the Hillsborough fair." He waved, then disappeared into the trees.

Robert tossed his pads and saddle onto Barstow's back, and secured the girth. "Eldswythe, by tomorrow evening we should be in Hillsborough. Gilroy cannot touch you there."

Eldswythe rubbed her throbbing head. Her chest tightening, she looked away, remembering the captain's warning. Robert had risked his life to come after her. He was not using her to get back at Gilroy, as the captain claimed.

Robert walked to Eldswythe's side. He put his hand around her neck and pulled her face to his, resting his forehead on hers. "Eldswythe, come what may at Hillsborough, never doubt that I . . ." He stammered, and then he lowered his head and kissed her hard on the lips, his mouth consuming hers.

The captain grunted and opened his eyes "What the devil . . ."

Robert lingered, before pulling away. He tossed the broken lance tip at the captain's feet. "Give this back to your lord, good sir. Tell him when next we meet in battle, I'll drive my sword through his heart."

Without another word, he lifted Eldswythe onto Barstow's
back, then mounted behind her. Kicking Barstow to a canter,
they raced from the spot where Gilroy's soldiers lay dead and
his naked captain lay squirming in the dirt.

Eldswythe sat in silence atop Barstow and leaned against
Robert's chest. The bright moon lit up the night sky like a
beacon and the air was still. The forest that edged the road
was quiet save for the sound of Barstow's hoofbeats. His head
bobbed in sync with his every step, just as it should. The
makeshift padding beneath his foot had done the trick and relieved the pressure on his sole. He was no longer lame. Eldswythe took a deep breath, thankful that the horse was sound
and the wide road on which they traveled was smooth and
free of shadows.

A flat-roofed inn sprawled in the trees at the crossroads not
far ahead. Slivers of golden light glowed from behind the
shutters, and the twang of a lute rose over laughter and
singing. Travelers were reveling before they settled in for
the night.

Robert's deep voice hummed in her ears. "We'll stop here.
The Bear and Fox is a modest inn, but with good food and
drink."

Startled, Eldswythe sat up. Robert had said little since her
rescue, though he kept his arm tightly around her waist.
Every now and then he turned and scanned the woods behind
them, on guard for Gilroy's men. It surprised her he'd take the
risk and stop here. Perhaps he was as fatigued as she. Robert
drew Barstow to a halt, then dismounted and lifted Eldswythe
down. "Will they have room?" she asked. "From the sound of
it, the place is full."

"They'll make room. The Earl of Hillsborough keeps a
running account with the innkeeper. My brother often brings
his hunting parties here to eat."

He led Barstow into a crowded lean-to, where a bedraggled,

obstinate-looking donkey refused to make more room until Barstow butted the beast with his head, and barreled his way up to the hay-filled manger.

Robert slapped Barstow on the rump good-naturedly, then turned and took Eldswythe by the hand. He walked in silence beside her, and when they approached the door to the Bear and Fox, he paused, then swung her round to face him. "Eldswythe, speak to no one here. Be quiet and do not draw attention. I'll do the talking."

Before she could respond, he threw the door aside and sauntered in. Her hand still in his, she had no choice but to follow. The voices in the room fell silent. The air was thick with the smell of sweat, sour ale, and smoke.

Weary travelers, men mostly but a few women, sat huddled at the tables, nursing great tankards of muddy beer. A man in a red and yellow striped cloak sat in the corner and softly strummed his lute, while a roaring fire crackled in the hearth.

Robert released her hand and strode across the room. He leaned over a greasy serving table and tapped a buxom young woman on the shoulder. She had her lips locked on the neck of a drunken knight, who, like her, had his eyes closed, his face rapt with pleasure.

"Where's Reynolds?" Robert's hand was on his sword's hilt, but his face was impassive.

A small round man, looking every bit the troll, waddled down the stairs from the loft. "Here I be . . . What the devil? Is it the Dark Rider come celebrate his return to the living? Sir Robert Breton, is it you or do I see a ghost?" He took his cap off his head and bowed repeatedly. "Good to see you here again, milord. We've missed you. And is this the Lady Mar— 'er, no. I can see it isn't." He looked at Robert as if he fully expected an introduction.

Robert shook his head. "The lady needs a room. Is there one to spare?" He answered curtly and offered no further explanation.

Reynolds glanced at the stairs, to the rooms above. "For

you, milord, of course. And I'll see you, uh, I mean the lady, has no intrusions."

He bowed, then trotted up the stairs and banged on a door. "Out, you rowdies! Your hour's up, and I've a lord and lady waiting."

A couple staggered out. A shop-worn woman with a dirty apron tied low on her ample hips tucked a coin into her bodice, then squeezed the man's buttocks before she tottered down the stairs. The man stumbled down behind her, smiling unapologetically.

Reynolds held his arm out, bidding them to enter. "All yours, milord. I'll fetch your lady fresh linens and some blankets."

Robert escorted Eldswythe into the tiny room. He drew his sword and checked beneath the bed, then threw the shutters open and surveyed the yard below. The moon filled the view from the window, the gentle light softening the roughness of the coarse furnishings inside. The crisp night air felt sharp and clean against her skin.

Reynolds reappeared in the doorway, holding a stack of blankets in his arms.

Robert waved him in. "We'll be needing food and drink. The best you have to offer."

The round man entered and laid the bedding down, then scurried out.

Eldswythe sat carefully on the foot of the bed. Drunken voices drifted from the tavern below, and in the dim light Robert's shoulders sloped with fatigue. Mother Mary, he looked as bone-achingly tired as she felt. Exhausted.

She wanted so much to tell him how part of her had wanted to die when she saw him lying on the ground, still and lifeless. She longed to throw her arms around his neck and cover him with kisses. But how could she say any of this to a man who might not welcome her attentions? Since he'd rescued her from the soldiers, he had kept his distance. Was he regretting the trouble she brought him? By the rood, he couldn't even admit to her that he was tired, that he needed to rest as much as she did.

Footsteps pounded up the stairs. "This should suit the lady and you both, milord." Reynolds thrust a tray with steaming bowls of soup, a leg of roasted mutton, and mulled red wine into her hands when she opened the door, then bowed and left.

The door closed behind him, shutting out the noise below, and the light.

Robert's eyes locked with Eldswythe's. The tray rattled in her hands. Wine spilled over the edges of the tall pewter cups. By God, she'd have her say with him and be done with it. Even if it meant rejection.

"I cannot believe I am about to say this." She set the food aside, her voice barely above a whisper.

"No." Robert took a quick step forward, closing the space between them, as if he were about to reach for her. Then he stopped, fists clenched at his sides. "Let it be, Eldswythe. We are both exhausted. Whatever there was, or is, between us must be kept in check. Say nothing that would make it harder, for you—or for me."

Eldswythe lowered her eyes. "I have to tell you . . . before tomorrow. Before we get to Hillsborough, for I fear I will never get another chance. Robert, I . . ."

Robert took her hands in his and pulled her to him, interrupting her confession. He pressed his face against her head and stroked her back, his warm hand sending a charge of desperate need through Eldswythe's heart. "God's peace, Eldswythe, be silent." His voice was a husky whisper. "I thought I'd lost you. When I awoke to find you gone, I could barely breathe."

Eldswythe flung her arms around his neck. "The last thing I saw was you lying on the ground, not moving. I thought Gilroy's men had killed you. From that moment on, I didn't care what happened."

Her heart pounding next to his, racing and erratic, she leaned against him, her knees wobbly and shaking.

He sucked in his breath.

"Robert," she whispered her voice nearly cracking. "I may spend eternity in hell begging God for forgiveness, but I cannot spend my life on earth not knowing . . . I nearly lost you, Robert. I cannot bear the thought of not knowing what loving you would feel like."

She lifted her lips and kissed him, hard and with complete abandon. Devouring the sweet taste of his mouth, her need urgent and unfettered.

Breathless and trembling, she broke away from his embrace, then pulled off her overdress. The laces at the neck of her chemise gave way beneath her shaking fingers. With a toss of her shoulder, the garment fell to her waist, past her hips, and landed in a heap at her feet.

Robert's eyes never strayed from hers, despite the temptation to lower his gaze and feast on the beauty of the woman who stood naked in front of him. Corpus bones, she amazed him. Most women who'd just survived what she'd been through would have collapsed in hysterics. But Eldswythe didn't cower or whimper. And God knew she'd suffered much these last few weeks. She was strong, in full command of her wits and her will. Neither had she accused him of failing her, of not protecting her as he'd promised. Instead she stood in front of him in naked honesty and declared how much she cared, setting aside what she knew he planned for her estate. Could her willingness to lie with him really be genuine? Was her invitation truly fired by need and sheer desire? Yet how could it not be? She'd naught to gain from bedding him, nay there was much she could lose. Why would she do this?

Her boldness touched his heart and her brazenness made his loins ache, but he could not let her offer herself to him. Not like this.

"Eldswythe," he said softly, "cover yourself. You don't know what you're doing. Remember what I want. You will hate me for it, and you will hate yourself for what you are about to do."

"I do know, Robert, exactly what I'm doing. I've not forgotten what you are about, but God help me, this is what I want." She stepped toward him and took the hem of his tunic in her trembling hands, then lifted it upward.

He caught her wrists and held them, forbidding her to move. "Eldswythe, if you should get with child—"

"I am strong enough, Robert. I know the risks. I choose to take them."

He could feel his own heart beating, and hear it thudding in the silence as she looked up at him, hopeful and with emerald eyes that shimmered with desire.

She had never looked so beautiful as she did at this moment. Long legs. Slim hips and round, smooth buttocks. Her shoulders lean and sculpted. Firm breasts with a rose-brown ring of color encircling their tips. Her nakedness awash in the moonlight, she looked vulnerable and utterly enticing.

Her scent filled his nostrils and he shuddered with raw desire. Would the physical possession of her body quench the fire that burned in his loins or would it only make it worse?

As if she sensed his struggle, she pressed her body full against him, breasts, belly, and thighs assaulting him. She stood on her toes and lifted her lips to his. There was no hesitation, no apprehension as she claimed his mouth—her purpose clear—to undermine his resistance. Her tongue darted past his lips.

His senses came crashing down.

He lifted Eldswythe in his arms and strode across the room. His mouth still covering hers, his hunger insatiable and growing, he lowered her onto the bed.

He prayed to God she had no purpose behind his seduction. He prayed that her motives were as honest and as open as they seemed.

"Eldswythe, the moon is already high," he said. "We must be gone by dawn. I've dreamed of teaching you, of showing you how rich loving one another can be, but tonight should not be rushed. The first time you might feel pain and I—"

"You say tonight as if there will be others. A false hope,

Robert, and you know it. I would rather love you for an hour, than not at all. I'm not afraid. Please, show me." She ran her hands down his back, then pulled his tunic over his head.

At the touch of her fingertips against his back, a head-clearing shiver rippled through his body. He almost raised himself from the bed. By God, he almost did. But then her lips were on his neck, moist and warm, kissing the scar that ran from his collarbone to his ear. Her hands fanned out across his shoulders and forced him to bend, to lower his chest to hers and he felt the softness of her breasts and her sweet breath was there against his mouth.

He could not resist her touch, her softness. He needed her—more than he had ever needed any woman.

With a deep-seated groan, he tore his lips from hers and kicked off his boots and hose. The cool night air braced him as he peeled his breeches off and freed his bulging shaft, casting aside all his honorable intentions, all his noble determination not to enmesh them further in an unhappy situation that had no solution.

She stared, her face filled with longing. He kissed her lips then hesitated, but she responded eagerly by sliding her hands over his bare buttocks. Robert lowered himself into her arms, the soft mound of hair between her legs brushing up against his belly. He was shaking like a boy, but she didn't seem to notice. He slipped his fingers between her legs, into the softness of her folds. A shocked cry slipped past her lips before she cut it off by sucking in her breath.

It was too quick, he knew, but there was no time to linger. Not tonight. Robert did what he could to make her ready. He caressed the core of her with his fingers while he held himself back. She was ready for him physically, but if he could, he would have given her more time to get used to the idea of what was to come as well.

"I would there were more time," he said out loud.

She closed her eyes and clutched him tighter. "I know not what to do."

Need rushed through him, almost ripping away every ounce of his control. "Trust me."

He gently pushed her legs apart with his knees and pressed his tip into the warm, wet hollow of her core. He paused, feeling the tightness as he entered.

She tensed. Her fingers dug into the bunched muscles of his back and he heard the air slip from her lips and he pushed deeper inside her. A low moan came from her throat as she threw her head back and closed her eyes.

"Put your legs around my waist," he whispered. "I am almost there." With one thrust he entered her completely, sliding deeper, until the length of him was buried in her folds and the weight of his hips bore down on hers.

He felt her tightness give way and she gasped as he slowly withdrew and sheathed himself again. With scorching need, he entered her again and again, until he thought he would die from the pleasure of it, from the sweet sensation that ebbed and flowed with every thrust.

Eldswythe groaned and lifted her hips, the rhythm of their union urgent and almost violent. The bedposts banged against the wall and the ropes beneath the mattress strained as he drove deep inside her, harder and harder with an aching need, blind and wild. Arching beneath him, she matched his pace, moaning as he gripped her buttocks and pulled her closer. A sheen of sweat erupted in the dusky cleft between her breasts and her cheeks flushed.

"Please," she murmured. "I want to know all of you. To feel what you feel."

He rubbed against her, his shaft impaled and he felt the tiny muscles deep inside her clench around him, quiver, then strengthen into something much more. She moaned, and shivered as the muscles constricted tighter around him and left him breathless, trapped by her passion.

A guttural sound, a low moan of complete satisfaction, rumbled from his throat as he came to rest inside her. Damp with sweat, he kissed her lightly on the lips and then he whispered in her ear, "I should have taken longer with you, Eldswythe."

Her cheeks radiant with a rosy flush, she said softly, "I would not have lasted another minute if you had. I might have soon expired without blessed release."

He laughed a low, throaty laugh. He kissed her cheek, his long legs still between hers, his upper body resting on her chest. "I would stay here forever, if I could. If we could . . ." His tone serious, he lowered his head to hers and ran his hand across her breasts, fondling the buds that grew round and hard at his touch.

She closed her eyes. "And I would have you stay here forever, if I could. Forgetting any place but this. But Crenalden is waiting. And your army. Both conspire to keep us tethered to our duty."

Robert laid his head down on her chest. "Let me savor another minute in your arms before the morning comes." He lifted the green stone that hung on a leather tie around her neck. "Where did this come from?" His voice was husky, his eyes still clouded with satiation. He traced small circles around her nipples with the cool smooth pebble.

"It was a gift. But, you are right, I am too trusting and naive. With that admission, I have another. I am falling in love with you, Robert Breton, though I've tried so hard not to. I know you hate my father, and that you want our lands. But I can't help myself. I love you."

Robert said not a word, but rolled onto his back and stared at the ceiling.

Would that he could tell her that he loved her, too. He dreamed not of this—that his heart would be captured by the horsewitch. Somewhere in these last few weeks she had infused him with hope and strength and, quite unexpectedly, renewed his spirit. She kept no secrets from him. She offered him her heart without expecting anything in return, knowing that if anything, he would take more from her. With her forthrightness, she'd earned his respect. With her body and her heart she'd won his soul. She was not like the other women in his life who'd kept secrets, hurtful secrets that placed their lives and his in peril. He'd paid the price for trusting Margaret of Suttony. What price would come with trusting Eldswythe?

He winced, the agony of his past still as painful as a fresh wound. Perhaps Eldswythe was not as honest or as noble as he believed. Perhaps she was hiding something from him and used her body to weaken his defenses. He couldn't trust his own judgment anymore. Where she was concerned, his brain was clouded by desire. But if she proved to be different, then how could he let go of the one woman he could love and respect? They both were sworn to paths that would keep them apart. How could he speak of love if they had no hope of a future without strife. And what if she were not what she seemed? Best to be certain before he spoke such words to her.

His head ached with confusion and he raised himself from the bed. "Eldswythe," he whispered, an edge of pain to his voice. "Eldswythe, I don't—"

Her slender hand skimmed across his back and came to rest on his shoulder. "Do you regret what we've done, Robert? What I begged you to do?"

He looked into her eyes. They were deep and dark green and filled with the afterglow of their loving. They were innocent and naive. She looked at him with love and hope. Could she be as true and honest as she seemed?

"No, Eldswythe. Good God, I don't regret it." He searched her face, tired but glowing with the afterlight of loving. He lowered himself back to the bed, and wrapped his arm around her, pulling her close. "But you deserve to be loved back," he said softly. "By someone who can love you freely and who holds no grudge against Crenalden. By someone you can trust completely with your land and with your heart. Who trusts you—without reservation. You deserve a better man than me."

He'd not meant to hurt her, but she gulped back a sob.

Images of a distant Hillsborough Castle closed around him as he kissed the tears clinging to her cheeks.

"I've given you no cause to doubt me. My father did not

leave yours to die," she whispered. "And you could ask the king for land other than mine, or take a gold reward instead."

He had no answer for her words. A cold, sinking feeling filled his hollow gut. She had accused him before, of seducing her for her land. Had she made love to him just now, hoping to make sure he would walk away from it?

Startled from an all-consuming slumber, Eldswythe disentangled her legs from Robert's and ran to the window, the clanging of the bell below shattering the silence. Men shouted and frantic figures raced about the sunlit yard. A small boy dragged a rope behind him and called up to Eldswythe. "Something's spooked the horses and some of them got loose. My lady, send your husband down."

Eldswythe turned to Robert. "Barstow!"

In an instant Robert jumped from the bed and pulled on his clothes. He grabbed his sword and kissed her on the mouth. "Stay here. Gilroy may be up to something."

He bolted from the room.

He searched for Barstow. Loose horses whinnied and darted round the trees and wagons. Men raced into the woods and others tried to calm a trembling horse they'd cornered by the well.

Robert grabbed the boy by the shoulder. "Have you seen a destrier, a chestnut with feet big as platters?" he yelled.

The boy pointed to the lean-to. "He's still in there, sir. Him and the donkey are the only ones that didn't run."

Robert strode into the lean-to and found Barstow standing free beside the hitching post. The reins of his bridle dangled in the straw. Though he wasn't tied, he hadn't moved a muscle.

The donkey hee-hawed, then continued eating the absent horses' share of grain.

Robert slowly let out his breath as he tied Barstow's head back to the post. "Whatever it was, I'm glad it wasn't bad enough to scare you off. Or mayhap you did not care to jump the donkey's back to leave and let him eat your supper?"

He laughed, then heard the deadly clink of a sword in its scabbard.

Robert's hand flew to his weapon and he braced himself to strike.

A deep voice called from the corner. "Hold, Robert! God's peace, man! It's Thomas!"

Robert lowered his sword and let his breath escape his lungs. "When I last saw you, you were racing from the frackus at Crenalden, to join Hugh and Eldswythe's maid. I take it you survived, but old friend, you don't realize how close I just came to taking off your head."

Thomas held up his hands. "Saints preserve me. When next we meet I'll make certain that I call out my name, else I end up like this fellow."

He pointed to the slumped body of a soldier, a short dagger protruding from his chest. Air still hissed from the wound.

Robert used the flat of his sword to push the man's cloak aside. "He wears John Gilroy's badge. Thank you for killing him before he made his way into the inn."

Thomas grunted. "I didn't kill him. I chased another one on foot into the woods, but this fellow . . . I didn't even know he was here."

"Then who . . . ?" A flash of white caught Robert's eye, a woman running—Eldswythe. She held a stick in her hand, her skirt thrown across her arm. Wild dark hair shining in the early morning light and dark green eyes aflame with fear, wide enough to swallow the sun.

"Robert! What's happened?"

He folded his arms and grinned. If ever Eldswythe of Crenalden Castle looked like a horsewitch, she did at this moment. Still rumpled and glowing from their lovemaking, she'd dashed out of their tiny room, hell bent on saving *him*. Ready for a battle.

He let a slow smile of satisfaction spread across his face. It felt good to have a woman care that much. "Nothing is amiss."

He strode out to greet her, hoping to shield her from the dead solider. "The other horses spooked, but the donkey and Barstow are still here. Eating."

Eldswythe came to a halt in front of him, panting. Lowering the stick to her side, her eyes darted left and right. They came to rest on Barstow, who stood with his nose in the manger, spilling greedy mouthfuls of grain back into the trough as he chewed.

Then her gaze fell on the soldier. Gilroy's man, a lifeless form with his helmet knocked askew and a dagger in his heart.

Robert rested his hand on her shoulder. "I found him thus. Thomas here chased the other one into the woods."

Her eyes wide and her voice trembling, she stared at Robert. "You are all right? No wounds?"

Robert smiled and put his hand behind her neck, drawing her face close to his. "I haven't felt this good in weeks. Tell me, horsewitch. What did you intend to do with that stick?"

Before she had the chance to answer, he pulled her into his arms and pressed her body close to his. He laughed a deep, rich laugh and he kissed her full on the lips, his mouth both hungry and tender. He lingered for a moment, then muttered. "It's time to go. We should leave while I still have power to resist taking you back to bed. Hillsborough is waiting for us."

Sir Thomas cleared his throat. "We've a garrison from Hillsborough on the road not far ahead. They'll be pleased I've found you."

He averted his eyes, staring at the road. By the color of his red cheeks, it was apparent he was embarrassed by what he'd seen. His friend, a Breton, kissing Lady Eldswythe. He spoke but he stared absently into the distance. "Robert, you should know . . . your brother has given Margaret sanctuary."

Robert stepped away from her. A look of dismay flashed

in his eyes. He took a deep breath, but the forced look of indifference on his face didn't fool her.

"Thank you, Thomas. We're ready to depart . . ." He strode toward his friend and put his hand on Thomas's shoulder. "I ask that you keep what you've witnessed to yourself. It would serve no purpose to reveal what you saw. The Lady Eldswythe and I have responsibilities. We've not forgotten the duties asked of us by others. We've agreed to go our separate ways from this point on. Whatever arrangements my brother has made for Margaret . . . I care not."

Though his stance remained the same, his back straight, his chin up, Eldswythe sensed a sudden change in Robert. That commanding knight he'd been on Dover Beach, a surly horseman called the Dark Rider reappeared. She'd not forgotten how he strode across the sand with a touch of arrogance in his manner. He'd argued with the clerk that day and barely checked his anger until he'd read the king's letter, then gained control of his temper by acting remote and superior.

In the awkward silence that followed, the faint sound of saddle bells, distant but familiar, tinkled from somewhere in the woods.

Eldswythe dropped the stick and whipped her head around to search the trees. God's peace. The bells sounded too familiar, and she thought she caught a glimpse of a yellow horse race into the shadows at the trees. Ceres? Impossible.

Thoughts of Crenalden suddenly came rushing in. Isolde. Khalif. Her father. The bells that tinkled in the trees reminded her of her duty, a vow she pledged to keep.

Robert strode away and an overwhelming sense of loss consumed her.

The sun pushed fuzzy stars from the dawn sky as Barstow thundered down the road, his pace quickening at the sight ahead.

Knights and horses milled about beneath the trees. A garrison of thirty, or maybe forty men. From the sweat on their mounts, it looked as if they'd been riding all night. Blue and silver standards flapped in the morning breeze, banners bearing the crest of Hillsborough: a rearing unicorn.

Sir Thomas traveled a discreet distance behind Barstow, allowing ample opportunity for Eldswythe to speak candidly to Robert. But her heart was locked with confusion. She couldn't find the words to tell him she was afraid.

She was the Horsewitch of Crenalden. How would the people of Hillsborough receive her? As a guest? Or prisoner? A wave of dread rolled over her.

Shifting in the saddle, the faint ache between her legs reminded her of how she'd spent her last hours with Robert Breton. But she'd no regrets, though the uncertainty of life at Hillsborough Castle loomed like a storm.

Robert slowed Barstow and raised his hand to hail the men. One by one, the knights came to attention. Some held their swords above their heads, others knelt before him.

Sir Hugh clapped his gauntleted hands across his chest as the members of the garrison cheered and Thomas galloped past, then reined his horse to a halt and saluted Robert.

Sir Hugh approached, his destrier champing at the bit. He laughed and slapped his thigh. Wooly brown hair sprang from his head as he pulled off his helmet. "Thomas finally found the elusive Sir Robert Breton and the Lady Eldswythe. Bloody hell, where have you been?"

Robert grinned and gripped the knight by the forearm. "Hugh, 'tis good to see you."

Sir Hugh grinned and returned the clapping. "God's feet! Robert. We've scoured the woods and sent a garrison to the west. If I didn't know you better, I'd think you did not wish to be found."

He looked at Eldswythe and stroked his bushy beard. "Lady Eldswythe, I forgive you for disobeying my command and racing from my side in Belway Forest. But the fair Bertrada will probably never speak to you again. She has been sick with worry and doesn't find Hillsborough Castle at all to her liking."

Eldswythe lowered her eyes. "I am sorry, Sir Hugh. I will try to make it right with Bertrada."

Sir Hugh shrugged and turned to Robert. "They are glad to have you back. The Earl of Gloucester was not the man to command Henry's army. Had you been with them, things would not have gone so badly. The rest of Henry's men, a hundred, maybe two, are recuperating at Hillsborough. Gilroy's troops killed at least another hundred."

Robert stiffened, assuming a soldierly countenance. "The king's men look haggard. Hillsborough's army will be the force that beats John Gilroy back."

Sir Hugh saluted. "They await your command."

Robert raised his fist. "All mount. To Hillsborough!"

Eldswythe watched the man who'd, just days before, had an easy laugh and later held her tenderly while they slept together. Here, in the shadow of Hillsborough Castle, Sir Robert Breton, a warrior, brooding and angry, a man they called the Dark Rider, was back.

Chapter 14

As dusk fell, the shadows from Hillsborough Castle, a fortress with seven turrets and towering keep, rose to meet the moon. Eldswythe untied the smooth green stone that dangled against her throat. She twisted in the saddle, acutely aware that Hugh sat not far behind. Lowering her voice she spoke to Robert. "My thanks, Sir Robert, for all that you have done for me. Now I would ask that what has passed between us these last few weeks be forgotten. You must lead an army to Crenalden, I must help to raise the ransom for the Earl of Gloucester and prepare to marry him and rule my father's castle. That was our bargain, that we should part thus." Her voice fell as she searched his eyes for some sign of his objection.

Barstow snorted.

Robert's face grew cold, his gaze distant. He continued to stare at the men ahead, but he nodded once.

Eldswythe took his hand and dropped the green stone in his palm, then closed his fingers over it. "I want you to keep this. I want to give you something for helping me. There is good in you, Robert Breton. You are a worthy and an able knight. A horseman like no other who will defeat John Gilroy, I am certain of it. My father, and yours, God rest his soul, would be proud of you."

Robert met her watery gaze with silence. His eyes flickered with anguish.

Sir Hugh approached. "I am ready to be home. With Sir Robert there, it will do much to improve my position at the feasting table. I might even rise to the level of the salt." He grinned at Eldswythe, then he narrowed his eyes and glanced at Robert, before looking back at her. "Why so somber, Lady Eldswythe? Has he been unkind? God at peace, Robert. You'll stay a lonely man if you do not change your ways."

Eldswythe felt the color rising to her face. "Sir Hugh, Sir Robert has behaved as a knight of the highest caliber. I have dust in my eyes, that is all."

Robert glared at Hugh, but he spoke to Eldswythe. "My lady," he said formally, "mayhap you would be more comfortable riding in the wagon from this point on."

Eldswythe arched an eyebrow. The man sounded heartless. Yes, why not ride in the wagon? There were thirty other knights on this patrol to guard her. No need to suffer this unbearable man.

Robert reined Barstow to a halt.

Not waiting for assistance, she jumped from Barstow's back and patted the horse on the neck. "Goodbye, Barstow. I thank you."

Without looking back, she strode toward the cart, weaving through the knights and foot soldiers who waited to resume the march.

The wagon jarred and bumped and reeked of swine. In truth, she would have much preferred a horse, a mule or even walking. But that was never offered as an option. Leaning against the backboard, she chewed on hard bread and jerky, soldier's rations. She hadn't seen Robert for hours and doubted if he had given her a second's thought.

The wagon creaked, then lurched to a halt. Scrambling onto her knees, she leaned across the sideboard. "Why have we stopped?" The squire who stood beside the wagon squinted and pointed to the road ahead of them.

"It is Sir Robert's horse, milady. He refuses to walk on."

"Is it Barstow? Is he lame?" She swung her leg over the sideboard.

"Dunno, milady, 'tis hard to tell from here. One thing is certain. If anything should happen to Sir Robert's beast, I wouldn't want to be the man that caused it."

She hiked her gown above her calves and lowered herself onto the muddy road.

"You cannot go up there, my lady. 'Tis no place for a woman. The men would want you to stay in the wagon."

Ignoring the squire, she hurried toward the soldiers who had gathered around the big destrier standing squarely in the middle of the road.

She exhaled. It wasn't Barstow—but it was Robert's big bay, the one that had carried their baggage and provisions back from Dover Beach.

The horse snorted and shook its head.

Two sweaty-faced men locked their well-muscled arms behind the horse's hindquarters and scrabbled in the mud as they tried to move the great horse forward. The bay planted all four feet and refused to budge.

Robert held the reins. Eldswythe watched as he stroked his horse's neck and tried to soothe it.

"Should we try the whip, sir?" a sweaty soldier asked, breathing heavily.

Robert glared at the man. "No. The horse will not be whipped."

The soldier wiped his face across his upper arm. "What's wrong with him, sir? You've let him rest three times within the hour past. Do you think he's got the Bane?" His eyes widened.

It was against her better judgment, but Eldswythe could not stay silent. "It is not the Bane," she said, stepping to the front. "I know what is wrong with him and I fear no better end."

"Do you?" asked Robert, who looked surprised to see her.

Eldswythe's throat went dry. "Yes. He's been elf shot. Colic in the belly. I am afraid he will not recover."

"How, exactly, did you come to that conclusion, Lady Eldswythe?" asked Robert.

"I know the signs, sir. His flanks are swollen and he is breathing too hard."

"These signs I've seen before. But they usually pass. How do you know he will not recover?"

Sir Hugh stepped in front of Eldswythe. "Robert, leave the horse. We can send a man to retrieve him later. We cannot delay here. Gilroy's men are but half a league behind us."

Robert shook his head. "Then send a runner on to Hillsborough and ask for reinforcements." He turned to Eldswythe. "How do you know that the horse will die?"

Eldswythe approached the great horse and laid her palm at his girth, low on the left side. "His heart is racing. Here you can feel it."

She took his hand and placed it over the horse's heart. Robert's face remained expressionless, though Eldswythe sensed that he was not convinced.

She lifted the horse's upper lip. "His gums are scarlet and turning purple."

Robert's face paled.

Gripping Eldswythe by the shoulder, Sir Hugh pulled her back. "Robert, leave the horse. Our man reports that Gilroy's garrison has entered the forest." He shot a guarded glance at Eldswythe, then back at Robert. "There are rumors in the ranks. The men believe you've been bewitched. They're saying *she* is the reason your bay is sick—she did it to slow us down. Gilroy is after all her half brother and her loyalties are in question. Be forewarned, Robert. She'll not be welcome at Hillsborough. Is there somewhere else to take her?" He looked sheepishly at Eldswythe, as if he had been forced to tell her what the men were saying, though he did not share their sentiments.

Was that a look of doubt that flashed across Robert's face?

Eldswythe's knees went weak. "No! It isn't true. Sir Hugh, Robert, surely you don't suspect me of—"

Robert cut her off. He spoke to Hugh with a vehemence that shocked her. "I've sworn to protect her. I am a man of my word. I shall keep my promise." He turned to face his men. "The Lady Eldswythe will go to Hillsborough. We will offer her protection on order of the king. If any man wishes to challenge me on this, step forward."

The troops stood in silence, not a single man contesting.

Suddenly, the great horse dropped to its knees and with a monumental effort, lowered its hindquarters to the ground. The animal rested with its muzzle in the mud, then groaned and began to roll.

Eldswythe turned to Robert. Her palms upturned, she pleaded. "Please, Robert, I know you cannot bear to see him suffer. Do not let him die in agony. He could linger here for hours."

"You are asking me to kill my horse?"

"There is nothing to be done. If we leave him here he will die a slow and painful death."

The horse rolled on its bloated side, legs extended, grunting with every breath.

Sir Hugh studied the road behind them. "Robert, we cannot afford to tarry. Staying longer will risk their lives and ours."

Eldswythe bent beside Robert, kneeling in the mud next to his horse. Moving closer, she snatched the dagger from his belt.

With a battle-ready reflex just as quick, he grabbed her wrist and held it in his powerful grip. Eldswythe did not release the weapon, but she was completely immobilized in his hold. She looked him in the eye, tears rolling down her face. "If you cut above the great vein, he will die quietly."

"I have seen both men and horses die by the sword, my lady, and some by my own blade. They do not all die quietly." He released her wrist. "Can you not save him? Can the horse-witch not restore him?"

It wasn't his anger that made her suck in her breath, it was the bitter, hurtful way he'd called her horsewitch. She lowered her eyes and spoke softly. "Were it in my power to cure him, you know I would. And I know you have a horseman's heart. Please. End his pain." She offered him the dagger.

Robert's face reddened. His jaw flexed. "Do not presume to know my heart, Eldswythe." He slipped the bridle from the horse's head and lifted the dagger from her hand. "You will be disappointed—in everything I do from this point on."

Eldswythe stroked the animal's cheek, then stood and turned to walk away in silence. Stung by Robert's words and even more by the change in him. She did not know this man—that he would speak to her this way in front of his men and in front of Sir Hugh, that he could be so harsh and doubt her loyalty.

"I will not let him suffer," Robert murmured, inaudible to others, but loud enough for her to hear.

She did not look back.

The moon hung low beneath the scattered clouds as the small garrison trooped across the drawbridge into Hillsborough Castle. Bowmen walked the battlements above and sentries watched from the two tall circular towers that flanked the gatehouse. The moat below was covered with a swill as thick as pudding. It glistened in the moonlight and stank of waste.

Eldswythe pinched her nose and strained to see stables just inside the courtyard. At least she found the stink of fresh manure, for there were piles of it, less offensive. And the stables. *Jesu*! There must have been three hundred horses here or more, judging by the barns and haystacks in the yard.

Beyond the inner wall, the bailey surged with shops and tents and two water wells, one for livestock and one for men. With the animals confined for the night in their pens, all was quiet in the bailey. Knights huddled around a bonfire outside the doors of the great hall.

Conversation ceased as the garrison approached. Men bowed to Robert and stared at Eldswythe as the wagon came to a jarring halt.

Sniggers emanated from the huddle. The tallest of the men ventured near the wagon and peered at Eldswythe.

"There she is, the Horsewitch of Crenalden castle! Had I known she was so fetching, I would have volunteered myself to go and get her." He winked, then smiled a toothless grin.

His scrubby squire peered across the sideboard. "I hear she can ride a warhorse as good as any man." His boyish voice rang clear and high.

The tall knight harrumphed. "She can ride my pony anytime. I'll even help her get upon it."

Laughter followed as Eldswythe climbed out of cart and moved to stand on the other side, away from leering eyes.

The knights fell silent and stepped aside as Robert strode around the wagon. "She is here under my protection. You will treat her with respect." He signaled for her to follow. "This way, Lady Eldswythe."

He shot a menacing look at the men. "I suggest you find your beds. Training starts at dawn. You, Pearson, are the horses fit and ready?"

The young knight bowed. "Yes, Sir Robert. We have been practicing for days, waiting for you to get here, wondering what you were doing with the horsewitch . . ." He lowered his eyes, as if he immediately regretted his flippant answer.

Robert took a step toward the young knight, then halted when a boy, not yet ten years old, beckoned from the doorway at the top of the stairs. "My lord!" he called. "We feared you were dead."

Robert climbed the stairs, his great stride advancing over three steps at a time. He smiled and tousled the boy's hair. "Good to see you, Jack. I think you've grown."

The boy grinned and bowed to Eldswythe. "M-m-m-my lady," he stammered, then looked away and turned to follow Robert up the steps.

Eldswythe climbed behind him. Robert had not spoken to her since she had left him kneeling in the road. His distance angered her. At the same time, she would have done anything to redeem herself if he'd only acted like he cared.

Exasperated, she blurted out, "I was not the cause of your horse's death. It was an act of nature. By Saint Eustace, I would have saved him if I could."

Robert appeared to not hear. He strode into the dimly lit hall and parked himself beside a massive table placed before the large stone hearth. The blazing fire cast a golden glow across the tapestries and heraldic flags that loomed from the porticos above. He poured brown ale into a pewter goblet and held it up. "A drink?" he offered. He waited a moment, then he drained the cup.

Exhausted, Eldswythe sank onto the cushioned bench next to the warming hearth. "No, thank you."

She lowered her tired head and studied the toes of her muddied shoes. The rich glazed tiles beneath her feet were painted French blue and white and bore the Earl of Hillsborough's crest.

A deep voice boomed from the shadowy tall-backed chair sitting on the dais. "Welcome, Robert. Brother."

A tall man, whose nose was red but whose features otherwise bore a striking similarity to Robert's, strode across the hall. "So, the king has called you back to defend Crenalden. I am sorry that you didn't get to take the cross. It might have cured your guilty conscience." He poured himself a drink. The bell-shaped sleeves of his green gown, trimmed with ermine and bejeweled, slid up to his elbows to reveal a claret-colored shirt beneath. It matched his woolen hose and leather ankle boots. The heavy gold medallion resting on his chest glimmered in the firelight as he stretched out and reached for Robert. "Come now, brother. Let us begin anew. I forgive you for your badly mangled dealings with the Lady Margaret. 'Tis her name that's sullied, not ours."

Robert stepped back, his eyes clouded with fury.

The man dropped his arms and sighed. "A successful mission, I see," he said, gesturing to Eldswythe.

Robert filled his cup again. "Lady Eldswythe, let me introduce you to my brother, Harold, Earl of Hillsborough." He stared into the cup, swirling the dregs.

Rising from the bench, Eldswythe dipped a curtsy. "My Lord, I am Eldswythe, daughter of the Earl of Crenalden. I am grateful to your brother, and to your great house, for coming to my aid."

Harold smirked and stared at her through his red-rimmed eyes. "The king commanded it, Lady Eldswythe. I think he hopes to make our families friendly. Courtesy demands that I inquire—how fares your father's lady wife, Isolde? I fostered with her brother."

From the tone in his ruthless voice, she knew he asked a question to which he already knew the answer. "Isolde is dead," she answered flatly, refusing to give him the satisfaction of detecting her grief. Harold smirked and in the awkward silence that followed, resentment reared up inside her, trampling her last vestiges of self-control. "Why didn't you send reinforcements to help the Earl of Gloucester? The king's army could have used the help of the knights of Hillsborough."

Harold spun to face the dais and placed his hands behind his back. A whiff of sour ale floated on his breath as he exhaled. "Lady Eldswythe, my knights were in Wales, defending King Henry's interests there. Whilst his princely son and my pious brother were preparing to crusade, I could not spare any men to help Crenalden."

Robert slammed down his cup. "The Earl of Gloucester was captured. You could have taken the command."

Hillsborough lifted his arms, feigning exasperation. "I was busy. Wales is a good distance from here. Gilroy marched on Crenalden sooner than the king expected."

"Busy? I'll wager you were hunting or drinking. You neglect your duty to the crown. Gilroy will set his sights on Hillsborough if no one stands against him." Robert seethed. "And you have done little here this summer. The moat stinks, the yards are rank with manure and I doubt you have given any thought to harvest. I can fathom what you have been up to and none of it is good."

The earl grinned, his fine white teeth shining in the shadows. "Hillsborough is *my* birthright, brother, to manage as I see fit. I've done what needed to be done. Our father may have favored you, but the law is the law. The earldom belongs to me. You are the second son. Stop meddling in my affairs."

Robert moved his hand to his sword's hilt.

Harold stepped back and fingered his gold medallion. "Come, let's not quarrel. I am truly glad you have returned. I find the business of running the estate and corralling our recalcitrant retainers a tedious effort. And feeding the remnant of the king's army has taken its toll. The men lounge around all day and chase our women. They game and drink at night and the next morning, they claim that they are sick or wounded and cannot train. No wonder Gilroy sent them home with their tails between their legs. They are lax without a leader. Undisciplined." Harold cleared his throat. "Since you speak of him, my spies tell me the Earl of Gloucester may be dead. At least no one has seen him since Gilroy locked him in prison. The men who guarded him have even been relieved."

Leaping from the bench, Eldswythe gripped the table, her face within an inch of the earl's. "I beseech you, Lord Harold, give me the money to pay his ransom. Gilroy will produce him, alive and well."

Robert glared at his brother and fixed both hands on his hips. "The king would appreciate your contribution."

The earl shook his head. "I see no point. Crenalden is lost and the Earl of Gloucester is as good as dead. Paying a ransom now will gain nothing. If you think he is alive and you wish to give Gilroy what he asks for, Lady Eldswythe, you must raise the money—from Gloucester's own family or get it from my brother here." He snapped his fingers. "Beg pardon. Robert has forfeited everything he owned for the crusade, and has only one horse left, I'm told. I guess he cannot help you either."

Eldswythe backed away, trembling. "Forgive me, I should not have asked you for the money. After all, you are a Breton, and I am the daughter of the Earl of Crenalden." She squared her shoulders. "Why do I get the feeling that you are pleased to see John Gilroy defeat us?" She pushed the table aside, unable to control her anger. "I think you hope he will win the day, but that would put a robber baron one step closer to your door. Be careful what you wish for."

The earl raised an eyebrow. "You overstep your welcome, Lady Eldswythe. If you wish for hospitality here, curb your tongue."

Robert took a breath. "Enough. We are both weary from our travels." He faced his brother. "I will take the Lady Eldswythe to the ladies' chambers. Nothing more can be done tonight."

Harold spun his emerald ring around his finger. "In a week, brother, we will celebrate St. Michael's feast. Lord Bernard, the Bishop of Cleves, will grace us with his presence. I hope you and Lady Eldswythe will be dressed accordingly, as befits your rank." He fanned his hand in front of his face, as if to shoo away a stench. "Meanwhile, surely by the time I see you tomorrow you should each take a bath. Make yourselves presentable, you are dressed like common farmers."

Eldswythe watched him stroll away, his hard-heeled slippers clacking against the stone pavers.

Robert exhaled. "I apologize for his behavior. My father would not have behaved as such." He poured himself another drink. "As for the bishop, he is no friend to Hillsborough. His visits here have always been contentious and they serve some political purpose. Be wary."

Robert set down his cup and gestured to Eldswythe, indicating that he wanted her to follow. They crossed the great hall, passed beneath the curtain behind the dais and climbed a narrow spiral staircase. He stopped before an arched door, where a single torch on the wall sputtered black smoke and threatened to go out.

He gently moved her in front of him, as he banged on the door. "Open. The Lady Eldswythe is to sleep here tonight."

The hum of women's voices chattered on the other side, then fell silent.

The door swung open and a slender woman with high cheekbones and lips as pink as cherries smiled widely at Robert. Wisps of honey-colored hair escaped her crisp white veil and curled around her face. She curtsied. Her finely woven yellow dress floated as she kneeled, then came to rest at her feet, like a cloud. A tiny prayer book swung from a golden chain around her waist. "Sir Robert, I am glad to see that you are well. I have prayed for you."

"Greetings, Lady Margaret," he said, his voice steely. He looked over her head into the room behind her, as if he were making mental note of who was there.

He pushed Eldswythe across the threshold. "I will leave you in Lady Margaret's hands. My brother has declared her chatelaine until my mother returns from pilgrimage. She will find you clothes and a place to sleep."

He leaned in low. His lips brushed against her earlobe. "Have a care," he whispered.

With that he turned and left.

The door slammed shut as Margaret ushered Eldswythe into the sleeping chamber, where no less than seven women shared two beds. At least both were draped with curtains, and piled high with covers, furs, and blankets.

Eldswythe stood there staring at the Lady Margaret, stunned as if she were looking at an apparition. Yet she was very much alive and she lived at Hillsborough!

The Lady Margaret gestured for a chair and lowered herself into it as if she were a slighted queen. "Lady Eldswythe, you look as if you've seen a ghost." She fanned herself with a linen hankie, and pressed it to her lips. "'Tis no wonder, considering what you've been through. Count your blessings that the king has commissioned Sir Robert to win your castle back." She placed her slender white hand across her breast and looked up at Eldswythe, smiling sweetly.

Eldswythe bristled. She detected something in the Lady Margaret's tone that hinted at jealousy and malice.

Margaret folded her hands in her lap, her doe-like eyes searching Eldswythe's. "I welcome you, Lady Eldswythe, and offer our condolences. The ladies of Hillsborough bear no ill will against the daughter of the Earl of Crenalden. We regret that you have come upon such unfortunate circumstances." Margaret's eyes roamed up and down the length of Eldswythe.

She felt her face grow hot, acutely aware of how unclean she must look and poor, dressed in a borrowed wheat sack. She pretended that it did not matter. "Thank you, Lady Margaret. The people of Crenalden, who now must bear the rule of Gilroy and his army, could use your prayers."

"Of course." Margaret smiled.

The youngest of the ladies, a slight girl with maple-colored hair and freckles on her nose, wrapped a coverlet around Eldswythe's shoulders. "Are you a horsewitch like they say?" she asked breathlessly. "Is it true you knew Sir Robert's horse would die from colic and you were about to cut its throat yourself before he prevented you?"

A collective gasp stopped the huddled conversation about the room.

"Lady Anne," Margaret snapped, "there will be no talk of horsewitches in our chambers and your knowledge of such gossip is most unbecoming." She stood and donned a sumptuous yellow velvet cloak, lined with rabbit fur. "You spend too much time milling about the gatehouse to learn what news the runners bring." She turned to Eldswythe. "I think she is in love with Sir Robert. At news of his return she could not refrain from waiting there to greet him."

Anne's face turned as red as beets, but Margaret continued, her gown twisting around her legs as she spun to glare at the girl. "Really, Anne, don't say I didn't warn you. You'll find you've lost your maidenhood and, worse, find yourself with child." Margaret held her hand up as if she would not hear a word in Anne's defense. "He will not care a fig for your predicament and you will be in ruin."

The room grew still as Anne's mouth hung open.

Margaret smiled sweetly at Eldswythe. "Rest now, Lady Eldswythe. You can take Anne's place in the berth with the Widow Alyce."

Eldswythe shook her head. Better to decline and not impose on anyone. She would need every friend she could get. "Thank you, but I would prefer to sleep here by the fire."

Margaret looked surprised. "You mean to sleep on the floor?"

Nodding, she pointed to the pallet. "If I could borrow one more blanket."

With a look of disapproval, Margaret handed her a fur-lined cover from the bed. Eldswythe smiled at the aging widow Alyce and the stricken Lady Anne, then spread the fur beside the fire. "I will be fine here. Thank you."

Margaret pursed her fine lips together. "First thing tomorrow morning you can bathe and don fresh clothes. I'll have your maid bring your bags to you."

Eldswythe's heart leapt. Was it possible she had managed to salvage a few of their possessions? "Bertrada? Where is she?"

"She is sleeping in the stables. We have no more room up here."

Eldswythe bit her tongue. Dear Bertrada, sent to sleep in the stables. It was meant as an insult to her as the daughter of the Earl of Crenalden, and poor Bertrada would suffer, so afraid of horses. No doubt Margaret had sent her belongings out there, too, after she had rummaged through them.

She forced herself to smile. "I have few clothes in my possession. No doubt you know that, and you also know that my bags do not contain charms, herbals or potions of any sort. I am not a horsewitch, despite what people say."

Several ladies smothered a laugh, but Margaret's elegant

face hardened. "Good night, Lady Eldswythe. I pray you've not left your manners in the barn and can conduct yourself at Hillsborough as is befitting to a woman of your station." She crossed herself and turned to leave. "Say your prayers, every one of you. God looks kindly on pious women." She headed for the door, then stopped and turned to Eldswythe. "Lady Eldswythe, I will do everything within my power to see that your stay here is as comfortable but as brief as possible. Of that you can be certain."

Eldswythe rolled over on her pallet and faced the fire. Shadows fell across the room as the ladies extinguished their candles. She'd spent more than half her life in a convent and oft slept on the floor. One thing she learned from her experience with the nuns was how to sleep on stone and that the truly pious were never so self-righteous, or as haughty as the Lady Margaret. When it came to godliness, the woman was a pretender.

Hillsborough did not appear as foreboding by the light of day. The hallways were covered with tapestry and sconces filled with new candles. The scent of freshly baking bread and herbs wafted through windows that were high and open.

Once Eldswythe had had a bath and dressed in her own clean clothes, she felt more like herself. Bertrada helped her dress in her dark green kirtle and pale blue undergown. Eldswythe lashed her silver girdle around her waist, and donned her favorite silver circlet to keep her white veil securely on her head.

Following the troop of women down the stairs to the great hall for breakfast, she listened to their quiet chatter. The ladies of the household proved unexpectedly kind, barring the Lady Margaret. Anne and the Widow Alyce exceedingly enjoyed gossip. The comings and goings of Sir Robert were a favorite topic. All of the women jostled for a seat next to him, each hoping to attract the attention of a man they considered both dangerous, and desirable.

A week passed without event, while they waited for supplies and horses from the king. Eldswythe missed Robert deeply and every time she entered the hall, she searched for his face. Occasionally he looked her way, but made no attempt to seek her company.

She pretended that she didn't notice and talked quietly with other women or with Bertrada. Her maid, it seemed, now pined after Sir Hugh and jabbered endlessly about his kindness and his prowess.

This morning, she was particularly effusive in gushing about Sir Hugh.

Distracted, Eldswythe listened as servants carried trays of baked apples, cheeses, and hot eel pie to the tables. She quickly took her seat and, as she had every day this week, and ate in silence. Next she would endure an hour of chapel with the ladies before, blessedly, she made her way to the stables.

The horse marshal there had at first been reluctant to let her enter. Dressed in finery, she didn't look like a lady who would work in a barn, and he was suspicious of a noble woman from Crenalden.

But Eldswythe had long learned it was better to appear in the barns in fancy clothes than to show up in a worn and dirty gown. Witches always dressed in soiled clothes and rags. Better not to look the part. It was safer to look every bit the daughter of an earl.

Besides, she would affront the clergy if she attended chapel in anything less than her best.

She'd promised the horse marshal to help steep and strain the herbs she'd convinced him would be needed to treat the sundry maladies of the three hundred horses that would soon go to battle. For all the wealth of Hillsborough, there was something lacking in the horses' care.

Lord Harold, it was rumored, had told the steward to limit the dispensing of the coin that was needed for the horse's keep. But she had entreated him to part with a sum of gold to improve the horses he loved to ride to hunt. There was coin enough left over for medicines and bandages for the rest. She'd earned the gratitude of the marshal and the steward was happy to make certain the earl continued hunting. It kept his lordship from overseeing the accounts as closely as he should have.

She passed her hours in the stable and today the taste and smell of agrimony, cumin, and anise would be on her clothes, and in her mouth and hair. But she'd earned the respect of the grooms and stable boys with her willingness to work. To help with the gentling of foals and with the colts newly put to saddle. Even the knights had begun to seek her out, to ask her opinion. Eldswythe lost herself in the place where she felt most at home. The work kept her mind off Robert. Off Crenalden. As long as her hands and head were busy, she'd little time to worry.

The sun already high and hot, she hurried into the barn with her head down. She rounded the corner to find herself faced with the broad chest of a knight—a man dressed in the familiar dark tunic. Robert.

Her heart leapt as her eyes locked with his. "Beg your pardon, Sir Robert."

He smiled and bowed a courtly bow. "Good morn, Lady Eldswythe. I see you are keeping busy. All is well with you and the horses?" There was a look of softness in his face, of longing but his tone was formal. Distant.

She lowered her eyes. "Yes. And how are you?"

Robert set the bucket at his feet. "I'm fine, though I chafe at waiting for the king to send provisions. We need more armor and more bowmen before we can attack Crenalden."

"All else is ready?" she asked, fearful he would soon be leaving, and anxious at the same time that he should go, knowing the people of Crenalden suffered every day that Gilroy ruled.

Robert waited until a groom passed by before he answered.

"My men are ready," he said, in a low voice. "As soon as we can, we will march. The longer the delay, the better the advantage for Gilroy. I've not made our plans well known. There are spies everywhere."

Eldswythe swallowed. He talked of business. Of war. But nothing else. As if they barely knew each other!

She picked up her skirts and backed away. "I'll leave you to your duties then. God willing, the provisions from the king will be here soon."

He stepped toward her. "Eldswythe—" Robert said, softly, his hand resting lightly on her shoulder.

A deep voice suddenly boomed from the yard. "Robert. The men are waiting on the lists."

"I must go," he said, lowering his hand and turning to wave at Sir Thomas. "But it's good to see you, Eldswythe, to know you are safe and well." He wheeled around and joined Thomas in the yard.

The horse marshal quietly sidled next to Eldswythe and handed her a bucket filled with steaming mugwort. "My lady, we need you in the south barn and Sir Robert needs to train."

Eldswythe exhaled as she watched Robert stride away. "Is it true, marshal, what they say about a horseman who's a knight?"

"What's that, my lady?"

"That every horseman needs a horse, a sword, and a woman, but he only loves the first two."

Chapter 15

Eldswythe and the other women strolled across the bailey to the chapel the next morning, the sky clear and bright, the yard humming with activity. Anvils clanged, horses whinnied, and the sound of clashing swords rang above the grunts and moans of exercising men. The day smelled warm and sweaty and the air filled with the metallic scent of hot iron and newly shod horses.

Soldiers stopped to stare at the passing women. Eldswythe bristled and steeled her nerves, preparing to hear the dreaded word, *horsewitch*. Miraculously, the crowd around her was silent. Not a whisper or a jeer fell across her ears. Robert's warning, it seemed, had been well heeded.

Then she spotted Robert sparring with Sir Hugh. Both men were engaged in swordplay, slashing at each other with a vigor and enthusiasm that a week ago, would have made Eldswythe worry for Robert's safety. But in the days that passed, he'd clearly grown stronger and more agile, his muscles honed and tight, ready for a fight.

Sir Hugh clapped his hand on Robert's back, "Ah, Robert, the Lady Eldswythe is especially fine to look at today." Grinning, he saluted the passing group of women, eliciting laughter as he posed a courtly bow.

Robert didn't answer. His penetrating gaze settled on Eldswythe.

She could not look away, just as she had not been able to stop thinking about him since the day before. The steaming bath this morning should have left her feeling stronger, more ready to face the trials of the day. She knew she looked her best. Bertrada had spent the past hour happily brushing out Eldswythe's long dark hair, though she claimed it would smell cleaner if she'd not spend every morning in the stables. Gleaming, it fell freely from beneath a creamy linen veil and tumbled down her back.

Eldswythe could not keep from walking closer to Robert. "Good morning, sir. I see you've been training hard. I am impressed with your prowess if not your manners. Will you not at least remove your helmet when ladies pass?"

Robert bowed, then pulled off his helmet. "Thank you, Lady Eldswythe, for reminding me of my manners."

Mother Mary! He looked as if he hadn't slept in days. Had he looked like this when they'd met in the stables yesterday? Had she been so surprised to see him then that she didn't notice? Even freshly shaven, dressed in a leather jerkin with a clean short tunic and new black hose, he looked as though he'd been up all night. His face was hollow and his gray eyes rimmed with dark circles.

She inclined her head and lowered her eyes, resisting the temptation to inquire about his health.

Stroking his ragged beard, Sir Hugh looked at Robert. "You've had enough, Robert. You've been swinging at me like a madman. I need a rest. I'll ask Bertrada to massage my arm." He glanced at Eldswythe. "And I feel as though I am intruding."

He bowed, then turned and left.

Eldswythe felt her cheeks begin to burn.

Robert spoke in a low voice. "Lady Eldswythe, having you watch me every day and hover close, but pretend that you don't see me is driving me insane. Please, let me train in peace."

"I, I . . . I haven't been watching you." She had never been too good at lying and she was disconcerted to learn that he watched her, too. Until this morning, he'd never given any indication that he noticed her presence when he trained.

Flustered, she spun around and fled into the chapel to join the other ladies. All the way, she had the uneasy feeling Robert was still watching—and he was staring at her backside.

A willowy priest with a balding head began St. Michael's mass, his monotone voice reverberating from the vestibule. Within the hour, most of the ladies appeared to be doing anything other than listening, except the Lady Margaret, who seemed to be sincerely engaged in the Latin recitations.

Anne counted seed pearls on the cuffs of her sleeves. The Widow Alyce snored, while her two young daughters, Clare and Margery, played with puppets they had fashioned from their handkerchiefs. The other ladies had all perfected the art of sleeping with their eyes open and could mouth the hymns at the priest's command.

Eldswythe tried to concentrate, but her mind drifted. The ledge was uncomfortable, the wall cold at her back. But it was better than standing, as other folk were expected to do. She was restless, eager to get to the stables. She studied the frescoes on the wall behind the priest. The Four Horsemen of the Apocalypse thundered down, each horse a different color, the black stallion and its rider looked much like Barstow and Robert Breton.

She winced, the fresco reminding her of the pleasure of riding Barstow while she nestled in Robert's lap.

The Lady Anne nudged Eldswythe and whispered, "I saw you speaking to Sir Robert, Lady Eldswythe. He is so handsome, is he not? They say he is the finest horseman in all England." A girlish giggle slipped from her lips. "I saw the way the two of you looked at each other. Everybody did."

Eldswythe stared ahead as warmth rose to her cheeks.

Anne spoke behind her hand. "I am not in love with him,

you know. I waited by the gates to see Sir Thomas." She blushed and lowered her eyes. "'Tis him I think I love."

Anne pretended to cough and raised her hand to cover her mouth. "Be careful, Lady Eldswythe," she whispered. "The Lady Margaret watches you and Sir Robert. I think she is displeased with what she sees."

Eldswythe looked askance.

Margaret sat prim and proper. In the shadows of the chapel, her soft blue eyes and golden hair made her look almost angelic.

Anne continued softly, "They were once betrothed, but neither she nor he will speak of it. The wedding was called off and she has been allowed to stay here until the countryside is safe. I think Margaret still pines for Sir Robert."

Puzzled, Eldswythe leaned a little closer to Anne. "Why is Lady Margaret chatelaine?" The words came out a little louder than she meant.

Anne clucked. "Harold. He hates his younger brother so much, he would do anything to spite him."

The Widow Alyce suddenly sat upright. A sneeze erupted from her head and blew the handkerchief that was folded in her lap onto the floor. Alyce bent down low to fetch it. "Lady Eldswythe," she whispered, "It isn't Sir Robert that the Lady Margaret wants. Nay, she has her eyes on Harold, the Lord Hillsborough, and it's rumored that already she shares his bed. Lord have mercy on us if he takes her to wife. We'll have her for a chatelaine for good and life here will be intolerable. We'll all be forced to spend hours in this damp and chilly chapel." She hiccupped and wiped her nose with her hankie. "My achy bones won't last."

The priest concluded with a melodic amen and the ladies began filing from the chapel.

A hundred questions raced through Eldswythe's mind. She wanted desperately to press the Lady Anne and the Widow Alyce for details, but now was not the time.

Anne walked next to Eldswythe as they shuffled toward the chapel door. She tugged on Eldswythe's sleeve. "Sir Thomas plans to ask my father for my hand," she whispered as they strode into the daylight. "I pray he has gold enough. I shall die if I cannot marry him!"

Eldswythe smiled and looked at Lady Anne's soft round face. She was younger than herself by at least five years, sixteen years of age, mayhap. And she was an honest soul, not in the least beguiling. She hoped, for Anne's sake, that as the youngest daughter of a nobleman, she would be allowed to marry for love.

She followed the giggling Anne as she picked her way across the muddied yard, then broke away from the pack of women and headed toward the stables.

Robert stepped before her. "Lady Eldswythe, the Bishop of Cleves has arrived and requests an audience with you."

Eldswythe frowned, in no mood for another game of cat and mouse with Robert. What business could the bishop have with her? She had never met the man, but she had heard he was stern and unforgiving when it came to women.

"Later," she said, stepping around Robert. "I have to see to the horses. Your captain's horse has rheumy eyes, and a coughing spell is sweeping through the barns."

"The bishop needs to see you now."

"I'll come as soon as I can."

Stepping in stride beside her, he spoke in a low and warning voice. "This way, Eldswythe." He took her by the elbow and steered her to the hall.

Saints preserve her. Had she been summoned to be skewered as a horsewitch?

The horses forgotten, she stumbled as they climbed the stairs to the great hall. "At least have the courtesy to slow your pace and help me," she called up to him. "It will draw less attention to our discourse than your huffing."

Robert halted. His eyes looked tired and bleary. "Eldswythe, if you knew how much I want to touch you. To take you in my arms . . ."

Without another word, he spun around and headed toward the side staircase leading to his brother's solar. "Follow me," he ordered softly. "And please be careful."

"I'll ask the bishop to pay William's ransom," she blurted, tromping up the stairs behind him. "The Earl of Gloucester and my father generously support the church. He should help us now."

Robert stopped, one foot resting on the last riser. "I wouldn't get my hopes up if I were you. Next to God and himself, the bishop has a love for gold. He usually comes asking for it, not offering to give it up." Robert headed down an arching hallway that was unfamiliar. She hurried after him, not certain where else to go.

The Bishop of Cleves, dressed in a scarlet cassock and a short white mantle trimmed in gold, was pacing just outside a pair of arched wooden doors. His knotty-pated head and thin sharp face, clean shaven, shone beneath the tallow torches that smoked on the wall. He glowered at Robert through narrow, calculating eyes. "Sir Robert," he said, without bothering to acknowledge Eldswythe. He threw open the doors.

The solar, a large, oak-paneled room was warm and smelled faintly of wood smoke and soured wine. Every wall was covered with a tapestry and a massive curtained bed dominated the cavernous space. Two yellow candles fizzled atop tall pedestals. A single padded chair, covered in silk brocade and deep enough for two people, sat beneath a slit window.

Eldswythe's eyes were drawn to an empty flagon and the clothes that were strewn across the floor, including a pair of women's silver slippers, all hastily discarded.

Robert strode across the room and leaned against the hearth, casually folding his arms.

The bishop pointed at Eldswythe, directing her to stand beside Robert, then clasped his hands behind his back. He had an air of superiority that made her instantly dislike him.

"Sir Robert, I am sorry that you did not sail to Acre," he said. "But then again, there are battles *here* to fight. Battles that are just as important to the king."

Robert grunted.

The bishop crossed the room. With a fling of his arm, he

swept back the pale blue curtains from the bed where a human form, buried under a mountain of furs and linens, moaned and rolled onto its stomach. "Get up, Lord Hillsborough. It comes as no surprise to find you still abed. The king sends his greetings and has asked me to relay an urgent message, the reason for my visit."

Harold sat upright, shirtless, rubbing the sleep from his face. On this rare occasion his nose wasn't red. With his dark hair cut just above his ears in a military fashion and his sparkling blue eyes, he was quite handsome. He groaned and massaged his temples. "Who disturbs me at this hour? It is not yet noon." His eyes focused on the bishop. With a look of disregard, he yawned and scratched his belly. "Ahh, *Jesu*. Already here, bishop? Did you fly with angels' wings this time or ride the devil's horse?"

The bishop scowled. "You have always been an insolent pup, arrogant and careless with your tongue. Had I not the patience of a man of God, I would have little tolerance for a miscreant like you. You do your father's name a disservice."

Harold flopped back into the pillows. "'Tis too early in the morning to have a conversation with a man who represents both our Lord in Heaven and the king. I'm bound to hang myself no matter what I say. Who else have you summoned to my chambers, my Lord Bishop? I smell a woman. She has an earthy scent. Of sweet green hay and of horses. Could it be a horsewitch? The one who advised my indecisive brother over there to destroy his suffering steed?" He waved his hand carelessly in Eldswythe's direction.

Robert grabbed his sword's hilt and stepping to the bed, flung the covers to the floor. "You are a wastrel, brother. I was hoping you'd reform during my absence. I see you haven't."

The bishop stepped in front of Robert and pushed his sword away. He shot a reprimanding look at Robert and glared at Harold. "God's teeth, you are of noble birth, a member of the king's high court, Hillsborough. Deport yourself with dignity and cover up your nakedness. There is a lady in your presence."

Harold laughed and put his hands over his privates. "I wager that I've nothing that she hasn't seen before." His looked at Eldswythe and tipped his head in Robert's direction.

Eldswythe felt the heat scorch her face. How could he know?

The bishop tossed a cover from the floor into Harold's lap. "Cover yourself, you immoral lout. No wonder the king cannot find a woman of noble birth who'll agree to wed you."

He turned to Eldswythe. "That brings me to the reason for my visit, Lady Eldswythe. I'll get right to it. You are now the Countess of Crenalden."

Eldswythe staggered, groping for a chair. She felt the blood pooling in her knees and feet. "My father's dead?" she asked, her voice trembling.

"Yes, Lady Eldswythe." There was no pity or remorse in the bishop's voice, and no sign that he recognized the news might be upsetting. He continued. "The king sends his condolences. He is still in Scotland battling the renegade's revolt, but he has not forgotten England or your plight. He desires you to find a husband immediately. Crenalden land and its water rights must remain entailed to the crown."

Eldswythe lowered herself to the chair, head spinning. Her father was dead! She hadn't heard another word the bishop uttered after that.

"How did he die?" she pleaded, grasping for an explanation. "Prince Edward and the crusade would not have yet reached the Holy Lands."

"Your father died in France, Lady Eldswythe. Someone put an arrow in his back."

Eldswythe screamed. "Gilroy!" She buried her face into her hands and sobbed. "He said he had assassins."

The bishop paced, his long red gown rustling around his feet. "The prince will find the killer, have no doubt. Your father was a valued ally. Now stop this womanly weeping and listen to what else I have to say."

He stopped in front of Eldswythe, face severe, eyebrows drawn together as if he were about to give instructions to a misbehaving child. "Lady Eldswythe, the king desires that you marry Harold, the Earl of Hillsborough. This house, like yours, has always been the crown's strong supporter. You are a countess and he is an earl. It is a reasonable match. You are of equal station."

Eldswythe clutched her skirts and sprang to her feet. Her chest tightened. "No! I promised my father that I would marry the Earl of Gloucester. I will honor my oath. I will not marry Lord Harold. I will not marry a Breton!"

The bishop shook his head, the tiny blue veins beneath his slanted eyes throbbing as he spoke. "Your vow to marry Gloucester has not been sanctioned by the king. He never gave consent despite your father's and the earl's repeated requests. You are not now and never have been betrothed to the Earl of Gloucester. Not in the eyes of the church or of the crown."

Robert's head snapped around. A look of surprise flashed across his face, replaced at once with anger and frustration. He stared at Eldswythe. "You were *not* formally betrothed to the Earl of Gloucester?"

She didn't answer, and turned her head to look to the bishop, her mouth agape.

"Lady Eldswythe, no one's seen Gloucester in more than a month. Gilroy has stopped sending demands for his ransom. We must assume that the earl is dead. That he died in Gilroy's prison. You will marry as the king commands."

Eldswythe backed away. "No! I will not marry the Earl of Hillsborough. I refuse."

The bishop exhaled, barely concealing his irritation. "The king suspected that you might." He stared down at Harold, who still lounged naked in the bed with nothing but a fur across his lap and a smirk on his face. "Frankly, I don't blame you. Most women at the king's court hide when they see him coming. He's usually drunk. Even sober, he's useless when it comes to managing his estate or an army. Hillsborough stays afloat because the people here are loyal to his brother. In the year that Robert Breton has been absent, Harold here has all but run the place into ruin." His eyes narrowed. "But you have no choice I'm afraid, Lady Eldswythe, unless . . ." He paused, and scratched his chin. "Unless you are prepared to marry his brother, a second son without lands or title."

Eldswythe stood in silence. Shock and dismay rolled over her, rendering her speechless. The king and bishop, it seemed, were both determined that she marry *someone* in the House of Breton.

The bishop clasped his hands behind his back. "The king is prepared to offer you Sir Robert for a husband. What's important to the crown is that Hillsborough and Crenalden unite and protect the royal interest. He doesn't really care which Breton you choose, just that you do it."

Robert clenched his fists. "The king assumes that *I* will comply? I've received no note from him, no instructions since the missive from the clerk at Dover."

The bishop cocked his head. "You know Henry. You'll get no note, just another promise. He ordered you to defend Crenalden Castle and protect the Lady Eldswythe. In exchange, he promised you the land along the River Greve that you wanted, and two-hundred hectacres of Crenalden's fertile farmland. Consider now that he is offering the whole pie, Crenalden Castle and its earldom, if you or your brother agree to take Lady Eldswythe as wife."

Harold sat up and crowed. "Tell the king I'll marry her, horsewitch or no! Another earldom suits me, and the lands and Crenalden Castle. Now that's a dowry I cannot refuse, even if she has ridden with the devil and has the mark to prove it."

There was greed in his eyes, and a softness about his belly that disgusted her.

She glanced at Robert. His eyes clouded with confusion and apprehension, and something else. He looked like a cat with a songbird in his mouth.

"Eldswythe," he said. He took as step toward her. "It isn't like it seems. I didn't know anything about this. The king maneuvers all of us at his whim. If you think I brought you to Hillsborough knowing what he planned—"

Eldswythe stepped away. "What a fool I've been. The king never meant for me to marry the Earl of Gloucester. He has betrayed me and my father, and the earl. I've been naive. But I am cured, and I have his highness to thank for that." She took a deep breath. "Regarding the Earl of Gloucester, I pledged to marry him. I promised my father I would as soon as the king gave his permission. I didn't know the king was against it from the begninning." She lowered her eyes, breath tight in her chest. "But I did not deceive you, Robert. Never."

The bishop cleared his throat. "You must choose, Lady Eldswythe, one brother or the other."

Eldswythe faltered, racked with guilt, betrayal, and a sense of failure. Isolde and her father were dead. Khalif lost. She'd never had the chance to defend Crenalden, marry Gloucester, or make her father proud. Worst of all, if he were alive, he'd disown her now if she wed a Breton.

She shook her head, heart torn in two.

The bishop slammed his hand on the table, sending the pewter cups tumbling. "Let me make the situation clear, Lady Eldswythe. If you refuse to marry as the king chooses, you will find yourself back in some remote and godforsaken abbey. Crenalden Castle and all of your family's holdings will be taken, divided and parceled out to the king's retainers. You will be left with nothing. It will be the end of your line and your family name. So I doubt your father would object, even from his grave, if you do as the king has ordered and marry a Breton."

He bent low and peered into her face. "Life in a convent, Lady Eldswythe, will be difficult for a horsewitch. I will see to it personally that you are properly converted."

He fingered the bead and leather belt that dangled from his waist.

Robert stepped in front of the bishop. "Do not threaten Lady Eldswythe. If you ever lay a hand on her, even in the name of God, you will rue the day. I promise." He moved his hand to his sword.

The bishop leaned away, then took a single step back, glaring at Robert defiantly.

Eldswythe swallowed. Robert stood so close that she wanted to reach out and take his hand, to rest her weary head on his chest. But all of that was long undone. Their chance at love squashed by ambition and politics.

She glowered at the bishop. *Horsewitch,* he had called her, and he all but threatened to beat her into submission. But no man had a hold over her now. Not her father nor her intended husband. Even Robert had rebuffed her and could not say he loved her.

She knew what she would do. Power rushed through her, sweeping away the weakness of grief and indecision. From where it came she wasn't certain. Perhaps from the same place where her gift secreted itself. Suddenly, she no longer felt helpless or alone.

She stepped in front of the bishop, standing to her full height. Her eyes bore down on him with anger and with pride.

"My Lord Bishop. Do not call me a horsewitch. I am a healer. And let me make it clear. Your threats don't frighten me. I've seen my people slaughtered, I've watched the Bane kill both man and beast, and I've been trussed and carried off as Gilroy's prisoner. I've lost everything I own—my lands, my castle, my horse and friends—and I've lost my father. Do you think, even for a moment, that the thought of a convent scares me? I've spent most of my life there, so it does not, sir, but I will not give up my family's birthright. If I must marry to try and save what's left of my father's estate. I will."

She folded her arms. "I will marry Robert Breton."

Harold cursed and muttered underneath his breath.

The bishop merely smiled, but his eyes were filled with the light of one who considered himself a victor. "Wise choice, Lady Eldswythe, not to defy the king. To do as you are told."

The bishop adjusted his red mantle and stalked to the door. He turned to Robert as he rested his hands on the iron pull.

"Do you agree then, to marry the Lady Eldswythe? Put that unfortunate business with the Lady Margaret to rest? The Baron of Suttony, her father, still has not forgiven the king for granting your abstention. He no longer contributes to the church and claims that he is too poor to pay his taxes. He has cast Margaret off and rescinded her dowry. Henry wishes now that he'd forced your hand. As do I. Perhaps this marriage to the Lady Eldswythe will make amends on all accounts."

Harold whooped and flopped back down on the bed. "Hah! My near-perfect brother will never live down that mistake. Loving Margaret of Suttony. I can do no worse than him when it comes to choosing women."

Robert's nostrils flared and the veins on his forehead pulsed. He grabbed his sword and took a menacing step toward the bed.

Then he stopped just short of drawing his weapon. He glowered at Harold. "Were you not my brother, I would challenge you to take a stand against me and settle our discourse by the sword, once and for all."

His deadly stare moved to the bishop. "Lady Eldswythe must agree freely to marry me. I will not take an unwilling wife. No one can force me on that issue. Not even the king."

Mother Mary, Robert was angry. The muscles in his jaw were flexing.

The corners of the bishop's thin mouth upturned, as if he enjoyed the sparring. "Lady Eldswythe? Do you willingly agree to marry Sir Robert?"

She didn't answer, too stunned into silence to respond.

Chapter 16

"I would expect your loyalty and I would give you mine. I will not enter the sanctity of marriage lightly." Robert crossed the room and stood before Eldswythe.

She leaned against the hearth. Her fate seemed unavoidable, as did Robert's unless she could dissuade him. "John Gilroy has Crenalden. If you marry me for my lands and a title, you must realize that you could end up with nothing—but me. Penniless and still a knight who has yet to earn his fee. Or worse. You could lose your life in battle."

He took her hand in his and kissed her open palm. His lips barely grazed her skin. "That is a risk I am willing to take." He smiled, careless that the bishop or his brother watched.

She pulled her hand away. The touch of his warm lips on her skin made her stomach flutter. She held Robert's stare with her own. "My Lord Bishop, tell the king I will marry Robert Breton freely, of my own accord. I consent without coercion. And you, Sir Robert, will have at last what you want, in it's entirety. My father's estate. I am loathe to give it to you, though I will be bound by the law of marriage to give it to you, I will never believe you did not scheme and set this whole thing up so you might have it."

She could almost hear her father groaning in his grave!

What else could she do? Hot tears welled along her lashes and she bit her lip to dull the pain of her consent.

Robert shook his head. Anger blazed in his eyes. "I am not guilty of conspiring against you in this. This is the king's doing, not mine."

The bishop headed toward the door open. "It is settled. The king will be pleased," he said over his shoulder. "We will have the betrothal feast tonight and post the banns. Come two weeks hence and you will be man and wife."

Harold frowned then cackled. "My brother's bound to a horsewitch. She suits him, my Lord Bishop. Why not marry them tonight and be done with it? I'll stand as witness. I will stand beside him naked if you like!"

The bishop slipped his hands inside his long bell sleeves and glared at Harold as if he were the stupidest clodpoll on the good earth.

Robert's eyes bore down on the bishop. "Tell him, my Lord Bishop. Tell him that you'll not marry me to the Lady Eldswythe tonight because Henry told you not to. Should I be captured by John Gilroy and held for ransom the king is too strapped to pay to free me and I doubt you'd bother. Thus, Lady Eldswythe, as a married woman with a husband who's alive but imprisoned, would not be available to dangle as a royal prize. Without the claimant heir to marry, what would be the incentive for any man to fight to regain Crenalden?"

Resignation flashed across his face, then Harold smirked and lowered himself onto his pillows. "It pains me that you think I wouldn't pay your ransom. You're right, of course. I wouldn't. At any rate, I'm more than happy to send you off with a betrothal feast. The sooner you leave Hillsborough, the better. I want you gone. Since you've been back, the good people of Hillsborough forget that I am the earl, their lord and master, not my younger brother."

Eldswythe clutched Robert by his sleeve. "Are you leaving?"

Robert gently took her hand from his arm. "I will explain later, Eldswythe. In private."

The bishop impatiently poured himself a drink of wine,

gulped it down and slammed the cup back on the table. He headed toward the door. "Sir Robert, come with me while I draft the betrothal contract. You must write a letter to the king. A runner waits to report the outcome of my visit and Henry wants to hear about his troops. You must remind him to send provisions. In his old age he oft forgets what he's promised. Let that be a warning to you."

Robert bowed to Eldswythe and touched his finger to her chin. "I won't be long. I promise." He followed the bishop out the door.

Harold threw the covers back and slipped on his shirt. His bare feet slapped onto the stone pavers as he searched for his slippers. "Pardon, Lady Eldswythe, I must take my leave and break my fast. Then go to chapel to give thanks that I have been spared again from marriage." He bowed low, his bare buttocks poking from beneath his shirt, golden hair hanging in his face.

"Forgive me," he said, looking up. "I mean no offense. You are a beauty and so very chaste I am sure." He laughed sarcastically, his mouth curling. "You have so much to offer, but I suspect you have already offered it to my brother."

The heat of anger rose from her neck and spread across her cheeks. She turned on her heels to leave, then halted when Harold's brittle voice rang out. "You hide your feelings poorly. You are as besotted with him as he is with you." He slipped his arms into his velvet robe. "The bishop is no fool and neither is the king. They did not intend for you to marry me. They knew you wouldn't. You've played into their hands, Lady Eldswythe, and my brother's, by doing exactly as they wished. They've even managed to get you to agree to do it willingly. Women. You are so easily deceived."

Suspicion and doubt suddenly wrapped around Eldswythe, squeezing the breath from her lungs. Had the scene that just played out been planned? God's feet! Robert, that blackguard who could make her senseless with his kisses, had known all along what the king was about, though he denied it. Robert would answer for this, one way or another.

She lifted her chin. "By all means, my Lord Harold, don't waste your time gloating. Go to your prayers and give thanks that you will not be my future husband."

Harold laughed. He pressed his hands together and looked to the heavens. "I will, and I will also pray for the soul of my dear brother. He has just agreed to take an angry horsewitch for a wife."

Eldswythe leaned across the gallery rail to watch the servants below. Dressed in new blue tunics and silver-gray hose, they scurried round the hall with organized efficiency, setting up the tables and dragging long oaken benches from their place along the wall. Children laughed and played with dogs that romped and barked, while the steward counted cups and plate.

Robert sauntered up beside her. "I hear the troubadours will sing tonight of a horsewitch who can make a warhorse dance and who knows a potion that will cure the Bane."

Eldswythe did not look up. "The stories of players are greatly exaggerated to make a better tale." She watched a servant girl spread fresh flowers on the tables.

Robert chuckled. "'Tis close enough to the truth, my lady, and I swear to keep secret the bits that aren't."

She leaned against the cold stone pillar by her side, the torch above her head so hot it made her cheeks warm. She watched a server carry steaming bowls of rich brown gravy, and platters of roasted game and fish to the dais. The table gleamed with gold and silver plate, and was draped with a crisp white cloth hemmed in ribbons of blue and silver.

Men and women milled about the vestibule, bejeweled and dressed in their finest silks and colored hose. A young girl pointed to the galley walk and whispered to her friends who turned to stare at Robert. God almighty! Did everyone here desire him? Tonight he was dressed in finery. He cut a striking figure in a black velvet surcoat with fluted sleeves and padded shoulders trimmed in sable. Yes, every woman in the castle couldn't help but notice. She couldn't help but notice either, and his nearness warmed her like a fever.

Aware that she would be scrutinized as his future wife, she smoothed her loosely plaited hair and brushed her hands down the front of her pale blue gown. The dress was of the softest wool with a neckline embroidered with a pointed band of silver that matched the edging on her flared sleeves and the scrollwork that trimmed the hem. It was her best gown and her favorite, tailored to fit her slim form and enhance her small bosom. The laced panels at her sides even showed a hint of the fine white linen underdress beneath.

She had planned to wear the gown on the morning that her father left for Acre, to see him off clad in her very best. She looked at Robert, wondering if he thought that she had chosen this dress because it was blue, in honor of the colors of the House of Breton.

His eyes wandered appreciatively up and down her form. He pressed a small velvet pouch into her hand. "A gift. In honor of our betrothal."

Eldswythe opened the pouch and withdrew a silver ring. On the face there was a rearing unicorn with a ruby for an eye, the figure set against an oval border of pearls and amethysts.

"I don't know what to say. It's magnificent."

A lock of his rich dark hair tumbled down onto his forehead and his smooth strong chin was set with pride. "It was the first prize I ever won at Smithfield," he said. "There was no one—" He looked across the galley rail. "There have been many prizes since, but this one I kept because it meant the most. I want you to have it." He slipped the ring on her middle finger. "It would please me if you'd wear it."

"I . . . I have nothing to give you."

He pulled the green river stone from beneath his tunic and dangled it before her. "This is your gift to me." He leaned down and kissed her, his mouth covering hers, hands roaming up and down her back. "And this," he muttered against her lips.

Her knees went weak. She pulled him closer, forgetting for a moment that he was a Breton, that she stood in the great hall of Hillsborough Castle and, as of this night, she had agreed to marry a man her father hated.

Trumpets pealed out the call to supper and Robert pulled his mouth from hers.

His smile was enough to dissuade her from doubting what she was about to do—to vow before the world that she would be his wife. In silence, he led her downstairs.

The doors opened to the great hall and nobles paraded to the dais, past the villeins, freemen and burghers, the craftsmen and their wives who stood beside the tables. Hornpipes played as Eldswythe fell into the procession with Robert at her side.

The bishop led the way. Just behind him, Harold strutted in a silver tunic, blue unicorns emblazoned on his chest. A small white plume bounced from his jaunty blue cap as he winked at Eldswythe.

Robert pulled her closer to his side. "My brother overly enjoys feasting. He will be asleep in his cups before the evening ends."

Eldswythe pressed her lips together. He was jealous. He thought she was admiring Harold. In truth, Robert was by far the handsomest man in the room.

The hall fell silent as the Earl of Hillsborough stepped onto the dais and stood in front of his tall chair. "Welcome, honored guests." He bowed to the bishop standing to his right. "In celebration of our visitor, enjoy the abundance of these tables and the company of friends."

The crowd erupted into cheers, then quieted as the castle priest, Father Beady, a wiry fellow with a large mole beneath his eye, stepped into the center of the floor. "First, good people, let us bow our heads. O Holy Father, bless this house and those gathered here. This eve we put our differences aside. We pray for a fruitful harvest, a gentle winter, and an early spring. Amen."

He crossed himself, then lifted his arms. "Time for gladness, time for play, a holiday we keep today. We thank the clergy most of all, who best would love a festival!" He looked impishly at the bishop who, by the look on his face, had decided not to chastise the popular priest.

To the loud applause and raucous amens, a steady stream of servants appeared, filling cups and offering ewers of water so the guests could wash their hands. Servers carrying platters of food paraded amongst the tables. Roasted piglet stuffed with green apples, a baked swan complete with plumage, larks' tongues and lamb stewed in goat's milk were all presented with great fanfare and flourish.

Eldswythe shared a plate with Robert and waited while he cut her meat. He speared a piece of venison, then held it to her lips. "Sweet and tender, from the fields of Hillsborough, near the river where *your* family hunts *our* deer." He smiled.

She swallowed, then said, "*Our* deer, Robert. Yours and mine together. I pray they will taste as good. After all, it is the hunt that makes you hungry," she said sourly.

A look of amusement flashed across his face.

A fire roared in the hearth behind the table, where squires and pages, ever ready to attend their lords, stood warming themselves and flirting from a distance with the girls.

The food did not appear to tempt Robert much, but the spiced and honeyed wine was to his liking. He drank freely and filled the cup again. Eldswythe averted her eyes from his dark gaze, and plucked a sugared plum from a silver bowl. God, how she missed the sweetness of the fruit, how the taste loosed memories of Crenalden. Memories that made her feel secure, and at the same time wistful.

The bishop rose from his chair and shot a glance at the Lady Margaret, who sat demurely, stroking the head of the giant hound sitting by her side. From the look on the bishop's face, Margaret's presence displeased him. He raised his silver goblet. "Honored guests, I propose a toast. On this day, the fifth of July, we announce the betrothal of Sir Robert Breton, the second son of Raulf, the late Earl of Hillsborough, and the brother of Harold, the current Earl of Hillsborough, to the Lady Eldswythe, Countess of Crenalden."

The room fell silent. Even the dogs appeared to settle. The bishop's voice echoed as he raised his cup. "To the House of Breton, and to Crenalden. Let there now be peace between them!"

An even deeper hush fell across the hall.

God, it was happening so soon? She glanced at Robert, who sat frozen at the table.

The bishop turned to Robert. "Stand, and take the Lady Eldswythe's hand in yours, Sir Robert."

Robert took Eldswythe's hand as they rose from their seats.

"With the blessings of the king, Lady Eldswythe, do you, the daughter of Aldrick, the Earl of Crenalden, consent to marry Sir Robert Breton, the son of Raulf, brother to the Earl of Hillsborough, Harold?"

Eldswythe's hand trembled, and Robert closed his fingers over hers. Her breath quickened. Mother Mary, this was hard. To pledge oneself, in body and in soul to a man, any man. Even Robert Breton. She reminded herself it could be worse. If she must marry someone, at least it wasn't Harold. A coward, interested in women, hunting, and his cups.

The bishop cleared his throat, snapping Eldswythe from her thoughts.

"I consent," she answered quickly, just wanting to get this over with.

He continued. "Do you bequeath to Sir Robert Breton, by right of marriage, all of Crenalden Castle and its holdings as your dower, recently bestowed upon you at your father's death?"

Eldswythe felt a sheen of sweat dampen her face. Her breath hitched in her chest as she forced herself to answer. "I will."

God's peace! What had she done?

The bishop's voice snapped her thoughts to Robert.

"Do you, Sir Robert, take the Lady Eldswythe as your betrothed, with the promise that you'll wed her and assume lordship of her property and her person?"

The last few words made her blood run cold. She'd have more freedom as an unmarried woman, without land or a title. Now she was bound by law to submit her body and soul to a man she wasn't certain she could trust. A man who had never once said that he loved her.

Robert squeezed her hand. "I will," he answered resolutely. "And I'll see John Gilroy routed from Crenalden and the land restored to she who has the right to claim it. Lady Eldswythe."

The bishop raised his cup and faced the guests. "Let the banns be posted. Come two weeks hence, Lady Eldswythe and Sir Robert shall be married!"

The crowd erupted into cheers. Cups banged on tables, servants hooted and dogs barked at all the ruckus.

Robert leaned close, raising Eldswythe's fingers to his lips. "The cheers are as much for you as they are for me, my lady. It appears you've made yourself quite popular amongst the people. Well done."

Eldswythe pulled her hand away. "Not everyone is pleased." She discreetly glanced in Lady Margaret's direction.

The Lady Margaret had turned as white as a sheet, and would have swooned had not the Lady Anne steadied her.

Robert balled his hands into fists. His eyes flared with anger. "What the Lady Margaret thinks of our betrothal is not—"

Harold jumped to his feet. "To my brother and the Lady Eldswythe! May you know much love, have many children and take joy in their making." He swayed slightly, then collapsed into his chair, much to the approval of the crowd.

Robert growled. He bowed to his brother, grimacing, his brow knitted in frustration. Eldswythe couldn't help but notice his thumb rested on the handle of his sword's hilt.

Blessedly, the musicians began to play as the servants passed out wrist bells. The guests diverted their attentions from Harold and Robert and left the tables to congregate on the center floor, where men and women stood in separate lines, facing each other, waiting for the drums to start.

Robert kicked his chair out from beneath him, standing as

servants tied the bells around his wrists. "A betrothal dance, my lady, for us," he said coolly.

Eldswythe pushed her sleeves up and held up her hands. A servant tied the bells around her wrists.

Robert led her to the floor. "Do you still keep the Earl of Gloucester in your heart, Eldswythe? Were you in love with him when you promised to be his wife? Are you still?"

Eldswythe circled Robert, clapping to the drums. Ah-hah. Now the reason for his moodiness. His brother had mentioned love.

"Did you love the Lady Margaret? Do you still?" she countered. She leaned in closer as they circled each other, the bells ringing at their wrists. "Do you love me? Or do you use me with the king to suit your purpose and achieve your goals. To rise above your brother and claim my land."

Suddenly aware that people on the floor were looking at them, Robert's face reddened. He lowered his voice. "I've pledged to be your husband, to take you and you alone as my wife. Shouldn't that be all that matters? I will be fair and rule your people with a gentle hand."

The warmth of his breath sent shivers down her spine, but Mother Mary, the man was frustratingly bullheaded! She snorted. "You have not won me over, Robert Breton, nor have you won my land or my castle yet. As I've said before, and so have you, we argue over something that may never come to pass."

"I hope for both our sakes it does. I want us both to get what we want, though we want it for different reasons."

The drums stopped. The tinkling of bells gradually diminished and Eldswythe felt the eyes of the guests upon them. Determined not to escalate their discussion in front of the entire castle, she smiled at Robert, then bobbed a curtsy.

He bowed stiffly in return and led her off the floor, his face pinched and strained.

The guests ambled back to the tables for more refreshments. Musicians moved to the center of the floor and a mandola player strummed a chord. "Now 'tis time for a song," he said, as he bowed to Harold and then to the bishop. "We are fresh from the king's court and this tune is a favorite of the queen herself."

The timbre of his tenor voice rippled through the hall. A lilting tune, sad but pretty. The disgruntled guests began to boo and bang their cups on the tables.

Harold staggered to his feet. "By God, play another one, good sir. The very nature of that pious song makes me want to kiss the heavenly Lady Margaret right on the lips." He puckered up his lips and groped in the direction of Margaret, who sat aghast and held a dainty hand across her mouth.

The bishop slammed his cup on the table. "Sit down, Lord Hillsborough. Act as befits your station. Troubadour, sing another tune."

The troubadour removed his bell-tipped cap, gave a grand bow to the bishop, then bowed again before the guests. "I'll sing a tale I've just written, performed for the first time here tonight."

His voice clear and strong, he sang with no accompaniment:

The Horsewitch of Crenalden Castle is a maiden still,
*   her heart is true and kind,*
She finally found a husband, cast a spell, his soul en-
*   twined.*
A horse's back will be their wedding bed, she'll ride and
*   sing a lusty song.*
Her groom won't be a horse, but she hopes he'll last as
*   long!*

The crowd howled and the hall filled with the sound of cups rapping on the tables. Drunken men hooted and ladies smothered their guffaws.

All eyes fixed on Eldswythe. The troubadour bowed again and stayed low, waiting there for some signal, it seemed, that his bawdy tune would not get him tossed out on his arse.

Eldswythe fingered the point of her eating knife and kept

her eyes low. She half expected Robert to bolt from the table and wrap his hands around the troubadour's frail neck. Instead, he jumped to his feet and held his chalice before her.

"A toast, to the lovely Lady Eldswythe, who this night has agreed to marry me and remain devoted to my household, and to my future heirs. A dutiful and faithful wife she'll be."

In a sweeping gesture, Robert wrapped his arm around Eldswythe's waist, hoisting her up. Before she could object, he lowered his face and pressed his lips to hers.

The crowd roared with approval as Eldswythe leaned into Robert and braced herself with her hand against his chest. His ragged breath brushed across her face.

He nuzzled at her ear. "They suspect we lust for one another. Let's not disappoint."

Eldswythe tipped her head back. She feigned a smile and spoke loud enough for everyone to hear. "Sir Robert, please, not until our wedding night." She batted her lashes and grinned. "Or at least give me a better sample to help me wait."

She clapped Robert's face between her hands and drew his mouth to hers. Her lips parted, she pressed herself full against him, inviting him to linger.

Guests hooted, while the musicians struck up a lively tune.

Pushing Robert's face from hers, she stepped away, but not before she brushed against the evidence that she had roused him thoroughly.

He growled. "Had I known what you were saving for me, I would have carried you upstairs three hours ago."

She turned away and spoke across her slightly dipped shoulder. "It would not do for me to sleep anywhere but the ladies' quarters. And the beds there are already full. There is no room for you."

The flutes and horns blared above the din. All attention shifted from Eldswythe and Robert to the great pastries the servants paraded around the hall. Sweet confections shaped like mythic beasts, ships and even one like Hillsborough castle were carried round. The butler set the servers to carving.

Robert drained his cup and scanned the room. "I predict there will be more insults hurled at me tonight. Someone put the troubadour up to that tune, and I intend to find out who did." His gaze focused on Harold, who leaned across the table to leer at a pretty serving girl.

The hall grew silent once again as a servant girl appeared, carrying a huge silver plate. She walked around the table and stopped in front of Robert.

His eyes grew wide and his face turned scarlet. The veins in his temples throbbed.

On the plate was a subtlety, a confection in the likeness of his great horse, the big bay, lying on its side, its legs extended, its bloated flanks draped with a black funerary cloth.

The girl dipped a shallow curtsy and held the plate out for Robert's inspection. "For you, my lord, commissioned in your honor by Lord Hillsborough."

Eldswythe held her breath.

Robert bolted up from his chair. "What's the meaning of this?" He glared at his brother.

Smiling, Harold stepped down from the dais and sidled next to the platter. "Why, Robert, dearest brother, I commissioned this in honor of your great horse so that we might remember it and pay homage to the valiant steed. Perhaps the Lady Eldswythe would care to take the first slice."

Harold palmed his dagger, then offered it to her. "Perhaps you could cut . . . right here." With that, he sliced through the neck of the equine form and loped off the horse's head. The heap of sugar landed in a great misshapen lump at his feet.

Before anyone could stop him, Robert leapt across the table, his dagger drawn.

Just as quick, Harold drew his knife. With one wide swipe, he slashed the sleeve of Robert's tunic. A scarlet splotch of blood oozed through the fabric. Robert thrust at Harold and pinned him against the dais, the tip of his dagger pressed against his brother's cheek.

The Lady Margaret jumped to her feet. "Robert, no! He's

drunk and meant no harm. Blame me. I hired the troubadour to sing the song that tipped your temper." She turned to Eldswythe. "I didn't know of your betrothal until it was announced. The song was rude, the insult unintentional. Forgive me." Her voice lacked sincerity, though her angelic face appeared repentant.

Eldswythe rested her hand lightly on Robert's arm. His muscles beneath her fingers tensed. She locked her gaze on his. "I know it isn't in your heart to kill him. You are his brother, his only kin, as loyal as he is cruel."

Harold offered up his neck and smirked. "You'll miss me when I'm gone. And our dear departed father would roll in his grave if his favorite son committed murder. You'd be hanged and never claim my earldom."

Eldswythe prayed to God to soften both their hearts.

But Robert's eyes turned steely. A hush fell over the hall and the crowd shifted, as if an imaginary line separated Harold's men from his. Sir Thomas and Sir Hugh moved to the front of the dais, their hands on their swords. They stood close to Robert's back, making their position clear.

Robert glanced first at Eldswythe, then he slowly scanned the crowd, assessing it seemed, who aligned with whom. Then his dangerous gaze came to rest on his brother. "Thank the Lady Eldswythe, Harold. I spare your life because she asked me to." He lowered his knife but his tone implied a threat that could not be mistaken.

Harold eased himself up, then snatched his hat from his head. He bowed to Eldswythe, his face filled with mockery and contempt.

Eldswythe took a deep breath, forcing the muscles in her face to show no expression.

A bench screeched against the paver stones. The bishop stood from his seat, determined, it appeared, to end the dispute. He raised his papal hand. "Depart in peace good friends. Go and find the comfort of your beds." It wasn't a request, it was a command. And it was obeyed.

Harold sauntered from the hall, a serving maid on his arm, the bishop and his entourage close behind him. Hornpipes blared and shocked guests obligingly filed out the doors leading from the hall, their voices low and hushed, disappointed. The men stole curious looks at Eldswythe and the women chattered excitedly behind their hands. Servants kept their heads down and cleared the tables.

Robert sheathed his knife and clamped his hand across his wounded arm, a trickle of blood oozing through his fingers. The veins in his temples were visible, the muscles in his jaw clenched. He watched every knight who lingered and the Lady Margaret, who made a great fanfare of her departure. Her ladies helped her from the dais and arranged her skirts. She glanced in Eldswythe's direction, her face veiled with disapproval.

Robert stepped in the way of her view, then took Eldswythe by the elbow. "Come with me. Upstairs," he said, while he kept his narrowed eyes on Margaret.

Eldswythe sensed the warning in his voice, that his request was a command. Dutifully, she moved along beside him, wishing this dismal night would end. When they reached the landing, he released her and strode ahead, down the corridor, then led her through a pair of arching doors that opened into a cavernous stony room. A private apartment, large and lushly furnished with tapestries, a scattering of Turkish rugs, and a single, wide-berth oaken bed. A small fire crackled from the man-sized hearth.

Robert ushered Eldswythe in and closed the door, then lowered the iron lock bar. He swung around and faced her, his short cloak tossed behind his shoulders. "You'll stay here tonight." Before she could open her mouth to protest, he continued. "I'll not leave you alone out there with my brother, nor will I send you back to Margaret's den." Disgust formed his face, then he scowled.

Eldswythe had last seen him look like this on the road outside of Hillsborough, when he'd been forced to destroy his bay destrier. She knew better than to argue with him this time. In truth, she was grateful not to have to sleep in the ladies' quarters. But she wasn't at all certain of why he had brought her here, or what he expected next. To cover her nervousness, she pushed her forever-straying tendril of her hair behind her ear, then she folded her arms, her hands clutching the laces on the sides of her gown.

He opened his mouth slightly, as if he meant to speak, then clamped his jaw shut and knelt beside the hearth. "The room will warm once the fire gets going." He added another log to the fire, rested his wounded arm across his bent knee and sat with his back to her, a slight stoop to his shoulders.

After all they'd been through together, Eldswythe knew him well enough to detect the emotion in his voice. He turned away to hide his worry, to hide how upset he was about the scene in the hall. Alone beside the fire, he looked tired and adrift. Not at all like the man who had challenged her to accept her gift as a horsewitch. Not at all like the Dark Rider who could sit in a saddle and still swagger.

Instead, she saw a man who was vulnerable, but who'd survived—a brutally harsh father, a vindictive jealous brother, and a woman who took his love then cast it off. He was determined to prove himself and make his way in the world. She longed to ease his troubled spirit, but she knew not how, so she stood where she was by the door, hoping he would ask for help, fearing that he wouldn't.

Eldswythe held her breath, but forced her feet to cross the room. She moved silently to stand next to a kneeling Robert, so close his hair brushed against the back of her hand.

"Please," she said softly, "your arm is hurt. Let me tend to it."

He didn't look up, but he rested his forehead on the heel of his palm. His wound had stopped bleeding and clearly, it wasn't his physical injury that pained him.

She ran her hand through his hair, down the back of his neck, then massaged his shoulder. Taut cords of muscles softened beneath her fingers. He rose, then turned to face her as her hand fell away.

"Had it not been for you, tonight I might have killed my brother."

"No, you wouldn't have. You could not—"

He held up his hand up. "I must tell you something else. Gilroy has garnered allies. He plans to march on Hillsborough. I must ride out with my army and cut him off."

Eldswythe grabbed a chair to steady herself. "When?"

"As soon as I can make the arrangements." His voice was strained. So low she almost couldn't hear his words. "Under the circumstances, there is no time to waste. It isn't safe here. I'm sending you away."

She drew a deep breath and forced herself to remain calm. "Where?"

"To London. With the bishop and his guards."

In the breathless silence that followed, she clasped her shaking hands, her composure on the verge of slipping. "And you? You'll be outnumbered. Will you be safe?"

His face was stoic, determinedly impassive, but his thumb drew tiny circles on the head of his sword's hilt. "I swore an oath to the king."

His expression might have been carved in stone, but something in his tone told her he had forced his personal feelings aside. Then his eyes fell to her hands, where she steadied them against her breast. Without thinking about it, she spun his ring around her finger. Then she saw the subtle movement of his hands. His fingers spread apart and he almost reached for her, then he clenched his fists and held his arms stiffly by his sides.

Her mind raced. While he spoke with cold conviction, his eyes flickered with a different message. Deep in her bones, she knew he felt the same undercurrent, the same tension that raged between them, as powerful as any code of honor, greater than any physical attraction.

By the saints, she couldn't help herself. She wanted him to

know how much he'd come to mean to her, how much she needed him. Tonight might be her only chance. She stepped deliberately closer, then she curled her arms around his neck and kissed him, hard and full on the mouth.

He captured her hands in his and halted her embrace. "Eldswythe," he muttered against her lips, "I didn't bring you here expecting to—"

"And I came here not knowing what to expect. But I know what I want. I have always known what I want."

"And so have I, lest you forget that you hate me for it."

"I do," she answered, but she held on tighter and planted soft kisses on his cheeks, his neck, along the hollow of his throat. The rise and fall of his chest quickened. His breath warm against her face, he closed his eyes and she could feel his defenses retreat, his resistance fall away.

She knew full well he had gotten what he wanted, Crenalden, a boon greater than his wildest dreams. But it wasn't possible for her to ever love another as she loved him and though yielding her father's estate cost her, she could not stop what she had started.

With a low groan, he crushed her to him. "God's breath, Eldswythe, I need you." Then he pressed his lips against her own and kissed her with a kind of passion she'd not felt from him before, urgent and achingly raw.

Mother Mary, how she needed him. All these long weeks apart at Hillsborough. Every hour, every minute. Every second.

He buried his face in her hair. "I've missed you. I can't sleep without you."

Eldswythe felt her legs melting. The blood coursed through her veins at a gallop. She leaned her head back and let him layer searing kisses down her neck.

Then his lips abandoned her, left her skin burning. He searched her eyes and his hands grazed her face, his touch tender and exploring, as if he were trying to memorize how she looked and how she felt. "God knows that if I'd had my way, tonight we would be married, but . . ."

Her chest tightened. She could barely breathe. The very thought of his leaving her alone tonight stole the air from her lungs. Wordlessly, she kissed his along his jawline, planting one light kiss after another until she reached that soft spot at his temple, while she moved her hands down his chest and lower, beyond the edge of his tunic, defying him to stop her.

A thin white line formed around his mouth. His gripped her arms, his fingers tightened with another warning. "If you should get with child and I die in battle—" His ragged voice broke. His face turned pale. "I cannot bare the thought of leaving you alone with a babe."

She put her fingers to his lips to silence him and shook her head. "You will not die," she pronounced, surprised by the strength in her voice. "And to be the mother of your son or daughter would bring me joy. As I said before, my love, I am strong enough. 'Tis my choice to make."

Robert turned his face away, his eyes closed and creased at the corners. He took deep breaths as if he needed time for her words to penetrate. And when he lifted his head she was struck by the look of relief, followed by the sheer wonder in his eyes. "You cannot know what it means to me to hear you say that, knowing that I've coveted your family's land, that I would stop at nothing short of battling Gilroy to take it back for you, then take it from you."

She tipped her head to lift her mouth to his. "You have a hold on me I do not understand. You tried to seduce me weeks ago because you wanted Crenalden and still, I am in love with you. And now I find myself thinking of this." She teased him, taunted him with her darting tongue and her hands on his buttocks. She felt him flinch at her touch and in the back of her foggy brain she heard him mutter, "God's bones, horsewitch, you've enchanted me," before he lifted her and carried her to the bed. "I cannot forget my father's death, and yet I find myself here with you, desiring the daughter of my greatest enemy. I know not what has possessed me."

He set her down amongst the furs and silks, then made

quick work of removing his clothes, the sleeve of his fine linen shirt stained with dried blood. She bit her lip at the sight of his wound, a cut that was small but deep enough to bleed.

He glanced at his arm and shrugged. "'Tis just a scratch, my lady. Another scar to add to my collection." He lowered himself to the bed. His masculine scent flowed over her, rich and arousing. Then his lips devoured her own, his mouth urgent and insistent.

She let his hands push her gown and chemise off her shoulders and bare her breasts. The warmth of his skin covered her and she leaned her head back as his mouth roamed down her neck. Heat winnowed its way from her belly up her spine. She ran her fingers through his hair and pulled his head closer, wanting to feel every scorching search of his tongue, all pretense of reserve shamelessly cast aside. If the cost of loving him tonight was betrayal of her heritage and her family name, she would gladly pay the price.

As she lay sprawled beneath him, Robert could think of nothing except how beautiful she looked, her face dusted pink by the fire and her hair shining, flowing over her bared shoulders. He could hear her breathing, feel the warmth of her smooth skin beneath his hand and a jolt of desire shot through him. She smiled, then moved her hand to rest on his chest for a moment before she trailed her fingertips down his belly. The torture of her touch was divine, too sweet to be real and he couldn't keep from sucking in his breath.

The very thought of what he was about to do made his body tremble. He wanted to see the bliss on her face and watch her body shudder with sweet release. If it took all night to get her to that point, so be it. He could rein in his own desire long enough to see her through, and his own pleasure would be that much sweeter.

His raised himself and slowly drew her skirts upward, above the edge of her stockings. "Close your eyes and think of nothing but the way you feel. I want to learn every curve, to study every freckle, every mark."

She stiffened. There was a look of willingness on her face, but also a hint of apprehension. The color in her cheeks deepened. She was embarrassed, perhaps a little frightened. He reminded himself that this was only her second time.

He ran his hand along her shin. "There is nothing to be afraid of. You're beautiful," he whispered reassuringly, "all of you, every part."

She moaned, the sound low and resonating and the corners of her mouth upturned with delight.

He chuckled, and turned his attentions to her stockings, taking the edge of one between his teeth. He breathed in her feminine scent as he dragged the fine woolen hose down her leg, inch by inch, to her ankles, then repeated his action with the other stocking. He tossed the hose on the floor and stared at her gloriously naked legs, creamy white and stretched languidly along the length of the bed. The sight took his breath away.

"You have lovely legs, Eldswythe," he said, running his fingers lightly up her calf, past her knees. She gasped and he slipped her dress down over her hips, down her thighs, leaving her completely naked, save for the ring he had given her and the swath of her dark hair spread over her breasts, to her waist.

A nervous laugh tripped across her lips. "I can feel your eyes upon me." She pulled a fur across her waist. "I'm cold."

Robert laughed and dragged the covers from her hands. "Then let me warm you." His kissed her knees and he separated her thighs with his hands.

A startled gasp slipped from Eldswythe's throat and her legs tensed. "'Tis not decent, is it, that I should let you do this?"

Robert kissed her shins, his lips trailing upward. "Do what, my horsewitch? What do you think I plan to do?"

"I, I don't really . . . Oh, by the saints, you're teasing me!"

Robert laughed again, his lips against the silken skin of her inner thigh. His kissed her lightly, his mouth coaxing from her little cries of pleasure. He came to the mound of soft black hair that delved into the cleft between her legs, then raised his head. He waited and watched her breasts rise and fall with the rapid pace of her breathing.

She moaned, and opened for him, her movement tentative. Hesitant.

He smiled and lowered his head. He used his tongue to taste her softness, to make her arch her back, and writhe with the joy of it, her fists grab at the covers, her legs draw up and open even more. He lifted his head and caressed her there with his hand as well.

"Eldswythe, relax," he whispered, his long fingers increasing the intensity of their work.

Feverishly, she tossed her head from side to side, her hips lifting, responding to his touch. He kept his hand between her legs while he covered her belly with slow kisses, traveling upward, kissing the valley in between her breasts, up her neck, to her chin.

"Remember this," he said huskily, as he trailed his lips to hers.

Her voice tight and breathy she answered "yes" and closed her eyes.

He felt her muscles close around his fingers. She cried out and with a convulsive arch, her body shuddered. Then she arched again, her face blissfully contorted and she moaned, lifting her quivering buttocks, pressing her mons against his hand. At the same time, his hunger drove to the surface. Demanding attention, declaring need that he'd kept locked away, deep inside him.

The corners of her full mouth tugged upward into a lazy smile, a thin film of sweat on her forehead. "That was the first time I've ever felt . . . felt . . ."

She didn't attempt to finish her sentence. She took a deep breath, stretched her arms above her head, nestling deep into the covers, as if she were prepared to settle back and sleep.

"Oh, no. You're not done. That was only the beginning."

Her eyes flew open. "There's more? Have you not seen all, and done everything you wanted?" She bit her lower lip and averted her eyes, half filled with hope and half with teasing. He could tell she knew full well he wasn't finished.

He moved his hand back between her legs and stroked her, moving it around in tiny circles while his fingers entered her again. Her lungs expanded with a deep slow breath. She dug her fingertips into his back. Little bursts of breath shot past her lips. "If you keep doing that, I shall lose my wits."

"Then turn over," he whispered. "There is more I want to show you."

She went still and let him lift her by the waist, turn her onto her knees. He reached for the candle beside the bed. His hands skimmed over her soft, round buttocks. She gasped and her buttocks tightened, but she didn't recoil.

"What are you doing?" she asked breathlessly.

"Just looking. You have a lovely horse bite, and I admit, this part is as much for my pleasure as for yours." He ran his fingers across the tiny pink scars and then lowered his lips, kissing every ripple. "Every part of you sets my loins on fire."

"Now you've seen my scars, as no one else ever has. Have you had your fill? Can we go to sleep now?" Her voice was groggy and low, but she wiggled her rump playfully.

Robert groaned. Her rump against him, his erection sprang full and upright. Throbbing. She was teasing him and she was anything but sleepy. He gently rolled her over, and lowered his body over hers, her breasts cushioned against his chest. "I want to see your face," he said as he lifted up, bearing his weight on his forearms.

Then he went completely still. Her fingers brushed his most sensitive parts, wrapped around his erection and stroked him. She stared into his eyes and smiled. "You're as big as a horse."

He grabbed her wrist and nipped her lower lip between his teeth. "Stop that, temptress," he muttered. "I'm not ready for this to end. Are you?"

She smiled. The word "no" formed on her lips and she opened her legs. He slipped his shaft into her, thrusting slowly, carefully, until he was completely buried deep inside her. A sweet whimper rolled off her lips and her muscles tightened, encasing him with her soft heat.

A torrent of desire rushed over him. Breath quickening, he withdrew and sheathed himself again. And again. Thrusting harder and faster, her tightness sustained and unyielding. His heart pounding against his ribs, his breath blowing, he could hear his panting and hers, and feel the sweat between them.

She wrapped her legs around his waist as he had taught her, and she pressed hard against him, gripping, meeting his every thrust. Her face pinkened. Her mouth opened, and she closed her eyes, her body trembling. She groaned. A deep, animal-like groan. At the sound, a current ripped through him. Sending waves, hot torrents, pulsing from his shaft into her. She dug her fingers into his back and buried her face in his hair, accepting everything he had to give. His name was on her lips as his body, and hers, shuddered.

Eldswythe let her legs fall as Robert rolled beside her. She lay absolutely still, with a look of complete contentment on her face, then she raised herself on her elbow and pressed her lips to his damp temple. Her scent, her warmth, her soft breath against his skin calmed him, soothed his passion while his breathing slowed.

He slipped his arm around her waist and pillowed his head against her breasts. Sleep, blessed sleep, came upon him.

Eldswythe roused from a dreamless slumber when the dawn light streamed through the leaded window. She was still entwined with Robert, her cheek nestled against his neck, her legs wrapped around his, her arm carelessly over his shoulder. Her eyes fluttered open and her gaze came in to focus on the man who slept beside her.

He looked different from the lonely knight who had sat

beside the fire last night with his brooding brow pressed into the heel of his hand. Gone was the stern set to his jaw, the worried lines around his eyes and the tightness of his mouth. A lock of his dark hair had flopped across his smooth forehead and against the white sheets he looked untroubled, restored. But the scars that striped his back and the larger wound that roped around his neck was a telltale sign of a life that had been anything but peaceful. She'd seen a glimmer of what he'd been through and how hard he'd worked to survive.

She wanted to let her hand skim down his arm, over his waist and come to rest on his hip, but she feared awakening him, knowing how much he needed sleep. So she let her eyes wander over him, study his strong male form, bold in contour and resilient. Mother Mary, he was handsome, as striking as he was the first time she'd laid eyes on him—in his thigh high leather boots and a black tunic split up the middle.

A warm flush rose to her cheeks and an urge to kiss him on his full mouth almost overtook her. Reluctantly, she carefully disentangled herself and slipped from the bed, deciding to let him sleep in these last few hours.

She found her clothes and dressed quietly, knowing there wasn't much she could do to restore her bed-tousled appearance. In truth, she didn't care if anyone knew what she and Robert had been doing. Neither was she the least embarrassed that she'd seduced him. There was no doubt about her feelings for him, even though she'd yet to rectify his craven desire to claim her land. By the rood, if he would only say he loved her, if she knew he loved her, had some sign, she might be able to put their differences aside. The house of Breton united with Crenalden. What were the odds of that without divine intervention?

She let out an anguished sigh, finger-combed her hair and then slipped on her shoes. On tiptoe, she headed toward the door when she saw Robert stretch then flop his arm over his head.

He stirred, his eyes half open. "Eldswythe?" he asked groggily.

She went to the bed and pulled a coverlet over him. "Go back to sleep. I need to pack. Unless you have a compelling reason for me not to, I'm riding with you to Crenalden. I love you, Robert, but I have the right. Until we are married, Crenalden is still mine."

She smiled and brushed a kiss against his lips, then spun on her heel and headed out the door.

Robert sat upright, his body shocked from its repose, as if someone had just doused him with a bucket of freezing water. He cursed and flung the covers from his legs. She was going to Crenalden with him? Like hell she was!

"Eldswythe!"

He sprang from the bed and pounded across the room, heedless of his nakedness, or of the sound of men and horses gathering in the yard below the solar.

He flung the door open and he stood there panting, not caring if he sent the startled chambermaids skittering for cover.

"Eldswythe!" he roared.

When he got no answer he stalked back into the room and found his clothing. He cursed and muttered beneath his breath while he dragged on his hose and his shirt.

A woman riding to the battlefield? Horsewitch or no, it was too dangerous. She'd not be adequately protected and he could not afford to be distracted. She'd seen what atrocities Gilroy was capable of. Hadn't the taste of battle scared her? Didn't she understand what might happen to her if she were captured?

There was no way on God's earth he would let her go with him. Of all the ridiculous notions she'd ever had!

He ran down the galley and turned the corner, his feet stomping down the stairs, taking two at a time. One night of passion had set her on a course he'd not predicted. Why in God's name had he bedded her last night? Because he thought he saw the pleading in her eyes, how much she wanted him to hold her, to love her? Was that the only reason?

He almost stumbled.

In truth, he needed her too much. More than he'd realized, in ways he hadn't allowed himself to think about since Margaret.

There was the core of it. God's bones, Eldswythe loved him without question. There was no deceit in her soul. She wasn't capable of malice, like the fair Margaret of Suttony, a woman who'd betrayed him then laughed at his pain. He almost pitied her now. For she lacked Eldswythe's strength of character, and despite her renowned beauty, she would never be as beautiful as the woman he had come to love.

Hugh had told him it was time to put his hatred for Margaret aside. Perhaps he was right.

He slowed at the bottom of the stairs, vaguely aware that his fellow knights and soldiers were in the hall, come to break their fast before they left for Crenalden. They were dressed in full armor and weaponry. They were staring at him, their mouths half open, half filled with bread.

In his haste he'd forgotten his boots, his sword, and his tunic. His eyes fell upon the bemused face of Hugh, who pointed to the great doors, still ajar. He mouthed the word "stables," then he turned back to his breakfast and spoke to Thomas.

With as much dignity as he could manage, Robert turned and climbed back up the stairs.

Damnation. Eldswythe was not going with him. She was going to London. And as soon as he was dressed and found the bishop, he would send her on her way.

Margaret's voice called from the landing at the top of the stairway. "Robert, please. I need to see you. It's urgent."

Robert paused, then moved past her. "God's peace, not now," he answered, in no mood to deal with Margaret.

Her slippered feet padded after him. "Please. Please let me talk to you."

Robert went into the room he'd shared so memorably with Eldswythe, threw his tunic on, stuffed his feet into his boots and pivoted sharply. "Why? What can you possibly want from me?"

He kept one hand on his dagger and made no attempt to hide his contempt. Margaret blushed, but if it was real or not, he had no way of telling.

"Robert, please. I beg forgiveness. I would do anything you ask if you would take me back. Don't marry the horsewitch. I love you. I have always loved you. Once I said I didn't, but that was over a year ago. Now I know I do."

Robert arched his eyebrows, surprised that he felt nothing at her plea. Not anger. Not remorse, not even pain. If anything he felt pity. "No, Margaret. What's done is done. There is nothing more between us."

Margaret's eyes filled with tears. "But I am desparate, Robert. The bishop and my father have arranged to send me to Covington Abbey! You have cast me off, no man wants me for a wife, now. I'll have to leave here as soon as it's safe to travel. I don't want to take the veil. I could not live a cloistered life."

"I'm sorry, Margaret, I cannot help you. Your circumstance is of your making. You chose another man, that day at the Smithfield tourney, because he was richer. You made your choice when you begged to be released from our betrothal."

"Then I will appeal to your brother. He was kind enough to let me stay here. I see how he looks at me. If you don't want me, then I will pursue him."

Unmoved, Robert shook his head as he fastened his short cloak over his shoulder. "Margaret, you fool no one with your devoutness. 'Tis common knowledge you've already shared Harold's bed. To think I nearly lost my life fighting for your honor. I laid wounded in the monastery, alone and thinking of you, while you dallied with another. What a fool I was." He sidestepped around her, and headed out the door, not looking back.

"You will not cast me off again, Robert Breton!"

Robert stopped and spun around. "I've kept your secret and spared you the shame of what you did. Now go home, Margaret. Beg your father for forgiveness. In time he may find another man who is willing to take you for a wife."

A bitter laugh fell from Margaret's pink lips. "You keep my secret, Robert, because it's your secret, too. You wouldn't reveal it, because you could not bear for anyone to know the truth—that the man who got me with child was not you."

Steel encased his heart, but it wasn't forged in anger. He'd spent the night with Eldswythe, the woman he loved and trusted. It calmed him, deflected the hatred in Margaret's words and her sick deceit. It was up to God to cure her heart.

He let a sad smile lift the corners of his lips. "It was my child, Margaret, and you know it. Tell the world, if you wish, but I know you will not, since you saw fit to rid the babe from your womb. I was only three months into my recovery when I learned what you did, or else I would have stopped you. Now there is nothing more between us. I bid you peace." He raced down the stairs, out the hall and to the stables.

Chapter 17

From the stable Eldswythe could hear the clamor of armor, men yelling, wagons creaking, and dogs barking. Horses whinnied and the hammering clank of iron against the smithy's anvil filled the yard. The army of Hillsborough was preparing for war. Robert was sure to be up and dressed by now, out there somewhere, seeing to the preparations.

She hurried from the barn and pressed her way through the crowd, hoping to find Robert, to make certain that he knew she was ready to ride with him in battle.

Hugh touched her on the shoulder, his great horse standing close beside him, as was Bertrada.

He smiled knowingly. "Robert's looking for you, too, but he's in an agitated state. Be careful of his heart. He loves you. He deserves to be loved back."

His voice trailed off and he looked away, then he took Bertrada by the hand. "I promised your fair maid here that I'd teach her how to ride a horse before we left. The lesson will be brief, but she'll know the basics."

Pupil and instructor walked away, talking quietly between them, with their heads together, closer than was proper for a teacher and his student.

Eldswythe smiled, then spun around and scanned the yard to see Robert, striding in her direction. He waved and she opened her mouth to call his name, when a young voice rang out behind her.

Young Jack limped across the yard, lugging Robert's high-backed saddle on his hip and a gilded bridle over his shoulder. He came to stand beside her and waited, his big brown eyes shy but bright.

He called out. "Sir, what do you want me to do with these?"

Robert took the saddle and lifted the bridle from the boy's shoulder. "'Twas meant for the bay's big head and will fit no other horse unless I cut it down. But I thank you for taking care of it. Someday, you'll make a fine squire."

Jack's face beamed with gratitude.

Eldswythe cleared her throat. "It would be a shame to cut it down, Sir Robert. It is a beautiful bridle. I have not seen so fine a piece ever." She ran her fingers across the gilded reins.

Robert flashed a smile at Eldswythe, then he turned to Jack. "The gold is only for appearance. Beneath it lies steel to prevent enemy swords from hacking through the reins. When you are older and are made a knight, you'll have one just as fine." Robert hitched the bridle higher onto his shoulder. "My thanks for watching over it."

He walked in the direction of the armory. "Come with me, Lady Eldswythe, I'd like to talk to you and there's something I want to show you."

Curious and praying that his complaisance meant he was taking her to Crenalden with him, Eldswythe followed as he crossed the yard and entered the armory, where all manner of mail, weapons, and tack hung from the walls. He opened the iron lock on a large upright chest bearing the Breton coat of arms and set the saddle inside but kept the bridle on his shoulder.

Robert stood directly in front of Eldswythe. "You left too early this morning, I would have rather stayed in bed with you all day, but there is much to do." He took off his gloves, reached to pluck a piece of straw from her hair, then he leaned to kiss her lightly on the forehead. "I have a wedding present for you."

"You've already given me a gift. My ring."

"There is more." He took her by the hand and pulled her outside, upstairs to the battlements. He pointed to the south fields, where the grass was dark green and the apple trees were heavy with fruit. "See there, beside the wood?"

Eldswythe squinted. In the distance, three horses wandered, grazing on the knoll, their bellies round and swollen from the rich summer grass.

"Mares?" She turned excitedly to Robert.

"Yes. All three from fine Spanish bloodlines. They belong to me. In a few months time, I'll breed them to Barstow. With luck and training, perhaps at least one foal will grow to have the strength and heart of its sire."

He lifted her chin and bent to kiss her. Eldswythe closed her eyes, drinking in his scent, his taste, and savoring the feel of him, his smooth lips against hers, the ache between her thighs a sweet reminder of their night of loving. The cool morning wind blew across the ramparts, lifted the hem of her gown and wrapped it around his legs. For a moment she forgot anything but this.

"Eldswythe, choose the mare you want and you can have her. Take her to London."

His words whispered against her lips and her breath rushed from her lungs. She pulled her mouth from his. "To London? Nay, not to London. I'm going with you to—"

Horns bleated, sounding from the watchtower as soldiers ran across the wall, bows and arrows drawn. A guardsman called from the steps above. "Soldiers approach. Be ready, all!"

Instantly the archers aimed their bows at the small party of mounted knights that approached the bridge.

Robert set Eldswythe from his arms and strode to the wall, his eyes focused on the travelers. Eldswythe moved quickly against the wall and peered through the loophole, all thoughts of London set aside.

The watchman bellowed. "Who goes there? Name yourselves."

A standard bearing the familiar clawed griffin fluttered against the breeze and the rider cupped his hand around his mouth to answer. "We come in peace. Lord Gilroy has a gift for his sister, the Lady Eldswythe of Crenalden."

Eldswythe's breath hitched. She craned her neck to get a better look and counted three men on horseback. The one who wore a dirty white tunic and had no weapons weaved and swayed atop his horse. His reddened eyes were sunken and his face unshaven; his thin frame slumped in the saddle. He looked as though at any moment he would lose the ability to stay upright.

Eldswythe's fingers gripped the wall's ledge. "By the saints! 'Tis the Earl of Gloucester!" She turned to race down the steps.

"No!" Robert grabbed her by the arm. "Watchman, draw up the bridge, do not let them pass, or let the Lady Eldswythe out!"

The heavy chains creaked. The drawbridge slowly lifted, the portcullis slamming down.

Eldswythe stared at Robert, the blood boiling in her veins. "What are you doing? Let the Earl in!"

"They are Gilroy's men. I will not let them enter."

A soldier in the road below called up to Robert. "We come in peace, good sir, escorting the Earl of Gloucester. His ransom has been paid."

Eldswythe leaned across the rampart wall as far as she could go. "Please, Robert, let him enter!"

"Eldswythe, this is a trick. Why else bring him here? Why not take him to his family?"

Robert called to the soldiers below. "Leave him by the road. You will not pass through Hillsborough's gates."

A soldier dismounted and dragged Gloucester from his horse, then dumped his limp body in the grass beside the road. If the earl was alive, he offered no resistance.

Eldswythe sucked in her breath.

The knight called up to Robert. "We'll take the horse back with us. He won't be needing it now." Without further discussion the small retinue of men spun their mounts around and galloped down the road.

Eldswythe shook with rage. "Let me out, Robert. The earl needs my help."

Robert held Eldswythe by the arm, his strong grip unyielding. "I'll not let you leave. Something is amiss." He called up to the watchman. "Does he still breathe?"

"No, Sir Robert, I think that he does not."

Robert's hand gripped his sword as his eyes searched the woods beyond the fields. "Summon the knacker and send word to my brother's hunting party not to return by the main road."

Eldswythe's chest tightened and she fought back tears. She tried to jerk her arm from his grasp. "I saved you. Perhaps I could save him, too. Let me go."

Robert held her tighter. "He's dead, Eldswythe. Now listen to me. I have not paid the ransom, nor has my brother. I suspect this is a trick. Eldswythe, Gilroy has used infected prisoners before. He sends them home into the arms of unsuspecting loved ones, infecting all with the contagion. I will not take the risk and bring the Earl of Gloucester inside. What if he has the Bane?"

Eldswythe's limbs stiffened. Tears streaming down her cheeks, she stared over the wall at Gloucester's lifeless form. "He was a loyal family friend. My life was to have been with him." Eldswythe gripped the wall to keep from shaking. "I will stay here until they cart him to the pits. He did not deserve the fate John Gilroy has dealt him. I owe him."

"Eldswythe, your vigil will not help the Earl of Gloucester. It will only make you miserable. Come away from here."

Eldswythe shook her head and watched the knacker, a man who earned his keep by burying the dead, men and beasts alike, slip from the gatehouse, pulling his two-wheeled cart along the hastily re-lowered drawbridge. He drew his hood down over his head, crossed himself, and set about the task of dragging the body onto the cart.

Eldswythe pleaded. "I must know why he died, Robert."

Robert spun around, tossed a coin over the wall and called to the lone figure who rolled the body into a tattered woolen blanket and heaved it onto the wagon. "Was he wounded?"

The knacker stood over the earl, studying his head and his chest. "No, milord."

"Do you see anything about the body that will tell us how he died?"

The man pulled his scarf around his mouth and nose before he pushed the blanket aside and lifted up Gloucester's head. Bright red blood trickled from his mouth and eyes and nose.

The knacker kicked the blanket back over Gloucester's head, "My lord, 'tis the Black Bane."

A blaze of hatred reared from Eldswythe's core. What kind of man was John Gilroy that he could do this, infect a man and plan to spread the disease to hundreds of others?

The soldiers on the battlements crossed themselves. Some uttered quiet prayers. Robert called out to the men. "The contagion did not breach the gates." He tossed another gold coin to the knacker standing below. "Take the body to the lime pit. Bury him. Quickly"

The knacker scooped up the coin and without another word, cart in tow, he headed down the road.

Robert put his cloak over Eldswythe's trembling shoulders. "Go back into the keep. I will see that the priest says a mass for the Earl of Gloucester."

Eldswythe hung her head. Her last hope, her last connection to her father and her former life . . . gone. The siege of Crenalden, and now the earl's death, extinguished the girlish dream of a quiet life as a wife and mother. She'd been foolish.

She shot a heated glance at Robert. "My so-called bastard brother will pay for this. I swear by the air I breathe, he will pay. He will never take Crenalden from me. He will have to kill me first."

She handed Robert his cloak, then picked up her skirts, spun around, and headed for the stairs.

Robert reached to catch her. "Eldswythe, don't go rushing off. I fear you think to hatch some plan. You will not—"

"I will do what I must." She jerked free from his grasp. "I am the Countess of Crenalden." She took a deep breath. "And I am a horsewitch. I am not powerless to stop my bastard brother."

"Damnation, Eldswythe, stop. I will not allow a wife of mine to—"

She halted with one foot on the riser of the last step. "I am not your wife—yet—Robert Breton. Now give me leave. I will not disrupt your battle plans, I will assist you in their execution." She let a small laugh cross her lips. "Must I remind you, I fight to win back my own land and my castle, and then I'll have to hand it over to my husband, a Breton. But better to you than to Gilroy." She looked to the sky. "I hope my father understands."

She raced across the bailey, ignoring Robert's calls.

Eldswythe slammed the tower door behind her and shoved the heavy iron latch into the locked position. She leaned against the cold stone wall and thought of the Earl of Gloucester, buried in the pits without a coffin. John Gilroy had killed her father and the earl without compunction, but the strength of her resolve grew with her grief and anger.

Distracted, she barely heard the great clatter tumbling down the stairs, nor did she see the face of the person who fell on her in full force, knocking her from her feet.

A hand across her mouth muffled her attempts to scream. Eldswythe fought the hooded figure who pressed her onto her back and held her down. She freed her arm with a vicious twist and with one great slam, she clouted her assailant in the head. Her attacker landed with a thud amidst the rustle of fine skirts, with her legs flying out from under a pale yellow gown. Silvered silk slippers tumbled from her white stockinged feet.

Eldswythe rubbed her aching knuckles. "Who are . . . ? Lady Margaret?"

Margaret sat up holding her cheek with her hand. "Horse-witch! You have bruised my face. I did not attack you, I did not see you!"

"You fell upon me like you meant it. You tried to keep me quiet!"

Margaret worked her jaw, then plucked a handkerchief from her sleeve and dabbed at the wound. "Think where we are. I didn't wish to call attention to it."

Eldswythe looked up the stairs, knowing full well that the closest room at the top was Harold's. A jagged shock of understanding rocked her bones.

The silver slippers she'd seen by Harold's bed were the Lady Margaret's.

Margaret crawled onto her knees and sat back on her heels. "Why are you running?" She looked at Eldswythe's face. "Have you been crying? 'Tis Robert Breton, isn't it? The jape. What has he done?"

Eldswythe shook her head and slumped against the stone.

Margaret patted her on the shoulder, then offered her a handkerchief. "Lady Eldswythe, he isn't worthy of you. I tell you from experience, he will break your heart and leave you when he has gotten what he wanted."

Eldswythe raised her eyebrows.

"'Tis true. We he lured me to his bed before the banns were read. I was so in love. I could not resist him. What did I know of men?" She lowered her head and her cheeks flushed. "When I told him I was with child, he cast me off, and claimed the babe was not his. Truth be told, he'd found a richer woman. The Countess of Wildemere, newly widowed. 'Twas rumored she fancied Robert. They dined together at the Smithfield tourney on the day he left me. He wore her favor on the lists when he was injured, not mine."

Eldswythe studied Margaret, and her distrust for the

woman faded into something akin to pity. By the rood, could she be telling the truth?

Margaret wiped a tear from her eye. "I lost the babe, but the bishop gave Robert absolution from our contract. The Countess of Warwick then married an earl, and then Robert set his sights on you. I am left alone. My father refuses to take me back to his house, and my dowry isn't large enough to readily attract another suitor. Please say naught of this to Robert. I begged him not to tell anyone I'd been with child. I fear what he would do in retribution. My shame is punishment enough."

Eldswythe touched Margaret's sleeve. She could understand the fear of being cast off by one's father.

Margaret sniffed. "Thanks be to God, Harold let me stay on at Hillsborough, though I think he does so just to gibe at Robert. If I don't find another man to wed me by springtime, the bishop will send me to a convent. He says I am a poor example of a godly woman."

Eldswythe held her breath. Good God, was this the secret Robert would not speak about?

A mountain of doubt rose up before her. It didn't seem like Robert to set aside the woman he had pledged to marry, but if this sad tale were true, then she should be worried. He'd planned to take Crenalden lands long before she'd agreed to the marriage. What would he do with her after he had what he wanted? A sickening feeling welled up from her stomach.

Margaret caught her by the arm. "Lady Eldswythe, do not mention our meeting here to anyone." She looked up the stairs, where the Earl of Hillsborough's laughter echoed. "He's just back from the hunt. His blood is hot, as it always is after a killing. He's asked of me things I daren't admit and allows me to stay here only so long as I consent. I suspect the bishop knows. Please, Lady Eldswythe, take pity on me. Keep what I have told you in confidence."

Eldswythe gaze turned to the dark and hollow rising stairwell. At the top, past Hillsborough's rooms, was the solar, where she had hoped to take refuge and devise a plan. After listening to Margaret, she had no desire to go up there, to sit alone in the solar and hear the laughing Lord of Hillsborough entertaining so close by.

She scrambled to her feet and dusted off her gown.

Without another word to Margaret, Eldswythe threw the door open and dashed out of the tower. She headed to the stables, where she knew she would find comfort and a friend.

Robert held the horse as the bishop put his slippered foot into the stirrup and hoisted himself into the saddle. A squire arranged his scarlet robes so that they draped over the horse's haunches, the folds and pleats arranged to best display the robe's gold embroidered border. The bishop turned his head, his wide-brimmed black hat shadowing his face.

Eldswythe came dashing from the stables and across the yard.

Robert handed the bishop the reins to his horse. "I trust you to deliver the Lady Eldswythe safely on to London. She is more precious to me than anything, or anyone else, at Hillsborough." Robert whistled, signaling for the squire to fetch the lady's palfrey. He patted the bishop's horse on the neck. "You've twenty men to guard you. Make haste and get to Windsor before nightfall. Our runners say Gilroy's scouts have already crossed the river. Hillsborough Castle is ill-prepared, and the army barely ready, thanks to my brother. I want Eldswythe as far from here as soon as possible."

The bishop gathered up his reins, his hands shaking. His face pinched with worry and the wrinkles around his squinty eyes were lined with fear. "Have no doubt, Sir Robert. I intend to be safe inside of Windsor before the moon is high. But if she slows us down . . ."

He didn't finish the sentence before Robert's hand gripped his wrist. "It is well within my power, bishop, to keep you here at Hillsborough. Unless you wish to *see* the battle, hold

your tongue. You'll find yourself hard put to keep up with
Lady Eldswythe. I've seen her ride. She could leave you in
the dust if she chose to."

Robert's gaze darted from the bishop toward Eldswythe,
who strode across the yard. She stopped and looked at
Robert, then her focus moved to the squire who held her
horse and to the retinue of armored guards that surrounded
the bishop.

The wrought iron gates of the portcullis screeched as the
raising chains were cranked. Horses whinnied and the men
assembled, forming rank and line around the bishop.

Her eyes grew wide with a sudden look of understanding.
She hurried toward him, veering away from the path that led
to the barn. He fully expected to be told she would not get on
her horse unless she was riding to Crenalden.

Robert folded his arms and prepared himself. He'd made
up his mind. She would not stay at Hillsborough, not with
Gilroy's army preparing to attack. Great fortress though it
was, Harold had been lax. The storehouses were not full
enough to last a siege, and there was no oil to burn or tar readied for defense. Nor was there enough water in the wells to
douse the fires. If Gilroy got close enough to attack Hillsborough, there would be a bloody and a vicious battle, but Eldswythe would not be here.

There was only one way he was certain he could get her
to go.

She stopped full on and tipped her head, her eyes studying
the bishop. "What's happening, Robert? Where is he going
and why is he leaving so soon? Why is my horse saddled?"

Robert reached out to touch that lock of hair on her forehead, that tendril that refused to be bound by braid or veil. He
took in every detail of her face, memorizing every freckle and
the way her eyebrows arched, high and regal.

"Eldswythe," he said. "Our scouts tell us Gilroy is perhaps
a day away. The bishop is going back to Windsor Castle

where it's safe. You are going with him. I'm going with my army to Crenalden."

Eldswythe's face turned stony. She didn't move, nor retreat. She said nothing, though he waited, as did his men. Not a single word of protest passed her lips, but her eyes flashed with fury and defiance.

Robert took her by the arm and pulled her to him. "Eldswythe, it isn't safe here. You cannot stay. I must face my greatest enemy and need to know that you are well beyond his reach."

A small cry escaped her lips.

Robert kissed her on the forehead. "Eldswythe, you will always be my horsewitch. Defiant, headstrong, and smart enough to know that Gilroy has the upper hand. Hillsborough is not ready for a siege. I will take my army out to meet them. We'll fight in the fields outside of Belway Forest and spare the village and castle folk the devastation of a battle."

He breathed in her scent, of horses and hay, and closed his eyes. "Do what I ask. Free me to fight without the fear that you might be captured."

Eldswythe leaned her head against his chest, tears rolling down her face, wetting the front of his black leather jerkin. She wiped her cheeks with the back of her hand and stepped away, looking into Robert's eyes. "I love you, Robert." She stared at him expectantly. "I love you," she repeated, loud enough for all to hear. "I do not wish to go to Windsor."

Robert kept his face stern, his heart unfeeling. He would only have to give the signal and his men would tie her to the palfrey that waited in the bishop's line. She would fight and scream and curse him, mayhap even try her magic to make the horse refuse.

Or he could say the words he knew would break her heart, and would make her ride away on her own volition.

Eldswythe's face clouded, first with hurt, then with anger. She spread her feet. Her arms stiff at her side, she raised her chin. "I am not going to Windsor. If I must go somewhere I'll go with you."

"Eldswythe, I made a pledge to the king to fight for Crenalden because I was promised a parcel of your land. You know that. What you do not know is how badly I wanted it. Marriage to you was not a part of my plan, though now I consider it an added boon, for as your husband I will rule *all* of Crenalden, and the river rights. My father's murder will at last be avenged. The House of Breton will have vindication." He waited before he continued, intending to allow a moment for the words to have their full effect. Then he added in a low tone. "I fight Gilroy for what is mine. Crenalden. Now go to Windsor. I will send for you when we have won the battle."

Eldswythe's face turned white. Her eyes narrowed and fury flared in their depths. "You are trying to provoke me so I will leave with the bishop. I know this is a ruse. I know you, Robert Breton."

"How can you be certain?" He stood with his arms at his sides and his hands balled into fists, his fingernails digging into his palms.

Eldswythe blinked. Her lips parted, then she clamped her mouth shut as if to bite back a retort. She faced him with the look of a she hellcat who had instantly decided she had lost this battle, and had chosen to retreat but who would not be defeated.

Robert fought to kept his face impassive. He signaled the squire standing by the bishop's horse. The boy led a roan mare forward, a palfrey with a huge head and straight strong legs. Eldswythe stood motionless, neither moving toward the horse to mount, nor stepping back.

It took all of Robert's will not to yell at her, to tell her how much he loved her and by God Almighty, throw her on the horse and beg her to be safe. Christ, he cared about nothing else but her. Damn the land and river rights. Gilroy would not stop until Eldswythe of Crenalden, the only true heir, was dead.

Resolve reinforcing his decision, Robert waved the guards to surround her.

Eldswythe locked her eyes with his, then without another word, she turned and mounted the mare. She sat rigid in the saddle, her eyes fixed on the gatehouse.

Robert rested his hand on the mare's neck and looked up. "Godspeed, Eldswythe. I will send your things and your maid as soon as it is safe to do so."

Her eyes filled with tears. Then she did the one thing he had not expected. She leaned down and kissed him, a passionate kiss that tasted of sugared plums, a kiss so filled with desire and longing, Robert felt the ache in his loins flare like a newly stoked fire.

She pulled away. "I will go. But my heart will stay with you."

Time stopped and Robert grappled with the urge to pull her lips back to his, to drag her from the saddle and hold her in his arms.

The wooden drawbridge banged to the ground. Chains clanked and the church bells rang out above the bailey, signaling the bishop's departure.

The mounted guards filed out of the gatehouse. Hoofbeats pounded mournfully across the bridge, while the blue and silver standards of Hillsborough waved from the battlements high above. Eldswythe dug her heels into her palfrey's sides and raced to the center of the column at the front. Knights and soldiers surrounded her and the last thing Robert saw was her white linen veil. Lifted by the gentle wind, it fluttered from her head and floated down, trampled in the mud by the feet of the horses.

Robert's head ached. It had been three hours since Eldswythe had left, but it felt like a lifetime. Had the danger of her staying on at Hillsborough not been so real, he would have raced out to bring her back.

As it stood, he'd barely have time to ready his army before

Gilroy's forces marched from Crenalden. Their spies reported Gilroy's troops were already on the move.

Damn his brother.

There wasn't food enough to withstand a siege, or men enough to post in numbers along the battlements, or at the gate. What had Harold been doing for the last year, besides hunting and carousing?

Robert stormed into the hall. If they left tonight there was a better chance he could move his army to Belway Forest and then to Crenalden before they were discovered.

His feet pounding up the stairs, he barreled through the doorway to find Sir Hugh and Sir Thomas by the hearth. They were cloaked and armed, talking quietly to each other. Sir Hugh arched an eyebrow and inclined his head, sending a silent signal that they were not alone.

There at the dais sat Harold, his cheeks and nose apple-red, a cup in his hand. The smell of wine soaked the air. He slurred his words. "Brother. I pray you save Hillsborough for me. Save me from Gilroy." His eyes were glazed, but behind their fog, Robert could see the fear. Fear like he'd seen in his brother the day their father discovered Harold had stolen a month's worth of rent collections from the steward's locked store box. Fear like he'd never seen before.

Robert narrowed his eyes. "What are you talking about? Why are you drunk and not dressed for battle?"

Harold raised his cup. "I'm an earl, brother. I've men to fight in my place. Besides, Gilroy seeks to slay me. He killed our father. I watched him do it. I've no desire to die like that." His voice trailed off.

Robert's blood ran cold. "You witnessed the murder of our father? You didn't try to stop it? Why?"

Harold rose from his seat, his knees buckling twice before he stood up straight. "Because I despised the man and I wanted to be the Earl of Hillsborough," he answered softly. "Because Gilroy promised me he'd give me back the land the Earl of Crenalden stole from us if I kept the crime to myself.

With that land, the very land you wanted for your blasted horses, we could be rich. I would be a man to be reckoned with. In favor with the king and no more beatings from a father who loathed me." He collapsed, sobbing in his chair, the pain on his face unmistakable, the cries from his throat like those of a child.

A wave of nausea rolled up from Robert's belly. "You coward. You let the man who gave you this life die—for a title and for the money. Rot in hell!"

He lunged at his stricken brother, sword drawn, only to have Sir Hugh and Sir Thomas grab him by the shoulders and haul him back. Hugh flung his thick arm around Robert's neck and held him like an iron lock. "Robert, leave him. What's done is done. He is despised and his death would end in your imprisonment. The people here need you. The king needs you. Lady Eldswythe needs you. Now."

Robert lowered his weapon, hate pulsing through him. God, how he loathed his brother. He was weak and undeserving. If ever a man knew greed and ambition, it was Harold. If ever a man knew shame—Harold did.

I pray to God I don't become my brother.

That thought set him back. What *was* the difference between him and his brother? By the saints, they wanted the same things. He had almost deceived the woman he loved, Eldswythe, to win her land and money, and yet in the end he couldn't do it. Not to her. What kind of man could live with such dishonor?

Suddenly, he pitied Harold, and the loathing that brewed inside him for years began to retreat.

He glanced at his friends. "Thomas and Hugh, had you not been here, there would have been another murder. You saved my brother's life. And Eldswythe of Crenalden has saved mine."

Chapter 18

"You say they left Hillsborough hours ago? Are you certain she was with them?"

John Gilroy scanned the woods as the scout knelt before him. "Yes, my lord. The bishop and the Lady Eldswythe, escorted by guards, are headed this direction. The rumors served us well, my lord. Harold believes your army is on the march and told his brother. Sir Robert sent the Lady Eldswythe from Hillsborough to shelter at Windsor Castle."

Gilroy smiled. Normally, he would have taken great pains to keep his plan to march on Hillsborough a secret. This time he'd let his enemy be forewarned. Robert Breton would be sure to march his army out of Hillsborough, into Belway and to Crenalden. He would not suspect that his opponent's army had grown by a thousand men. Or that they were waiting, prepared to fight. And as predicted the Lady Eldswythe had been sent away for safety. She'd be an easy target and there was no greater tool for bargaining than a lovely hostage. Robert Breton would be enraged, though the Dark Rider had not become a champion on the lists because he could not control his temper. Nay, chivalry would kill him, as it almost did that day at the Smithfield tourney last summer.

Gilroy wiped the sweat from his nose, the earthen smell of the muggy summer forest an irritating distraction. Lady Eldswythe captured and held as a hostage might offer no advantage, but it didn't really matter. At this moment, his bowmen and footmen, his cavalry of four hundred, and his archers, waited at Crenalden for his orders to prepare for battle.

The crows shuffled from one tree to another and Gilroy rubbed his neck. Hell to the devil, he was roasting beneath his chain mail.

He called to his horse boy, the poor peasant who traveled on foot with his scouts to serve their horses.

"A drink," he ordered.

The boy fetched the wineskin from the sack slung over his back. The liquid slid down Gilroy's throat like velvet. He tossed the skin back to the ragged boy, who asked for none for himself and slinked back into the shadows, until he was called to care for the horses. What more could a man want from a servant?

Gilroy exhaled. Thank God summer would soon be over. He had grown tired of the fighting season. This battle with Robert Breton would be his last campaign this year and by all accounts the Lady Eldswythe should pass across this trail at any moment.

He jerked his horse's head up and held the reins tight.

The sound of galloping hooves growing closer, he raised his hand to silence his men.

His soldiers sat still as statues, bows drawn and swords ready.

Lady Eldswythe at the front of the column, surrounded by knights and guards, came flying down the narrow road on a leggy palfrey.

Without missing a stride, her roan mare pricked her ears and snorted, as if she sensed the danger. Eldswythe's eyes darted toward the woods.

It had taken hours for Eldswythe to regain her composure after her goodbye to Robert. Riding in silence, oblivious to the heat, she recounted Robert's words a thousand times. Each time, the pain of his admission stole her breath, and made her eyes fill with tears. Things had not gone as she had planned. She'd not counted on his thinking she would *refuse* to leave. She'd not counted on the hurtfulness of his speech, calculated and meant to drive her away, but deeply wounding nonetheless. There'd been no opportunity to steal away from the castle and ride to Crenalden, alone as she planned.

By the Saints, they would be in Windsor by nightfall. And locked behind the walls of London's fortress-palace, she would have a hard time getting herself captured by John Gilroy. If she could not be captured, what chance did she stand at getting inside Crenalden Castle, and putting the rest of her plan into place?

Swords clattered in the ranks around her, jolting her from her thoughts. Men shouted and in an instant, Eldswythe found herself surrounded by the guardsmen from Hillsborough and the enemy alike.

Gilroy's troops descended, arrows raining down, the bishop and his guards taken by complete surprise. Eldswythe screamed. Five of the fifteen men from Hillsborough took an arrow in the chest before they drew their swords. The others fought wildly, falling quickly out of line, hacking and thrusting at their attackers, struggling desperately to protect her and the bishop. Eldswythe crouched low on her horse, shielding her body from the arrows whizzing past. God's bones! She wanted to be captured, not killed!

"It is me you want!" she screamed at a visored knight, who swung his blade and seemed not to hear.

The bishop pulled a dagger from beneath his cassock and slashed at one of his attackers. The soldier, with a snake-like arm quick as lightening, struck with purpose and precision. A bloodcurdling yell pealed from the bishop's throat. He arched, frozen in mid-strike. "Damn you to hell!" He groaned, then slumped. An axe protruded from his back. Eldswythe spun her mare around. *Plans for capture be damned! Escape!*

She caught a glimpse of a figure cloaked in red, sitting atop a great white horse. John Gilroy beat the sides of his mount, and the animal reared, then leapt from the woodside onto the road. "Get the woman, lame her horse if need be! If she escapes again, I will see you quartered, to the man!"

Men descended. A tall but blocky soldier threw himself from his mount, grabbed Eldswythe's horse by the bridle, then dragged her from the saddle. Two men held her by the shoulders, then forced her to her knees just inches from the wicked hooves of the manic white horse that danced beneath John Gilroy.

Eldswythe resisted, panicked with the realization she might not live the day.

Gilroy stared down at her. "So, Lady Eldswythe, we meet again. Did you think you would escape me?"

Eldswythe tossed her head. Better to meet death fighting to the end than to grovel before the enemy. "You have no right to Crenalden."

He laughed. "But I do, Lady Eldswythe. I am the product of an unholy union between your father and my mother. Then she was forced to marry far below her station, wed to a man who was a beast and who was stingy. Crenalden Castle is my due. Robert Breton will not keep it from me. Nor will you." Malice flickered in his narrow eyes. He puffed up his chest.

Eldswythe raised her eyes and glowered at the man. "You cannot claim Crenalden. It belongs to me. Robert Breton's army is on the march."

Gilroy's face turned brilliant red. "Watch me. I sent our father straight to hell, dear sister. I'll send you and Robert Breton there to join him." He raised his riding whip. "A taste of what's to come. Unless you swear fealty to me, you'll stand before all of Crenalden and feel the lash until you beg for your life."

Instinctively, Eldswythe raised arm to shield her face, but she locked her eyes on the eyes of Gilroy's hot-tempered horse. A blur of a whip shot through the air. In that instant, the horse stepped sideways. The whip fell just short of its mark. A gush of warm blood rolled down from the corner of her eye.

Gilroy wheeled his frantic horse in circles and brought the whip across the horse's flank. "Horsewitch!" he bellowed, as he spun the uncontrollable horse in circles. "I'll beat the horse to death if you exercise your magic again. Hold yourself in check."

Fearful for the mount, Eldswythe lowered her eyes, but willed the horse to stand. The horse whinnied, then planted all four legs squarely underneath him.

An unerring sense of power swept over her. God's bones! The horse had done her bidding, as if he'd heard her thoughts. She'd not looked him in the eye, and this time, she'd not been left weak, or dizzy like before. Instead, her body surged with strength.

The great beast champed at the bit, as if he awaited her next command. By the heavens, if she could control this *one*, mayhap she could control two, or three, or more, without the need to see their eyes!

Gilroy gestured to the two men holding Eldswythe. "Bind her hands. She'll ride back to Crenalden with me. If she dares cast a spell on a horse—" He spun his horse around and whistled at the small figure who stood at the edge of the woods, then he whirled the horse around to face Eldswythe. "The horse boy dies," he bellowed, "and so does the beast."

The lad, dressed in a dirty brown cloak and beaten wooden shoes, hurried to his master's side. He kept his head bowed and his face hidden in the hood of his mantle. He all but cowered as he bowed.

Eldswythe sucked in her breath. Gilroy's threat was simple but effective. He could not control her thoughts, but he could control her actions, though he gave no indication he understood what she'd just discovered about her gift.

He pointed his whip at her. "I am ready for a fight, horse-

witch. I would kill you now, but you are of more use to me
alive. A bargaining tool. When Robert Breton marches to
Crenalden with his meager army, I will be waiting for him,
with three times the men and horses. When he learns I have
you, he will be enraged. He'll want to fight. But if you concede your property and fealty to me, and Robert agrees to retreat, perhaps I'll let you live . . . and he might survive."

Robert's body tensed like a drawn bowstring. "What say
you? What's happened?" He kept his pace toward the armory,
no time to waste. He would ride out with his troops within the
hour and the last of the weapons needed to be loaded into the
wagons, secondary pikes, maces, and shields, meant to replace those lost by knights and footmen during the battle.
Hillsborough had quantity enough, as long as nothing out of
the ordinary happened—they could not suffer a *huge* loss of
men or horses, because unlike the weapons, there were no
replacements.

Hugh strode beside him. He didn't answer for a moment,
then Robert stopped and faced him. "Out with it, friend. What
news? It can't be any worse than Gilroy's plans to siege Hillsborough."

Hugh drew a deep breath. "Robert, Gilroy ambushed the
bishop. Lady Eldswythe has been captured. One of our men
survived and made it back. He lost an arm in the battle."

Sweat covered Robert's brow. His hand flew to his sword's
hilt and he drew his weapon. The blade arced aimlessly in the
air as he swung and yelled, a primal sound of rage that made
men stop what they were doing and step back. He stabbed the
weapon's point into the dirt, burying the blade halfway before
he stopped. Robert spun around to face his friend. "She was
well guarded, was she not?"

Speechless, Hugh merely nodded.

"I hold myself responsible. I swore an oath to the king."

Hugh's face turned solemn. "There is more to this than

oath to the king, Robert. Gilroy holds her hostage to incite you and to use as a bargaining chip."

"I will not bargain!"

"You may have to."

"What do you mean?"

"Gilroy has threatened her with torture if she does not swear an oath of fealty to him and concedes her property. He's used the whip on her already."

His mind roiling with fury, Robert yanked his sword from the ground and swung at a wagon wheel leaning against the armory wall. The wheel spokes shattered on impact with the steel, and the wooden pieces went sailing, splintering.

Every vessel in his neck and face felt as if it were about to burst, and every sinew in his back and shoulders, where once his father had whipped him bloody, felt like it was on fire. He yelled, his rage contemptuous and deadly. "I would take every lash for her, ten for one. I would lay my back bare to Gilroy if I could. I would do anything to spare her from that. She does not deserve this, any of this. A woman used as a pawn in men's war. I'll kill Gilroy. I will do it with my last breath."

Hugh set his hand on Robert's shoulder. "I tell you this now so that you may plan for battle with a calm, precise mind. One prepared to meet an enemy, unlike any other."

Robert gripped Hugh by the wrist but said nothing, the fury almost driving him to madness. He broke away from his friend and strode through the armory door, the air inside cool and metallic. He took a deep breath, forcing the image of Eldswythe tied and whipped, her back bare and bleeding, from his mind.

"Jack! Fetch my tourney silks. The blacks. And ready Barstow. Don him in the saddle cloths from summer last, and my gold gilt bridle."

Jack scampered from the corner where he'd been mending tack. His eye sparked with excitement. "Yes, Sir Robert. I knew one day you'd want them back. The troops will fight like madmen with the Dark Rider at the helm."

* * *

Eldswythe sat unmoving, her hands tied behind her back. She let herself feel nothing, not the throbbing in her head, or the ropes that cut into her wrists. Mother Mary. She should have been terrified. Instead she squeezed her eyes shut to close off the anger and channel all her efforts to keeping her thoughts in check. She dared not try her magic on Gilroy's horses. The horse boy, pitiful in his efforts to keep up, had fallen behind and tested Gilroy's patience. Any provocation on her part, real or imagined, would not bode well for the boy. Like a frightened turtle, he kept his head withdrawn into his hood.

Her back as straight as a reed, she sat in front of her captor and thrust her chin upward. She leaned slightly forward and balled her hands into fists, lest her fingers touch between his legs.

Gilroy laughed. "Lady Eldswythe, you struggle not to touch me, but 'tis a hard ride that way from here to Crenalden. I wager by the time we get there, you'll be willing to do anything I ask." His tongue grazed her earlobe as he lowered his head and spoke softly. "It did not take long to convince Margaret of Suttony to do what I wanted. She was just as unaccepting of my charms at first. I had to work to earn her love." He nibbled Eldswythe's ear. "I prefer a woman who presents a challenge." Breathing on her neck, he spurred his horse into a gallop.

Nauseous, Eldswythe gripped the great horse with her knees, and prayed she had the strength to ride for the miles to come.

The warmth of the sun had long faded by the time they reached the edge of Belway Forest. They were but a few hours from Crenalden and every muscle in Eldswythe's body ached from sitting rigid in the saddle.

Gilroy reined his lathered horse to an amble and stroked Eldswythe's arm. "We'll rest here, then travel on as soon as the horses have recovered." He halted, then dismounted, pulling Eldswythe down with him. He stood so close she could see the dust on his eyelashes as he ran his fingers over her mouth. "You have lovely lips, Lady Eldswythe." He leaned in, his warm breath grazing her cheek. "I should like to know you better, sister."

A chill rippled up her spine. She kept her gaze focused on the ground. Hoping to distract his thoughts, she stepped away and turned her back to him, presenting him with her bound wrists. "I will not run. I swear it. But my hands are numb from the ropes."

"Rest assured, Lady Eldswythe, if you run, your attempt will cost another's life." He shot a glance at the bedraggled boy, who sat in the grass and rubbed his feet.

To her surprise, cold steel grazed her skin and the ropes fell from her wrists. By the devil, if there was a way to escape, she would and she'd take the boy with her. But the brambles here were as thick as thatch.

Gilroy perched on a rock and produced an apple from the pouch at his waist. He cocked an eyebrow and withdrew his eating knife from his belt. "Did you enjoy your stay at Hillsborough? How fares the lovely Lady Margaret?"

Eldswythe squinted. A trickle of fresh blood oozed from the cut above her eyebrow and rolled down her cheek. She lifted her chin, determined not to show her fear. All that mattered now was that Gilroy take her inside Crenalden so she might assess the strength of his army firsthand and find a way to send a warning to Robert.

"Lady Margaret?" she answered, feigning disinterest, but noting with surprise the yellow handkerchief Gilroy pulled from his sleeve bore Margaret of Suttony's initials. "Why do you ask?"

He dabbed the apple juice from his mouth, then he spit out the seeds and stood up. "She loved me, and I loved her," he said flatly, as he twirled the yellow cloth. "I used to wear my lady's favor on the lists." He paused, then sighed and tucked the handkerchief back into his sleeve. "I should throw it out, but it's hard to forget the woman who betrayed my heart."

Eldswythe raised her eyebrows. "Betrayed *your* heart?"

"She was meant to be my wife. But she took to Robert Breton's bed and got herself with child. Three months pregnant and she tried to tell me that the babe was mine. Lying bitch. Let me show you why." He pulled aside his cloak and thrust his hand into his breeches. He held his shaft, throbbing and erect, its mauve head curved sharply to the left.

Eldswythe backed away. She'd seen this condition once in a stallion. The horse could barely breed, and had never sired a foal.

Gilroy threw his head back and laughed. "My surgeon tells me he can fix it with a single swipe. The ladies tell me my deformity brings them extra pleasure. And they need not worry, for no spawn has ever come from this. Margaret enjoyed it well enough." He frowned. "She was hoping I would plant a babe in her womb to give me an heir and spur me into marriage. I would have married her without one. In fact I found it hard to give her up, even after she got rid of the Breton's spawn. We continued our liason for months while Sir Robert nursed the wound I inflicted. She underestimated how much I cared. But in the end, I could not forgive her betrayal. I finished what there was between us."

Eldswythe's head, spinning with the revelation, began to ache. Margaret had used Robert, hoping to trap Gilroy into marriage? And to think she had sympathized with the desperate woman. No wonder Robert would not speak of their revoked betrothal. He kept her secret to protect her reputation—and he was ashamed. Cuckolded by a man he hated, a man who almost killed him on the very day Margaret asked to be released from their bethrothal.

She squared her shoulders and looked Gilroy in the eyes.

He smiled. "What, no maiden's blush? Has Robert Breton already bedded you?"

Warmth heated Eldswythe's cheeks.

He smirked. "I see he has. Since you have already been initiated, I will not hesitate to introduce you to more unusual delights. I've never bedded with my half sister, much less a horsewitch. And since Robert plundered Margaret . . ." He licked his full lips, then shoved his member back into his breeches and called to his watching men. "Mount up! I am eager to get to Crenalden." Glaring at Eldswythe, he sneered. "I expect by now that Robert knows I have you. He should have his army on the march." He grabbed her arms, then forced them behind her back and wrapped the rope around her wrists.

She grimaced. "Do not bind me. I will ride with you and not cause trouble. I wish no harm to your horse."

Gilroy loosened the ropes, but did not free her. "Free you? No. I can be a gentle man when it comes to women, but know this . . . the captain who let you get away is now swinging by his neck in these very woods. The riders who failed to catch you and Robert Breton on your way to Whickerham—they, too, met a most unfortunate end. Should you think to try and escape, more lives will be forfeited on your account."

He motioned to a stooped servant boy who held his ghostly white horse by the reins. Gilroy spat at the boy's feet, the spittle splattering the poor child's battered wooden shoes. "You walk beside us." He turned his gaze toward Eldswythe. "If you struggle with me, or manipulate a horse, the boy dies. Is that understood, Lady Eldswythe?"

She nodded. "As you've said before. I'll not forget."

Gilroy mounted, then dragged her onto the white horse. "I am not a fool. One suspicious move by you, and the boy pays the price."

The boy didn't flinch at the words, but he hurried to take his place beside the horse.

A sinking feeling settled in Eldswythe's stomach. She got

the strange sense that the silent servant boy who walked at her side did so with more than a self-preserving interest.

Dusk fell quickly and the sun passed behind the horizon like a fiery sinking ship. Crenalden Castle loomed in the distance and torch lights flared from the battlements along its crenellated walls. In the darkness and shadows, her home looked as it always had—an imposing stone fortress, its three towers rising over a silver river. Eldswythe shuddered, wondering what she would find inside.

She'd passed the last two hours thinking about Robert, replaying their last night of lovemaking, and the exchange between them just before she'd ridden out with the bishop. To have experienced and felt that kind of all-consuming love— the harsh events of the exchange that followed seemed incomprehensible.

Heartbreak and rising fear threatened to undo her. She needed to stay strong, needed to remind herself of her commitment to her purpose—her capture, though not as she planned, presented the opportunity to learn of the size of Gilroy's army, how many men and where, and to find a way to get a message back to Robert.

The sound of men yelling from the gatehouse jerked her from her thoughts. The drawbridge lowered and the garrison passed beneath the portcullis, horses' hoofs clattering across the stoned pavers. The yard swelled with soldiers, makeshift tents, and horses. The stench of war was in the air, the smell of blood and sweat. A great cooking pit had been dug outside the armory and filled with spits bearing pigs, chickens, and slabs of beef. The castle folk labored at the site, bringing wood to the fire and tending to the roasting meats. Her father's smithy glanced in her direction, alerted to the horsemen who came pouring through the gatehouse. Neither he nor the young apprentice at his side acknowledged the daughter of their former master—who now rode with their conqueror,

Lord John Gilroy. Eldswythe had never been sure the smithy liked her, or if he had merely tolerated her presence in the stables because he had to. Though he never said much, he'd always done as she asked when it came to nursing sick horses.

As they rode past the stables, Eldswythe made a mental note: Every stall was full, and the surrounding yard was filled with destriers. There were three hundred, maybe four hundred horses behind Crenalden walls and at least three times as many men, counting the archers, foot soldiers, and bowmen who loitered in the bailey.

A sickening smell, a stench so foul Eldwythe covered her mouth and nose, drifted over the yard. A wagon full of the dead, Crenalden's and Gilroy's men alike, rested by the well. Had Isolde been buried in the churchyard, or tossed without last rites into the great stinking trenches used as graves in the fields? Had Khalif survived?

Gilroy reined his horse to a halt and dismounted. Eldswythe dismounted, too, and Gilroy cut the ropes from her wrists before he led her up the steps to the great hall. "Welcome home," he said, hauling her along. "Now, mayhap you could show me where your father hid his plate. We've searched for weeks and turned up little. I cannot believe you were as poor as the furnishings suggest."

Eldswythe's legs trembled. Bone aching fatigue and an overwhelming sense of loss made her weary. Her voice almost cracked when she spoke. "We sold everything to raise gold for the Holy Cause. I see you ruined or destroyed everything else."

He shook his head as they passed through the great wooden doors and swept into the hall. "Sold your wealth for the Holy Cause? What a shame, Lady Eldswythe. That venture was doomed before it started. I knew it when I paid for the ships, but the gesture afforded me an opportunity to take what I wanted. I am the new Lord of Crenalden Castle. I have waited years for this. The profits from the river commerce alone will refill my chests with gold." He leaned over and kissed her, his rough lips covering her mouth. His breath smelled of sour apples and when pulled his head away, he laughed bitterly. "Our father had the son he wanted. 'Twas a shame he ignored me. It should not have come to this, sister. We should be exchanging a kiss of welcome, two long lost kin reunited."

Eldswythe fought the urge to retch as she wiped her mouth. "You are not the Lord of Crenalden. And do not call me sister."

Gilroy laughed. "I *am*, Lady Eldswythe. Perhaps I need to show you."

He dragged Eldswythe to the end of the hall, past heaps of soldiers' pallets scattered in the rushes. The smell of stale ale, sweat, and smoke settled over the vast space, though a fire blazed in the huge hearth.

"Bring a tub and water to my rooms," he bellowed to the horse boy, who bounded through the hall, and hurried toward the door to the kitchen.

A moment later, Mathilda, her father's portly cook, appeared with the servant standing discreetly behind her. Thanks be to God, Mathilda was still alive!

Mathilda held her fists clenched at her side and walked slower than she should have, her dirty, voluminous rough hewn skirt sweeping through the rushes. She glanced at Eldswythe, then dipped a curtsy to Gilroy. "Yes, my lord," she said in a careful tone. "A bath. I'll get the water heating right away." She kept her head low but cast another furtive glance at Eldswythe.

Eldswythe's voice shook. "Mathilda. Are you well?"

Mathilda kept her head down, but answered in a strong voice. "Yes, my lady." Her eyes flickered between Gilroy and the soldiers, knights, and military men who sat beside the fire.

Gilroy laughed. "She fares as well as any servant who swore an oath to serve me. Maybe better. My men aren't interested in one so wrinkled and so fat. Now off with you, old woman.

Make my chambers and my bath ready. And fill the tub deep enough for two." He flashed an evil smile at Eldswythe.

Mathilda hurried back to the kitchen. The horse boy slipped into a poorly lit alcove at the end of the hall, seeking refuge it seemed, from more duties.

A sword point jabbed Eldswythe's back. Gilroy directed her up the stairs and down the hallway that led to the wood paneled chamber that had once been hers. She found the room unchanged, the furniture intact, the tapestries on the wall still in pristine condition. Her precious books, all six of them, save for her lost *Hylica*, were as she'd left them on the shelves beside the hearth, but her chests were open and her clothes and furs were gone.

Gilroy slammed the door shut and spun around to face her. The booted feet of guards outside came to a halt and in the silent pause Gilroy's ragged breath quickened. His gaze roamed over her, and Eldswythe backed away, fearing his intent. She'd seen enough of his mercurial temper—one moment he threatened to kill, and the next he changed his mind. No one here would dare come to her aid even if they heard her screaming.

"Take your clothes off, sister. I intend to finish what I started by the river and I want you clean. Robert Breton will know the pain he caused me by despoiling Lady Margaret. Afterwards, *you* might find fealty to me more tolerable and thus spare yourself the whip. I've been told I am a good lover."

The hair on the back of Eldswythe's neck prickled. The thought of this man touching her made her nauseous.

Eldswythe lifted her chin. "I will not submit to you."

Gilroy flung off his cloak and strode across the room, where a large chest, marked with his coat of arms, a gryphon with a dove between its talons, sat beneath the narrow window. He unbuckled his belt and pulled his dirty tunic from his head. Bare-chested, he threw open the trunk and rummaged.

"Here they are. I have not used them in a while. Margaret didn't like them."

He pulled out a set of iron manacles, the velvet-lined wrist bands small enough to be bracelets. A ring of pearls glistened around the ornate locks.

He dangled the manacles in the air. "Either you do as you are told or I will lock you to the bedposts, and do what I will. I know how much you hate being bound."

Eldswythe stepped away. Her back against the cold stone wall, there was nowhere for her to run.

He took her hand and jerked her forward. "Get on your knees and swear your oath to me. I'll not lash you if you acquiesce in private."

"No. *I* am the Countess of Crenalden, the rightful heir. I will not submit to you."

His face crimson, he raised his hand to strike. She raised her knee, planting it hard between his legs.

The door flew open as Gilroy howled and collapsed, moaning at her feet.

Mathilda stood holding a wooden bucket of steaming water. She glanced at Eldswythe, then took a step and tripped, slopping hot water into Gilroy's lap. A smile raced across her face, then vanished.

Gilroy roared like a wounded bear and staggered to his feet as the guards came rushing in. "Chain the horsewitch to the hitching post outside the stables!" He pointed to Mathilda. "And chain her to the wall in the dungeon."

The guards grabbed Eldswythe by the arms and two men hauled Mathilda to her feet.

Anger boiled inside of Eldswythe. Hatred, deadly and vicious, rose up from her, the depth of her vehemence was one that surpassed any other she had ever known. "There is no man as vile as you in all England, John Gilroy. Leave Mathilda be. Thrash me and leave her alone."

A sheen of sweat glistened on his brow as he massaged his crotch. He walked to his chest and pulled out a coiled whip, the end of it a bundle of thin leather strips. "I plan to do exactly that, horsewitch. If you want to save your life, you will kneel before me and beg to live. The people of Crenalden, what's left of them, will witness your defeat. We will do this in the yard before my army rides out to battle."

Footsteps pounded into the room. A large man, a gatehouse guard with blood on the sleeve of his tunic, bowed to Gilroy. "My lord, Simon de Montfort has arrived. He brings another three hundred men and horses. He demands to see you. He wants the terms of payment for his service in advance. He claims you owe him."

Gilroy halted. "De Montfort? God bless him, he is here just in time!" He clapped the guard on the back. "Send the old woman back to work in the kitchen. She's my only cook and tonight I'll dine with my new ally, then we'll settle." Turning on his heel, he pointed at Eldswythe. "Chain her to the post outside the stables. I will attend to her as soon as I am able." He pitched the whip to the guard. "If she balks, use it."

The guard shoved Eldswythe across the yard, a yard filled with blazing campfires, round tents, and men.

She tried to jerk free, but his massive hand had locked around her arm. "I am the daughter of the Earl of Crenalden, the Countess of Crenalden!" she shouted. "You will beg my forgiveness when this is done!"

He laughed, hauling her to her feet when she stumbled over a muddy rut.

St. Genevieve, help me!

Eldswythe dragged her feet to buy some time. She whispered out of the corner of her mouth. "Good sir, I'll tell you where we hide our plate, just help me get out of the castle."

The guard halted, but he held on tight to her upper arm. "I heard you tell Lord Gilroy your plate was sold. I could see in your eyes that you spoke the truth. If I let you go, Gilroy would kill me as quick as he killed the Earl of Hillsborough.

He would track you down and kill you, too, before you made it to the woods."

Eldswythe legs gave way and she faltered. Surprise, followed by relief washed over her. *John Gilroy* had killed the Earl of Hillsborough? She closed her eyes and bit down on her lower lip. Blessed saints, Robert's father had not been killed by hers. How had Gilroy done it, and why?

The guard hauled her up again. "Come along, Lady Eldswythe. You've no one here to help you. Best you help yourself and swear an oath to your bastard brother."

His last few words sank in. The man was right. There was no one who could help her. And with de Montfort's troops riding with John Gilroy's army, the knights of Hillsborough would suffer a severe defeat. A foreboding vision flashed across her mind. Carnage and the sickening sight of dead men and horses would soon fill the fields outside the castle. Her personal danger paled before what was to come.

A hard yank on her manacled wrists jerked Eldswythe against the block-sized hitching post. She let out a yelp as she stumbled and fell against the corner of the square beam. Pain bit into her shoulder.

The burly guard wagged the whip in front of her face. "The whole army is watching you, and the few Crenalden castle folk we've seen fit to keep alive. Now set a good example and kiss Lord Gilroy's boots when he comes to visit. Spare yourself a whipping."

The guard left her sitting in the mud, with her arms aching and chained by a short length to the post, the closest campfire too far to impart warmth. She watched the shadowy figures in the yard. Knights huddled around crackling fires and talked, while squires tended to heaps of armor and counted weapons. A laughing camp washerwoman entered a tent and emerged a few minutes later adjusting her skirts. Restless horses stood tethered in groups. A few had grain sacks tied to their heads but most were pawing at the mud, looking for grass or weeds. If she could spook them, cause havoc in the camps, she might use the opportunity to—to what? Chained here like a dog, there was no hope of escape, no matter what she commanded of the unsuspecting horses.

Eldswythe's stomach rolled, hunger and fear rising from her belly, her head light and dizzy. Pray to God, she would see Robert once more before she died.

She closed her eyes, exhausted, remembering the warmth of the summer evenings past here at Crenalden, the hot long days, the sweet smell of freshly cut hay. She was young then and a different person—the girl who left this place for Dover Beach barely a month ago was gone. In her place was a woman, chained without hope or a chance for a normal life, or for any life at all. Especially not a life with Robert Breton, the man who consumed her soul. She squeezed her eyes shut. *St. Genevieve let him live, even if I do not.*

"Eldswythe," a soft voice whispered in the darkness. "Eldswythe, I've brought bread and some wine."

Eldswythe's eyes snapped open. "Who's there? Mathilda?"

The stooped horse boy, the same boy who'd walked for miles beside Gilroy's great white mount, pushed his hood from his face, though not completely. Closely cropped silver hair caught the light, and his deep blue eyes filled with the moon's reflection.

Eldswythe sucked her breath in, stunned.

He whispered. "It was better that you didn't recognize me." He tugged the cloak hood back over his forehead. "The big guard sent me to watch you while he tended to his needs before the battle." She gestured to a nearby tent, where the guard now shared a cup with the boisterous washerwoman. He kept the whip tucked beneath his arm.

Eldswythe glanced at the distracted guard, then turned her gaze back to the boy. "Safia? It's you?" she asked softly, barely able to rasp out the words.

Safia locked her eyes with Eldswythe's. "My heart leapt when you first passed through Belway Forest a month ago. I have been close by ever since."

"God's breath! It was you at the inn who killed Gilroy's scout!" She squeezed her eyes shut, longing to cradle her cheek in Safia's hand and at the same time, fighting back the bitterness of one who felt abandoned. "I pray you've come to help me," she whispered. "Or will you leave again?"

Safia hung her head. "I could not find the keys to your shackles, but daughter of my heart, leaving Crenalden—leaving you—was the hardest thing I've ever done." She raised her eyes to meet Eldswythe's. "I was pregnant with your father's child."

Eldswythe's breath caught in her chest. She stared at Safia.

"The castle folk would have killed the babe, a child born to a horsewitch who would not name the father. He was furious and ashamed of me, and of what we'd done. He'd pledged to marry Isolde and he already had a bastard, John Gilroy." Safia cast a glance across her shoulder, as if she still feared the truth. "He didn't want another."

Eldswythe groaned, tears welling in her eyes. She'd never believed her father had committed murder, but had she ever really known the man?

Safia moved as if to touch Eldswythe's cheek, then lowered her hand. "When Isolde lost the babe, your father thought it God's punishment. He took the cross and joined the Holy Cause as atonement for the sin he and I committed."

"Where is your child?"

Safia shook her head, the look in her eyes pained and grieving. "I let the Weeper Women take him away. I feared your father. My son is safe, grown big and strong. He knows not of his sire, or of his mother, a horsewitch." She lifted her eyebrows, her words clear and meant as a confession.

Eldswythe's mind reeled. Somehow she'd known all along that Safia was what they said she was, but the disenchantment, the disappointment with her father was almost more than she could bear.

"If my father truly loved me, or you, he would not have sent you away. You were like a mother to me. When he brought me home from the convent that first year, I had no friend but you, no one to talk to but you."

"Eldswythe, your father did not understand the bond between us, or your gift. He ignored your gift and let you dabble because he knew not what else to do. Perhaps he thought if I left your talent would go away, too."

Eldswythe closed her eyes and leaned her head against the post. The camp was quiet and no one seemed to care much that a small and dirty horse boy huddled by the prisoner and talked. She could hear the horses, hundreds of them, breathing. They shifted, restless as if they knew tomorrow they would ride in a battle.

Safia raised the wine cup to Eldswythe's parched lips. The drink soothed her throat and calmed her. She lifted her face to the only one on earth who could answer her question. "These last few weeks I've discovered I can make a horse do what I want with just my thoughts." She lowered her eyes. "I am a horsewitch, like you," she whispered. "If you knew I had the gift, why didn't you tell me?"

"I wasn't sure. You've lived a sheltered life. Until now, you had no need to discover what you could do."

Eldswythe gripped her chains, stomach turning. "Are the Weeper Women a horsewitch coven?"

"No. But the women look to us for protection. There is one like us amongst them, a beauty, a girl named Mahaut who wants to be their leader, but her heart is prone to jealousy and envy. You are blessed, Eldswythe, with a good soul and born with the powers of observation and intuition that make you a gifted healer. In time, you will be able to control many horses at once with just your thoughts. I am old. My gift is waning. I cannot command a league of horses as I used to. Be careful of the wickedness that comes with the talent."

Eldswythe winced. "A leader? When I might not live the night? Besides, I could never cause a horse to suffer. You taught me, Safia, to use my knowledge for their good. Tell me I will never inflict disease. Tell me that *you* have never done it."

Safia shook her head, her face shadowed. "You will be tested, Eldswythe, as I have been. You will find that power can be intoxicating, inciting greed and meanness." She blinked back tears.

Eldswythe straightened, her spine aching, her arms all but numb. Her gift might be dangerous, but still, she had a power, untapped and undisciplined, but a power nonetheless. Perhaps, she could after all, use it to free herself and help the people and the man she loved.

Robert Breton.

"Safia, I love Robert Breton more than my life." She glanced around her. "Gilroy's army is massive. It will not be a battle, it will be a slaughter. I would do anything to turn the tide."

Safia shuddered. "Eldswythe, be careful. If you use your power in that way, you will be forever tempted. Tempted to change the outcome of events to your satisfaction. You can't always determine who is right and who is wrong. I wasn't strong enough to resist the evil in my own heart. In Acre I killed scores of horses to save my village from invaders. I've been tempted time and time again. I was so angry with your father." She paused, tears rolling down her cheeks. "I almost killed Khalif."

Eldswythe sucked in her breath. "It was you who made him so sick that even I couldn't help him. He almost died and only just recovered. We couldn't risk sending him to Acre."

Safia closed her eyes, the shame on her face undeniable. "I tell you this as a warning. Please, be careful how you use your gift." She cast a furtive glance across the camp, then pulled her cloak around her narrow shoulders. "I turned Khalif loose outside the castle. I did what I could for him."

The sky closed over, turning from gray to black as thunder rumbled. Murmurings of "horsewitch" echoed across the yard as men looked to the dark clouds, then looked at Eldswythe.

It was a bad omen to have it rain on warhorses the night before a battle.

Eldswythe raised her head as two men headed in their direction. They were drunk and they staggered, one man stepping on the other.

Safia cast a glance across her shoulder, her gaze following Eldswythe's. She pulled a dagger from beneath her cloak and slipped the weapon into Eldswythe's boot. "Take this. I sent word to Sir Robert you are alive," she said quickly. "He is beside himself. I pray he is not rash in the coming battle."

"Did you warn him, tell him his army is outnumbered?"

"I did. But de Montfort had not arrived yet, so he knows not of him. There is little Robert Breton can do with the king's army in Scotland and most of the rest of the loyalist knights on ships to Acre."

"Ask the Weeping Women to come to the battlefield. Have them lie in ambush at the edge of the forest. If they will help us, I will be forever in their debt."

A sly grin spread over Safia's face. "Robert Breton is worthy of you, Eldswythe."

A cry escaped Eldswythe's lips. "Soldiers are coming! Run! You'll be discovered. Go!"

Safia hesitated, then gathered up her cloak, pride beaming from her unlined face. "I love you, Eldswythe. When this is finished, come to us, or stay with him. Whichever you choose, I understand."

In an instant, she disappeared into the shadow-darkened yard, weaving her way between the horses, tents, and the men.

The drunken soldiers seemed to have forgotten where they were or where they were headed, distracted by a horse who raced in front of them. His broken lead rope trailing in the mud, the men scrambled to get out of his way.

He nearly ran them over.

Chapter 19

The morning sun barely glowed behind heavy clouds that filled the sky. Soon the yard would be filled with sucking mud and water.

Eldswythe crouched against the post. Blood drained from her outstretched arms, she'd spent the sleepless night struggling to come up with a plan to give the army of Hillsborough an advantage. She fought the urge to cry, the pain of her frustration overwhelming. By now, Robert would be less than a league or two away.

Women's voices chattered, rising above the stirring camp sounds.

Mathilda stumbled across the yard. She carried dirty pots in her apron. Behind her came the castle steward, Alfred, and the baker's wife, Karlene, with stacks of wooden bowls and cups. They dumped their dirty dishes in the horse trough not ten feet away, and started scrubbing.

Mathilda spoke with her eyes downcast. "My lady, we woulda tried to find some keys and set you free but we been locked up in the kitchen all night, cooking for Lord Gilroy and de Montfort."

Alfred pretended to wash a tankard. "Lady Eldswythe, we have not always treated you with fairness, but your father was a good man. He would be rolling in his grave if he could see you thus. His castle taken by a traitor and murderer. He would never call this bastard his son!"

The wind rolled across the yard, whipping Eldswythe's hair and tunic. Rain splattered on her face. She focused on the little group, her brain fogged with fatigue. Despondent, she could barely manage to acknowledge their presence.

Karlene grunted. "God's bones, Lady Eldswythe, what I wouldn't give for a feast like your father used to give. I am so hungry that I'd even eat the bread Gilroy makes me bake for his horses, except he keeps it guarded and rationed to his beasts. He'd beat me if I dared."

Eldswythe raised her head, a glimmering of an idea rising up. Her heart skipped a beat. "Karlene, how much horse bread is left?"

Karlene rubbed her lower back and looked toward the clouds. The raindrops started to grow in size and number. Thunder cracked in the distance.

"Not much, my lady. It rots my bones to cook for Lord Gilroy's horses when our own men are starving in the dungeon. I pray Sir Robert and his troops get here soon. What's left of us won't last much longer, but who'd 'ave thunk we'd look to Hillsborough to save us?"

Eldswythe bit her lower lip. She lifted herself to her feet, her chained arms folded behind her head. "I think I know a way we can give Sir Robert's troops a fighting chance."

Alfred, Karlene, and Mathilda slowed their tasks. Mathilda tipped her head toward Eldswythe and raised a quizzical eyebrow.

She lowered her voice. "Alfred, take Karlene and Mathilda to the storerooms. Bring up the barrels of the rye seed. The first cleanings, not the barrels with chaff and husks."

The steward's eyes grew wide. "I was hoping I could save the rye."

"I know, Alfred. This isn't for Lord Gilroy or his troops. It's for his horses."

Alfred paled. "His horses? Why? They use their mounts to kill us!"

Mathilda smiled. A look of comprehension swept across her watery face. "The horses! Of course!" She grabbed Karlene by the hand. "Back to the kitchen. Get the ovens ready."

Karlene grumbled. "To bake rye bread for horses? When barley bran will do? Why feed Lord Gilroy's horses like we feed the king?"

Mathilda grinned at Eldswythe. "Rye bread, Karlene, baked with seed from last year's harvest."

Alfred's eyes widened. He smiled, triumph on his face. "I know which ones to use, Lady Eldswythe. Yes. Yes. We need some two hundred loaves to start. At least!"

Eldswythe took a deep breath. "Be sure to undercook the bread a little. It should be soft in the middle."

Karlene wrung her hands. "Aye! We will, my lady. An' we'll tell 'em we're running outta bran and barley—cause we are!"

Mathilda chuckled as the rain poured down, dripping off her chin and flattening her wild gray hair to her head. "An' the rain will give us time to bake. They won't be marching till it stops." She scooped the pots into her apron and faced Eldswythe. "I've faith that a horsewitch and the Dark Rider can best John Gilroy. I'm glad we got both of 'em on our side. God be with you and Sir Breton, Lady Eldswythe. We are."

Mathilda, Karlene, and Alfred hurried toward the kitchen as raindrops, round and hard as pebbles, came pouring from the sky. Thunder rumbled and men shouted. Horses whinnied while man and beast took cover.

Eldswythe let the stinging rain hit her face, but she felt no pain, though her shoulders trembled and tears flowed down her cheeks.

May God forgive her. She could not resist the power, the temptation. And many, many horses were about to suffer.

* * *

By noon, the yard was a slog of mud and water. The great hall, the stables, the chapel, and the kitchen were filled to capacity with captains, noble knights, and any man of rank. Everything and everyone left outside was wet. Tents. Horses. Armor. Men.

Soldiers huddled round sputtering fires and cursed, their squires and pages using anything to keep shields and weapons dry. Eldswythe knew they considered the storm a bad omen. Occasionally a man-at-arms would kneel and pray, looking up to the heavens. Others would eye her suspiciously, as if she had something to do with the storm. The men kept a wary distance when they walked past her.

Smoke curled up from the kitchen chimneys. Mathilda and the others would be busy with the preparations for the last meal before the battle—and baking bread for the horses.

Soaked to the bone, she clamped her jaw shut to keep her teeth from chattering and replayed her strategy. Reconsidering every outcome, every possible flaw in her irrevocable plan. Even if it worked, she did not expect to live. And when she died, she did not expect to go to heaven. But what she'd done was worth the cost if she saved one life. One man.

Robert Breton.

Mathilda and the others filed from the kitchen. Loaf by loaf, they spilled the bread on the ground beneath the lines of knight's and captain's horses.

Eldswythe closed her eyes, her thoughts encouraging the beasts to eat, to fill their stomachs. The animals ate ravenously and licked the ground for crumbs. She slumped, heart heavy and racked by guilt.

Mathilda sidled beside her and laid an empty bread sack in Eldswythe's lap. "'Tis the only thing we have that's even close to a blanket. But we've been busy, my lady. We've baked two hundred loaves of bread, enough to feed every horse in the yard. Every captain's horse has eaten and every knight's horse that will lead a column in the army has had its fill."

Eldswythe prayed that just one round of bread would be enough and that the seed was still as potent as it was last summer. The horses who'd sickened on it then had eaten it for days before they showed the signs.

Mathilda sighed. "The castle folk, what's left of us, pray to God that the Horsewitch of Crenalden and her horseman will win the day. If you have to use your magic, you'll hear no jeers from us. 'Twas God sent, Lady Eldswythe. You're blessed." She patted Eldswythe's knee and hurried to the kitchen.

Eldswythe leaned her head back and prayed it was indeed God's will they win this day.

Silver armor glinted in the hazy sunlight. Gilroy, surrounded by his captains and two guards, marched in her direction. Dressed for battle, he wore a red and black checked tunic over his fine mail shirt, and steel and leather plates around his elbows, knees, and shins. He veered toward the watch guard, the burly knight who'd sat all night close by the fire, his attentions oft divided between watching her and watching the washerwoman conduct her dubious business in the tent. Gilroy grabbed the whip from the guard, and without another word, stalked in her direction.

Eldswythe felt the blood draining from her face. She was not afraid of pain, but she hated the thought of the humiliation of being forced to kneel in front of him. If the toxin hadn't worked on his horses, then she would be forced to swear an oath to her bastard brother. There was no other way.

Gilroy squatted, his face less than an inch from hers. "Get up, Lady Eldswythe." He fingered the feather end of the leather whip he'd tucked beneath his arm.

"I'll not swear my fealty to you, John Gilroy. It would not change Sir Robert's resolve. He will fight. As my future husband, Crenalden will be his. He'll not give it up. You should kill me now."

He laughed. "You'll have to wait for death. Your lover has called me out. He's in the fields with his army, waiting. I go to greet him." He rolled the whip into a tight coil and tied it to his belt.

Trembling, she glanced at the knights, Gilroy's retainers dressed in red and black, who readied their destriers. Squires hoisted banners and troops assembled in formation, those at the front of the line waited for the gatehouse doors to open. War drums pounded. The sound of steel clanked and horses whinnied. Horses, wagons, and columns of knights, footmen, bowmen, and archers filed beneath the raised portcullis.

Gilroy pulled Eldswythe up by her hair. "I'm told Robert Breton has donned his tourney blacks, had his horse draped in silken saddle cloths, and his armor shines and glitters. He has resurrected the Dark Rider because he hopes to intimidate me. He does not. I've beat him once before. This time when I knock him from his horse, I will not grant quarter. I wish to put an end to this game of cat and mouse."

Eldswythe pushed her shoulders back and straightened. "You beat him in a tourney, not a war. And you cheated. You are not the better knight."

Seemingly indifferent, he smirked, then whistled and his squire came running, pulling the great white warhorse behind him. Gilroy mounted and used his foot to push the squire aside. He lowered his visor, then spoke to Eldswythe. "We will see who is the better knight. But you will not be there to watch. You will stay here with a guard." He pointed to the common soldier who stood by the fire and warmed his hands. By the look on his disgusted face, he did not relish his assignment.

"I'll send for you when the time comes. I'm not fool enough to take you to the field, though it would enrage Robert Breton. But I cannot let you get close to my horses during the battle."

With that, he wheeled his mount around and raced toward

the gatehouse, his remaining captains and retainers riding close behind him. Mud churned and flew out from the horses' great feet and footmen and armor scattered as they thundered past.

Eldwythe watched Gilroy and his knights ride out of Crenalden. Not a one took a misstep, nor trembled. No sign that the toxin had taken its effect. Mayhap it never would.

The mist drizzled down and she braced herself against the wave of hopelessness that rose up from her heart. Standing as straight as the slackless chains around her wrists would allow, she closed her eyes and prayed for Robert and the knights of Hillsborough. They would be faced with the biggest army in all of England.

She stood there listening to the clatter of horses' hooves race through the gatehouse, and the sound of Crenalden's chapel bell ringing out the call to battle. What seemed like hours passed before all was quiet in the yard, except for the cackle of smoldering campfires and the watchmen on the battlements calling out the hour.

The sound of footsteps coming closer altered her senses, and she turned her head to see the smith, striding in her direction. His sour, pockmarked face as harsh as she'd ever seen it, he led a flea-bitten horse behind him and carried a swatch of cloth in his free hand.

"Lady Eldswythe," he called. "Lord Gilroy has sent for you."

The soldier who been assigned to watch her sat beside the fire with his arms folded. He looked up, his face expectant, as if he knew Gilroy would ask for her before the battle was decided. He was a small man with a crude sword and a small, round old-fashioned shield. A mercenary with hand-me down weapons. He glanced at Eldswythe, but didn't bother to get up as the smith strode toward her and said, "You're ta come with me." He held the swatch of cloth up. "I've orders to blindfold ye, so you ye don't cast a spell on any horses."

Eldswythe stared at him, studying his eyes and the way they seemed to ask her to comply. She lowered her head, allowing him to tie the dirty cloth around her eyes. "You've a key?" she asked softly, raising her wrists.

She could hear the smith draw a breath. "Not to those," he whispered. "But I've one for the chains to the hitch loop. I'm the smith. This post is meant for horses and for oxen. Not the Earl of the Crenalden's daughter."

A spark of hope flickered deep inside her. Had the smith come to help her?

The chains fell free and dangled from her wrists.

The smith jerked her by the shoulder and slapped her hands against the saddle. "Get on. Ya don't need yer eyes to do this, do ya, horsewitch?"

Eldswythe climbed into the saddle and the smith swung up behind her. He whispered in her ear. "Act afraid."

She lowered her chin and slumped, swaying just a little. "Where are you taking me?" she asked in a low voice, desperately hoping he intended to bring her to Robert.

He kicked the horse into a trot. "To the woods at the edge of the battlefield. Stay hidden in the trees but find Sir Robert and his men to guard you if they can. I'm off to find my wife and children. They were in the village before the siege. I've not heard from them since." The anxiousness in his voice apparent, the smith kicked the horse into a gallop. Guards called as they passed through the gatehouse, voices questioning why the lone smith would be sent back to fetch the horsewitch. "Open the portcullis!" yelled the smith in retort. "Lord Gilroy wants her. Now. He gave me this to show you. Let me pass."

The guard's voices died down, and the chains to the portcullis creaked. Eldswythe felt the horse beneath her bolt forward, then race across the wooden drawbridge. Once they reached the road, the sounds of the battle ahead rose up like thunder. She ripped the blindfold from her face and stared at the yellow handkerchief, embroidered with a distinctive M and S, the smith clutched in his hand.

"Where did you get this? It's Margaret of Suttony's favor."

"One of Gilroy's hounds found it in the rushes. Seems Lord Gilroy cast it off or lost it."

The horse pounded through the trees along the edge of the field. Just beyond the gentle hill ahead came the sounds of men, clashing swords, armor, and squealing horses. The smith veered their mount into the brush and squires leading horses draped with the wounded appeared on the knoll. "I'll leave you here, my lady. Out of the fray but close enough to find Sir Breton. 'Tis the best I can do."

Every sound, every smell, and every color she could sense bespoke the violence of war—smoke, steel grating, men screaming, and splashes of scarlet against the green earth and dark sky.

The smith dismounted and tossed Eldswythe the reins.

Eldswythe called, "Before you go, why help me?"

The smith raised his weary face. "Because you saved Khalif, my lady. Had the horse died, your father would have strung me up. And as much as I looked to the Earl of Crenalden for my family's food and shelter, I hate John Gilroy for what he's done. To all of us."

He bowed, then ran off into the woods.

Eldswythe's heart leapt as she turned away to face the field. From the cover of the trees, she watched. The battle well underway, Gilroy's pikemen scattered at the site of Hillsborough's mounted knights approaching, and archers raced forward to fill the break in the line. Arrows rained down, while foot soldiers surged onto the field. The archers worked to reload and fire another volley, but some fled in groups of twos and threes, though their stations quickly filled with more of Gilroy's footmen.

Eldswythe urged her skittish horse through the trees, to move toward Hillsborough's front line. She searched for Robert, her eyes desperately scanning men and horses. The dead and wounded lay unattended, though a few brave squires had scrambled through the melee to drag their masters from the field.

A wave of nauseousness swept over Eldswythe. She'd never seen a battle up close, let alone so many men gored and speared. The grass ran with red, blood pooling beneath the fallen, and for every casualty from Hillsborough, it seemed as if five more of Gilroy's men raced into the battle.

Eldswythe reined her horse to a halt. Riders, hundreds of them bearing Gilroy's black and red standards, advanced in a line. The sound of drums pounded over the field and in an instant, the combat lulled, Gilroy's and Hillsborough's footmen falling back.

An eerie silence fell over the field. Hillsborough's mounted knights appeared on the knoll opposite of Gilroy's men. They took their places in a line that stretched for half a league, but Gilroy's men outnumbered them, almost three to one. Lances lowered, both sides prepared to charge.

God's peace! Her magic wasn't strong enough to command four hundred enemy horses.

Her heart raced. Robert suddenly rode to the front of the line, his black surcoat a standout amongst the many heraldic colors. Barstow snorted, his nostrils flaring as he champed at the bit. The great horse stood a hand higher than all the others. Bedecked in shimmering blacks, his tack studded with gold and silver, he looked like the devil's horse himself.

Robert held his lance low, his men battle-ready and poised to strike at his command.

The air crackled with the tinkling of saddle bells and horses snorted. A sparrow swooped low in front of Eldswythe. Her mount sidestepped and retreated into the trees, reminding her of her failed attempt to change the likely outcome of this fight. Gilroy's horsemen adroitly moved their mounts into position. There was no sign they had been poisoned. Not a single mount faltered.

A damp breeze, heavy with the smell of blood, rustled

through the trees. Eldswythe rubbed her temple, her hand shaking, her eyes locked on the scene before her.

St. Genevieve, is there nothing I can do?

Robert raised his fist. A trumpet blared a single note. Men roared and horses whinnied as the mounted knights charged across the field.

Eldswythe's frightened horse pranced and spun in circles, uncertain which way to go as men and horses rushed across the field. *Stay calm! Stay still!*

Horses and footmen thundered by, and the sounds of shields cracking, steel slashing, and men and horses screaming filled the air. Eldswythe strained to see the field. Puddles, once full of rain, now ran red.

God's peace! Gilroy's troops had Hillsborough's army surrounded and Robert fought with fury in the middle of the clash.

A knight in green, splattered with mud and blood, hacked his way toward Robert. The attacker was Simon de Montfort, the Earl of Leicester, whose rivalry with the king had united him with a traitor like John Gilroy.

Eldswythe screamed and clenched her fists, her body rigid and her spine erect. She focused on the Earl of Leicester's destrier. The horse whipped his head around, and stared, unblinking, just as de Montfort raised his axe, and then brought it down on Robert's shield, splitting it in two. Steel slashed across Robert's arm, slicing chain mail and padding. A crimson trail flowed down Robert's gauntleted hand.

Robert gripped his arm, dodging the attack as his enemy's horse reared, his great feet striking Barstow in the neck.

Eldswythe wailed. "No!"

The horse came down, one knee buckling beneath him, then the other, spilling Simon de Montfort from his back. The horse landed on his side, pinning his rider beneath him.

His face ashen, Robert stabbed his sword point into the

Earl of Leicester's neck as men in red tunics descended, thundering across the field.

"Retreat!" Sir Hugh's voice bellowed as he galloped to Robert's side. "Lady Eldswythe! Run!"

By the saints she'd been spotted! But she would not run, no matter what he commanded. Robert's arm was fractured!

Robert swayed, his weakness from loss of blood apparent.

Sir Hugh grabbed Barstow's reins and pulled the horse toward a group of knights from Hillsborough, who defended their place behind a line of upturned wagons. Eldswythe held on tightly, and steered her mount from the trees toward the wagon.

She bolted on her horse across the field, suddenly aware that the horses around her were stumbling. Gilroy's army was retreating. Like leaves carried by the wind, they scattered.

She caught a glimpse of one of Gilroy's knights, his horse shaking, its muscles trembling. The great beast staggered, then fell to his knees. The knight jumped off and drew his long sword to fight off Hillsborough's men as Eldswythe raced behind the line toward the wagons.

One by one, Gilroy's horsemen dispersed, their abandoned animals staggering aimlessly around the field. Muscles shivered beneath sweating skin, and every riderless destrier had a look of panic about its eyes. Crazed and manic, they ran wildly about the field, trodding over Gilroy's banners. Footmen, archers, and bowmen were undefended. They dropped their weapons and begged for quarter, or turned around to run.

The knights of Hillsborough, their blue and silver standards rising, charged across the field chasing Gilroy's men. Eldswythe drove her horse into the enclave of Hillsborough's knights, their archers firing arrows from behind the upturned wagons. She raced to Robert's side. He slumped in the saddle, with his sword in his bloodied hand, as Hugh dragged him off Barstow.

Choking back a sob, Eldswythe snapped an arrow shaft in

two and splinted Robert's arm, then bound the wound with banner silk. "God's peace, Robert, 'tis a bad break."

Robert's eyes widened. "Eldswythe, what in God's name are you doing here?" He touched the cut above her eye with his good hand and winced. "He used the whip? Devil take him, I'll kill him."

Eldswythe, held a wineskin to his lips. "'Twas the only strike. I am not hurt, Robert." If he noticed the manacles still around her wrists, he made no sign of it. "I told you I would come to Crenalden. It is my right. And I believe we are victorious."

Robert tried to smile, his face drained of color and his mouth smeared with blood. "You caused the staggers? How did you do it, horsewitch?" he asked breathlessly.

Her voice wavered. "Rye seed from our north fields. It made our horses sick last summer. Christ be willing, the beasts will recover in a day or so. But Gilroy's army will be no more."

The look in his eyes told her she'd misspoken. Robert took a deep breath. "I fear not, my love." He pointed to the field.

Gilroy thundered in their direction with a line of knights behind him, horses who ran like the wind and showed no signs of staggers. Hundreds of knights raced across the field, far more than Hillsborough's remaining men, enough red knights and unaffected horses left to mount a second wave of attack.

A cold shock of sweat broke out over Eldswythe. *I cannot let this happen.*

She dashed from behind the wagon, standing before the line of charging horses. She raised her bound hands and closed her eyes.

Please, please, help me turn them back!

Robert's voice boomed from behind her. *"Eldswythe!"* His faltering boot steps raced in her direction.

She glanced across her shoulder to see a man enraged and fearless, his skin as pale as death. He was reaching for her, but what caught her eye was just beyond him—figures at the edge of the wood—the Weeping Women dressed in green and leggings, with bows raised to fire, and swords ready in hand. Safia, dressed in a flowing green cloak, emerged from their ranks riding Ceres, her golden mane strewn with beads. Beside her rode a red-headed girl, the one Safia called Mahaut. Even from the distance, there was no mistaking the pride in Mahaut's face, a warrior's face, framed with hair the color of burnished copper.

With a nod, Safia raised their arms, as did Mahaut.

Eldswythe felt a jolt of white-hot energy track through her. She spun around and lifted her arms higher, and the surge of power that passed over her made her feel almost weightless. Forces joined with her own, streaming from Safia, and from Mahaut.

Robert stopped at her side. "My God," he said, in a low voice.

The charging horses, just yards away skidded to a halt. They reared and wheeled around, their riders cursing, thrown off balance and unable to gain control. Wild-eyed and manic, hundreds of horses turned and sidestepped, refusing to cross some imaginary line, refusing to do anything the knights who rode them asked. Everywhere Eldswythe looked, horses balked. Some lay down, trapping their riders beneath them. Some turned and raced back toward the castle, unstoppable.

Robert turned around to face his men and yelled, waving his good arm over his head with his sword clutched in his fist. "Attack."

His men thundered forward, their horses bearing down on those retreating. Riders slashed at fallen knights and those who fought for their lives on foot. Horseless men were no match for a league of warriors on destriers and those who chose not to fight and ran into the woods were met by a new army, unlike anything they'd ever seen before—Weeping Women who waited at the forest edge, with their swords and shields, their bows and arrows ready.

Robert grabbed Eldswythe and shoved her behind him.

John Gilroy's great white horse bolted forward, grappling to stay afoot. His shoulder muscles trembled. His eyes grew wild at the sight of Eldswythe.

Gilroy flung himself from his useless horse and roared. "Robert Breton, let's finish what there is between us." He raised his sword in one hand and held his whip in the other. "To the death! I'll not grant quarter."

Robert staggered, his strength waning. His kept his eyes locked on Gilroy but he spoke to her. "I love you, Eldswythe. I live for you. I breathe for you. I fight for you. I care not about the land or the castle. I will not take it from you once I've cut him down."

Eldswythe swallowed. "Don't fight him, Robert. I don't want Crenalden. I want you."

Calm resolve resonated in Robert's voice. "Margaret and I were to be married when she told me the babe she carried was his." He pointed his sword at Gilroy. "She said she loved him. I ended our betrothal because she asked me to. It took the work of God himself to get the bishop to give me dispensation. Then Gilroy refused to marry her. Before I learned he could not have sired the child, she got rid of it. My child, Eldswythe, a life I would never know, but a life I had a hand in making. I've spent the last year hating. But in these last few weeks with you, I have come terms with . . . forgiven Marg—"

Gilroy spread his feet and raised his sword. "You tell a twisted tale, Robert Breton. I'll not yield Crenalden without a battle. Enough talk. Fight!"

Robert took a deep breath, and glowered at the enemy who stood before him. "Lady Eldswythe will not be safe until you are dead. I will fight."

He tipped his head toward the wagon. "*Adieu*, horsewitch. Take cover. You are forever in my heart." He pulled the small green stone necklace, the only gift she had ever given him, from beneath his surcoat, raised it to his lips, then braced his bruised and battered body to face John Gilroy.

* * *

Robert stood, his feet planted firmly in the ground, his shoulders thrown back. He ignored the pain that shot like lightening up the length of his broken arm. Hell to the devil, he'd felt worse, though the slight bump beneath his chain mail sleeve and the flowing blood that dripped off his fingertips was sure sign the fractured bone had poked through the skin. His arm all but useless, it hung limp at his side. But it wasn't his injury that made the sweat erupt on his upper lip, or the scarred muscles in his neck draw up like cords.

His eyes focused on Gilroy's unfurled whip.

Thoughts of the past, of searing pain delivered with efficient calculation, the lashes sharp enough to break the skin but not to cut the muscle raced through his mind. No horse, and no man, no woman—or child—should ever suffer the whip. That Gilroy dared to strike Eldswythe ignited a hellbent fury. Rage suddenly replaced his cold-sweat fear and overpowered any sense of physical weakness, of pain in his shattered arm, obliterating the bitter, debilitating memories of punishment endured as a boy.

He swung his sword, the steel point arcing just short of Gilroy's belly. The familiar snap of the whip cracked the air, and in an instant, Robert felt the leather wrap around his wrist and jerk his arm forward. There'd been no sting on contact, his skin protected by his metal gauntlet. But his sword arm was immobilized, and the only way to break free was to drop his weapon.

Eldswythe gasped at the sight of Robert with the whip wrapped around his wrist. Unable to move, she stood frozen in terror, then Hugh hauled her behind the wagon. "Stay back!" He drew his sword, ready to defend her.

Her gaze fixed on Robert, she hiked up her skirt and

pulled from her boot the knife Safia had given her. She moved as if to dart from behind the wagon, then Hugh's strong eyes settled on her face. She halted and stared at the knife in her hand. What did she think she could do? The knife would be useless against an armored John Gilroy, and she'd no chance of getting close enough to cut the whip from Robert's sword arm.

Hugh lowered his eyes to her knife. "Let him fight. He has a score to settle. I admire your courage, but your interference will distract him." Hugh slowly turned away, giving her the choice to go, his silence telling her he would not stop her.

Eldswythe swallowed. God in heaven, she'd gone rushing in before and only made things worse. She dropped the knife and knelt beside Hugh, wanting to bury her face against his strong shoulder, but unable to tear her eyes away from the battle.

Gilroy slammed his sword against the edge of Robert's blade, the force of the impact causing Robert to stumble. Gilroy drew back on the whip, jerking Robert's sword arm, still tethered by the wrist.

Robert roared, struggling to right himself. Then with the strength of an ox he yanked his arm backward. The whip snapped taut. Surprise flickered over Gilroy's face as his weapon jerked from his hand and he stumbled, then slipped in the mud, falling forward.

Eldswythe screamed as Robert ducked and lunged, propelling his sword into Gilroy's side. Blood splattered. The gaping hole in Gilroy's chest sucked in air as he drew a painful breath. He gasped, then fell to his knees, his eyes raised in disbelief. He landed face down, his fist still wrapped around his sword.

Robert clutched his wounded arm and knelt. He swayed, the rapid rise and fall of his chest alarmingly shallow.

Eldswythe bolted to his side.

His wounded arm bled heavily and a scarlet stream soaked the sleeve of his surcoat. Through heavy lidded eyes, he looked at her. "I love you, Eldswythe. If I die, bury me here at Crenalden." He closed his eyes and slumped.

Eldswythe strained to prop him up. She ripped the belt from his waist and cinched it round his upper arm to staunch the bleeding. "Hugh! Hugh!" Her voice felt like gravel, dry with panic and the cold feeling death imparts.

Hugh at her side, he thrust Barstow's reins in her hands, then hoisted Robert into the saddle. "Get him to the castle. Quickly."

They picked their way between the knights of Hillsborough who rounded up survivors and carted off the dead. The price paid today was high for both sides. There was silence on the battlefield except for the moans of the wounded. A victory cry rang out from the woods, and Eldswythe scanned the tree line. The women were gone, though she sensed Safia stayed near.

They passed through the gatehouse, and into the yard. Hugh called across his shoulder. "Is he breathing, Lady Eldswythe?"

"He is," she answered in a broken voice, tears filling her eyes. Robert teetered in the saddle. His breath was thin and raspy, but he breathed. She kept her eye on him to make sure.

Robert's voice rumbled. "Eldswythe after you've attended to my cuts and scratches, fetch us ale and send for stew. I'm hungry."

Hugh shook his head, a smile of relief spread over his bearded face. "Love keeps his heart alive, Lady Eldswythe."

A sense of reprieve threaded through her. "Nay, 'tis not for me, Hugh." She chided. "He has always been overly concerned for his stomach."

Hugh led Barstow into the yard, where Mathilda, Karlene, Alfred, and the others stood waiting. One by one, they bowed.

Chapter 20

The sound of hammers and workmen's shouts hummed from the yard. Masons and carpenters had already started repairs on the castle walls and set the scaffolding to build new towers. Bertrada offered Eldswythe a stool, then picked up an ivory comb. She gestured to Eldswythe to sit down. "It's good to be home, isn't it, my lady?"

Eldswythe lowered herself onto the stool and spread her skirts across her knees, then she tucked the small green stone that matched the one Robert wore, beneath the neckline of her gown. The rich blue cloth settled over her feet, the hem trimmed with silver cording. The bodice was decorated with pearls and silver beads, the gown opulent and flowing. One of many Robert had demanded she purchase for their wedding. He'd spent a good portion of the king's reward on her and Crenalden, and three boxes of gold and a chest full of silver plate were filled to the brim and sitting in the corner of the room. The hoard had arrived two weeks ago, a week before the wedding. And with it came another missive—one that transferred the Earldom of Crenalden to Sir Robert Breton. Eldswythe felt the warmth in her cheeks. Gratitude to the king was superseded by the love for her new husband.

Bertrada, dressed in green with a silver belt around her

waist, a gift from the new Earl of Crenalden, ran the comb through Eldswythe's hair. "I have never seen you look so beautiful, my lady. It isn't just the dress. Your cheeks are glowing and your hair is as shiny as polished coal. Even that troublesome curl that always slipped from beneath your veil and dangled on your forehead is cooperating today."

Eldswythe fidgeted, unable to contain her excitement. A secret she was bursting to reveal, one that might explain why she couldn't stop eating sugared plums. She had consumed so many in the last week, she'd had to scrub the purple stains off her lips and fingers. "It pleases me to see you happy, too," she managed to say to Bertrada, then she placed her hand on her maid's forearm.

Bertrada lowered the comb. "This dress is the finest thing I've ever owned, my lady. Sir Robert is most generous. And I am truly happy, but not just because I have new clothes." She laughed, then cleared her throat. "Sir Hugh, my lady, means to ask for my hand." She stifled a giggle. "He made me swear to learn to ride a horse first, and it surprised him when I did. I even asked him to buy me a proper lady's saddle for my wedding gift."

Eldswythe grinned. "I thought as much. The two of you have been inseparable. It will be good to see you settled."

A knock pounded on the door. Booted feet tromped across the room, not waiting for permission to enter the private quarters.

Robert stopped just in front of Eldswythe, straddling her knees. God's legs! He was handsome. The edge of a new white linen shirt showed beneath his black tunic. He wore new leather boots, freshly oiled and gleaming, and he smiled with a look that told her he found her appearance more than pleasing—and he was up to something, his bandaged arm was tucked suspiciously behind his back.

He leaned toward her. His dark hair smelled like mint and sage, his scent totally entrancing. Her heart beat as wildly as it did the first time she laid eyes on him.

Robert's mouth upturned into a wicked grin. "For you, my lady. Two more gifts, delivered by runners just this morning."

Eldswythe's breath hitched as she reached to take a letter and a book, a copy of the *Hylica* like the one she'd lost so many months ago. "Where did you get this?"

He shrugged. "I wish I could take the credit, but I know not who sent it. I found them both outside the door."

Her hands trembled. She opened the book to read the inscription inside the cover. "Eldswythe, daughter of my heart, he is worthy of you."

"Who is it from?"

She smiled at Robert, a man she'd known from the moment she had met him would claim her soul. "It doesn't say," she answered, tucking the book beneath her arm. She pulled the letter open and raised her eyes to meet Robert's. She was utterly overwhelmed by the words on the parchment.

"What it is wife?"

"It's from the king. He is sending me a string of horses. A gift for my service to the crown. Purebred stock. The best horses in all of England!"

Robert pulled her to her feet. "And well deserved, my love. The king sees in you what I have come to love. A resilient spirit and a gift I'll never understand, but have come to respect. Now I have another surprise. There is a man in the yard asking for a horsewitch. I'm of a mind to turn him out."

Eldswythe tipped her head and grinned. "He asks for me?" Then she crossed the room to look out the narrow window that overlooked the bailey.

She spun around and threw her arms around Robert's neck. "Khalif! You've found him! 'Tis the best of all my wedding presents." She covered Robert's face with kisses while tears rolled down her cheeks.

He laughed and captured her hands in his. "I am afraid he's lost a stone or two and has some singed hair. Other than that, the gypsy I hired to find him seems to have cared for him as best he could."

Straining her neck, she peered back out the window. Jacques de Littean stood holding Khalif's lead.

She wiped her cheeks with the back of her hand and let a slow smile spread across her face. "He is forgiven." She broke from Robert's warm embrace and headed for the door, her hand entwined with his. "I want to see my father's horse! Come with me!"

The words "my father's" slipped from her mouth and made her halt, her feet frozen to the pavers. For the first time in weeks, she had the urge to tell the world that her father was the great Earl of Crenalden, a noble knight who bred the finest horses in all of England. A man who loved his daughter so much, he let her, however reluctantly, be what she was meant to be . . . a horsewitch and a healer.

Robert pulled her to his chest, nuzzling her temple. "Eldswythe, I love you. More than life. It makes my spirit sing to see you happy."

Heart melting, she almost forgot about her secret. "Robert there's something I need to tell you—"

He held up his hand. "First, news from Hillsborough. My brother has been captured . . . into marriage. By Margaret. She's spent the lot of Hillsborough's reserves preparing for the wedding. When de Littean last saw the happy couple, they were bickering over her meager dowry. It seems my brother lost every bit of it on a horse race."

"What will they do? Winter's coming."

"I'll send provisions, if my wife agrees."

"Of course. Their struggle with each other will be hard enough. I'll ask the Lady Anne if she might come for a visit. I will need her."

His gray eyes held her gaze, warm and loving. "Eldswythe, you should know *I* have everything I need. No horse, no amount of gold or land, no title could buy what feeds my soul."

Worry suddenly tamped her gay mood. "Will the Dark Rider take to the lists come tourney season, next? Will he wear my favor on his sleeve?" she asked with a seriousness that surprised her, driven she suspected by new concern for the future.

"No, my love. The Dark Rider is retired. Forever. He'll not risk his horse, or his life, for sport. He has a wife now, who brings light to his heart."

Bertrada's footsteps padded from the room. Eldswythe smiled. Her maid always knew when to leave.

She shrugged her cloak from her shoulders, then pulled Robert onto the bed. "Khalif can wait a little longer. I need to give my husband a proper thank you."

His hands already working on the laces at the sides of her gown, she straddled his lap and laughed. "Husband, how much gold is left?" She pointed to the locked chests against the wall.

"Enough. Why do you ask?" His fingers were busy on her ties.

She patted her belly. "We'll need a dowry. *She* will have the gift, I am certain."

Chuckling, Robert pulled her to him, covering her bare shoulders with kisses. He muttered against her neck. "I'm her father. I'll keep my jewel of a daughter locked away until I find a horseman who needs a horsewitch for a wife. Then her gold or lands won't matter."

"Say it, Robert Breton. Say the words I love to hear."

"I love you, Lady Eldswythe, the Horsewitch of Crenalden Castle. I will say it over and over, until you beg me to stop."

Eldswythe closed her eyes and let her horseman's silken voice and gentle touch command her soul.

Author's Note

Epidemics of anthrax have been recorded throughout history. At least two such episodes were documented in France and England during the twelfth and thirteenth centuries, when thousands of cattle and horses died of the disease.

Anthrax-contaminated soil is frequently the source of the disease in grazing livestock. It has long been known that anthrax outbreaks repeatedly occur in certain areas known as "anthrax districts," where unique conditions in the soil and sudden changes in the climate induce the changes that activate dormant anthrax spores. Warm weather followed by heavy rain is a condition that favors anthrax outbreaks. Anthrax disease in man has been called Miltzbrand (German), charbon (French), wool-sorters disease, and the Black Bane, as it was in medieval England. True to fact, a poultice of dried prunes would have been the treatment of choice for the anthrax lesions on Sir Robert Breton's hand.

Rye-grass staggers has also been recorded in horses and cattle since ancient times. Coarse grain breads were commonly fed to horses in medieval England. I have taken the liberty of having the people of Crenalden mix mycotoxin-infected rye seed into the bread they fed to Gilroy's horses. Rye-grass staggers is rarely fatal, but it does cause a transient "drunken" gait in affected horses.

For more information see http://equestrianne.com/kdennis.

—Kathrynn Dennis